FIVE DEAD CANARIES

As thousands of Brits are fighting on the Front Line, a new breed of woman emerges to hold the Home Front together. Fiercely independent and fiery-spirited the munitionettes, or 'canaries' are easily recognisable by their chemically-stained yellow faces. Among the raucous group of women is Florrie Duncan, who plans to celebrate her birthday in style in the Golden Goose pub. Tragically, the celebrations are cut short when all but one are killed in a brutal explosion. Scotland Yard suggests it's the work of a German spy but Detective Inspector Harvey Marmion and Sergeant Joe Keedy remain unconvinced, believing something more complex and sinister to be at work.

FIVE DEAD CANARIES

FIVE DEAD CANARIES

by

Edward Marston

Magna Large Print Books
Long Preston, North Yorkshire,
BD23 4ND, England.

British Library Cataloguing in Publication Data.

Marston, Edward
    Five dead canaries.

    A catalogue record of this book is
    available from the British Library

    ISBN   978-0-7505-3940-1

First published in Great Britain by Allison & Busby in 2013

Copyright © 2013 by Edward Marston

Cover illustration by arrangement with Allison & Busby Ltd.

The moral right of the author is hereby asserted in accordance with the Copyright, Designs and Patents Act, 1988

Published in Large Print 2014 by arrangement with
Allison & Busby Limited

Magna Large Print is an imprint of Library Magna Books Ltd.

Printed and bound in Great Britain by
T.J. (International) Ltd., Cornwall, PL28 8RW

In memory of the women who worked and died in munitions factories during the Great War

CHAPTER ONE

1916

Maureen Quinn usually had to drag herself reluctantly out of bed at five o'clock but it was different that morning. Having slept fitfully, she was up earlier than usual and had a decided spring in her step. She dressed, used the outside privy, washed in the kitchen sink, ate a meagre breakfast, brushed her teeth and applied powder with great care to soften the yellow tinge of her face. Before the rest of the family had even stirred, Maureen was walking briskly in the direction of the railway station. Lost in thought, she was at first unaware of the diminutive woman who came out of a side street. Agnes Collier had to call out her friend's name three times before she finally got a response.

'It's me, Maureen!' she yelled. 'Have you gone deaf?'

'Oh, hello,' said the other, jerked out of her reverie. 'I'm sorry, Agnes. I was miles away.'

'I know what *you're* thinking about.'

'Do you?'

'Of course – it's Florrie's birthday. We're going to have a party.'

'Oh, yes.'

'Well, sound a bit more enthusiastic,' chided Agnes, falling in beside her. 'How often do we get the chance to celebrate? After the best part of ten hours at the factory, I can't think of anything nicer than going to a pub to have some fun. What about you?'

Maureen manufactured a smile. 'I've been looking forward to it all week.'

They were part of a gathering mass of people who converged on the station, jostled each other in the long queue, bought their tickets and moved out onto the platform. Like all female munition workers, they collected a variety of glances and outright stares, some hostile, some sympathetic and some charged with a grudging admiration. It was their faces that gave them away. Even with her make-up on, Maureen could not fully disguise the distinctive yellow hue, and Agnes's cheeks were positively glowing. Both were canaries, two of the countless thousands of women whose exposure to TNT and sulphur had dramatically altered the colour of their skin. It was the un-mistakable mark of the so-called munitionettes.

Maureen was a startlingly pretty young woman of twenty with lustrous dark hair turned almost ginger at the front. Tall, slim and shapely, she moved with a natural grace. The plump Agnes, by contrast, tended to waddle along. Five years older than her friend, she had a podgy, open face and fair hair brushed back severely and held in a bun. While Maureen was single, Agnes was married and had been quick to answer the call for workers at the rapidly expanding Munitions Filling Factory No.7 in Hayes, Middlesex. Her mother looked after the baby for her, allowing Agnes to bring a regular wage into the house.

'Any word from Terry?' asked Maureen.

'No, we haven't had a letter for over a month now,' said Agnes, worriedly. 'Mam keeps saying that no news is good news but I'm not so sure. I keep dreading that a telegram will arrive one day. Be grateful you're not married, Maureen. Having a husband in the army is murder. I have the most terrible nightmares sometimes.'

'And me – I've got two brothers at the front, remember.'

'Poor things – let's hope they all come home safe. However,' she went on, brightening, 'I'm not going to let sad thoughts spoil Florrie's big day. We always have a laugh with her. It's been one of the few joys of taking a job at the factory. I've made some wonderful new friends.'

'Yes,' said Maureen, quietly, 'and so have I.'

'Florrie Duncan is a scream.'

'She has so much energy. Nothing seems to tire her.'

Agnes laughed. 'Whereas I'm exhausted before I even get up.'

'How's the baby?'

'Oh, he's a Turk but I can't help loving him. When I come home from work, I get a lovely welcome. Only trouble is that – with this yellow face of mine – he must think his mother is Chinese!'

Her cackle was soon drowned out by the thunder of the train as it surged into the station and juddered to a halt. Doors were snatched open and the passengers clambered aboard. Dozens of other munitionettes were on their way to Hayes along with men who also worked at the factory and who wore a badge in their lapels to indicate that they were engaged in war work, thus making them immune to routine abuse and to the humiliation of being given a white feather. The train was soon packed with half-awake travellers. When Maureen and Agnes sat side by side in a compartment, the well-dressed man opposite shot them a look of frank disgust and hid behind his newspaper. His reaction brought out a combative streak in Agnes Collier.

'Let *him* try filling shells and keeping his complexion!'

Maureen didn't even feel the nudge from her friend. Her mind was elsewhere.

Until the end of the nineteenth century, Hayes had been a predominantly agricultural and brick-making area but, since it boasted a major canal and was on the route of the Great Western Railway, it was ripe for industrial development. By 1914, several factories had opened but the outbreak of war played havoc with their business plans. Under pressure from the government, some had to adapt their facilities to help the war effort and, as the supply of male employees dwindled as a result of enlistment, they began to recruit women in large numbers. Maureen Quinn and Agnes Collier were therefore part of a huge female workforce at the munitions factory. As the hordes walked or cycled through the gates, the chatter was deafening, amplified by the swish of tyres and the clack of heels on tarmac. Another long day had begun.

For some, however, their shift had just ended. Those who'd worked hard throughout the night to keep up the non-stop production of shells were now clocking off, thinking about their breakfasts and their beds. Women clocking on gritted their teeth as they braced themselves for another punishing day. The first thing that Maureen and Agnes did was to change out of their clothes and into the plain and unbecoming work overalls. A cap of the same blue material covered their heads. Because her fringe poked out from under it, Maureen's hair was only gingery at the front. It was the same with other women. Their faces, hands and exposed hair all changed colour over time. There was the usual banter and the usual ear-splitting litany of complaints, then they were herded into their respective buildings. Maureen, Agnes and their friends worked in the Cartridge Section, a place where well over four hundred thousand items a day were made. Understanding the crucial importance of their work, they were proud of their output.

Florrie Duncan was first to her bench. She was a big, boisterous woman in her late twenties with an infectious grin and a deafening laugh. No matter how long the shift and how tiring the work, Florrie never flagged for an instant. As well as being the natural leader of her group of friends, she was also its inspiration. When she saw Maureen and Agnes, she beamed at them.

'Ready for the party?' she asked.

'Yes,' said Agnes. 'Happy birthday, Florrie!'

'Happy birthday!' echoed Maureen.

'My birthday begins the moment we clock off,' said Florrie, waving to some other newcomers. 'I'm going to drink until I drop. Then I'm going to find two handsome young men to carry me

15

home and put me to bed. That's *my* idea of a perfect birthday present.'

Florrie's coarse laugh reverberated around the whole building.

Since opening hours had been severely curtailed by war, patrons made sure that they got to their local pubs on time. The Golden Goose was therefore quite full that evening and, apart from the inevitable moans about another unpopular government edict – watered beer – the talk turned to the munitionettes. Leighton Hubbard, the publican, was a short, skinny man in his fifties with a reedy voice and eyes that kept roaming the bar like miniature searchlights. When he announced that six canaries were about to hold a birthday party in his outhouse, he set off a heated argument.

'Bloody women!' cried Ezra Greenwell, an embittered old man with a flat cap shadowing a grim face. 'They got no place in here. They ought to be at home, looking after their kids or washing the shit out of their husbands' underpants.'

'Some of them are not married,' said Hubbard, reasonably, 'and those that are have got their blokes at the front. They're entitled to let off a bit of steam.'

'It's indecent, if you ask me. Pubs are for the likes of us.'

'I'm in business, Ezra. I turn nobody away.'

'Well, you should. Those harpies just don't belong here.'

'Fair's fair, Ezra,' said Tim Burnham, a stocky young man in army uniform. 'They do a vital job.

16

I should know. I've seen what's happening over there. When the war first started, the Germans had far more shells than us. It was a right old scandal. We were always short of ammo. Thanks to the ladies, that problem has been solved.'

'They're not ladies,' insisted Greenwell. 'They're stupid women trying to behave like men and,' he added with searing envy, 'they're paid far too much money.'

Hubbard shook his head. 'They get half of what the men get.'

'That's still a lot more than me,' said Burnham. 'It's embarrassing. I agree with Ezra on that score. First day on leave, I'm having a pint in the Red Lion and these two canaries walks in. When I offered to buy them a drink, one of them tells me to put my money away because it's *her* treat. Then she opens her purse and takes out this wad of notes. Honestly, I thought she'd robbed a bleeding bank.'

'There you are,' said Greenwell as if he'd won the debate. 'It's unnatural, giving them wages like that. If they'd bought *me* a drink, I'd have poured it all over them. They get above themselves. You should refuse to serve them, Leighton.'

'I need all the customers I can get,' admitted Hubbard. 'The war has already killed some of my regulars. Besides, these girls will be no trouble. They'll be tucked away in the outhouse with their booze and their sandwiches. The missus has even baked them a little cake.'

'What did she use – canary seed?'

They were still laughing at Greenwell's sour joke when the door opened and the six women marched in. Florrie Duncan was in the lead. Agnes Collier, Enid Jenks, Shirley Beresford and Jean Harte were right behind her, with Maureen Quinn, looking rather apprehensive, at the rear of the group. Florrie had the most vivid yellow complexion of all but the others were also identifiable canaries. They got a mixed reception from the exclusively male customers. Some, like Ezra Greenwell, glowered in disgust, others pointedly ignored them, a few just goggled at them in wonder and Burnham, their sole supporter, clapped his hands and grinned amiably. The publican moved swiftly to avoid any possible friction.

'This way,' he said, going to a door at the side of the bar and opening it. 'I think you'll find everything ready for you.'

'Thank you, Mr Hubbard,' said Florrie, slapping some money down on the counter. 'That's the price we agreed. Keep the change.'

He scooped up the cash. 'Oh, thanks – very kind of you.'

She led the way through the door. 'Come on, girls. The party starts now.'

'Happy birthday, Florrie!' Hubbard called out.

'Yes,' added Burnham as they hurried past him. 'Happy birthday!'

When all six women had gone, Hubbard tried to close the door after them.

'Leave it open, Leighton,' shouted Greenwell. 'We need some fresh air in here to get rid of the stink. Those women are six good reasons why this bloody country is going to the dogs. They're freaks. They should be locked up in a cage.'

Loud murmurs of approval filled the bar. The

canaries had enemies.

It was not long before the party was in full swing. Separated from the pub by a cobbled courtyard, the outbuilding had originally been three stables, now converted into a single room. Though it was bare to the point of bleakness, had an undulating floor and aromatic memories of its earlier existence, the women didn't complain. The trestle table in the middle of the room had a bright red cloth and was covered with plates of sandwiches cut diagonally. Pride of place went to the little birthday cake at the centre of the table, its solitary candle flickering away. What caught the attention of the visitors, however, was the alcohol on display. Having clubbed together for the occasion, they'd spared no expense. Florrie Duncan and two of the others favoured port and lemon. Jean Harte and Shirley Beresford opted for ginger beer while Agnes Collier and Maureen Quinn preferred a nip of gin.

There was a convivial atmosphere. The food was tasty, the drink was plentiful and they were soon having a lively party as they sat around the table. The only person who didn't seem to be enjoying it to the full was Maureen, who only nibbled at one sandwich and took a brief sip of her drink. Florrie was in her element.

'We ought to have a party like this *every* week,' she said.

'Why not have one every day?' suggested Agnes.

'We could never afford it,' warned Jean over the laughter.

'Well, we need *something* to help us put up with

the hell we go through at that factory,' argued Florrie. 'It's not just the work. I'm happy enough to do that. It's the way we get pushed around by the men. They're always inventing new rules to make our lives a misery.'

'I don't like the way that clerk in the wages office leers at us,' said Agnes. 'You know, the one with the long nose and glass eye.'

'Leering is fine by me, Agnes. Men are men and I like to get noticed. What I draw the line at is them as takes liberties. Mr Whitmarsh is the worst. Don't ever get caught alone with him or his hands will be everywhere.'

'I might like that,' said Jean, giggling.

'Wait till you smell his bad breath. That will put you off.'

'It's Les Harker that I can't stand,' volunteered Shirley. 'He's always making nasty remarks about us. I mean, we do almost the same job as him yet he gets paid a lot more. It's just not fair.'

'Then it's down to us to do something about it,' said Florrie, decisively. 'We should demand higher wages. If we threaten to go on strike, they'd probably cave in. Let's face it, girls,' she went on, raising her glass in the air, 'they can't do without us.' She stood on a chair. 'Who *are* we?'

The others replied by breaking into song, their voices rich with conviction.

'*We are the Hayes munition girls,*
Working night and day,
Wearing the roses off our cheeks
For very little pay.
Some people call us lazy

But we're next to the boys on the sea,
If it wasn't for the munition girls,
Where would the Empire be?'

They rounded off with a concerted cheer. While the others had sung with gusto, Maureen had only mouthed the words. Though she tried to keep a smile on her face, she was increasingly uncomfortable.

'There you are,' said Florrie, climbing down from the chair, 'we not only look like flaming canaries, we *sing* like the little buggers.'

The drink flowed, the excitement quickly rose in pitch and the sense of camaraderie was overwhelming. Within half an hour, they'd forgotten their aching limbs and put the multiple horrors of war out of their mind. All that mattered was the rare chance to enjoy themselves and they took it with relish. When it was time to cut the cake, they chanted the ritual words and Florrie blew out the candle with a monstrous puff before wielding the knife. After cutting slices for each of them, she passed the plates out. Maureen was the last to receive hers.

'What's wrong?' asked Florrie, noting her friend's pained expression. 'This is a party, Maureen. Join in.'

'That's what I'm trying to do,' said the other, 'but the truth is that I've got an upset stomach. In fact, I've had it for most of the day.'

'Another glass of gin will help to settle it.'

'I've had enough already.'

Florrie hooted. 'Hear that, girls? Someone's had enough. We can *never* have enough booze. It's the one thing that keeps us alive. Come on, Maureen,' she urged. 'Get another glass inside you and let your back hair down. Yes, and it's about time you let your knickers down as well, if you ask me.'

The comment caused an eruption of mirth and made Maureen cringe with embarrassment. Everybody was looking at her and some of the older women began to offer her crude advice. Even Agnes, her best friend, joined in the general teasing. It was excruciating. Trembling all over, Maureen got to her feet, snatched up her handbag and rushed to the door.

'I'm sorry,' she said, 'I really do feel ill. I've got to go.'

Ignoring the pleas of the others, she left the building, trotted across the courtyard and went into the pub. Curious eyes looked up as she hurried through the bar to the exit and let herself out. It was only when she was well clear of the Golden Goose that her heart stopped pounding and the prickly heat began to fade. Facing her friends at work on the following day would be something of a trial but she couldn't have stayed to endure any further mockery. Her only consolation was that the other canaries would soon forget her when they'd had more drink and exchanged more stories about work at the factory. They'd bonded in a way that she'd simply been unable to do. As she walked along the pavement, she rehearsed the apology that she'd have to make to Florrie Duncan for storming out of the party. Valuing her friendship, Maureen didn't want to lose it. But she was right on the verge of doing so.

Thirty yards from the pub, she turned a corner and lengthened her stride. It was then that she heard a violent explosion from somewhere behind her. It made her blood run cold. Maureen dashed back to the corner and looked down the street at a scene of utter devastation. Glass had been shattered, bricks thrown far and wide and roof slates turned into deadly missiles. Flames were visible and thick smoke was curling angrily up into the air. The outhouse from which she'd just fled was now on fire with five dead canaries trapped somewhere beneath the rubble.

Sickened by what she saw and seized by a clawing despair, Maureen lost all control of her body and collapsed to the ground in a heap. She never even heard the anxious cries of neighbours and the clanging approach of the fire engine.

CHAPTER TWO

Harvey Marmion was just leaving Scotland Yard when he heard hurried footsteps behind him. He turned to see a uniformed constable coming at speed towards him. Marmion's heart sank. He sensed an emergency and that meant his wife would not see him home as early as promised. Marmion would be on extended duty.

'Excuse me, Inspector,' said the constable, 'but there's an urgent message from Superintendent Chatfield. He'd like to see you immediately.'

'I don't suppose you could tell him that I've

already gone, could you? No,' said Marmion, seeing the baleful look in the other man's eye, 'that would be unfair on you because you'd get the blame.' He heaved a sigh. 'All right, I'll go. Thanks for the message and goodbye to a restful evening in my armchair.'

Minutes later, he was tapping on the door of his superior's office. Marmion had an uneasy relationship with Claude Chatfield, not least because they'd both applied for the same promotion to the rank of superintendent. In the event, Marmion had decided that he didn't really want a job that would keep him chained to a desk for most of the time so he deliberately fluffed the interview. Unfortunately, that left Chatfield with the feeling that he'd been the better candidate and it fed his already inflated sense of self-importance.

'Come in!' he snapped in answer to the knock.

'You sent for me, sir?' asked Marmion, entering the room.

'Yes, I did, Inspector. I want you to go to Hayes immediately.'

'What's the problem?'

'There's been an explosion at a pub called the Golden Goose.'

'Has a Zeppelin tried to bomb that munitions factory again?'

'This has nothing to do with an air raid,' said Chatfield. 'Early reports say that a bomb went off in an outhouse, killing five people and wounding others inside the pub. And before you ask me,' he continued, seeing the question form on Marmion's lips, 'this is nothing to do with a burst gas main. It was definitely a bomb. The fire brigade found fragments.'

'Isn't this something the local police can handle?'

'I think it might involve Special Branch. If the bomb turns out to have been planted by enemy aliens, then it's out of our hands. In the short term, however, we need to establish the facts of the case.' Chatfield's face darkened. 'That's why the commissioner recommended you.'

'That was very good of him,' said Marmion, gratified.

Glad that Sir Edward Henry had shown such faith in him, he was sorry to disappoint his wife yet again. But the incident in Hayes sounded serious and had to take precedence. He had the strong feeling that Chatfield would have preferred to assign someone else to the case but had been overruled. That fact did nothing to remove the latent hostility between inspector and superintendent. It only made Chatfield more resentful. He was a tall, stick-thin man with bulging eyes and thinning hair. Fond of dramatic gestures, he rose to his feet and pointed to the door.

'Well – what are you waiting for?'

'Do you have no more details to give me, sir?'

'You know as much as I do, Inspector.'

'Then I'll round up Joe Keedy and be on my way.'

Chatfield smirked. 'A little bird tells me that you and the sergeant have had a tiff. I hear there's been some domestic upset.'

'Then you heard wrong,' retorted Marmion.

'I could always move Keedy to another position, if you wish.'

'That won't be necessary. He's an outstanding detective and I enjoy working with him.' He turned on his heel. 'I'll be on my way.'

'Keep me informed of all developments,' ordered Chatfield.

'I wouldn't *dare* to keep anything from you, Superintendent.'

After giving him a cold smile, Marmion left the office and walked down the corridor. He was still smarting at the comment about his private life and wished that Chatfield had not heard the rumours. Marmion had been caught on the raw. There was unresolved tension both in his family and work life. Joe Keedy, a man with whom he'd built up an impressive record of success, had been unfailingly loyal, reliable and enterprising. His loyalty had now been called into question because he and Alice Marmion had formed an attachment that alarmed her father. It was not merely the age gap between his daughter and the sergeant that worried him, nor was it the fact that Keedy had a reputation as a ladies' man with a string of conquests in his past. What irked Marmion was the knowledge that the man who worked closely beside him had kept the relationship secret for so long. Adding to her father's disquiet, Alice had joined the Women's Police Service. It had made him very unhappy.

'Damn you, Joe Keedy!' he snarled to himself. 'London is full of pretty girls. Why the hell did you have to choose my daughter?'

Much as he loved her, Alice Marmion was very far from Keedy's mind. All that concerned him at that moment in time was potting the red and making sure that the cue ball didn't snooker itself behind the cluster of remaining reds. Studying the table, he worked out the angles with care before he bent his tall, wiry body into his familiar crouch. At the precise second that he played his shot, a voice rang out.

'Hey, Joe – you're wanted! The inspector's waiting outside for you.'

'Shit!' exclaimed Keedy as the cue ball followed the red into the pocket. He turned to confront the man who'd called out to him. 'Look what you made me do, you idiot! I ought to have that shot again.'

'You're joking,' said his opponent. 'It was a lousy shot and it's left the table at my mercy. So, if you're about to go charging off, I want my money right now.'

'But we haven't finished the game.'

'You're forty points behind and you just committed suicide. Pay up, Joe.'

Keedy conceded defeat with a grimace. He reached for his coat and slipped it back on before taking his wallet out of the inside pocket. After handing over the money, he apologised for having to break off in the middle of the game. Grabbing his hat off the peg, he put it on at a rakish angle and went quickly out to the waiting car. As he climbed in beside the chunky figure of Marmion, he was in a frosty mood.

'You just cost me ten bob, Harv,' he complained as the car set off.

'What are you on about?'

'Thanks to you, I had to abandon a snooker

27

game that I could've won.'

'Sorry, Joe, but police work comes first. By rights, I ought to be at home with my slippers on. Instead of that, we're on our way to Hayes.'

'Bit outside our territory, isn't it?'

'The commissioner wants us to investigate.'

'Is it that bad?'

'It could be, Joe. For a start, we have five murder victims.'

'Crikey!'

'We're going to a pub called the Golden Goose.'

He gave the sergeant the outline details of the case and aroused both his interest and sympathy. Five deaths and a number of associated injuries added up to a serious crime. Then there was the extensive damage to property. Keedy dismissed the snooker game from his mind. What he was hearing about was a major incident. His frown deepened.

'Who'd want to blow up a pub?' he wondered. 'Was it a temperance fanatic?'

'No, Joe. It was the outhouse that was destroyed in the blast and not the pub itself. The place went up in flames.'

'Did Chat have any theories?'

'The superintendent thinks it might possibly be the work of a German agent, in which case we let Special Branch take over.'

'What's your feeling, Harv?'

'I'm keeping an open mind,' said Marmion, 'though, if I was in the pay of the enemy, I'd try to blow up the munitions factory in Hayes, not part of a pub. I reckon that this might have nothing whatsoever to do with the war.'

'In other words, we're in for a long night.'

'It's on the cards, Joe.'

'What a pity!' said the other. 'I promised to see Alice later on. She's going to be very disappointed.'

'Then she shouldn't have got engaged to a policeman,' said Marmion with a tinge of bitterness. 'My daughter should have known better.'

When the bomb had exploded, pandemonium had ensued. Everyone within earshot felt that it was an air raid. Windows in the neighbouring houses had been blown out and people felt tremors worthy of an earthquake. Crowds had soon poured into the street. While the outhouse had taken the worst of the blast, the pub itself had not escaped unscathed. One wall had been badly damaged and half the roof had been ripped off, leaving the chimney standing at a perilous angle. Inside the bar, everything had been shaken up hard. Bottles had fallen off shelves, glasses had smashed on the floor and drink was spilt everywhere. Customers had been injured by falling bricks and plaster, and by horseshoes dislodged from overhead beams. Ezra Greenwell had been in the act of supping his beer when he felt what seemed like a giant hand slapping his back. It caused him to bite involuntarily through his glass and cut his mouth open. The noise of the roaring fire nearby made them all evacuate the premises as fast as they could.

By the time the fire brigade arrived, the two uniformed policemen first on the scene were trying in vain to hold back the crowd and still the

29

tumult. When word spread that some canaries had been holding a party in the outhouse, there were shrieks of horror and vows of revenge. Speculation as to the cause of the blast was loud and contradictory. Everyone from foreign agents to landlords of rival pubs were blamed. It was only when police reinforcements arrived that the fire engine was able to get through to the Golden Goose. Intense heat kept onlookers from getting too close but curiosity made them surge forward in waves. For the first half an hour, the chaos was almost uncontrollable.

The journey from central London was much faster than the permitted speed limit but Marmion ignored that fact. It was imperative to get to Hayes as swiftly as possible, even if it meant upsetting other drivers and frightening pedestrians. When their car finally found its way to the correct address, scores of people were still clogging up the street. The fire was more or less under control and an ambulance was just leaving the site. Jumping out of the car, the detectives identified the senior officer and found themselves speaking to the burly Sergeant Edwin Todd, a man whose broad shoulders seemed to be about to burst out of his uniform. Sweat was dribbling down his face and his eyes were blazing. When the newcomers had introduced themselves, Todd waved a brawny arm at the crowd.

'If only this bloody lot would get out of our way,' he said with vehemence. 'They seem to think it's a sideshow laid on for their benefit.'

'Tell me about the fatalities,' said Marmion.

'They were five canaries from the munitions

factory, sir. According to the landlord, they were celebrating someone's birthday. He put them in the outhouse because some of his customers don't take too kindly to women with yellow faces.'

'Five dead, you say – do we know any names?'

Todd referred to his notebook. 'The only one the landlord could remember was Florence Duncan,' he replied. 'It was her birthday and she handled all the arrangements with the landlord. He's Leighton Hubbard, by the way.'

'What sort of state is he in?'

'Still filling his pants, I expect.'

'Have all the bodies been taken away?' asked Keedy.

'Yes, sir – and the other woman's been taken to hospital as well.'

'What other woman? I thought there were only five.'

'Six of them went into that outhouse, Sergeant. What you might call a real flock of canaries.' He gave an incongruous chuckle. 'But Leighton told me that one of them came flying out minutes before the bomb went off. Apparently, she was found lying on the pavement. They took her off to hospital, suffering from shock.'

'Do we know her name?' asked Marmion.

'No, we don't, but she's a very lucky woman.'

'We need to speak to her. Joe,' he went on, turning to Keedy, 'take the car and get across to the hospital. See if she's still there. If she's not, go on to the factory and make enquiries there. *Someone* must have an idea who these six women were. Ask about friends of Florence Duncan.' He looked at Todd. 'Miss or Mrs?'

The policeman sniffed. 'A bit of both, according to the landlord,' he recalled. 'She was Mrs Duncan till her hubby was killed at the battle of Loos. Hubbard described her as a real live wire who preferred to be called "Florrie". She sounds like something of a merry widow, though she had little enough to get merry about.'

'That's enough to go on,' said Marmion. 'Off you go, Joe.'

Keedy nodded. 'What about you, Inspector?'

'I'll have a chat with the landlord. Meet me back here.'

'Right you are.'

When Keedy went off in the car, Marmion looked at the smoking ruin that had once been the outhouse. It was no more than a pile of stones and charred timbers now.

'Nobody could have survived that blast,' he said.

'No,' agreed Todd. 'And the Golden Goose will need some repairs before it can reopen. A real pity – they served a good pint in there.'

Leighton and Yvonne Hubbard lived above the pub but neither of them felt that it was safe to stay there until the building had been properly inspected. Accordingly, they moved around the corner to the house of some friends. Hubbard had gradually adjusted to the crisis but his wife – a nervous woman by nature – was close to hysterics. At the suggestion of their hosts, she'd retired to bed. When Marmion got to the house, the front door was opened by Dennis Cryall, a swarthy man of medium height and middle years. Marmion identified himself and explained that Todd had directed him to the house. Cryall was amazed.

'You've come all the way from Scotland Yard, Inspector?'

'We felt that it was a necessary precaution.'

'I'm glad that you're taking it so seriously. Hayes always used to be such a sleepy little place until the war broke out. Nothing ever happened here.'

'I'd like to speak to Mr Hubbard, please.'

'Yes, yes, of course – do come in.'

Cryall moved back so that Marmion could step into the passageway. He was then shown into the cluttered front room where Hubbard was seated with a glass of whisky in his hand. Like his friend, he was impressed that the incident had aroused the interest of Scotland Yard. Cryall waved their visitor to a chair then withdrew. Seated opposite the landlord, Marmion appraised the other man. Hubbard looked pale and drawn. The bomb had not only destroyed part of his property, it had injured some of his regular patrons and shaken up everyone else in the bar. He was justifiably worried about how much money he would get by way of insurance. It was his wife's condition that really troubled him. The explosion had turned her into a sobbing wreck. There was no compensation for frayed nerves in the insurance policy.

'How do you feel?' asked Marmion.

Hubbard lifted his glass. 'Much better after a drop of this,' he said.

'What state is the pub in?'

'Don't ask, Inspector. We'll be closed for weeks.'

33

'Tell me about the outhouse.'

'It's three old stables knocked into one. As a rule, we use it to store crates of empty bottles in. Then we had this request for a private room. To be honest, I was glad the ladies wanted to be on their own,' admitted Hubbard. 'Some of my regulars hate the sight of those munitionettes. It's very unfair, really. It's not their fault that they look as if they've got a nasty attack of yellow jaundice. Anyway,' he added, 'Florrie made the booking and I was happy to accept it.'

'Do you happen to have an address for her?'

'I don't, I'm afraid, but she lives locally some-where. I remember her coming into the Goose with her husband when he was alive. That's why she chose our pub for her party. It held good memories for her.' He rolled his eyes. 'Not any more.'

'Did you know any of the friends who came with her?'

'No – never set eyes on them before.'

'So you can't give me any more names?'

'I'm sorry, Inspector. I wish I could.'

'Go through it very slowly,' invited Marmion. 'Tell me exactly what happened from the time they arrived until the moment the bomb went off. There's no rush. Set your own pace.'

Hubbard took a long sip of his whisky. Having gathered his thoughts, he gave a somewhat laboured account of events, even including details of the row involving Ezra Greenwell. When he heard that the old man had needed treatment for the wound in his mouth, Marmion could muster no sympathy for him. He found Greenwell's anti-

34

pathy to the women quite disgraceful. As far as he was concerned, they were doing a dangerous job at a time of national emergency and should be applauded for their efforts, not jeered at by some resentful bigot. Marmion was all too aware of the deficiencies in the army at the outbreak of hostilities. His own son, Paul, was among an early eager batch of volunteers to join the army. On his first leave, he'd been very critical of the shortage of ammunition.

Having made some notes during the account, Marmion closed his pad.

'Six of them went into that room,' he said, reflectively, 'but only five remained there. Have you any idea why the sixth young lady left early?'

'Yes,' said Hubbard, ruefully. 'There's only one explanation.'

'Is there?'

'You're the detective – you should have worked it out by now. That girl ran out as if she was fleeing a ghost. It's obvious, isn't it? She *knew* there was going to be an explosion there,' he claimed with a surge of anger. 'There was a plot to bomb my outhouse and that bitch was part of it.'

Joe Keedy was in luck. When he got to the hospital, Maureen Quinn was still there. Having been treated for shock, she'd been discharged but had felt too numbed by the experience to do anything more than sit in the waiting room and brood. The full implications of what had happened were terrifying. At a stroke, she'd lost five good friends at the factory. Their lives had been snuffed out like candles in a matter of seconds

35

and, if she'd stayed a little longer at the pub, Maureen would now be lying beside them on a slab in the hospital morgue. It was a sobering thought. She was still wrestling with recriminations when Keedy joined her.

'Miss Quinn?' he asked, gently.

She looked up. 'Yes, that's me.'

'I'm Detective Sergeant Keedy from Scotland Yard and I've been called in to investigate the explosion at the Golden Goose.' Maureen shrunk back as if in fear of arrest. 'There's no need for alarm. I just want to ask a few questions.'

'Oh, I see.'

'May I sit down?'

'Well, yes – if you must.'

'It's such a help to us to have a survivor,' he said, taking the seat beside her. 'It means that we can identify the victims. The only one we know by name is a Mrs Florence Duncan.' He smiled softly. 'I believe you called her "Florrie" at work.'

'Everyone did, Sergeant.'

He flipped open his notebook. 'Could I have her address, please?'

Before long, he had the names and addresses of all five women and – because of the way that Maureen's voice modulated each time – he had some idea of how she related to each one of them. Evidently, Agnes Collier was the biggest loss to her whereas Jean Harte seemed to be no more than an acquaintance. Having taken down Maureen's own details, Keedy could see from his notes that she and Agnes lived fairly close to each other.

'Next of kin will have to be informed,' he said. 'Who will that be in the case of Mrs Collier?'

'Her mother – a Mrs Radcliffe – she looks after Agnes's baby son.' Tears filled her eyes. 'This will come as a terrible blow to her. Then there's her husband, Terry, of course. He's in France some-where.'

'What about you?' he asked solicitously.

She was defensive. 'What about me?'

'Do you live alone or is there someone to look after you?'

'I live with my parents and my younger sister.'

'So you'll have plenty of support at home.'

'Yes, yes, I'll be fine.'

'With respect, Miss Quinn, you don't *look* fine.'

'I'll be all right, Sergeant,' she said, keen to end the interrogation.

'I'd be happy to give you a lift home,' he offered.

'No, no, you needn't do that. It's only a few stops on the train.'

'Naturally, the factory will have to be informed that they've lost five of their employees. Could you tell me who to contact?'

'Mr Kennett is the works manager. Speak to him – though he won't come on duty until six tomorrow morning. But,' she went on, thinking it through, 'they'll have his home telephone number at the factory. You could contact him this evening.'

'That's a good suggestion – thank you.'

Anxious to leave, she rose to her feet. 'I must be off now.'

'Are you sure that you feel well enough?'

'Yes, I'm much better.'

'Then let me ask a last question,' said Keedy. 'I saved it until the end because it's the most im-portant one. Why did you leave in the middle of the party? Weren't you enjoying it?'

'I was enjoying it very much, Sergeant.'

'So why did you walk out when you did?'

'I had this upset stomach,' she replied, putting a hand to her midriff. 'It's been troubling me all day. I hoped that it would wear off but it got steadily worse. There was a point during the party when I felt I was going to be sick. *That's* why I had to leave. I simply had to get out of there.' She pulled her coat around her shoulders. 'Can I go now, please?'

'Yes,' he said, 'please do. And thank you for your help. I'll be in touch.'

Her whole body tensed. 'Why? I've told you all I can.'

'There may be some small detail that slipped your mind.'

'But there isn't, Sergeant. I'll swear it.'

'Then I'll let you go,' he said, pleasantly, getting to his feet. 'Goodbye.'

'Goodbye.'

Having stayed at the hospital longer than she needed, Maureen now left it as if she had an urgent appointment elsewhere. Chewing on his pencil, Keedy watched her go. He felt profoundly sorry for her. Having dealt with survivors of explosions before, he knew how consumed with guilt they could become, blaming themselves for escaping from an accident that had claimed the lives of others. Not that the bomb at the Golden Goose was in any way accidental – it was deliberately designed to kill and wreck. Maureen Quinn had been extremely fortunate to leave the building when she did and she appeared to have had a good

38

reason for doing so.

Keedy wondered why he simply didn't believe her.

CHAPTER THREE

It was just like old times. Ellen Marmion was seated in her kitchen, having a cup of tea with a member of the police force. However, it was not her husband on this occasion but her daughter who was nibbling a ginger biscuit beside her. Having established that Joe Keedy had been sent off to investigate a crime that evening, Alice had sighed resignedly in a way she'd seen her mother do a hundred times. Instead of going back to her flat, she went back home so that she could commiserate with Ellen about their absent partners. Having joined the Women Police Service on impulse, Alice was now having regrets. Her duties were strictly circumscribed and seemed to consist largely of taking orders from her superiors and carrying messages to and fro. Longing to be given some operational role, she was confined to clerical work. It made her look back on her time in the Women's Emergency Corps with fondness. The work had been onerous but it had a wonderfully unpredictable range to it.

'Did you find out *where* they were going?' asked Ellen.

'No,' replied her daughter, 'but it must have been a major incident or they would have sent someone less senior than Daddy.'

'That's one way of looking at it.'

'What do you mean?'

'Let's just say that Claude Chatfield is not your father's greatest admirer. He takes pleasure in unloading awkward cases onto him. To give him credit, he does his job well but there's a nasty streak in the superintendent.'

'That's because he knows, in his heart, that Daddy is a much better detective. At least, that's what Joe believes. They call him "Chat", by the way.'

'Oh, I've heard your father call him a lot worse than that, Alice.'

They shared a laugh and reached for another home-made biscuit. Ellen was delighted to see her daughter again. Since she'd moved into a flat of her own, Alice's visits had become less and less frequent. With her son away in France and her husband on call at all hours, Ellen was well acquainted with loneliness. An unexpected evening with Alice was therefore a bonus. She bit into her biscuit.

'Have you set a date yet?'

'We've set it a number of times, Mummy, but we keep changing our minds.'

'Why is that?'

'Things sort of come up.'

'What sort of things?'

'Oh, I don't know,' said Alice with a weary smile. 'One minute I find a reason to change the date; next minute it's Joe's turn. It's a question of finding a time when both our families can be there. My stipulation is clear. I'm not getting

40

married unless Paul is back home from France.'

Ellen pulled a face. 'Well, that's in the lap of the gods.'

'This war can't go on forever.'

'How many times have we both said that?'

'Then, of course, there's Joe's family. They have commitments.'

'You didn't really take to them, did you?'

'It wasn't that,' said Alice, remembering her visit to the Midlands. 'I just never got to know them. When Joe told me that his father was an undertaker, I thought that he'd relax when he was off duty but he couldn't, somehow. It was the same with Mrs Keedy – she chisels the names into the headstones so is very much part of the business. She and her husband are both grim.'

'Maybe they'll improve with a drink inside them.'

Alice grinned. 'No chance of that – they're both teetotal.'

'I can see why Joe didn't stay in the family trade. He was born to enjoy life.' She put her hand on her daughter's arm. 'I'm *so* glad that this has happened, I really am. Your father may be against it now but he'll mellow in time. He loves Joe. He just doesn't like the idea of having him as a son-in-law.'

'Would he rather that we just lived together?'

'Heaven forbid!'

'I was only joking, Mummy.'

'Well, for goodness' sake, don't joke about it in front of your father. He's very sensitive on that subject at the moment. Working with Joe always used to be a real joy for him. Now there are definite tensions between them.'

41

When he finally got back to the Golden Goose, Keedy found Marmion deep in conversation with a uniformed inspector who kept nodding in agreement. The crowd had drifted away now and the area was cordoned off with ropes. Two constables were on duty to ensure that nobody tried to loot the pub or poke about in the rubble. One of them chased away a dog that tried to urinate over the inn sign that had been knocked off its iron bar by the force of the blast. The golden goose looked outraged at the sudden change in its fortunes. Marmion excused himself and came over to Keedy.

'You were gone a long time, Joe,' he observed.

'I know,' replied the other. 'After I'd talked to Maureen Quinn, I went over to the factory. They gave me the number of Mr Kennett, the works manager, and let me phone him at his home. He was knocked sideways by the news, Harv. He knew who Florrie Duncan was. She must have been a real character to stand out from the thousands of other women employed there.'

'Was this Maureen Quinn the sixth guest at the party?'

'Yes, she was still at the hospital when I got there.'

'How would you describe her?'

'She's a very pretty girl but – not surprisingly – stunned by what happened.'

'What did you learn from her?'

'Lots,' said Keedy, taking out his notebook.

After moving into the spill of light from a nearby lamppost, he translated his scrawl into a terse

42

account. Marmion was relieved to hear that all five victims now had names. Since four of them lived in Hayes itself, he delegated the task of informing their next of kin to the local police, who'd locate the addresses far more easily. Thankful to learn the identities of the dead women, the uniformed inspector said that he would pass on the bad news in person to each of the respective families.

'We'll go to Agnes Collier's address,' said Marmion. 'She lives some distance away.'

'Her mother will be there, looking after her grandson. She's a Mrs Radcliffe. I hope she's got a husband or some good friends,' said Keedy. 'She'll need someone to help her get through this.'

'Yes, the birthday party has turned out to be a nightmare.'

'What have you been doing, Harv?'

'I spoke to the landlord, Leighton Hubbard. You only have to look at the pub to imagine how *he* must be feeling. The worst of it is that he thinks he's somehow responsible for the deaths.'

'That's silly. It wasn't his fault.'

'He did give us one valuable clue.'

'Oh?' Keedy's interest quickened. 'What was that?'

'That outhouse was almost never used. He only rented it out two or three times a year. That narrows down the possibilities at once, Joe.'

'Does it?'

'Of course,' said Marmion. 'It means that those five women were not just random victims. One or all of them were intended targets. The person who planted that bomb knew the time they'd be here and he could rely on them not being too inquisi-

43

tive. When you go to a birthday party, the last thing you do is to search every nook and cranny for a bomb. They had no chance. They were sitting targets.'

'Why should anyone want to kill five harmless women?'

'The original intent was to kill *six* of them, remember.'

'In that case, Maureen Quinn was very lucky to escape.'

'According to the landlord, it wasn't luck at all but design. He tried to persuade me that *she* was the bomber and knew exactly when to get out. It sounds like a fanciful theory to me.'

'And to me, Harv,' said Keedy, recalling his conversation with Maureen. 'I don't think she's capable of anything like that. She seemed like a decent, honest, law-abiding young woman. There was no real spark in her. She was shy and unassertive.' A memory nudged him. 'On the other hand...'

'Go on,' prompted Marmion.

'It's always wise to double-check, I suppose.' Keedy reached a decision. 'When we've been to Agnes Collier's house, perhaps we should go on to have another word with Maureen Quinn. I'd like to see what you make of her.'

They couldn't believe it. When Maureen got home and told her family the news, they found it impossible to accept. On the previous Sunday, Agnes Collier had come to the house for tea with her baby son. They'd all had a very enjoyable time. Yet they were now being told that they'd never see the

woman alive again and that the child would have
to grow up without a mother. Their sympathy
went out to him. When Maureen told them about
the other four women who'd died in the bomb
blast, she had to force each name out and her
voice trembled as she did so. Seated beside her on
the sofa, Diane Quinn, her mother, kept a com-
forting arm around her shoulders and offered her
a handkerchief whenever she lapsed into tears.
Eamonn Quinn, her father, sat opposite in silence,
his face blank, his mind in turmoil. Sitting cross-
legged on the floor was fourteen-year-old Lily
Quinn, not understanding the full import of what
she'd been told but realising that something truly
terrible had occurred and that her elder sister was
at the heart of it.

'Will they put your name in the papers,
Maureen?' she wondered.

'Don't ask such a stupid question,' said her
father, reproachfully.

'Mrs Fenner's name was in the Standard when
she got knocked down by that car and all she did
was to break a few ribs.'

'Be quiet, Lily.'

'But our Maureen is going to be *famous*.'

'It's not the kind of fame we want,' said Diane,
tightening her grip on her elder daughter. 'Whenever she goes out, people will point at Maureen
and say that she was the one who escaped from
that dreadful explosion. Yes, and the tongues will
wag about the rest of us as well. The whole family
will suffer.'

'I'm not worried about being stared at,' said
Maureen, solemnly. 'I'm used to that. It's the gos-

45

sip that will hurt me. I'm bound to be blamed.'

'No, you won't, love. You didn't plant that bomb.'

'But I was the one who walked away without a scratch on me. Agnes's mother will be the first to blame me. I know exactly what Mrs Radcliffe will say. "Why was it *her* and not my Agnes? What's so special about Maureen Quinn?" And the other parents will be the same. They'll all hate me.'

'Well, they'd better not say anything against you when *I'm* around,' warned her father, bunching his fists, 'or they'll have me to answer to. It's a miracle you got saved, Maureen, and I'm not having anyone criticising you as a result.'

Quinn was a beefy man with deep-set eyes in a florid face and a rough beard. His wife was also carrying too much weight but she still had vestiges of the good looks inherited by her daughters. Hailing from London, Diane had a light Cockney accent whereas her husband had a whisper of an Irish brogue in his voice. Maureen and Lily had grown up talking more like their mother.

A protracted silence fell on the room. It was eventually broken by Lily.

'Do I have to go to school tomorrow?' she asked.

'No,' decided her mother. 'I'm keeping you at home.'

'But everyone will want to ask me about Maureen.'

'That's exactly why you're staying here. Word will have spread by tomorrow. I'm not having you pestered by questions at school. Apart from anything else, you might say something out of turn.'

Lily flushed. 'What do you mean?'

46

'Your mother's right,' confirmed Quinn. 'You'll stay at home – and the same goes for your sister. The pair of you will keep out of the way for a while.'

Maureen sat up. 'But I think I *ought* to go to work, Daddy.'

'Then you think wrong. Your place is here.'

'I'm not going to hide.'

'It's the sensible thing to do,' advised her mother. 'You've had the most awful shock, Maureen. You can't expect to shrug it off so soon.'

'But they need me at the factory – Mr Kennett will want to hear the details.'

'Then he'll have to wait. It's a police matter now. They'll tell him all he needs to know. In the circumstances, he'd never expect you to turn up.'

'Florrie Duncan would go, if she was in my position.'

'That may be so, love, but poor Florrie is dead and won't be going anywhere.'

'We keep ourselves to ourselves,' decreed Quinn.

'Does that mean you're staying off work as well?' asked Lily in surprise.

'No, it means that anybody who bothers me will get a flea in his ear.'

Quinn had a job delivering coal and there were several specks of it embedded in his beard and under his fingernails. He was a surly man at the best of times. The latest development would do nothing to improve his manner or his temper.

'And that goes for the coppers,' he added. 'We don't want them poking their noses into our business. Maureen has said her piece to them.

47

That's all they get.'

Imparting painful news to grieving relatives was something he'd had to do a fair amount in his career and Joe Keedy always found it difficult. He was, therefore, grateful that Marmion took over when they called at Agnes Collier's house. The inspector was older, more experienced and always seemed to find the right words. Invited in by Sadie Radcliffe, they went into the living room and noticed how scrupulously tidy it was. Sadie had been knitting and a half-finished jumper stood on the arm of a chair. Like her daughter, she was short, tubby and fair-haired. She wore a pinafore over her dress and a turban on her head. Marmion suggested that she might like to sit down but she insisted on standing. There was an indomitable quality about her that suggested she was used to hearing and coping with distressing news. While Marmion cleared his throat, she stood there with her arms folded and peered at him over the top of her wire-framed spectacles.

'Something's happened to Agnes, hasn't it?' she said, stiffening.

'I'm afraid that it has, Mrs Radcliffe.'

'Is it serious?' He gave a nod. 'I knew it. I expected her back over an hour ago. My husband will be wondering where I am.'

'Would you like us to contact him before we go into any detail?'

'No, Inspector, all he's interested in is his supper. Tell me the worst. I've been bracing myself for this ever since she went to work at that factory. Agnes has had a bad accident, hasn't she?'

'This is nothing to do with her job – except indirectly, that is.'

'So what's happened to her?'

Speaking quietly, Marmion gave her a brief account of events at the Golden Goose. Keedy, meanwhile, positioned himself so that he could catch the woman if she fainted but his services were not required. Sadie stood her ground and absorbed the bad tidings without flinching. Her first reaction was to look sorrowfully upwards as she thought about the implications for her grandson. He would wake the next day to discover that he no longer had a mother. Sadie pressed for more details and Marmion obliged her, even though he was uncertain how much of the information she was actually hearing because she seemed to go off in a trance.

When she eventually came out of it, she fired a question at Marmion.

'What were the names of the others?' she demanded.

'Sergeant Keedy has the full list.'

'Yes,' said Keedy, taking out his notebook and flipping to the correct page. 'Here we are, Mrs Radcliffe. The other victims are as follows – Florence Duncan, Enid Jenks, Shirley Beresford and Jean Harte.'

'What about Maureen Quinn? She was there as well.'

'She was fortunate enough to leave before the bomb went off.'

'That's just the kind of thing she'd do,' said Sadie with asperity. 'Talk about the luck of the Irish. It *had* to be Maureen, didn't it?'

49

'You should be pleased to hear that someone escaped the blast.'

'I am, Sergeant, but why wasn't it my daughter? Why couldn't *she* have left that pub in time? It's so unfair. Agnes has got a husband at the front and she works at that factory all the hours that God sends us. Doesn't that entitle her to a bit of luck? Hasn't she earned it?' she went on with undisguised bitterness. 'Why does it always have to be Maureen? Who's she that she gets special treatment time and again?'

'There's no answer to that, Mrs Radcliffe.'

'Agnes lost her first baby and damn near killed herself bringing her little lad into the world. It was one thing after another. She always seemed to be the one who got hurt most.'

'In this instance,' Marmion noted, 'there were four other victims.'

Sadie lowered herself onto the arm of the settee. 'Yes, I know,' she conceded, 'and I'm sorry for their families. They'll feel the way I do.' She drifted off again for a few moments then gave a wan smile. 'Funny, isn't it?'

'What is, Mrs Radcliffe?'

'The one thing I feared most was that Agnes would be killed in an explosion at work. It happens in all the munition factories, only they keep it out of the papers most of the time. There have been two cases at Hayes, though they were in the Cap and Detonator Section. I used to thank God that my daughter didn't work there.'

'It's a dangerous place,' said Marmion. 'The mercury fulminate they use is highly explosive and can be very unstable.'

'Yet it was *outside* the factory that Agnes came to grief.'

'Yes, it is ironic, I agree.'

'Who did it, Inspector?' she asked, getting up again.

'It's too early to say.'

'You must have some idea.'

'We've already set an investigation in motion. That means we have to gather evidence slowly and painstakingly.'

'But you will catch him, won't you?' she pleaded. 'You will arrest the devil who did this terrible thing to my daughter.'

'We will, Mrs Radcliffe.'

She fixed him with a glare. 'Is that a promise?'

'It's both a promise and a firm commitment,' said Marmion. 'This is a heinous crime. However long it takes, we'll get the person or persons behind it.'

Superintendent Claude Chatfield expected his officers to work hard but he also pushed himself to the limit. Long after the time when he should have gone home, he was still at his desk in Scotland Yard, reading his way through a sheaf of papers and making notes in the margin. When the telephone rang, he snatched it up and barked into the receiver.

'Is that you, Marmion?'

'Yes, sir,' came the reply. 'I'm ringing from the police station in Hayes.'

'What have you discovered?'

'The situation is very bad. It's also rather confused.'

51

'Have you identified the victims?'

'Thanks to the sole survivor, we have the names and addresses of the other five women. Next of kin have been informed in all five cases.'

'Give me the full picture.'

Taking a deep breath, Marmion launched into his report. He kept one eye on the notes in front of him and confined himself to the known facts. There was nothing that the superintendent hated as much as uninformed guesswork and the last thing that Marmion wanted to do was to arouse his ire. When he'd heard the full report, Chatfield was ready with a crucial question.

'Should we call in Special Branch?'

'I don't think so, sir.'

'Why?'

'That's my considered opinion.'

'Does it have any basis in fact?'

'I believe so,' said Marmion. 'This outrage was specifically aimed at one or all of the six people who attended that party. There's no propaganda value whatsoever for the enemy. These were ordinary young women who simply wanted to celebrate a birthday. For reasons unknown, someone objected to the occasion and was ready to go to extreme lengths to stop it.'

Chatfield was irritable. 'What are you trying to tell me, Inspector?'

'The killer was a local man with a good knowledge of explosives.'

'There's no shortage of people like that in Hayes.'

'Quite – that's why the munitions factory will have to be put under the microscope. We may well find that the person we're after works there. It would put him in the right place to hear about the time and place of that birthday party.'

'Have you made any contact with the factory?'

'Sergeant Keedy paid a visit there earlier on. They allowed him to use their telephone to ring the home of the works manager, Mr Kennett. He's been apprised of the details and promised to give us all the help we need.'

'That's a relief,' said Chatfield. 'Strict security always surrounds munitions factories. Just getting through the front gate is an achievement. They work on the theory that everyone is a potential spy.'

'It's probably the safest thing to do, sir.'

'I daresay it is. Thank you, Inspector. You seem to have been to the right places and asked the right questions. I'll draft a report and leave it on the commissioner's desk.' He sucked his teeth. 'Five young lasses blown to smithereens at a party – the press will go to town on this story. Make sure you don't tell them too much.'

'I never do, Superintendent.'

'If you're heading back to Scotland Yard, you may find me still beavering away in my office.'

'Don't wait there for us,' said Marmion, anxious to avoid seeing him at the end of a long day. 'We still have a lot of work to do here, sir. The sergeant wants me to meet Maureen Quinn. Something about her troubled him somewhat.'

'Why?'

'That's what I'm off to find out. I'll report to you first thing in the morning.'

'Good,' said Chatfield, suppressing a yawn.

'And you're quite sure that we're looking for a local man.'

Marmion was adamant. 'I'd stake my pension on it, Superintendent.'

Midnight found the two constables still on duty outside the Golden Goose. It was lonely work. The disaster had exhausted the curiosity of those in the vicinity so nobody came to pry. They chatted, complained about the chill wind, then moaned when a steady drizzle began to fall. Huddled in the doorway of the pub, they exchanged a few jokes to pass the time. Neither of them even saw the figure that approached silently on the other side of the street and kept to the shadows. When he reached the Golden Goose, the man stopped, looked at the debris, then walked on with a smile of deep satisfaction.

CHAPTER FOUR

When he heard the knock at the front door, Eamonn Quinn thought at first that it was a nosy neighbour who'd caught wind of the explosion at a pub in Hayes. Ready to dispatch the caller with a few choice words, he was taken aback when he opened the door and saw two well-dressed strangers standing there. Marmion performed the introductions and asked politely if they might speak to his daughter.

'She's gone to bed,' said Quinn, abruptly.

'I'm sorry to hear that, sir. We were very much hoping for a word with her.'

'Well, it's not convenient. Maureen will be fast asleep by now.'

'Then we won't disturb her.'

He was about to turn away when Maureen came into the narrow passageway.

'Who is it, Daddy?'

'Hello,' said Keedy, recognising her. 'It seems that your daughter is not quite so tired after all, Mr Quinn. May we come in and talk to her?'

'Only if I'm present,' insisted Quinn, annoyed that he'd been caught lying.

'You and your wife are most welcome to sit in on the discussion, sir.' He smiled at Maureen and indicated his companion. 'This is Inspector Marmion who's in charge of the investigation. He was keen to meet you face-to-face.'

'Good evening,' said Marmion, removing his hat. 'I'm sorry that it's rather late to be calling but this is in the nature of an emergency.'

Quinn grudgingly invited the detectives in, took them into the living room and asked his wife and younger daughter to leave. He and Maureen then sat together on the settee opposite their visitors. Arm around his daughter, Quinn adopted a protective pose and glared at them. The detectives could see that he might be a problem. Marmion turned to Maureen, perched nervously on the edge of her seat.

'We've just come from Agnes Collier's house,' he explained. 'Her mother is now aware of the tragic events at the Golden Goose. She bore up surprisingly well.'

'Sadie Radcliffe is a tough character,' said Quinn.

'So is your daughter, from what I hear.'

'She's been brought up proper, Inspector. We don't mollycoddle children.'

Maureen eyed them anxiously. 'What do you want to know?'

'Well,' said Keedy, taking his cue, 'we'd really like a bit more detail about the other people at the party. Essentially, all that you told me earlier were their names and addresses. Because you were in such a delicate state, I didn't want to press you too hard. But the inspector feels that we can't leave without some indication of the sorts of people your friends were. We know a little about Agnes Collier, of course, from her mother – but what about the others?'

'For instance,' said Marmion, 'tell us about Florrie Duncan. I understand that it was her birthday. How old was she?'

'Twenty-nine,' replied Maureen. 'She was the oldest of us.'

'What about you?'

'I was the youngest.'

'I spoke on the phone to Mr Kennett, the works manager,' said Keedy. 'He was horrified at the turn of events. The one name that he recognised was Florrie Duncan. He described her as the kind of person who'd make an impression anywhere.'

'That's true,' agreed Maureen, brightening a little. 'She was always so full of life. Florrie looked out for us. If there was ever any trouble at work, she'd always step in and help.'

'What kind of trouble?' asked Quinn, bristling.

'Oh, it was nothing serious, Daddy. It's just that some of the men–'

'Did they pester you, Maureen? You should have told me. I'd have put a stop to that right away. I won't let anyone hassle my daughter.'

'Florrie kept an eye on me,' said Maureen. 'She could see off anyone. And if some of the managers got too bossy, she'd stand up to them. Nobody pushed Florrie Duncan around.'

Marmion was interested. 'Were you in the National Federation of Women?'

'Yes, Inspector – Florrie made us join even though trade union activity was banned at the factory.'

'Now that's something I *don't* agree with,' Quinn interjected. 'I mean, it's bad enough making women work in a place like that until they turn bright yellow. Getting them into a union is going too far.'

'They're entitled to protect themselves, Mr Quinn,' said Keedy. 'That's what trade unions are for – to stop workers being exploited. Well, you must be in one yourself.'

'No need, Sergeant – I deliver coal. Only a fool would try to exploit me. But you take my point? Trade unions for *women* – well, it's just not right.'

'Thank you,' said Marmion, crisply, 'your opinion is noted but it's not really relevant. It's Maureen we want to hear, Mr Quinn. She worked alongside these young women. She has information about that birthday party that nobody else has.'

Quinn was peevish. 'Please yourselves.'

'Go on telling us about Florrie Duncan,' said

57

Marmion, nodding at her. 'It sounds to me as if she was a kind of mother to the rest of you.'

'Yes, she was, Inspector,' replied Maureen as if it was the first time that the idea had every occurred to her. 'That's exactly what she was. If you had a problem, you'd always turn to her. I remember when Enid – that's Enid Jenks – was having terrible rows at home with her father. She asked Florrie for advice and things got a lot easier after that.'

The detectives let her ramble on. Now that Quinn had been silenced, his daughter was able to talk at will. Slow and hesitant at first, she became more animated, talking about her friends with a mixture of affection and sadness. The individual characters of the murder victims began to emerge. Evidently, Florrie Duncan was the dominant personality. Jean Harte was a pessimist, always fearing the worst and prone to a succession of minor ailments. Enid Jenks was a gifted violinist and had ambitions to be a professional musician until a patriotic urge had taken her into the munitions factory. Maureen was quite fluent until she reached the last of the victims. When she came to a sudden halt, Keedy had to prompt her.

'What about Shirley Beresford?'

'She was ... very nice.'

'Tell us a bit more about her.'

'Yes,' said Marmion, gently. 'Was she single or married? What did she do before she came to work at the factory? Who were her closest friends? Did she have any hobbies? What do you remember most about her?'

It was all too much for Maureen. Having exhausted her ability to bring the women back to life, she was now overcome by the horror of their deaths. It was borne in upon her that she'd never see any of them and hear their lively banter. They'd been wiped instantaneously out of her life. Hands to her face, she burst into tears and bent forward. Her father put an arm around her and pulled out a grubby handkerchief to thrust at her. As his daughter continued to sob, he looked accusingly at the visitors.

'Did you have to badger her like that?' he said.

'Your daughter has given us a lot of important information, Mr Quinn,' said Marmion. 'Until now, she was doing extraordinarily well. But I can see that we've gone as far as we can now,' he added, getting up. 'Thank you, Maureen.'

'Yes,' said Keedy, also on his feet now, 'it was very brave of you. We're sorry to intrude at such a time but you'll appreciate that this is a criminal investigation. We need all the help we can get if we're to bring the person who planted that bomb to justice.'

'Make sure you catch the bastard before I do,' growled Quinn. 'If I get my hands on him first, there won't be anything left for the hangman.'

In search of more comfort, Ellen and Alice Marmion had adjourned to the living room. Every so often, one of them would glance up hopefully at the clock on the mantelpiece, only to be jolted by the lateness of the hour. Ellen had been very unhappy at the notion of her daughter giving up her job as a teacher to join the Women's Emergency Corps. While she admired the sterling work

59

performed by the organisation, she feared – wrongly, as it turned out – that it would be filled with militant suffragettes who'd have a bad influence on Alice. She was even less pleased with her daughter's move into the ranks of the police force, believing that law enforcement was primarily a job for men. They not only had the necessary strength and stamina, they were less likely to be shocked by some of the hideous sights they'd inevitably see and more able to cope with situations of grave danger.

From Alice's point of view, there was one great drawback to the move. She was under the strict supervision of someone who clearly disliked her.

'Who is she?' asked Ellen.

'Thelma Gale,' said her daughter, 'or, as she insists on being called, Inspector Gale. If you met her, you'd see why her nickname is "Gale Force". When her temper is up, she's like a one-woman hurricane.'

'And she treats you badly?'

'She treats *all* of us badly. Power has gone to her head.'

'But you said that she keeps picking on you.'

'Yes, I can't do anything right for Inspector Gale.'

'Have you complained?'

'What's the point?' replied Alice. 'Her job is to give orders and mine is to obey them. That's all there is to it.'

'I don't like the thought of you being harassed by her all the time.'

'I'll survive, Mummy.'

'Why not ask your father to intervene?'

Alice smiled. 'Daddy is at the root of the problem.'

'Oh? I can't see why.'

'Everyone at Scotland Yard knows and respects Inspector Marmion. When he solved those murders in Shoreditch, he became really famous; and people still talk about his other triumphs. It was the first thing Inspector Gale told me,' recalled Alice. 'She warned me that I wasn't to expect any favours because my father was in the Metropolitan Police. And she said it so nastily. That's what upset me.'

'Is there a Mr Gale?'

'No, she's not married. She'd frighten any man off.'

Ellen was disturbed. 'She's not one of those suffragettes, is she?'

'Yes, and it's the one good thing in her favour,' said Alice before correcting herself. 'No, that's unfair. Gale Force is very efficient at her job and works like a Trojan. Women police are still very much there on sufferance but she won't let any of the men patronise us. She'll even stand up to the commissioner.'

'That takes a lot of doing.'

'I just wish that she wouldn't keep throwing her weight around.'

'Have you told Joe about this?'

'No, Mummy. I can look after myself.'

'He might be able to give you advice.'

'Joe has his own problems with Superintendent Chatfield — so does Daddy, for that matter. Superior officers always like to pull rank. I'll just have to grin and bear it.' Alice glanced at the clock

61

once more. 'Heavens! Is it that late? I'd better go.'

'You can always stay the night,' suggested Ellen. 'Your bed is made up.'

Alice spoke with quiet firmness. 'It's not *my* bed any more, Mummy.'

'Well, it is to me.'

'I must be off.'

The moment that Alice rose to her feet, the telephone rang. Ellen got up and rushed into the hallway to grab the instrument. Her daughter could hear the mixture of pleasure and fatigue in her voice. When she eventually came back into the living room, Ellen was beaming.

'Your father's on his way back – and so is Joe. You'll have to stay now.'

Marmion and Keedy sat in the back of the car as they were driven in the direction of central London. It gave them an opportunity to review what they'd so far established.

'Let's start with the positives,' said Marmion.

'I didn't know there were any, Harv.'

'We've just talked to one of them.'

'Maureen Quinn?'

'She's a survivor, Joe. She was in that outhouse only minutes before it went off. Without realising it, she's a source of valuable information. If her father hadn't been there, we'd have got far more of it out of her.'

'Yes,' said Keedy, 'he was an awkward customer, wasn't he?'

'More to the point, he doesn't like policemen. He made that clear. As a rule, that means one thing. He's been in trouble.'

'Is it worth checking up on that?'

'I think so.'

Keedy lurched sideways as the car went around a tight corner.

'Right,' he said, sitting up straight again, 'what are the other positives?'

'The local police were very cooperative. They don't always put the flags out for what they see as overpaid detectives from Scotland Yard.'

Keedy snorted. 'Overpaid! Is that what we are? I can't say I've noticed.'

'We've got them on our side, Joe. That will save a lot of time arguing over boundaries. They accept that we're in charge. Another positive is that man you spoke to when you went to the factory?'

'Mr Kennett is the works manager.'

'According to you, he promised all the help we'll need.'

'He sounded like a thoroughly decent man, Harv. He was close to tears when I told him that five of his female employees had been blown up at that pub.'

'Then we come to the last and best positive.'

'And what's that?'

'We don't have to go back to the Yard to tell Chat what we've been up to.'

Keedy laughed. 'That's a huge relief,' he said. 'Chat is bad enough in the daytime when he's full of beans. By late evening, he gets tired and that makes him even more fractious. He's like a bear with a sore head.'

'That's why I advised him to go home.'

After exchanging a few jokes about the superintendent, they turned their minds back to the case in hand. Marmion listed all the things they had to do on the following day. They had to deliver a comprehensive report to Claude Chatfield, then appear at a press conference, asking crime correspondents of newspapers to broadcast an appeal for anyone who saw any suspicious activity near the Golden Goose recently to come forward. Detectives would be deployed to go from house to house in the area in search of potential witnesses.

'That outhouse was kept locked,' said Marmion. 'How did the bomber gain access to it to plant his device?'

'And how sophisticated was the bomb?'

'It was sophisticated enough to do the job, Joe. That's what really matters. But it will be interesting to see what the experts say when they've collected enough bomb fragments. It should tell us if we're looking for a rank amateur or for someone who works at the factory and is used to handling explosives.'

'Do you still think someone had a grudge against one of those women?'

'Yes, I do – against one or all of them. It may be some crank who objects to the very idea of women doing jobs always done by men in the past.'

'There's another way of looking at this,' mused Keedy.

'Is there?'

'What if the real target was the landlord? Somebody could have fallen out with him or been banned from the pub. When he blew up that outhouse, he might have been completely unaware of the fact that someone was inside.'

'It's an idea worth considering, Joe, but there's

one thing against it.'

'What's that?'

'Anyone who hated Mr Hubbard enough to plant a bomb on the premises would surely want to cause maximum damage. He'd blow up the pub itself,' said Marmion, thoughtfully. 'And I reckon he'd do it after dark so that no customers would be injured. If the landlord was the target, the best time to set off an explosion would be when he's completely off guard, snoring in bed beside his wife.'

'I still think we shouldn't rule him out, Harv.'

'Agreed – we keep every option on the table.'

'That brings us back to the five victims.'

'Yes,' sighed Marmion, 'and it confronts us with a massive problem. You know how people are when they're bereaved. They withdraw into themselves. The parents of those girls won't like it if we start prying into the private lives of their daughters – well, look at the trouble we had with Mrs Radcliffe. She was very defensive. Like her, the others will just want to be left alone to mourn. We'll be seen as intruders.'

'There's nothing new in that.' Keedy was struck by a sudden thought. 'Let's suppose you're right, Harv, and that one of those six girls *was* the target.' He turned to Marmion. 'What if it had been Maureen Quinn? Amazingly, she survived. When he discovers that, will the bomber have another crack at her?'

Though they tried to relax, Ellen and Alice were on tenterhooks. Every so often, one of them would go to the window and peer through the curtains.

65

Marmion had rung home from Uxbridge police station. The two women tried to work out how long it would take a car to drive back to the house, assuming that it was keeping to the speed limit. Because her knowledge of geography was poor, Ellen's estimate was wildly optimistic. During her time with the Women's Emergency Corps, Alice had driven a lorry all over London and well beyond it. She had a clearer idea of how long it took to get from place to place. She was nevertheless impatient and chafed at the delay. When they heard a car approach the house and slow to a halt, it was Alice who leapt to her feet and rushed to the door. She was in time to see the detectives getting out of the vehicle and ran into Keedy's embrace.

'I'm so glad you're back at last,' she said, breathlessly.

'Sorry about this evening, Alice,' he apologised.

'There'll be other times.'

She kissed him on the cheek, then became aware of her father standing there.

'Don't I get a welcome home?' he asked with a slight edge.

'Of course, you do,' she said, hugging him. 'Hello, Daddy.'

The car drove off and the three of them went into the house. Ellen collected a routine peck on the cheek from her husband then took him into the kitchen. Keedy and Alice followed them.

'There's a meal in the oven, if you're not too tired to eat it,' said Ellen. 'And there's more than enough for you, Joe.'

'I'm starving,' said Keedy.

'We haven't had a thing since we heard the

news from Hayes,' said Marmion, inhaling the aroma that came from the oven as Ellen opened the door. 'That smells good. Thanks for having something ready for us, love.'

'I know how hungry policemen can get.'

'But where've you been?' asked Alice. 'And why did you go there? Tell me everything. I can't wait to hear the details.'

'They're not very pleasant,' warned her father.

'Why is that, Daddy?'

He exchanged a glance with Keedy. 'Let's get some grub inside us first.'

'I second that, Harv,' said the other, rubbing his hands.

It was not long before all four of them were seated around the table. While Marmion and Keedy devoured their food, the women had yet another cup of tea. It was an odd situation but one which was likely to recur time and again now that Keedy was about to join the family. Ordinarily, Marmion would say very little to his wife about the cases on which he was working. He took special care to keep any horrific details from her but he could hardly do that now. Since his daughter was pressing him for information, Ellen was bound to hear it as well. She gave him an encouraging smile, as if indicating that she had no qualms about what he might say.

Choosing his words carefully, Marmion told them about the crisis that had made them hare off to Hayes in a fast car. Both women were appalled. The idea of one female victim was enough to upset them. The fact that five had been blown to pieces made them shudder. They found it difficult

67

to imagine how gruesome the scene of the crime must have been. Alice was the first to recover from the shock. Ellen was numbed and left all the questions to her daughter.

'Why would anyone want to murder some munition workers?' she asked.

'That's not what they'll be called in the papers,' said her father. 'They'll be described as canaries. They'll be robbed of their dignity and simply be lumped together as munitionettes.'

'That's terrible, Daddy. They were five separate individuals.'

'We discovered that from the survivor,' said Keedy. 'She told us how different they all were from each other and Mrs Radcliffe – the mother of one of the girls – told us a little about her daughter. In the normal course of events, all six of them would probably never have been friends. Well,' he corrected, 'two of them might have been because they lived so close to each other in Uxbridge, but the rest were scattered all over the place in Hayes. What brought them together was the war.'

'It brought them together, then killed them,' remarked Ellen.

'What a terrible way to lose their lives,' said Alice, face taut. 'They went off happily to a birthday party without realising that they were walking into a death trap. It's dreadful. What kind of a monster could do such a thing?' She swung round to face her father. 'Do you have any idea who he could be?'

'No, Alice,' admitted Marmion, 'but his signature tells us something about him. He's cold, ruthless, calculating and has no concern for the value of human life. The chances are that he was ready to sacrifice innocent young women in order to kill the person he was really after.'

'And who was that?'

'We haven't worked it out yet,' said Keedy. 'We're still at a very early stage of the investigation.'

'Needless to say,' cautioned Marmion, 'everything that we've told you has been confidential. Nothing – not a single word – must be repeated to anyone at work, Alice. When your colleagues know that I'm in charge of the case, you're bound to be asked. You must lie your head off.'

'That's not easy for someone as honest as her,' said Ellen.

'Yes, it is, Mummy,' said Alice. 'When I know how important it is to be discreet, I can be. I won't tell a soul.'

Marmion put a hand on her arm. 'Good girl.'

'But that doesn't mean I want to be kept in the dark from now on.'

'What do you mean?'

'Well,' she said, eyes glistening with interest, 'this case is fascinating. It's all about six young women of my age or thereabouts. I have some idea of how they might think and act. It's the one advantage I have over you and Joe. I don't want to be co-opted on to the investigation – that would be impossible – but I would like to know about any developments. Who knows? I might be able to offer some useful ideas.'

Marmion was caught momentarily off balance and Keedy looked less than enthusiastic about her offer. Both of them were having second thoughts about the wisdom of discussing the case so freely with her. Alice wanted to be included. They traded a look of mild desperation, neither of them knowing quite what to say.

Alice was forceful. 'What have you got against me?' she demanded. 'I might actually be able to help. I'm in the police force as well, remember.'

CHAPTER FIVE

Since neither of his daughters was leaving the house that day, it was Eamonn Quinn who was the first to get up. He liked to get to the coal yard early so that he had the pick of the bags. After he'd had a swill in the kitchen sink, his face was relatively clean. It would be black by the time he came home in the evening. Like his elder daughter, he had a job that changed his colour completely. The difference was that Maureen's yellow patina could not be washed off with cold water. On his visit to the privy, he had his first cigarette of the day and reflected on the distressing events at the Golden Goose. They'd give Maureen a worrying prominence. He'd feel the effects himself as his customers bombarded him on the doorstep with questions about what exactly had happened and how his daughter was coping with the fraught situation. It was the kind of interest that he'd never willingly seek. Others might bask in it but Quinn was a man who shunned attention.

By the time he returned to the kitchen, he

found the kettle on the gas stove and his wife preparing his breakfast. Diane was still sleepy, moving as if in a dream and yawning intermittently. She tried to shake herself fully awake.

'It feels funny, doesn't it?' she said.

'What does?'

'Most mornings, Maureen would have left hours ago. She'd be at work before either of us got up. It seems strange having her still here.'

'It's not strange, Di, it's necessary.'

'I know that.'

'She's had a terrible time. She needs to recover.'

'Maureen was shivering all over when I put her to bed last night.'

'I blame *them*,' said Quinn, curling a lip. 'Those coppers were wrong to keep on at her like that. They wore the poor girl down.'

'What do I do if they come back, Eamonn?'

'Keep them away from her.'

'But they're from Scotland Yard.'

'I don't care where the buggers come from,' he said, rancorously. 'I don't want them battering her with questions again. Maureen is not up to it.'

'She's stronger than she looks,' said Diane, turning off the gas and pouring hot water into the teapot. 'Working in that factory has made her grow up fast. Well, you've noticed it yourself. Maureen used to be very shy but she's got a lot more confidence now.'

'That doesn't mean she's up to being interrogated by those two.'

'They need information, Eamonn.'

'Whose side are you on?' he snarled. 'This is

71

our daughter, Di, and we've got to protect her. You know what I think about coppers. Don't let them into the house.'

'What am I to say to them?'

'Any excuse will do. Just get rid of them.'

'I don't want to get us into any trouble,' she said, nervously.

'Shut up and do as you're told, woman.' He sat down at the table. 'And get on with my breakfast. I've got a hard day ahead. I need some grub inside me.'

Diane went through her usual routine, pouring his tea, cooking his food and setting it in front of him. All that Quinn did was to gobble it down in silence then end with his usual belch. He'd changed and his wife made allowances for it. He was never the most congenial of men but the war had made him even more churlish and self-centred. She put it down to the fact that their two sons had both enlisted and were facing unknown dangers at the front. Quinn missed them dreadfully. He was now the only man in the household. The balance had tilted sharply against him. Instead of being able to spend time with two strapping young men who shared his interests, he was stuck with a wife and two daughters and felt isolated. He still loved Diane after his own fashion but he made no attempt to show it, considering any display of affection to be somehow unmanly. What Maureen and Lily had to put up with was his uncertain temper and a series of gruff commands. Like their mother, they'd learnt to read the warning signals and keep out of his way.

'I'm off,' he announced, washing down his last mouthful of food with a swig of tea. 'Expect me when you see me.'

'Yes, Eamonn.'

'And – at all costs – don't let those coppers over the threshold.'

'I'll do my best.'

'You'll do as I bloody well say.'

On that truculent note, he hauled himself up and walked out. Diane heard him putting on his coat and his cap before letting himself out of the house. The door was slammed even harder than usual. Other wives might have baulked at such brusque treatment but she was accustomed to it, always finding an excuse for her husband. It was not simply his underlying anxieties about their sons this time. The main cause of his anger, she told herself, was his concern for Maureen. Their elder daughter had escaped being blown up by the skin of her teeth. It was a shattering experience for her and Quinn was struggling to come to terms with it. As in all crisis situations, he reverted to aggression and bullying. His wife forgave him as a matter of course.

Diane had her own fears for Maureen. Just when the girl was starting to blossom and mature, she'd been thrown into disarray. There was no telling if she'd ever be quite the same again. She'd survived a disaster but would be scarred by it for life. It had already kept Diane awake in the small hours. It would, inevitably, cause Maureen nightmares. The loss of Agnes Collier would be particularly wounding because the two of them saw each other every day. A massive gap had suddenly opened up in

73

Maureen's life. Diane felt an urge to console her and went padding upstairs in her slippers, expecting to find her elder daughter lying in bed. When she tapped on the door and opened it, however, she was given a profound shock.

There was no sign of Maureen. Her mother flew into a panic. She searched the rest of the house in vain, recruiting Lily to help her and even dashing out into the tiny garden. It was bewildering. Without any explanation, Maureen had vanished.

Quick to criticise Marmion whenever the opportunity arose, Claude Chatfield had to acknowledge that the inspector knew how to control a press conference. Marmion remained calm and even-tempered throughout, winning the crime correspondents over by referring to each of them by their Christian names and producing the occasional quip. He fed them enough information to fill their columns while holding back some significant details. Chatfield knew what those details were because he'd seen the full report that Marmion had put on his desk earlier that morning. He marvelled at the way that questions were fielded and answered. What irritated him was the exaggerated respect that everyone was showing Marmion. It was not always the case. During a previous investigation – the brutal murder of a conscientious objector – the newspapers had been highly critical of what they saw as inertia on the part of the police. Marmion had been the scapegoat. When both the crime and a subsequent murder were solved, however, he was given full credit and his reputation was greatly enhanced. It remained to be seen whether he could succeed with what, on the surface, appeared to be a more complex investigation.

A hand went up and another question was fired at him.

'Are you certain this is not the work of foreign agents, Inspector?'

'I'm absolutely certain,' replied Marmion, levelly.

'Yet the women were canaries. Killing them was a way of weakening the workforce at a munitions factory.'

'I can see that you've never been to Hayes. It's an enormous factory, employing well over ten thousand workers, the vast majority of whom are women. Blowing up five of them will hardly have an adverse affect on production.'

'Point taken, Inspector.'

Keen to get back to the investigation, Marmion wound up the session by reminding them that an urgent appeal for help needed to be made. He also stressed that it would be both unkind and unproductive of them to pursue the families of the individual victims. They – and Maureen Quinn – needed to be left alone at such a sensitive time. Though everyone in the room nodded in agreement, Marmion was not sure if they'd actually obey his instruction. There was always one journalist who'd go to any lengths to get an exclusive story.

When it was all over, Chatfield stepped in to congratulate him.

'Well done,' he said. 'That was exemplary.'

'Thank you, Inspector.'

'You've obviously picked up a lot of tips from me.'

'Of course,' said Marmion.

It was not true but there was no point in arguing about it. In fact, Chatfield was not at his best during a press conference. He was too bossy and kept far too much back. Instead of wooing the press, he usually managed to antagonise them. Sublimely unaware that his manner was condescending, he always wondered why he received less than lavish praise in the newspapers.

'What's your next move, Inspector?' he asked.

'My first port of call is the Golden Goose. I want another chat with the landlord.'

'What will Sergeant Keedy be doing?'

'He's going to talk to Mr Kennett, the works manager at the factory.'

'I wish I could put more men at your disposal.'

'We'll manage, sir,' said Marmion. 'One trained detective is worth half a dozen uniformed constables who've spent most of their time pounding the beat and arresting drunks. We've a small but experienced team.'

'But will it deliver a result? That's my concern.'

'All that I can guarantee is that we'll do our utmost.'

'I suppose I've no need to ask this,' said Chatfield, raising an eyebrow, 'but I hope you haven't discussed this case with your daughter. I know that she's followed in your footsteps and joined the police but she's a complete novice and has no part to play in a murder investigation.'

As he looked Chatfield in the eye, Marmion's face was impassive. 'As you say, sir, there's no need to ask that question.'

'I'm relieved to hear it. In any case, she's probably too busy thinking about her forthcoming marriage, isn't she? Talking of which, I trust that the prospect is not distracting the sergeant in any way.'

'Joe Keedy is a true professional, Superintendent.'

'Yes – he reminds me of myself at that age.'

'I can't say that I see any similarity,' said Marmion, waspishly. 'You are quite unique, Superintendent. The car is waiting,' he went on, moving to the door. 'If you'll excuse us, we have five murders to solve.'

Bernard Kennett was a tall, stooping, middle-aged man in a crumpled blue suit. He looked rather careworn and had a habit of running his hand through his hair. Invited into his office, Keedy was quick to make an appraisal of him, deciding that the works manager was more or less exactly as he'd imagined him to be when they spoke on the telephone. Kennett was polite, educated and eager to be of assistance. He waved his visitor to a chair, then sat behind a desk piled high with invoices and correspondence.

'Let me get one thing clear, Sergeant,' he began. 'I'm not in overall control of production here. That duty falls to Mr Passmore. He's the factory manager. I'm in charge of the section where the five unfortunate young women used to work.'

'And you actually remembered one of them.'

'Oh, nobody could forget Florence Duncan. She was their spokeswoman. I recall her sitting in

77

that very seat and demanding a longer lunch break.'

'Did she get it?' wondered Keedy.

'That's immaterial.' The older man combed his hair with his fingers then reached for a folder on his desk. 'Knowing that you were coming, I did a bit of detective work on my own behalf. I spoke to some of the women who worked alongside the five victims and made a few notes.'

'That will be extremely helpful, sir,' said Keedy. 'Thank you.'

'It's only anecdotal, of course, but it will tell you something about their characters.' He opened the folder. 'I need hardly say what the mood is like in the Cartridge Section. Those five young women were very popular. The whole place is in mourning for them.'

'That's understandable.'

Kennett glanced at his notes. 'The one I feel sorry for is Enid Jenks.'

'We were told that she was a fine musician.'

'That's why she would have been so disappointed to miss the occasion. We're not just slave-drivers here, Sergeant. Productivity must, of necessity, be kept up to a high level but we do try to take care of our workforce. They're engaged in rather dull and repetitive work,' he continued, 'so we endeavour to take their minds off it by giving them periodic treats during their lunch break.'

'What sort of treats?'

'The one I have in mind is the visit of Madame Tetrazzini. Does that name mean anything to you?'

'I'm afraid not,' confessed Keedy.

'Then I can see that you are not an opera lover. Madame Tetrazzini is a famous Italian soprano. She has an international reputation. We were lucky enough to secure a booking with her. She's due to entertain our workers here next week. I fancy that Enid Jenks would have been thrilled to have the opportunity to hear the lady. It's a complete contrast,' said Kennett with a note of pride. 'The women go from filling shells for long hours to listening to arias from Verdi and Rossini. We may tire their limbs but we also feed their souls.'

'I wouldn't know about that, sir. I've never been to an opera. But I'm glad that it's not uninterrupted toil here.' He extended a hand. 'Can I see your notes, please?'

Kennett passed them to him. 'Take them away, Sergeant. My handwriting is not too atrocious. Now, then, what else can I do to help?'

'I'd be interested to see what the five victims actually did when they were here,' said Keedy, careful not to reveal that he believed the bomber might also work at the factory. 'I'd like some insight into their daily routine.'

'That can be arranged.'

Before he could stand up, Kennett was diverted by the urgent ring of his telephone. Apologising for the interruption, he picked up the receiver and listened. Keedy watched his expression change from interest to sudden concern.

'Yes,' said the works manager at length. 'By all means, allow her in. I'll see her immediately.' He put the receiver down. 'That was the security officer at the gate. There's a Mrs Quinn asking to see me. She seems quite desperate.'

79

'Would that be a Mrs Diane Quinn?' asked Keedy.

'It is, indeed. It appears that her daughter has disappeared from the house. Mrs Quinn is wondering if she came to work in spite of the fact that she was ordered not to by her father. Excuse me,' said Kennett, moving to the door, 'while I instruct my secretary to establish the facts. I want to put Mrs Quinn's mind at rest.'

Keedy took the opportunity to glance at the notes he'd been given. They were written in a neat hand and consisted largely of a series of quotations from friends of the deceased. They fleshed out the portraits that he and Marmion had been given at the Quinn house. He noted the kind words that were said about Maureen herself. Most of the praise was reserved for Florrie Duncan but Enid Jenks was admired for her musical talent – she also played the piano – Agnes Collier was remembered for her girlish giggle and Jean Harte was liked best for her morose humour. Keedy was very interested in a snippet of information about Shirley Beresford.

It was minutes before Kennett reappeared. When he finally did so, he had an anguished Diane Quinn with him. She was startled to see Keedy there. He stood up so that she could have his chair and listened intently to her tale of woe.

'It's my fault,' she said, chewing her lip. 'I should have checked the moment I got up. Better still, I should have heard her sneaking out of the house. It never crossed my mind that she'd go anywhere. Maureen was dog-tired last night. After what she'd been through, it's not surprising. But, when I went into her bedroom this morning, she simply wasn't there!' Apprehension darkened her features. 'My husband will be so cross with me when he finds out. I must get Maureen back before he comes home. Where on earth can she be, Sergeant?'

'I don't know, Mrs Quinn. I assume that you've conducted a search?'

'I've been *everywhere.* I even called on Sadie Radcliffe and that was a mistake. She was very spiteful about Maureen – don't know why. Anyway,' she continued, 'I remembered reading this article once about people who have a dreadful experience being drawn back to the place where it happened. So I caught the train to Hayes and asked where the Golden Goose was. It was frightening. Well, you've seen the mess that the bomb made, Sergeant. It made my knees go weak. If Maureen had been caught in the blast, we'd never have been able to recognise her remains.'

'That *is* posing a problem,' admitted Keedy, 'and I'm sorry that you had to see that pile of debris. What made you think your daughter may have come here?'

'It was what she wanted to do but Eamonn, my husband, forbade it.'

'I'm fairly certain that's she's not here,' said Kennett, 'because the other girls would have mentioned the fact when I talked to them. We'll soon know the truth. My secretary will find out if she clocked in.'

'She *has* to be here, sir. Where else can she be?'

Diane continued to insist that her daughter was in the factory somewhere and the two men consoled her as best they could. When the telephone rang, Kennett moved across to pick it up. The conversation was over within seconds. After putting the receiver down, he shook his head sadly.

'Maureen is definitely not on the site, Mrs Quinn,' he said.

She was devastated. 'Are you quite sure?'

'Yes, I am. If she *had* turned up here this morning, she wouldn't have been allowed to carry on as if nothing had happened. For her own sake, we'd have turned her away.' He looked at Keedy. 'People sometimes think that we force our employees to work until they drop but we're very humane. We always try to show compassion.' His eyes flicked back to Diane. 'You'll have to look elsewhere, Mrs Quinn.'

'But *where?*' she wailed. 'There's nowhere else left.'

'Yes, there is,' said Keedy, 'and it's possible that it never occurred to you. If you were thrown into a panic, you probably just ran around in circles.'

'That's exactly what I did, Sergeant. I was like a dog with its tail on fire.'

'Let's see if we can put that fire out, shall we?' He moved to the door and opened it. 'Thank you for your help, Mr Kennett. I'll be back in due course. At the moment, the search for Maureen takes priority.' He smiled at Diane. 'Are you ready, Mrs Quinn?'

Harvey Marmion was pleased to hear that many bomb fragments had been found and that they were being carefully pieced together. He would eventually know if they were dealing with an ama-teur or with someone who had some expertise in handling explosives. Looking at the rubble, he found it difficult to imagine where the bomb had actually been placed or what sort of timing device it must have had. The scene was a graphic illustration of cause and effect. A knot of people looked on with ghoulish curiosity. Uppermost in the mind of Leighton Hubbard was revenge. Standing beside Marmion on the pavement opposite his pub, he was quivering with fury.

'Catch him, Inspector,' he urged. 'Catch him then hand him over to me.'

'Let the law take its course, sir.'

'Hanging is too good for an animal like that.'

'We may be talking about more than one person,' said Marmion. 'It's something we can't rule out. Planting a bomb in its hiding place would have taken some time. The bomber might have needed a lookout.'

'He needs a hand grenade up his arse, if you ask me.'

'How did he gain access to the outhouse, that's what puzzles me? You claim that it was kept locked.'

'It's supposed to be,' said Hubbard, 'and I always make sure that it is. So does the missus, for that matter. We protect our property. Because he only works here now and again, Royston is not so careful.'

'Royston?'

'He helps us out, Inspector. He's a willing lad but he's not very bright. When he tried to join the army, they turned him down on medical grounds but it could equally have been because of his stupidity.'

83

'What does he do, exactly?'

'He fetches and carries. That's about all he can do. I'd never let him behind the bar and he'd be hopeless dealing with money. What he can do is donkey work. Royston cleans beer glasses and moves crates of empty bottles.'

'Where does he store the crates – in the outhouse?'

'Yes,' replied Hubbard.

'Does he ever forget to lock it?'

'I'm afraid that he does. Every time it's happened, I threaten him with the sack but...' the landlord hunched his shoulders '...well, the truth is that I feel sorry for the lad. You can't help liking him.'

'Where is the key to the outhouse kept?'

'It hangs on a hook in the corridor.'

'Where does the corridor lead?'

'It's the way to the Gents – that's out in the courtyard. Well, it was,' said Hubbard, bitterly, 'but that went up in smoke as well. It's only a shed with a corrugated iron roof. Thank God nobody was taking a piss out there at the time.'

The landlord was still simmering. Marmion gave him a few minutes to expel his bile about the temporary loss of his livelihood. Hubbard blamed everyone he could think of for the disaster, ending with an attack on the police for not guarding his premises. Marmion leapt to their defence.

'How were they to know that your outhouse was in danger?' he challenged. 'Police resources are very stretched, Mr Hubbard. They have to identify the most vulnerable targets and keep an eye on them. No disrespect to the Golden Goose but your pub hardly merits comparison with the munitions factory. Had a bomb been planted there, far more deaths would have resulted.'

Hubbard had the grace to look shamefaced. He even shrugged an apology.

'Right,' said Marmion, 'now that you've calmed down, you can start to help us and, by extension, help yourself.'

'Eh?'

'I'm bound to ask the obvious question. Do you have any enemies?'

'Yes, Inspector – I'm in business. Every other landlord in Hayes is my enemy.'

'Would any of them go to the length of bombing your outhouse?'

'No, they wouldn't – but I daresay they're rubbing their hands with glee now that the Goose is out of action for a while. As for customers I might have upset, there have been plenty of those but most of them are in the army now and the others wouldn't dare do a thing like this to me.'

'How many people knew about the birthday party in advance?'

'Apart from me and the wife, almost nobody was told. There'd have been strong objections from a few of the regulars, especially Ezra Greenwell. Oh,' he added as he scratched his head, 'Royston would have known, of course. He was there when the booking was made.'

'Would he have spread the word about the party?'

'I told him not to but that probably went in one ear and out the other. Royston lives in a world of his own. He goes around with this half-witted grin on his face. It was still there last night when he was watching my outhouse blazing away.'

'What's his full name?' asked Marmion, taking out his notebook. 'And where does Royston live?'

'He can't tell you anything, Inspector.'

'Nevertheless, I think that it's time he and I got acquainted.'

CHAPTER SIX

Alice Marmion schooled herself to be patient. In joining the police, she realised, she'd expected too much too soon. The concept of a female constabulary was still relatively new and the force had an ill-defined role. Again, it was fiercely resented in some quarters, as Alice had swiftly discovered. The war which had depleted the police force had given women the opportunity to move into its ranks and show what they could do. At best, they faced a grudging tolerance from male counterparts; at worst, they had to endure stinging criticism of their limitations. Alice had learnt to ignore their acid comments and simply get on with her job. She'd made some good friends among the other women but their support was offset by the hostility of a superior officer.

Meeting her in a corridor, Inspector Thelma Gale pounced on Alice.

'There you are,' she said, 'dawdling as usual.'

'I'm taking this report to Sergeant Reeves,' explained Alice, holding up some sheets of paper.

'She wants it urgently.'

'"Urgency" is not exactly your watchword, is it?'

'What do you mean, Inspector?'

'I mean that you trudge instead of walking briskly. I mean that you're slow of mind and even slower of body.'

'That's unfair,' said Alice, smarting at the reproof.

'I'm not the only one who's noticed. Others have complained as well.'

Alice knew that it was untrue but she was in no position to argue. The more she defended herself against the inspector, the harder she'd be slapped down. Thelma Gale was a stout woman in her forties with short hair and a flat, plain face twisted into an expression of permanent disapproval. Her natural authority was enhanced by the smartness of her uniform. She was a formidable character in every way and few people got the better of her in argument.

She tapped Alice's shoulder. 'What did I tell you?'

'You've told me a vast number of things, Inspector.'

'This concerned your father.'

'Oh, that – yes, I remember.'

'I warned you not to trade on the fact that you're the daughter of Detective Inspector Marmion. Admirable as his achievements have been, they don't entitle you to any preferential treatment.'

'I neither expected nor sought it.'

'And don't you dare go running to Daddy with complaints about cruel Inspector Gale,' said the other, wagging a finger, 'because it will have no effect. I don't answer to your father. I rule the roost here. Is that clear?'

'You've made it abundantly clear, Inspector.'

'Try to do *your* job properly for once and let your father get on with his. He obviously has his hands full at the moment.'

'Yes, he does.'

'Five young women blown to pieces – it's an appalling crime. They were already risking their lives and ruining their looks by working in that munitions factory. I regard them as unsung heroines.'

'So do I, Inspector.'

Thelma leant in closer to her. 'What has your father said about the case?'

'He hasn't discussed it with me.'

'Inspector Marmion must have said *something*.'

'When he comes through the door at home, he leaves his work outside. My mother appreciates that. Besides,' Alice went on, 'I don't live there any more. I have a flat of my own.'

'But you're also engaged to Sergeant Keedy. What has *he* told you?'

'Nothing at all.'

'Come now – you must have wheedled something out of him.'

'It's not my place to do so, Inspector.'

Alice's face was expressionless under the searching stare of the other woman. To admit that she had taken an interest in the case would have been foolish. It would have unleashed a torrent of denunciation from the inspector, accusing her of trying to get involved in something that was totally outside her remit as a police officer. Behind the censure would be a deep envy. Thelma Gale would be suffused with jealousy at the notion that a junior member of her force was engaged, even tangentially, in such an important investigation. Alice got an even harder tap on the shoulder.

'Get about your business,' said Thelma, 'and be sharp about it.'

'Yes, Inspector,' replied Alice. 'Do excuse me. Please.'

Stepping past the older woman, she strode along the corridor and turned a corner, gasping with relief. The first thing she saw was one of her colleagues coming in through the main door and letting in a blast of cold air as she did so.

'It's so windy today,' said the woman, straightening her hair.

'Yes,' agreed Alice. 'Gale force.'

Marmion had no difficulty in finding Royston Liddle. He lived with his widowed mother only two streets away from the Golden Goose. When his visitor called, Liddle was feeding two rabbits who were scrabbling about in their hutch. He opened the side door of the yard and called up the entry that ran between the houses.

'Who is it? I'm down here!'

Marmion peered down the entry. 'Mr Liddle?'

'That's me,' said the other, grinning broadly.

He was a short man with a compact frame. Though still young, he was totally bald. He had large protruding eyes with the gleam of innocence in them. Beneath his snub nose was a pencil-thin moustache that looked like a supplementary eyebrow. On a chill morning, Liddle wore nothing more than a collarless shirt, a pair of crumpled trousers and some dog-eared slippers.

'I was just feeding Mild and Bitter,' he said. 'They're my rabbits. When people go to the pub, they ask for mild or bitter. I like both, see? So that's what I named them.' He gave himself a congratulatory giggle. 'Clever, isn't it?'

'Yes, Mr Liddle.'

Marmion introduced himself and explained why he was there. The grin never left Liddle's face. He invited his visitor into the house and took him to the living room, a small, cluttered space with hideous green wallpaper and an abiding smell of boiled cabbage. Royston Liddle had to move a pile of clothing off the settee so that Marmion could sit down. Perched on an upright chair, he nodded away.

'Mummy isn't here at the moment,' he explained. 'She works in the shop.'

'Actually, it's about *your* job that I came, Mr Liddle.'

'Everyone calls me Royston.'

'So I gather.'

'Which job do you mean, Inspector? I've got five altogether.'

He chuckled as if it was some sort of record. It transpired that he worked part-time at two pubs other than the Golden Goose. He also helped to deliver milk every morning and did two afternoons at a furniture warehouse. Liddle was anxious to display his full range of abilities.

'Mummy cleans the big house on Wednesdays,' he said, 'and I sometimes help her, though of course, I don't get paid for that.'

Marmion could see that the landlord had got the man's measure. Royston Liddle was a willing simpleton. His glaring lack of intelligence was balanced by a burning desire to please, in whatever mundane station in life. Jobs that others might view as beneath them constituted a legitimate career in his view. When Marmion talked about the explosion at the Golden Goose, Liddle expressed shock and outrage but his grin nevertheless remained intact.

'Where were you at the time?' asked Marmion.

'I was down the cellar of the Black Dog,' said Liddle. 'I was moving a barrel when the explosion went off. I heard it clearly even though I was five streets away.'

'Mr Hubbard said that you did some work earlier for him.'

'That's right. I had to sweep the floor of the outhouse and put up that table. There was a birthday party there.'

'And you did that when the pub was closed, I understand.'

'Yes, Inspector.'

'Did you lock up after you?'

'Oh, yes, I have to or Mr Hubbard gets angry.'

'Did you notice anything unusual when you went to the outhouse?'

Liddle was baffled. 'Unusual?' he echoed.

'Was there anything out of place?'

'No, Inspector, there was just the usual pile of crates. I moved them out of the way so that the girls had some room. Oh, and I used the brush to get rid of the spiders in the roof beams. I know

91

that some people are scared of them.' He thrust out his chest. 'I'm not. I like spiders.'

'Tell me about the key to the outhouse.'

'It hangs on a hook in the corridor.'

'I know that. Has it ever gone missing recently?'

Liddle became furtive. 'I don't know what you mean.'

'Well,' said Marmion, 'from what I hear, it would have been easy for any of the customers to take that key and let themselves into the outhouse. Is that true?'

'I suppose it is.'

'Mr Hubbard confirmed it.'

'Then it could happen.'

Marmion watched him carefully. The grin had now become sheepish and Liddle's body had hunched protectively. Patently, he was hiding something.

'You do realise that this is a murder investigation,' said Marmion, putting some steel into his voice. 'You are aware that withholding evidence is an offence, aren't you?'

'I've done nothing wrong, Inspector,' bleated Liddle.

'Let me be the judge of that.'

'I just looked the other way.'

'What are you talking about?'

Royston Liddle wrestled with his conscience and ran a hand across his pate. It suddenly occurred to him that he might be in trouble and his mother was not there to speak up for him, as she habitually did. He was alone and hopelessly unequal to the situation. He started to bite his nails and his grin was almost manic.

'I think you're holding something back, Royston,' said Marmion. 'You can either tell me what it is right here or we'll go to the police station and have a formal interview. Is that what you'd prefer?'

Liddle emitted a squeak of terror. Having lived a blameless life, he'd never had the slightest trouble with the police. He was a fixture in the area. Constables on patrol treated him with amusement. The idea that he might be arrested by a detective from Scotland Yard sent a shudder through him. He got apologetically to his feet.

'It only happened a few times, Inspector,' he confessed. 'And it wasn't really my fault. I mean, he's a friend of mine. I just did him a favour.'

'Who are we talking about?'

'He gave me two shillings once but that's all.'

'What did you have to do to earn it?'

'I had to pretend I didn't notice,' said Liddle, 'and say nothing to Leighton.' He put his hands together in prayer. 'You won't tell him, will you, Inspector? If you do, I could lose my job there.'

'It all depends on what you actually did for this friend of yours.'

Liddle breathed in deeply and gnashed his teeth. 'I didn't report it when that key disappeared on the hook. They wanted to use the outhouse.'

'Who are *they?*' pressed Marmion.

'I don't know her name but she lives in Hyde Road somewhere. On Tuesday, they were only in there for half an hour. I know that because I checked that the key was back on the hook. No harm was done. It wasn't a crime or anything like that.'

'What you're telling me is that someone had unauthorised access to that outhouse and that you were aware of it.' He stood up to confront Liddle. 'Who is this friend of yours and where can I find him?'

Maureen Quinn sat in the gloom with her hands in her lap and her head on her chest. Time meant nothing to her. She was so preoccupied that hours slipped past unnoticed. Unknown to her, people had come and gone throughout the morning. When the heavy door squealed back on its hinges yet again, she was unaware of it. Even the clang of the iron latch being replaced failed to rouse her. It was her mother's voice that finally brought her out of her meditation.

'Maureen!' cried Diane Quinn. 'Thank heaven we found you!'

'I had a feeling that she might be here,' said Keedy.

Diane rushed to the pew at the rear of the church and embraced her daughter. It was a poignant reunion, both of them weeping copiously. It was some while before Diane was able to offer an explanation. She indicated Keedy.

'When he came to the house yesterday,' she said, 'the sergeant noticed that you were wearing a crucifix. I told him that we don't go to church very often because your father hates it. That's why I never even thought to try here. It was Sergeant Keedy who suggested it.'

'How are you, Maureen?' he asked, gently.

Her voice was distant. 'I'm fine, thank you.'

'Why didn't you tell us you were coming here?'

demanded Diane.

'Daddy would have stopped me.'

'I thought you'd gone to work.'

'I wanted to,' said Maureen, 'but I came here instead.'

'I was at the factory when your mother came looking for you,' said Keedy. 'I went to see Mr Kennett. He was able to tell me something about … the people at that birthday party. He'd gathered a lot of information about them. People said some very nice things about you, Maureen. You have a lot of friends there.'

'The best ones have all gone.'

'Is that why you came here – to pray for them?'

Maureen nodded. 'I needed to think.'

'I'll take you home now, darling,' said Diane, hugging her.

'I'd like to stay for a bit, Mummy.'

'But you've been here for ages. You must be famished.'

'I don't want anything to eat.'

'At least come away with me. You can think at home.'

'It's not the same.'

Maureen continued to protest but her mother wouldn't be denied. She wanted her daughter where she could see her. Keedy was anxious to return to the factory but he stayed long enough to hear Maureen's desperate plea.

'Don't tell Daddy about this, will you?' she said. 'He wouldn't understand.'

It was Marmion's turn to meet the works manager. Like Keedy, he found him both pleasant and

95

accommodating. Bernard Kennett answered all his questions readily and offered him free access to the site whenever he wanted it. Factories involved in the war effort were not always so welcoming. Marmion had had tussles with hidebound security systems on more than one occasion. Some managers sought to put the preservation of their rule book above a police investigation. Kennett took the opposite view. In the interests of solving a crime that had unsettled the entire workforce there, he would bend the rules to the full extent. In fact, Marmion drew a blank on his visit but he wasn't dismayed. Establishing a rapport with Kennett was important. It was something he'd not yet managed to do with the irascible landlord of the Golden Goose.

Taking his leave, Marmion left the building and headed for the main gate. No sooner was he let out than he saw Keedy approaching with his usual jaunty stride.

'It's all right for some,' complained the sergeant. 'You have use of the car whereas I have to travel by Shanks's pony.'

'Mr Kennett told me you'd gone off with Mrs Quinn.'

'You've met him, have you?'

'Yes, and he's as helpful as you said.'

'What brought you here, Harv?'

'Tell me about Maureen Quinn first. Did you track her down?'

Keedy explained that he'd followed his instinct and reunited mother and daughter. The incident had shown him just how afraid they both were of Eamonn Quinn. They'd agreed to say nothing about Maureen's disappearance and to make Lily hold her tongue as well. When he got home, Quinn would be unaware of the female conspiracy in his household.

Marmion explained that what had brought him to the factory was a name that had been given to him by Royston Liddle. It belonged to one of the drivers who worked there. Unfortunately, Alan Suggs was not on the premises. He'd driven off with a consignment of shells and would be away for some time. Keedy was not sure that the man was worth pursuing.

'I reckon he's in the clear, Harv,' he said. 'If he only used that outhouse as a place for a rendezvous with his girlfriend, he wasn't really breaking the law.'

'He was trespassing, Joe.'

'We can't arrest a man for spending half an hour in an empty outhouse. Apart from anything else, it would blight his romance.'

'I just want to talk to Suggs.'

'Well, show a bit of sympathy. Think back to the time when you were courting Ellen. According to Alice, her parents were not exactly impressed at first by the idea of you as a future son-in-law. I bet that you had a few secret meetings when and wherever you could.'

'That's beside the point,' said Marmion, unhappy at the reminder. 'We didn't hide in a place where five women were blown up only days later.'

'Are you saying that Suggs is a suspect?'

'I'm saying that we should check every lead we have. While I'm waiting for him to drive back here, I'm going to call at the homes of some of the victims and see what I can unearth. I thought I'd start with the one person that Maureen Quinn told us so little about and that's Shirley Beresford.'

'Well, I can tell you two significant facts about that young lady,' said Keedy. 'The works manager did some research on our behalf. I have his notes.'

'Excellent – what do they tell you, Joe?'

'Shirley Beresford was married and she was their star player.'

'Star player?'

'Believe it or not, this factory has its own women's football team. They not only finished top of the league, they're due to play in a cup final next week against a team from Woolwich. They take the game very seriously.'

'That *is* interesting,' conceded Marmion. 'What about the other women at that party? Did any of them play in the team?'

'Yes, they did. Maureen Quinn is their goal-keeper.'

'Is she any good?'

'She's one of the reasons they won the league, Harv. She keeps out shots at one end of the pitch while Shirley Beresford scores goals at the other. They were both crucial members of the team. See what I'm starting to think?'

'With two of their best players out of the way, they'd be badly weakened in that cup final. Woolwich would be clear favourites.'

'It all sounds so far-fetched, though,' argued Keedy. 'I know that passions run high in sport but would anyone really stoop to something like this?'

Marmion needed a few moments to consider his answer. Weighing heavily with him was the fact the munitions factory at Woolwich would employ lots of people who knew how to handle explosives. Cup finals did tend to intensify feelings.

'All's fair in love and football,' he concluded.

Diane Quinn sat on the bed with an arm around her elder daughter. She'd been so frightened by her disappearance that morning that she didn't want to let her go. Maureen's bedroom had blue patterned wallpaper, much of it covered by sepia photographs of the works football team and accounts of their progress cut out of the local newspaper. Her football kit was on a coat hanger on the back of the door and her goalkeeper's gloves were on the bedside table. A football was tucked in a box among a pile of assorted items. The room was small but it had seemed vastly smaller when Maureen had shared it with her sister. The departure of their brothers to the army allowed the girls to have a room each. It was a boon to Maureen. While she yearned for the safe return of her brothers, she revelled in her new-found privacy.

'Don't feel you need to speak until you're absolutely ready,' said Diane.

After a long, uneasy, painful silence, her daughter finally spoke.

'I'll never forgive myself,' she said, dully. 'I was ashamed.'

'You've nothing to be ashamed of, Maureen.'

'I forgot. I only slept for a couple of hours last night but, when I woke up, I forgot. I thought it was a normal day so I got up as usual, got ready and let myself out. It was only when I stood on the corner waiting for her that I realised Agnes wasn't going to come. Can you see how awful that was, Mummy?' she asked. 'My best friend was murdered yesterday and I somehow managed to forget. That was *terrible*.'

'Not at all,' said Diane, rocking her gently to and fro. 'In a way, it's only natural. You were so harrowed by what happened at the pub that you had to put it out of your mind – nothing wrong in that. A lot of people would have done the same.'

'I felt that I'd betrayed Agnes – and the others, of course.'

'You should have come straight back home. I'd have taken care of you.'

'I was too frightened. Daddy would have known what I did.'

'He loves you, darling. He's just not very good at showing it.'

'I stood on that corner in the cold for ages. People were staring at me.'

'Ignore them. Having that complexion is not your fault.'

'Do you know what I felt like doing?'

'What?'

'I felt like going round to Mrs Radcliffe's house to apologise. I wanted to say sorry that I'd made a dreadful mistake waiting for her and that it didn't mean I didn't care for Agnes. I cared for all of them – they were my friends.'

'Maureen,' said her mother, taking her by the shoulders and turning her so that they faced each other, 'I want you to promise me something.'

'What's that?'

'Don't – on any account – go to see Mrs Radcliffe.'

'Why not? I always got on well with her.'

'That was when Agnes was alive. Things are different now. When I was searching for you, I called on Mrs Radcliffe and got a real mouthful from her. She said some nasty things about you and I left before I lost my temper with her. I know she's bereaved but that doesn't mean she can abuse my daughter.'

Maureen was hurt. 'What did she say?'

'It's better that you don't know. Keep away from her.'

'I loved Agnes – and the baby.'

'That's all in the past now, Maureen. Get used to it.' She released her hold on her daughter's shoulders. 'Why did you go to church?'

'I remembered what Father Cleary said to us at Sunday school once. He said that church wasn't just a place where we held services. It was a place of comfort and it was open twenty-four hours. If any of us was in difficulty, that's where we had to go. So I did. It's why I went there, Mummy. I wanted solace.'

'Did you find it?'

Maureen fell silent and picked up the football, fondling it in her arms as if holding a beloved child. It was minutes before she gave her answer.

'I don't know,' she said.

CHAPTER SEVEN

During his many years in the Metropolitan Police Force, grief had been a constant feature of his work. It came in many disguises. Marmion had seen the pain of those who'd been assaulted, the horror of women who'd suffered sexual violation, the shock of those who'd been burgled, the indignation of those defrauded, the disbelief of those whose handbags had been snatched and the searing agony of families informed that one of their members had been murdered. Elderly people had suffered heart attacks on hearing bad news and even the most robust of the younger generation had been physically and emotionally shaken. What Marmion had not witnessed before was someone who was, literally, prostrate with grief. When he called at Neil Beresford's house, he was admitted by the man's mother, May Beresford, a doughty woman in her fifties with the look of someone who'd endured more than her share of anguish and become inured to it. Her face was granite hard. At first, she'd tried to turn the visitor away, but was eventually persuaded to let Marmion see her son. Her one stipulation was that she should be present at the interview.

Fully clothed, Beresford was lying on his bed and gazing sightlessly up at the ceiling. He was a slim, handsome young man whose features were distorted by a sorrow that had robbed him of thought and movement. Introduced to Marmion, he gave no indication that he even heard the visitor's name. May prompted him.

'Inspector Marmion is here to help, Neil,' she said, sitting on the bed and stroking her son's arm. 'He's determined to catch the evil man who planted that bomb and just needs to ask you a few questions. For Shirley's sake, I think you should make the effort. You want her killer caught, don't you?'

'Yes,' murmured Neil.

'Then listen to the inspector.'

'Well,' said Marmion, 'the first thing I want to do is to offer my sincere condolences. This must have come as the most appalling blow.' Beresford gave a barely perceptible nod. 'I want you to know that we'll do everything humanly possible to bring the person or persons behind this to court so that the ultimate punishment can be meted out. That won't, of course, bring your wife back but it may give you a degree of relief.'

'It will,' said May. 'We'll both be relieved. Do you have any suspects?'

'It's my belief that the target was one or all of the young women at that birthday party. What I'm looking for, in the first instance, is a local man with a grudge and with some experience of handling explosives.'

'Hundreds of men at the factory could make a bomb.'

'I'd like to hear from your son, Mrs Beresford.'

'He'll tell you the same. Neil works at the munitions factory. He and Sheila used to go off early every morning for their shift.'

'Mr Beresford,' said Marmion, leaning in closer to him, 'can you think of anybody who bore a grudge against your wife?'

'No, Inspector,' he mumbled. 'Shirley was wonderful. Everyone loved her.'

'I can vouch for that,' added May. 'She was a saint.'

'Don't know how I can live without her.'

'They were inseparable, Inspector – at work and at play. Neil coached the football team that Shirley was in. She was top scorer.'

'Then you must have been very proud of her,' said Marmion, seeing a spark come into Beresford's eye. 'Equally, you must have been proud of your own success as a coach. I'm told that your team won the league and is in a cup final.'

'We could have won,' asserted Beresford with unexpected force. 'We'd have beaten Woolwich for certain.' He sat up. 'We put five goals past them in a league match. Shirley got a hat-trick. She was amazing.'

'Tell me about her.'

Marmion had at last uncorked the bottle and words came pouring out of it. As he talked about his wife, Beresford's pride got the better of his grief. Having been a gifted player himself, it had fallen to him to mould the Hayes team into a winning combination. Marmion was struck by the fact that young women who worked nine-and-a-half-hour shifts could still find the time and energy to hone their skills on the football field. Beresford clearly had talent. None of his team had even seen a football match – let alone played in one – until he picked them out and taught them from scratch.

Both for him and his players, the game had been a joyous escape from the humdrum routine at the factory. It had taken over their lives and that of their supporters. May was one of their most devoted fans.

'I used to wash their kit,' she boasted. 'It makes a difference, sending the girls onto the pitch looking smart. Some of the teams we play don't bother. They're a load of scruffs. Neil set high standards. That's why we're the best.'

'Is there much rivalry between the various teams?' asked Marmion.

'Oh, yes,' said Beresford.

'Give me an example.'

'We've had footballs stolen, vile things painted on the shed where the girls change and some of our goalposts were sawn in half.'

'I hadn't realised young ladies could be so mercenary.'

'It's not the players,' said May, 'it's their supporters. They're mad. They'll go to any lengths to win.'

'So it seems,' said Marmion. 'Would they go as far as planting a bomb to kill your best players?'

Mother and son were both stunned by a question that they'd evidently not asked themselves. Inclined to dismiss it out of hand at first, they began to take it more seriously. Marmion watched the two of them having a silent conversation with each other. He wished that he knew what they were thinking.

'After all,' he resumed, 'it wasn't just your best player who was killed in that explosion. Your goalkeeper was at that party as well. If she hadn't left early, then you'd have lost two members of the team.'

'Three,' corrected May. 'Jean Harte was only a reserve, as usual, but she might have played in the cup final because Sally Neames was injured.'

'There you are then, Mr Beresford. Losing three players would have been a crippling blow to your chances. Do you think that someone from Woolwich would deliberately set out to deprive you of the services of your wife, Maureen Quinn and Jean Harte? Is that conceivable?'

But Marmion had got all that he was going to get out of Beresford. He put his head on the pillow and stared upwards again, mind numbed and body motionless. His mother gave a signal to Marmion and the pair of them went back down-stairs. In the living room, he spotted something he hadn't noticed before. On the mantelpiece was a large framed photograph. Expecting it to be of the couple at their wedding, Marmion saw that it was instead a full-length portrait of Shirley Beresford in football kit. She was a lanky girl with a long, narrow face and she was beaming in triumph at the camera.

'He's been like that since he found out,' said May with a glance upwards.

'Ask him to think over what I put to him.'

'Oh, I can answer that question, Inspector.'

'Can you?'

'Yes, yes, yes,' she affirmed. 'Some devil from Woolwich *could* have set out to ruin our chances. It's not just the cup, you see. There's the money.'

'But it's an amateur sport, Mrs Beresford. The players don't get paid.'

'They don't need to, Inspector. The money comes from the bookies. If the team you pick wins, you can make a tidy sum. I support Hayes through thick and thin but, if I had any sense, I'd bet everything I could on Woolwich for the cup final.'

Keedy could only watch in mute admiration. Taken on a tour around the Cartridge Section by Bernard Kennett, he saw what the women actually did when they clocked on for work. They were in part of an industrial complex that extended across all of two hundred acres. The buildings were so numerous and of such differing sizes that it was impossible to count them. The first National Filling Station to start production, Hayes was like a small town in itself, employing, feeding and – now and then – entertaining a workforce that ran into vast numbers. It was divided into five sections. In the West Section, eighteen-pound shells were assembled, whereas the East Section specialised in filling fuses, friction tubes and exploders. Pellets were also manufactured there. The Cap and Detonator Section was such an important part of the whole operation that it had a separate fence and its own guards. Primer caps and detonators were made there. The workshops in the Amatol Section were larger than most and spaced well apart. Warm liquid amatol – an explosive mixture of ammonium nitrate and TNT – was poured into shells of varying sizes. Danger was ever present.

Before he could pay full attention to what was happening in the Cartridge Section, Keedy had to get used to the pounding noise and the pervading stink. Women were working in serried ranks, helping to fill shell cartridges with explosive material. The numerous safety precautions were unable to protect the staff completely. They were continuously exposed to highly toxic materials. As a means of countering their effects, the women were given a daily ration of milk but it failed to halt the steady discolouring of their skin. To Keedy's eyes, it was like a vision of the seventh circle of hell, unceasing toil in an unhealthy atmosphere with constant targets to meet. Male workers were very much in the minority. The bulk of production came from the women, the youngest of whom was eighteen.

In their matching uniforms, it was difficult to tell them apart. Maureen Quinn had been part of this female army and might, in time, return to it. Florrie Duncan, Agnes Collier, Jean Harte, Shirley Beresford and the musician, Enid Jenks, would never come back to the Section. Keedy thought the work unsuitable for women and bewailed the fact that war had dulled the sensibilities with regard to what was appropriate to the two genders. As he was led around by Kennett, the workers went up in his esteem. In spite of their unflattering clothing, he could see that many of them were young, shapely and very attractive. But they were committed to a job that would round their shoulders, put furrows in their faces and paint them with such a telltale yellow sheen that their social lives would be badly affected. Even the most loving husbands would be repelled by the change in their wives' appearance and those in search of marriage proposals would be severely handicapped. In serving their country so willingly, they'd made unwitting sacrifices.

Keedy was glad to step out into the fresh air again. He turned to Kennett.

'Thank you for showing me round,' he said.

'Now you know what those five women did when they were here.'

'I had no idea that conditions were so bad.'

'They compare favourably with conditions in any of the other factories,' said Kennett, defensively. 'We do everything possible to minimise the danger to our workforce and to treat them with consideration.'

'Granted – but it's still worrying to see women doing such work.'

'It's an unfortunate necessity.'

'What will happen when the war ends?'

'Demand for munitions will cease,' replied Kennett, 'so we won't need to maintain such a high daily output. Men who return from the front will naturally expect jobs and they'll take priority over women, many of whom will have to be released to search for other employment.'

'The damage will already have been done,' said Keedy, sadly. 'Who'll take on women who look like yellow jaundice victims?'

'That's a regrettable side effect of working here.'

'Shouldn't they be able to claim compensation?'

'No,' said Kennett, sharply, 'that's out of the question. They understood when they first came here what the job entailed. The women accepted the risk. They can't turn round now and say that they deserve some sort of compensation. Where's the money to come from to pay them? We'd go bankrupt. If we set a precedent with munition workers, it would be disastrous thing to do.'

It would also be a civilised gesture, thought Keedy, but he didn't wish to have a dispute with the works manager. Sympathetic as he'd been to the plight of the five victims, there were clearly limits to Kennett's compassion. First and foremost, he had to maintain production at whatever cost. Workers were therefore seen as mere cogs in a machine rather than as human beings with needs and rights. One of Keedy's questions was answered. When Florrie Duncan had come to his office to demand longer lunch breaks, she obviously got very short shrift from Bernard Kennett.

After thanking his guide once more, Keedy took his leave and walked off the premises. The tour had served its purpose. He'd not just been interested to see how hard and unremittingly the women had worked, he was keen to note how often they came into contact with male employees. The latter were not just confined to management roles. Many worked alongside the women, doing the skilled tasks that were beyond them. Then there were drivers, porters, cleaners, kitchen staff and dozens of other men at the factory. Many of them came into daily contact with the munition-ettes. Keedy had observed more than one of them shooting sly glances at the women. Could the bomber they sought be working somewhere on the site? Thwarted passion was a powerful emotion. Keedy had seen it drive people to do incredible things. The shells manufactured at Hayes were lethal but unwelcome sexual desire could be

110

destructive as well. Was that what had cost five women their lives? It was an open question.

Ellen Marmion did what she could to help the war effort by working as a volunteer with groups that organised food parcels to be sent to the front or knitted gloves and other items for the soldiers. Aware of the privations suffered by those trapped in deep, muddy, rat-infested trenches, she strove to ameliorate their lot in her small way. On her way home after another session with the knitting needles, she passed a newspaper vendor and saw the headline emblazoned on his display board – FIVE DEAD CANARIES. Since the lunchtime edition related to the case on which her husband and future son-in-law were working, she bought a copy and glanced at the front page. Marmion looked up solemnly at her from a stock photograph but it was tiny by comparison with the photo of the doomed outhouse in Hayes. Seeing the extent of the damage made her stomach heave. It was the work of someone cruel and pitiless. Marmion and Keedy were in pursuit of the man. Not for the first time, she was reminded of the perils that came with a job at Scotland Yard. Someone who could kill five young women in cold blood wouldn't hesitate to murder two detectives. Folding up the newspaper, she thrust it under her arm and scurried home.

Ellen was not simply worried about their safety. She was alarmed that her daughter was, as she saw it, being bullied at work by a jealous superior. There was nothing that could be done to alleviate the situation. She was also disturbed by her husband's reluctance to fully accept Alice's choice of husband. 'While Ellen had been thrilled at the news, it had been an unpleasant surprise for Marmion and his unspoken objections remained. Most troubling of all, of course, was the eternal anxiety about their son, Paul, stationed in France near the Somme and sending infrequent letters that complained of boredom and bad living quarters. Some of the friends who'd joined up with him at the start of the war had either been killed or sent home with missing limbs. She prayed daily that Paul's name would not be added to the casualty list.

Trying to subdue her nagging concerns, she soon had something else to worry about. It started to rain and she had no umbrella. Almost without warning, the skies opened and the downpour began. Ellen had a coat and hat but they were inadequate protection against the driving rain. She was soaked within minutes. The storm put more speed into her legs and she practically sprinted over the last fifty yards. When she reached the shelter of her porch, she paused to get her breath back. Having spent its fury, the storm now abated and patches of blue sky peeped through the clouds. It was too late for Ellen. She'd been well and truly drenched.

When she let herself into the house, however, she saw something which banished all of her anxieties at once. It was a letter with distinctive handwriting on it. Paul had written to them again at long last. With a whoop of pleasure, she snatched up the letter from the floor. Dripping over the hall carpet, she tore it open.

'When were you told the news, Mr Jenks?'

'It was when I got back from work last night.'

'You have my utmost sympathy.'

'Thank you, Inspector.'

'Is that a photo of Enid on the piano?'

'Yes,' said Jenks. 'If she wasn't practising on her violin, she'd be sitting at the piano. Music was everything to Enid. She could play anything. It was because she was so well taught. My wife was a wonderful pianist as well. She wanted one of the children to learn how to play and the boys weren't interested. Enid was. She had enough interest for both of them.' He touched Marmion's arm and lowered a voice as if about to impart a secret. 'The vicar approached us, you know. He asked if Enid would be interested in learning the organ.'

'I daresay she'd have been proficient at any keyboard instrument.'

'Are you musical, Inspector?'

'No, sir,' replied Marmion. 'The only piano I could play is one with a handle on the side.'

Once the joke about the barrel organ had slipped out Marmion regretted it but the other man found it amusing enough. Jonah Jenks was quite unlike Neil Beresford. Where the latter had been knocked senseless by the enormity of what had happened, the former had merely accepted it and sought to carry on. He loved his daughter deeply but her death was not going to become an obsession. Having already lost a wife and a second daughter to diphtheria, he knew all about pangs of grief. Another child had died, leaving him to look after the two surviving boys. That's

113

what mattered most to Jenks. They were the ones who were really suffering. Though they'd argued constantly with their sister while she was alive, they were dumbstruck at her death, all the more so because it had been as a result of a crime. Jenks had kept them home from school and they were upstairs in the bedroom they shared.

'I just wanted to assure you that the investigation is well under way,' said Marmion. 'I have a team of detectives working under me.'

'That's good to hear.'

'You'll appreciate that I'm under a slight disadvantage. I don't know anything about the five victims. I'm trying to find out all I can about each one of them. I've spoken to Agnes Collier's mother and to Maureen Quinn's family.'

'Agnes came here once or twice. She was a nice girl.'

'What about Maureen?'

'Oh, I've never met her.'

'Who was Enid's best friend?'

'That would be Shirley Beresford. She used to go and watch her play football. Enid was very clever but she was hopeless at sports. Her brothers used to tease her about it. Shirley, on the other hand, was a good all-round athlete.'

'So I've been told. I called on her husband earlier.'

'I see.'

Jenks glanced at the photograph on the piano then sat opposite his visitor. He was a spare man in his fifties with hair neatly slicked back over a domed head. His spectacles gave him an owlish appearance and he had a scholarly air that inclined Marmion to think that he was a teacher. The well-stocked bookshelves indicated a reading man. In fact, however, Jenks was the manager of a large hardware store. Wearing a three-piece suit indoors, he kept his thumbs in the pockets of his waistcoat.

'What do you want me to tell you, Inspector?'

'Describe your daughter, please, if you will.'

'Enid was a lovely girl. I can't speak too highly of her.'

Jenks spoke in a low, measured voice. He talked fondly about his daughter's achievements and about his ambitions for her. A religious man, he took all three children to church every Sunday, then the family visited the graves of its missing members. A new one would now be added. Instead of being in regular use, the piano would act as a memento to Enid. Marmion was at once interested and saddened by the effect that factory life had had upon her. Putting her music aside, she'd dedicated herself to the production of arms. Jenks was a mild-mannered man who seemed at variance with the image of him that Maureen Quinn had conjured up. She had recalled the help given by Florrie Duncan at a time when Enid was having terrible rows with her father. Yet Jenks was giving his visitor a detailed picture of a household where perfect harmony prevailed. He even boasted that he never had to raise his voice to Enid.

Jenks became practical. 'Isn't there something you've forgotten?'

'I don't think so.'

'Where foul play is involved in a death, I

thought that next of kin would be asked to identify the body.'

'Ordinarily, that's the case, sir,' said Marmion, 'but the remains are not really recognisable. When a bomb goes off in a confined space, it causes the most unimaginable injuries. We wish to spare the families such a disturbing sight.'

'That's very wise of you, Inspector – wise and considerate.'

'Identification will have to be made by items they owned, by watches, bracelets and so on.'

'Enid wore a silver crucifix.'

'I'll remember that.'

'When will the bodies...' Jenks gave an apologetic half-smile. 'When will the remains be released to us?'

'Very soon,' said Marmion. 'The post-mortems have not yet been completed. When they have been, the undertakers can take over. They're used to this sort of thing. Not that they'll have seen many victims of a bomb blast, of course, but they can take a dispassionate look at ... human remains in whatever form.' He looked across at the photograph of Enid. 'She was a very pretty young lady.'

Jenks was nostalgic. 'She took after her mother.'

'Enid must have had a lot of admirers.'

'Everyone liked her. She was so outgoing.'

'I was thinking of boyfriends, Mr Jenks,' said Marmion. 'I have a daughter of my own so I know what happens when they reach a certain age. Was there anyone special in Enid's life?'

'No, there wasn't,' snapped Jenks.

'Are you certain of that?'

'Enid had no room in her life for that sort of thing.'

'Then she'd be most unusual.'

'There was nothing unusual about my daughter. Haven't you been listening to what I said? Enid was a good girl.' Hearing the anger in his voice, he tried to control it. 'I'm sorry, Inspector. You're entitled to ask such a question. But I've given you the answer. Enid was just not interested in young men. It probably stems from the fact that she had two brothers. All she wanted was her music.'

'Then we'll leave it at that, sir.'

Getting up from his seat, Marmion took a step nearer the piano so that he could have a closer look at Enid Jenks. She was not simply pretty. When the photo was taken, she was beautiful. Marmion simply couldn't believe that none of the young men at the factory had failed to notice the fact.

CHAPTER EIGHT

They met by prior arrangement at a café not far from the Golden Goose. Having sacrificed lunch in the interests of advancing the investigation, they were having an early tea. Keedy munched a pasty and Marmion sipped his tea while eyeing the cakes on the display stand and wondering if he should have one. It was time to compare notes. Marmion talked about his visits to the respective homes of Shirley Beresford and Enid Jenks and how differently their families had responded to the untimely deaths. As the inspector was talking, Keedy opened the folder given to him by the works manager.

'Everything you say about the two of them accords with what Mr Kennett found out,' he said. 'Shirley was the captain of their football team and Enid was good enough as a musician to make a living at it. They were both well liked by the others, Shirley in particular.'

'That's not surprising, Joe. She was their goal-scorer.'

'At least that would have killed off any complaints.'

'Complaints?'

'Yes, Harv. If, as you say, Neil Beresford was their coach, he couldn't be accused of favouritism by putting his wife in the team. Shirley was obviously their best player. I must say, I don't envy her husband.'

'Why not?'

'Coaching a soccer team is a real headache. When I used to play as a kid, we drove our coach to distraction. He reckoned we'd taken ten years off his life. I remember him tearing his hair out on the touchline as we made silly mistakes and gave away ridiculous goals. Neil Beresford must be a tough character to take on a task like running a women's team.'

'That's the strange thing, Joe,' said Marmion as he pictured the man lying on the bed. 'Physically, he looks wiry and he must be strong-willed to create and nurture a team that wins the league.

Yet he's more or less collapsed in the wake of the disaster. People like his mother and Mrs Radcliffe have coped far better – and so has Jonah Jenks. Why is that?'

'Beresford and his wife must have been very close.'

'He looked really ill when I left him.'

Keedy smiled. 'We can't all be like you, Harv.'

'What do you mean?'

'Well, *you've* been where they are – losing someone you loved, that is. When your father was murdered on duty, you didn't sit around and mope. You went after his killer and discovered that you had a detective's instinct.'

Marmion was rueful. 'I'd prefer to have found it out a different way. I never thought I'd follow Dad into the police force but his death changed my mind. It made me so *angry*, Joe. I felt that I simply had to do something.'

'Alice feels the same. She takes after you.'

'Let's keep her out of this,' said Marmion, sharply.

'But she has the same attitude as you.'

'That's as maybe. Tell me about your second visit to the factory.'

Keedy puffed his cheeks. 'It really opened my eyes.'

He went on to describe his visit to the Cartridge Section and how he felt that the women deserved far more than they earned. It was well below what men doing identical jobs took home at the end of the week. Keedy talked about the noise, the smell, the inherent dangers and how he found it difficult to reconcile the idea of a sex

119

that created human life making shells that would destroy it.

'It was weird, Harv – sort of unnatural.'

'Blame the war for that. When so many of our young men are wounded, killed in action or still serving at the front, women have had to step into the breach. I applaud them for that.'

'What about the ones who joined the police force?' Keedy saw the glint in his companion's eyes and quickly changed the subject. 'Where do we go next?'

'I'd like you to go to Jean Harte's house,' said Marmion. 'I called there earlier but drew a blank. Either nobody is at home or, if they are, they're not answering the door. Once we've crossed Jean off the list, there's only Florrie Duncan left. We'll visit her family together.'

'What will you be doing before then, Harv?'

'I'm going to the factory. Alan Suggs will be back soon.'

'Oh, yes, he's the phantom lover, isn't he?'

'He may turn out to be more than that, Joe.'

'His girlfriend must be very keen on him. There aren't many young women whose idea of a romance is a tryst in some converted stables. Most would expect something more comfortable than that.'

'He works as a driver, Joe. He can't afford a suite at the Ritz.'

At that moment, a waitress came to clear the plates from the table. Wearing a black dress and a white apron, she was an attractive young woman in her early twenties, the average age of the murder victims. Keedy couldn't help noticing the sharp contrast between her and those at the factory. The waitress had pale, spotless skin and there was a bloom on her cheeks. If any of the munitionettes had applied for a job at the café, they'd have been turned down because their appearance was likely to offend customers. It was grossly unfair.

'Right,' said Keedy as the waitress moved away, 'I'm ready. Is there anything particular you'd like me to find out about Jean Harte?'

'I want you to see where she fitted into that group of friends.'

'Maureen Quinn told us that Jean was teased a lot because she was always moaning about something. And she often had something wrong with her – not that that surprises me. That factory is an unhealthy place to work.'

'See what you can learn about the other girls. Which one was Jean's best friend, for example? Who did she see outside of work hours? And why was it that Enid Jenks and Shirley Beresford were so close?'

'Is there any reason why they shouldn't be?'

'Yes,' replied Marmion. 'From what I can gather, they had little in common. Enid was a musician who spent all her time practising while Shirley was a real sportswoman. One was single while the other was married. One was still under the thumb of her father while the other lived with her husband. I suppose you could call it an attraction of opposites,' he went on, getting up, 'but it seems odd somehow. I would have thought that Enid and Maureen Quinn were more natural friends.'

'Why is that, Harv?'

'They're both religious.'

121

'How are you feeling now, Maureen?'

'My mind is a blank most of the time.'

'That's understandable. You're still in shock.'

'It's just so painful to remember what happened,' said Maureen, 'so I've tried to block it out. But I can't do that for ever, Father.'

'Indeed, you can't.'

'Sooner or later, I'll have to face their families. They'll detest me.'

'That's not true at all,' said Father Cleary, gently squeezing her hands. 'They'll be glad that – by the grace of God – someone managed to escape the horror of that explosion. It's only natural that they'll wish that it had been *their* daughter, of course, but there should be no antagonism towards you.'

'Yes, there will,' said Maureen, thinking of Mrs Radcliffe.

'What brought you to church this morning?'

'I needed to be alone.'

'You're never alone in God's house.'

'I know that but I wanted...'

'A place of sanctuary?' he asked as her voice tailed off. Maureen nodded. 'Well, you came to the right place. We haven't seen as much of you or of your family as we'd like recently and I'm sorry that it's taken a tragedy like this to bring you back there. But you're very welcome, Maureen. You were much brighter than everyone else at Sunday school – especially your brothers. How are they, by the way?'

'We don't know. They're still at the front somewhere.'

'We'll remember them in our prayers.'

In obedience to her husband, Diane Quinn had already turned many callers away, both inquisitive neighbours and persistent reporters. The one person in whose face she couldn't shut the front door was Father Cleary, a stringy old man with a biretta that he never seemed to remove perched on a mop of silver hair. When word reached him that Maureen had spent hours in St Alban's church, he paid her a visit. Seated opposite her, he held her hands and offered sympathy and understanding.

Maureen was bewildered. 'Why was *I* spared, Father?'

'God moves in mysterious ways.'

'It's what I keep asking myself. In one way or another, they were all better than me. Florrie was our leader, Enid was a brilliant musician, Agnes had a gorgeous baby son and so on. Unlike me, they all had full lives.'

'Don't underestimate your importance in the scheme of things, Maureen,' said Cleary, peering over his spectacles. 'You were spared for a reason. These things are never random. The Almighty chose you for a purpose. It's only a matter of time before that purpose is revealed to you.' He sat back. 'Will I see you in church on Sunday?' Maureen hesitated. 'Yes, I know that your father keeps you away but I'll talk to him about it. If I do that, will you attend Mass?'

'Yes, Father,' she said with passion. 'I will, I promise.'

Joe Keedy knew that someone was inside the

house. He could not only hear them moving about, he caught a glimpse of someone through the net curtains on the bay window. Since he failed to get a response from several knocks on the front door, he took out his notebook, wrote his name and rank on it, then tore out the page and posted it through the letter box. After a long wait, the letter box opened and a reedy voice came through it.

'How do we know that you're a detective?' asked the man.

'I'll show you my warrant card.'

'We had someone earlier who claimed that he was from Scotland Yard.'

'That would have been Inspector Marmion, who's in charge of the investigation. He told me that he called here.'

'I didn't like the look of him. He was shifty. I thought it was another one of those reporters trying to trick his way in here so we ignored him.'

Keedy was amused at the idea that Marmion had been repelled on the grounds of his appearance and he vowed to taunt him about it later. Showing his warrant card to the pair of suspicious eyes in the open letter box, he finally pierced the defences at the Harte household. The door swung back just wide enough to admit him and he went in. Reuben Harte quickly shut and bolted the door. He was a slight man in his fifties with thick, dark hair and a bushy moustache. He wore shirt, trousers and a waistcoat that was unbuttoned. His eyes were pools of sorrow.

'What do you want, Sergeant?'

'Do we have to talk in the passageway?'

'Yes,' said the other, firmly.

'As you wish,' decided Keedy, removing his hat. 'As for reporters, they've been warned to leave you alone. Next time one of them bothers you, make sure that you get his name and we'll make a point of reprimanding him. At a time like this, the last thing you need is the press baying at your heels.'

'Thank you – I'll remember that.'

'However, since we wish to catch the person who set off that explosion, we need to learn as much as we can about the victims. Do you understand that?'

'No, I don't, but go on.'

Keedy glanced towards the living room. 'Is there a Mrs Harte?'

'My wife is staying with her sister, who used to be a nurse. She's not at all well, Sergeant, and this has only made her condition worse.'

'Tell me about your daughter. I believe that she was plagued with minor ailments. Is that true?'

'They weren't minor,' said Harte. 'Jean had some serious problems.'

Mother and daughter clearly didn't enjoy the rude health that Harte seemed to show. He was slim, straight-backed and looked younger than his years. There was no trace of grey in his hair. Keedy learnt that he was a bank clerk. When his daughter had wanted to work at the munitions factory, he opposed the idea at first but was eventually talked around. Paradoxically, her health seemed to improve slightly in the harmful environment of the Cartridge Section. Harte ascribed it to the reassurance of having such good friends. In previous spells of employment, Jean had always been the odd one out. Her father talked selfishly rather than fondly about her, recalling what he'd done for her throughout life instead of what she'd achieved on her own. It was almost as if he were trying to justify his role as a parent.

The verbal photograph he was given was recognisably that of the woman described in Kennett's notes. Jean was an integral part of a tight group, liked for her cynical streak and mocked for her endless whining. Her closest friend, it emerged, was Florrie Duncan. On the strength of what he knew about them, they seemed an unlikely pair to Keedy. While Florrie was an irrepressible optimist, Jean always feared the worst in any given situation.

'They got on famously,' said Harte. 'We liked Florrie.'

'Did they have much in common?'

'They had the most important thing, Sergeant.'

'Oh – what was that?'

'They both lost the person they loved most. Florrie's husband died at the front and so did Jean's young man. They got engaged during his last leave, then he went off and got himself killed. Florrie managed to get over it,' said Harte, enviously, 'but it cast a shadow over Jean's life. Maurice – that was his name – worked at the bank with me. I taught him all he knew.'

Harte came close to smiling without actually managing it. There was a possessiveness about him that made Keedy feel sorry for his daughter. It was as if he'd only allowed Jean to embark on a romance because he'd chosen and groomed the young man in question. Harte was not unintelligent but had obvious limitations and Keedy could see why he'd never risen above the level of a bank clerk. At a time in life when his contemporaries had become managers, he stayed in the shadows.

'How well did you know the other girls?' asked Keedy.

'Oh, I met all of Jean's gang,' said Harte, 'and encouraged her to invite them here. My wife and I are creatures of habit, Sergeant. We always go out on a Saturday night to visit my sister-in-law and her husband. Bert is disabled so walking all the way here is out of the question. Anyway, Jean often had one or more of her friends around. Florrie Duncan was always here and so was Enid Jenks. She used to play our piano and they'd have a sing-song. We'd join in when we got back.'

'What about Agnes Collier and Maureen Quinn?'

'They came now and again but neither were regulars. They don't live in Hayes, you see, and Agnes has a baby to look after. She brought him here once. He's got a good pair of lungs on him, I know that.'

Keedy sensed that he was claiming to know the women rather better than he actually did. He spoke about them with an affection that – Keedy suspected – was not entirely reciprocated. Harte was too dry and humourless to mix easily with characters like Florrie Duncan and Agnes Collier, both reportedly given to constant laughter. What he did do was to describe aspects of the five victims' characters that didn't appear in the notes provided by Kennett. Jean Harte had had ambitions of being a dress designer. Florrie

Duncan lived alone in a two-room flat because – in spite of her gregariousness – she preferred her own company. Shirley Beresford had been a suffragette before the war. Agnes Collier was an expert cook and had won a number of local competitions. Enid Jenks had twice tried to move out of the family home but had been baulked by her father on both occasions.

Keedy soaked it all in, then remembered the question that Marmion put to him.

'Why were Enid and Shirley such close friends?'

'I used to wonder about that,' admitted Harte.

'Did you reach a conclusion?'

'No, Sergeant. It's something I just can't explain.'

Alan Suggs was a thickset man in his late twenties with curly black hair and a beard that gave him a faintly piratical air. When he pulled the lorry into the parking bay, he switched off, took out a cigarette, lit it then jumped out of the vehicle. He was just locking the door when Marmion strolled across to him.

'Mr Suggs?' he enquired, politely.

'That's me. Who wants to know?'

Marmion introduced himself and noted the man's reaction. Suggs stiffened, drew nervously on his cigarette then exhaled a cloud of smoke. He decided that the best means of defence was stout denial.

'If someone's told you I've been giving unauthorised lifts to people,' he said, 'then he's lying through his teeth. I'd never do that. I know the rules and I've signed to say I'd never break them. Anyway,' he went on after another puff of his cigarette, 'why is Scotland Yard worrying about drivers misusing their lorries? It's small beer to you lot. Haven't you got anything better to do than that?'

'I've been talking to Royston Liddle,' said Marmion, meaningfully.

'Don't listen to anything that poor bugger tells you. Royston is soft in the head. My dog has got more brains than him.'

'He claims to be a friend of yours.'

Suggs laughed harshly. 'Royston is no friend of mine.'

'Then why did you ask him to look the other way when you borrowed the key to the outhouse at the Golden Goose?'

'That what he told you, Inspector? It's rubbish.'

'He didn't strike me as a practised liar.'

'Royston doesn't know what day it is.'

'He knows that he'd lose his job if the landlord discovered that he'd helped you to make use of that outhouse with someone. And before you deny it, Mr Suggs,' he continued, locking his gaze on the driver, 'let me warn you that I'm investigating the explosion at the Golden Goose. You had access to the place where they died.'

'It was nothing to do with me!' roared Suggs.

'Then why were you in the outhouse on the eve of the blast?'

'That's private.'

'There's no such thing as privacy in a murder investigation.'

Suggs was scarlet. 'I didn't murder anyone.

129

What the hell d'you take me for?'

'I take you for someone I'd never care to employ,' said Marmion, levelly. 'I think you're vain, shifty, dishonest and untrustworthy. If, as you claim, you had no connection with that bomb, all you have to do is to give me the name of the person with whom you spent half an hour in that outhouse. A lot can happen in thirty minutes, Mr Suggs. You'd have plenty of time to hide a bomb with a timing device.'

Having been quick to protest, Suggs now fell back into a sullen silence. Marmion could almost see the man's brain whirring as he sought for a plausible tale to explain his presence at the Golden Goose. He stared at Marmion with an amalgam of dislike and apprehension. Suggs had a glib manner that had suddenly let him down. After a last pull on the cigarette, he dropped it to the ground and stamped on it.

'You obviously have a problem with your eyes,' said Marmion, pointing to the sign on the wall. 'That says No Smoking. You also seem to have trouble with your memory. The best way to revive it is for us to have this discussion in the presence of Royston Liddle. Mr Hubbard would also be an interested observer.'

'Keep him out of this,' begged Suggs. 'Leighton would strangle me.'

'You look as if you'd like to inflict the same fate on Liddle, so let me say now that if any harm befalls him, I'll come looking for you with an arrest warrant. Now then,' Marmion went on, folding his arms, 'why don't you dredge up something resembling the truth?'

Suggs swallowed hard. 'I didn't plant that bomb. I swear it.'

'Did you advise the people who did?'

'No!'

'Did you tell them where the key could be found?'

'Of course, I didn't.'

'Where were you when the bomb went off?'

'I was fast asleep at home, Inspector. I work long hours. I need my rest.'

'You didn't need any rest on the previous evening. My guess is that you were feeling quite vigorous.' He took out his notebook. 'What was her name?'

'There *was* no "her". I was in there on my own.'

'Royston Liddle saw a young woman being hustled in there.'

'Are you going to rely on the word of a halfwit?'

'It's far more dependable than anything you've told me so far.' Marmion put the book away. 'Let's go and find Mr Hubbard. He has a right to hear the truth.'

'No, no,' said Suggs, both palms raised, 'anything but that.' He pursed his lips for a few moments. 'Okay,' he said at length, 'maybe there *was* someone in there with me on the night before that explosion.'

'Ah – we're making progress at last.'

'But I'm not in a position to tell you her name.'

'It's very gallant of you to protect her anonymity, Mr Suggs, but I'm afraid that I can't let you do that. Unless you tell me who she is, I can't get corroboration.'

Suggs blinked. 'What's that mean?'

131

'It means that I need someone to confirm what you tell me.'

'Can't you take my word for it?'

'No, sir – I fancy that you're a congenital liar. Indeed, that may be the reason you won't divulge the name of the young lady. Perhaps you've been telling her fibs as well.' He put his head to one side as he fired his question. 'Are you married?'

'No!' retorted Suggs.

'Are you sure you haven't led her to believe that you're single?'

'I'd never do anything like that.'

'Then let me have a name.' There was a lengthy pause. 'Or are you holding it back because the young lady is the one who's married?'

Suggs licked his lips then examined the ground for a full minute. When he raised his head, he scratched at his beard then smoothed the ruffled hairs down. Marmion could see that he might now get an approximation to the truth.

'Lettie and me are both single,' Suggs began. 'I'm hoping that one day we can get engaged but her parents don't like me. I don't know why. They refuse to let me anywhere near the house. That won't stop Lettie and me. We arranged a few secret meetings and the only place I could think of was that outhouse.'

'Why not invite her to your home?'

'I live with my parents.'

'Surely, they'd like to have met your girlfriend?'

'We wanted privacy.' He nudged Marmion. 'You were young once, Inspector, weren't you?'

'Yes, but I drew the line at courting in some disused stables.'

'It suited us.'

'What's Lettie's surname?'

'You don't need to know. I'll tell you every-thing.'

'Then let's start with the facts, Mr Suggs.'

'I'm giving them to you,' claimed the other.

'If you live with your parents,' observed Mar-mion, dryly, 'there must be a very nasty smell in the house because, according to your neigh-bours, they both died years ago. You live alone and that raises the question of why you didn't invite Lettie – or whatever her real name is – to your home.' He narrowed his eyelids. 'What are you trying to hide, Mr Suggs? And what were you *really* doing in that outhouse?'

CHAPTER NINE

Having finished her shift, Alice Marmion was still in uniform as she made her way back to her flat. On a previous bus journey there she'd once been stalked, but her new status protected her from unwanted attention. It was an important bonus. The uniform had another advantage. It reassured her landlady, a watchful old woman who believed that the virtue of all four young female tenants under her roof was in constant danger and who'd devised a system of rules to keep men at bay. They were only allowed onto the premises between limited hours and confined to the drawing room, a place in which all the chairs were deliberately set apart from each other to discourage any form of intimacy. Alice had entertained Joe Keedy there once and their conversation had been interrupted at regular intervals by the landlady, checking to see that her rules were being obeyed.

Notwithstanding the strict regime, Alice liked living there. The rooms had generous proportions and she got on well with the other tenants. While she'd lost all the comforts of her own home, she'd gained a precious independence. That made the move there very worthwhile. She could spread her wings. When she got to the house and let herself in, she intended to climb the stairs to her room but she was intercepted by her visitor. Ellen came bounding out of the drawing room, waving a letter.

Alice gasped in surprise. 'What are you doing here, Mummy?'

'I just had to tell *somebody*. We've had a letter from Paul.'

'That's wonderful – what does he say?'

'Read it yourself,' said Ellen, thrusting it at her. 'He's coming home on leave next week. I can't wait.'

Alice took the letter then moved into the drawing room to read it. Her brother had spidery handwriting and a shaky grasp of grammar but that didn't matter. He was coming home. Having been away in France for what seemed like an inordinately long time, he'd finally been given leave. It would be a blessed relief for Paul himself and a delight for the rest of the family. Thrilled by the good news, Alice was also slightly disappointed by the letter. Though her brother had been told about

134

the two major changes in her life – her move to the police and engagement to Joe Keedy – there was no mention of either. Did that mean Paul disapproved of both? It troubled her.

'I hope you didn't mind me coming,' said Ellen.

Alice returned the letter. 'Not at all, Mummy,' she said, brightly. 'I'm so glad you did. If Daddy had been in his office, of course, you could have phoned him there from home but he's out of reach at the moment. He'll be so pleased.'

'The same goes for Joe. He and Paul always liked each other.'

'Yes, they did.'

'Anyway, I have something else for you as well. Knowing the interest you took in the case, I bought the lunchtime edition.' Taking the newspaper from her bag, she handed it over. 'I wish that they could find a better photo of your father.'

Alice studied the front page. 'It does make him look sinister, doesn't it?'

'You'd think he was the bomber instead of the person who's after him.'

'Thank you, Mummy. I'll enjoy reading this.'

'That's more than I did. Some of the details are very upsetting and you can see the damage that was done by the explosion. I know I've said it a hundred times but I'd never make a detective. I'm far too sensitive.'

'You have to develop a thick skin.'

'Then I'll stay as a housewife. I'm good at that and it suits me.' She looked Alice up and down. 'What kind of a day have you had?'

Folding up the newspaper, Alice clicked her tongue then sighed.

'Oh, it was a lot less exciting than being involved in a murder investigation.'

'Did you have any trouble with the inspector?'

'There was a little bit of friction but it soon passed.'

'She ought to be grateful to have you there.'

'Gratitude is not her strong suit,' said Alice, rolling her eyes. 'She tackled me this morning about the explosion. Had I been discussing it with my father? Did I have any inside information? Was I overstepping my authority? And so on.'

'What did you do?'

'I denied the accusations, of course. I admit nothing to Gale Force.'

'You could always apply for a transfer.'

'That would mean conceding defeat and I won't give her that satisfaction. The inspector will get fed up with chivvying me one day and find a new victim. However,' she added, 'that's enough about me. Now that you're here, I'll make you a cup of tea. Then we must talk about the welcome we're going to lay on for Paul. We must really push the boat out for him.'

While he sat in the back of the car outside the police station, Joe Keedy flipped through his notebook to refresh his memory. In terms of gathering information about the victims, it had been a productive day. On the other hand, they seemed no nearer to identifying the bomber. Marmion had told him about the interview with Alan Suggs and how he was certain that the driver wasn't in any way connected to the crime. A prime suspect had therefore been removed. He needed to be replaced. Keedy could imagine what Marmion was doing. Having rung the superintendent to bring him up to date with developments, he'd now be listening to an irritating series of complaints and commands from Claude Chatfield. Nothing short of an arrest would placate him and that seemed to be a very long way off.

Putting his notebook away, Keedy took out his wallet and extracted the sepia photograph of Alice that he carried everywhere with him. He turned it over to read the message she'd written. After all this time, he still found it touching. It was strange to think that, when he first met her, she was barely into her teens. Neither of them had ever thought for a moment that their destiny was to be together. Turning the photo over again, he let his eyes dwell lovingly on her face until a dark shadow fell across it. Harvey Marmion was standing beside the car with such a look of displeasure that Keedy hastily put the photo away in the wallet. Marmion opened the door and climbed in beside him.

'What did Chat have to say?' asked Keedy.

'I'll give you one guess.'

'He wants a visible sign of progress.'

'He wants more than that, Joe. He's demanding a blooming miracle. This case has aroused national interest. Chat insists on a swift resolution.'

'Then he should lend us his magic wand. We certainly haven't got one.'

'The phone call wasn't entirely made up of the usual diatribe.'

'You mean that he actually had something

useful to say?'

'Yes,' replied Marmion. 'Enough of the bomb and the timer were recovered to send back to the lab. First reports suggest it's a fairly sophisticated device. In short, we're up against a pro.'

'Well, there are plenty of those at the munitions factory. It's their trade. Are you sure that one of them wasn't working hand in glove with Suggs? He could have got an accomplice into that out-house and kept watch.'

'The only accomplice that Suggs had was young, compliant and female. He has quite a private life, it turns out. Royston Liddle told me that Suggs took a woman in there on a few occasions but he missed out a significant detail.'

'What was that, Harv?'

'It wasn't always the *same* woman.'

Keedy laughed. 'You mean that he's a lady-killer?' he said. 'From what you told me about him, it didn't sound as if any woman would give him a second glance.'

'Appearance isn't everything, Joe. Suggs was coarse, ugly and as cocky as they come but that obviously attracts a certain sort of woman. I feel sorry for them, especially for the regular girl-friend.'

'Who's she?'

'The one who spends the odd night at the house,' explained Marmion. 'When he told me that he was in bed at the time of the explosion, he was being honest for once. What he omitted to tell me was that someone else was in bed with him.'

'He obviously likes variety,' said Keedy in amazement. 'You've got to admire the man's stamina. He has a production line.'

'It's not the way it looks, Joe. That's what Suggs kept telling me. He admitted that he was getting rather bored with his girlfriend and has been searching for a replacement. What happened in that outhouse was a series of auditions.'

'Where on earth does he find all these women?'

'They're from the factory. Where else? Look at the numbers,' suggested Marmion. 'There must be five women to every man. Suggs said it was like picking apples off a tree.'

'Did you remind him what happened to Adam and Eve?'

'I didn't need to because I fancy that the serpent was named Alan Suggs. He'd corrupt anyone.' Marmion leant forward to give the driver some instructions then sat back. The car started up and moved away. 'Let's see what we can learn about Florrie Duncan.'

'Yes,' said Keedy, 'and let's hope we actually get invited properly into the house while we're doing it. Mr Harte didn't let me anywhere near the living room.'

'Perhaps he didn't like the look of you.'

'That's where you're wrong, Harv. At least I got through the door. When you put a slip of paper through the letter box with your name on it, Harte didn't believe you were a detective. He thought it was a trick to lure him out.' Keedy's grin spread from ear to ear. 'He said that you were shifty.'

Marmion was offended. 'Shifty?'

'That was the word.'

'I take exception to that.'

139

'It's why he didn't let you in. You'll have to take some lessons from Alan Suggs.' Marmion bridled. 'He's obviously a master at turning on the charm.'

Everyone had a good word to say about Royston Liddle. Tolerant of his severe limitations, they found him harmless, likeable and unfailingly helpful. As he walked past the Golden Goose, he exchanged a few words with the glazier repairing some of the shattered windows of a neighbouring house. Farther down the street, two old women were chatting on the doorstep. They broke off when they saw him coming and gave Liddle a warm greeting. One of them slipped indoors to find some lettuce leaves she'd saved for his rabbits. When it was time to move on, there were other cheery waves and kind comments to collect from friends. He felt looked after. Wherever he went in Hayes, he was given a welcome. Liddle's famous grin was never wider.

There was, however, one person who had taken against him and he was lying in wait. When Liddle turned down an alleyway, he walked straight into the arms of Alan Suggs and was shoved unceremoniously against a fence. With one hand to his captive's throat, Suggs held a menacing fist inches from his nose. Caught unawares, all that Liddle could do was to splutter and tremble. The driver was bigger, stronger and much more aggressive than he could ever be. Suggs looked as if he was ready to inflict a terrible beating.

'Hello, Alan,' said Liddle, weakly.

'You're a numbskull, Royston.' He squeezed the throat. 'What are you?'

140

'I'm ... whatever you say.'

'You're a stupid, flea-brained, loud-mouthed, bloody nuisance.'

Liddle was in pain. 'You're hurting me.'

'I ought to cut you into little bits and feed you to those rabbits of yours. *They've* got more sense than you have. They know how to keep their traps shut.'

He released his hold and took a step back. 'I thought you were a friend.'

'I am, Alan, I always will be.'

'Not any more. You landed me in trouble.'

'I didn't mean to,' said Liddle, rubbing his throat.

'Why did you have to talk to the coppers?'

'But I didn't – it was that inspector who talked to me.'

'Yes,' said Suggs, pushing him against the fence again, 'and what did you do? You broke your promise and opened your trap. Inspector Marmion grilled me for over an hour. Thanks to you, he thought I'd planted that bomb.'

'Oh, no, I didn't say that. I told him that you only went into that outhouse to be alone for a bit with your friend.' He recovered his grin. 'What's her name, by the way?' Suggs went for the throat again. 'Sorry,' croaked Liddle, 'what have I done wrong now?'

'You behaved like the imbecile you are. Someone should have locked you up years ago. It's not safe to let you out.' He swung Liddle round and smacked the side of his head. 'Why I trusted you, I'll never know.'

'I did you a favour,' argued Liddle. 'I kept

141

watch for you.'

'I paid you to keep your gob shut, not to spill the beans to the coppers. When I came off work today, the inspector was waiting for me. He did everything but slap a pair of handcuffs on me. And it was your bloody fault!'

'I couldn't tell a lie to the police.'

'You didn't need to tell them anything at all.'

'But that detective frightened me.'

'That was no reason to blab about me borrowing that key,' said Suggs. 'What happened was private, see? It was nobody else's business. Then you betray me to Inspector Marmion and he bullied the truth out of me.'

Liddle tried a smile of appeasement. 'I won't do it again.'

'You *can't* do it again, you fool. The outhouse was destroyed. I'm not going to be taking anyone into a pile of rubble, am I?'

'What I meant is that I'll remember what you tell me next time.'

'There won't *be* a next time, Royston,' said the other, vehemently, 'because I'd never trust you again. Keep out of my way from now on or I'll give you the hiding you deserve.' He made a threatening move towards him. 'Now bugger off!'

With a cry of alarm, Liddle scuttled down the alleyway until he felt that he'd put a safe distance between them. Upset at his treatment and wounded by the cruel way Suggs had spoken to him, he felt an uncharacteristic urge to strike back.

'I know what you did in that outhouse,' he taunted, 'because there's a hole in the back wall. Last time you went in there, I watched the pair of you. She had big tits and I saw both of them wobbling away.' He giggled at the memory. 'I'm not that daft. I know what you were up to. You and her were doing what my rabbits do. I *saw* you, Alan.'

Enraged by the information, Suggs let out a roar of anger and charged down the alleyway. Liddle bolted at once, disappearing around the corner as if a runaway lorry was on his heels. Suggs went in pursuit but he was slower than his quarry and was soon panting at the exertion. Something brought him to a sudden halt. Marmion had warned him not to wreak revenge on Royston Liddle or there'd be repercussions. It was a warning that had to be taken seriously but Suggs wanted to inflict punishment somehow. Liddle would not escape completely.

The detectives were not only invited into the living room of the house, they were given tea and biscuits. In spite of the grief weighing her down, June Ingles was hospitable. Judging by the black-draped photograph of her daughter that stood on the sideboard, she bore a close resemblance to her. Florrie had inherited all of her mother's salient features. Had she not been so pale and drawn, June would have looked like an older version of her daughter. Both detectives noted with sadness that, when the photograph was taken, Florrie's complexion had been as clear as her mother's. She was a lovely young woman with an enchanting smile.

Brian Ingles had bequeathed none of his features to his daughter. He was a tall, well-built man with an expression of despair on a pock-marked face. Head bent forward and eyes wandering aimlessly, he looked as if all the life had been sucked out of him. It was left to his wife to do most of the talking. June sat beside him on the settee and held his hand for comfort. Ingles had a senior position with the Great Western Railway but he was bereft of authority now. Every question made him twitch defensively. While his wife sought to put on a brave face, he seemed haunted.

Marmion and Keedy had both noticed the difference. Every other house they'd visited in connection with the investigation had either been part of a terrace or semi-detached. The Ingles residence, however, was detached. Boasting four bedrooms, it had a small garden at the front and a larger one at the rear and, unlike most of the others, indoor sanitation. The detectives were impressed with the size and relative luxury of the living room. It had been recently decorated and had a new carpet. Brian Ingles's wage was clearly much larger than that of someone like Eamonn Quinn, the Irish coalman, or Jonah Jenkins, the officious bank clerk. The size of the home raised an obvious question.

'Why didn't your daughter live with you?' asked Marmion.

'Florrie and her husband wanted a place of their own,' explained June. 'When they got married, they moved into a flat. They were saving up to buy a house. Brian was going to lend them some money, weren't you?'

'Yes,' muttered Ingles, wincing.

144

'We offered to have them here, of course, but Florrie wanted them to set up on their own. And when she decided on something, there was no changing her mind.'

'I can understand her moving out when she married,' said Marmion, 'but why didn't she come back when she lost her husband?'

'It's what we both wanted, Inspector. Our other two daughters have married and moved away so we have three spare bedrooms here, but Florrie wouldn't hear of it. Having left home, she wanted to keep her independence.'

'Sounds a bit like Alice,' said Keedy, involuntarily.

'There's no need to mention her,' said Marmion, testily. He dredged up a smile for their hosts. 'The sergeant was referring to my daughter. She, too, would prefer to live on her own.'

'It wasn't like that in our day,' said June, 'was it, Brian?' Her husband shook his head. 'You stayed at home because you had to. I couldn't have afforded to rent a flat and my parents would never have let me move out. They were right.'

'Tell us about your daughter, Mrs Ingles.'

She smiled sadly. 'I could go on for hours about Florrie.'

'We're in no hurry.'

'She was a girl in a million. Florrie more or less ran this house when she was here. That's true, isn't it, Brian?'

'Yes,' he agreed, 'she had more energy than the rest of us put together.'

'We couldn't keep up with her. She was like a whirlwind.'

145

Once embarked on her daughter's life story, there was no holding June Ingles. Out came the photograph albums and the school reports and every other record they'd kept of her. Of the three children, she was clearly the favourite. Having mastered basic commercial skills very quickly, Florrie had worked as a secretary in a legal practice. When she was in full flow, June managed to shake off all hint of bereavement. She talked about her daughter as if she were still alive and well. Brian Ingles, however, sank deeper into his sorrow. Each treasured memento shown to the detectives had an adverse effect on him. He drew back, gritted his teeth and seemed to be in actual pain. When called upon to ratify one of his wife's fulsome claims about Florrie, the most he could manage was a reluctant nod.

Recalling his visit to Reuben Harte, Keedy tried to shift the focus slightly.

'Perhaps I could ask *you* a question, Mr Ingles,' he said. 'When I spoke to Jean Harte's father, he told me that her best friend at work was Florrie. Is that true?'

'I suppose that it is,' said Ingles, uncomfortably.

'They'd both lost someone at the front, I gather.'

'That's right,' said June, rescuing her husband from the ordeal of having to engage in a conversation. 'They were at school together, you see. I don't mean Florrie and Jean. I'm talking about Roger – that was Florrie's husband – and Maurice. They joined up together and were in the same regiment. On his last leave, Maurice got engaged to Jean and that was the last she ever saw

146

of him. They had a telegram weeks later. Roger had been killed earlier and Florrie was still in mourning yet, as soon as she heard about Maurice, she went straight round to Jean's house to console her. That was the kind of person she was. Florrie always put others first.'

'She sounds like a remarkable young woman,' said Marmion, 'and you're right to be proud of her. Did you approve of her taking the job at the factory?'

'Not entirely, Inspector.'

'Why is that?'

For once, she hesitated. The pause was unexpectedly filled by Ingles.

'We didn't like the idea,' he said. 'We'd heard about the dangers and we didn't want Florrie to spoil her good looks in that factory. Also, she had a good job. I paid a lot of money for her to learn secretarial skills. There were plenty of others ready to work as drudges because that's what they really were. They took women with no real education. Florrie was above such things.'

'It's what she wanted to do, Brian,' soothed his wife.

'It was wrong – and look where it got her.'

Feeling that he'd won the argument, he sat back and folded his arms. It was the first whiff of disagreement between him and June. The detectives realised that he could be more assertive than he looked and wondered if Brian Ingles was one of the reasons why Florrie hadn't wished to return home after the loss of her husband. Patently, her father felt that working at the factory was far beneath her. Left to him, she'd still be typing letters for solicitors.

'Mr Ingles raises an interesting point,' said Marmion, looking from husband to wife. 'There were five victims of that explosion and – had Maureen Quinn stayed there minutes longer – there would have been six. Why were they picked on? Was one or all of them a target?'

'We've established that the outhouse where the party was held was very rarely used,' said Keedy. 'In other words, whoever set off that bomb *knew* that someone would be inside it at a particular time.'

'What are you trying to tell us?' asked June, anxiously.

'The bomber must have hated someone at that party.'

'Well, it couldn't have been Florrie. Nobody could hate her.'

'Are you certain of that, Mrs Ingles?' probed Marmion. 'Even the most popular people can sometimes have enemies. Indeed, their very popularity can arouse envy in some twisted minds. The fact is that it was your daughter's birthday party. Everything revolved around her. I want you to think very carefully before you answer this question,' he said. 'Can you remember *any* occasion – any occasion at all – when Florrie upset someone by deliberately being rude or hostile to them?'

All that June could do was to stare at him openmouthed but the question infuriated her husband. Leaping to his feet and shaking all over, he pointed to the door.

'I'd like you both to leave right now, Inspector,'

he said, forcefully. 'Our daughter has been mur-dered. Don't you think we've got enough to put up with? Coming here and asking questions like that is an insult to Florrie. It's disgusting. Please go away and leave us alone.'

After a flurry of apologies, the detectives left the house and got back into the waiting car. Marmion wondered what had prompted Ingles's extreme reaction. Turning to him, Keedy gave a wry smile.

'I shouldn't mention that to the superintend-ent, if I were you,' he said.

CHAPTER TEN

When he got home that evening, Eamonn Quinn found a kettle of hot water waiting for him on the stove. He poured it into a chipped enamel basin and washed off the grime of a day's work. As he dried himself with a threadbare towel, his wife came into the kitchen.

'What sort of a day did you have?' she asked.

'It was terrible. Everyone wanted to ask about Maureen.'

'Well, it's only natural.'

'They kept on and on. I couldn't stand it, Di.' He hung the towel on a hook. 'What about you – any visitors?'

'We had lots,' she replied, 'but I didn't let any of them in. Well, not until Father Cleary called, that is. I couldn't turn him away.'

Quinn glared. 'What was that old fool doing here?'

'He came to offer his condolences.'

'Well, he could have done that on the doorstep.'

'Father Cleary wanted to speak to Maureen.'

'I told you to let nobody in.'

'He's our parish priest, Eamonn. He has rights. In any case, Maureen was willing to talk to him and I thought that was a good sign. She's even agreed to go to Mass on Sunday.'

He was aggrieved. 'What on earth did she do that for?'

'It's what she wanted,' said Diane. 'I may go with her.'

'Well, don't expect me to be there. I've had my fill of Father Cleary and his interference. I'm not having anyone telling me how to live my life.'

'But you were baptised and married in a Roman Catholic church. You made vows. We both did. We promised to bring up our children in the Catholic faith.'

'I agreed to a lot of things when we were younger,' he said, dismissively. 'Then I realised that most of them were a waste of time.' He rolled down the sleeves of his shirt. 'No sign of those detectives?'

'None at all.'

'Good – they're worse than that damn priest.'

'They need help, Eamonn. We can't stop them questioning Maureen.'

'Yes, we can. Say that she's too ill to talk to anybody.'

'But she might be able to tell them something useful.'

'How can she?' he demanded. 'Maureen doesn't have a clue who set off that bomb. The only thing we need worry about is the fact that she didn't die in the blast.'

'That's being selfish,' she protested. 'What about the victims?'

'They're not our concern, Di.'

'Yes, they are – especially Agnes. Have you forgotten how often she used to come here with the baby? She was a good friend to Maureen. They did everything together. If it had been our daughter who'd been killed instead of Agnes Collier,' she said, 'I bet that Agnes would have been round here like a shot to offer her sympathy.'

He curled a lip. 'Well, don't ask me to offer any sympathy to Sadie Radcliffe. She was always jealous of Maureen. I never liked the woman.'

'That's beside the point. She's in need of comfort.'

'She won't get it from me – and neither will the other families.'

Diane was stung. 'There are times when you sicken me, Eamonn Quinn,' she said, confronting him. 'As long as you can have meals put in front of you and go off to the pub every evening, you don't give a damn about anybody else.'

'Family comes first.'

'Those five girls were blown up. Doesn't that matter to you?'

'Not as long as Maureen is still alive.'

'That's shameful,' she said, fully roused for once. 'It's not us that should be going to church on Sunday, it's you. I think you ought to get down on your knees and thank God that our

151

daughter was spared.'

'Calm down, Di,' he said, putting a clumsy arm around her. 'There's no need to get so upset about it. And yes, of course I'm grateful that Maureen left that party when she did, but I'm not going to make a song and dance about it. As for the pub,' he added, 'they won't see me there tonight. It'd be like facing the Inquisition. I'll have to get some bottled beer instead and drink it here.' When he tried to kiss her, she pulled away. 'What's wrong now?'

'I'm not in the mood.'

'It's not like you to argue.'

'You can be so maddening sometimes, Eamonn.'

'Anyone would think that *I* planted that bomb,' he whined. When his wife continued to stare at him with disdain, his self-pity turned to anger. He reached out to grab her shoulder and pull her closer. 'Don't you *dare* say a word about that.'

'It happened,' she said, coldly. 'You can't deny it.'

'You're to say nothing,' he decreed. 'If the coppers come sniffing around again, tell them that Maureen is ill and send them on their way. Don't answer any questions. Do you understand?'

Diane regarded him with mingled fear and disgust. Their daughter's escape had not just reminded her of the importance of religion in their lives. It had told her something very unpleasant about the man she married.

'I'll make your tea,' she said.

Seated behind his desk, Claude Chatfield read the article with mounting annoyance until he

152

reached the point where he could bear it no longer. He flung the newspaper aside and fumed in silence. When there was a tap on the door, he barked an invitation.

'Come in!'

'Good evening, sir,' said Marmion, entering the room and closing the door behind him. 'I knew that I'd find you still here.'

Chatfield indicated the newspaper. 'Have you read this?'

'I try to read very few papers when I'm involved in an investigation. They're not good for my blood pressure.'

'This nincompoop was at the press conference because I remember seeing him there, but he obviously didn't listen to a word you said.'

'Did he appeal for witnesses? That's all I care about.'

'It's the one valuable thing he did do,' said the superintendent. 'In his article, he's trying to solve the case for us.'

'On the basis of what evidence?' asked Marmion.

'Why bother with evidence when you have a vivid imagination? You made it perfectly clear that you believed one, or all of those women, was deliberately killed by someone with a grudge. That's too prosaic a murder for this chap. He thinks it's the work of dissidents from central Europe.'

Marmion snorted in disbelief. 'What are they doing at a pub in Hayes?'

'There *are* immigrants living in the locality, it seems. He got that bit right. The rest of the article is arrant nonsense. It hangs on the debatable claim that bombs are the favoured weapon of political hotheads in places like Austria-Hungary. In other words,' said Chatfield with heavy sarcasm, 'all you have to do is to round up any wild-eyed Serbs in the area and the case is solved.'

'If only it were that easy!' said Marmion.

'Forget the press. Since they won't work with us, we'll manage on our own. Now then,' he went on, sitting upright. 'When we last spoke, you were about to interview the parents of Florence Duncan.'

'That's right, sir. It turned out to be a shorter interview than we thought.'

'Oh – why is that, pray?'

Marmion described what had happened and how the subdued Brian Ingles had lost his temper and, effectively, thrown them out. His wife had been embarrassed and apologised profusely as she showed them to the door. She told them that her husband had been paralysed with grief when he first heard the news and that neither of them had had a wink of sleep since. Chatfield listened, pondered, tapped the ends of his fingers together, then showed a real grasp of detail.

'So what we have are five victims and five varying responses to their deaths from the respective families. Agnes Collier's mother was hurt and resentful,' he recalled, 'Shirley Beresford's husband had to take to his bed, Enid Jenks's father showed no real emotion and denied that she might have welcomed male attention, Jean Harte's father didn't let Sergeant Keedy get any further than the mat inside the front door and Florence Duncan's parents found the notion that she might actually have enemies to be tantamount to slander.'

'Nobody was prepared to admit that their daughter could possibly have upset someone enough to provoke an attack on their life.'

'It all comes back to one thing, Inspector. How well do we actually know our children? The brutal answer, I suspect, is we have only limited insight. It's rather humbling. I have five children but I'd never claim to know the inner workings of their minds. And look what happened with your daughter.'

'I don't think that's at all relevant,' said Marmion, quickly.

'Of course, it is. Alice is the same age as some of those victims. She probably has the same interests and similar ambitions. I'm sure that you thought you knew her inside out, yet she pulled the wool over your eyes.'

'That's not what happened, Superintendent.'

'I heard the gossip. She and the sergeant were carrying on behind your back.'

'They're engaged to be married,' said Marmion, struggling to keep his composure, 'and my wife and I are very happy about it. As for gossip, it's never reliable. For instance, I heard a rumour that you were about to resign because you couldn't cope with the pressures of the job.'

'That's a vicious calumny!' snapped Chatfield. 'I've never felt fitter and wouldn't dream of walking away from a job that I love and do extremely well.'

In fact, Marmion had invented the rumour just to bait him. It had the desired effect and distracted the superintendent away from Alice. He spent minutes defending his record as a senior officer and asked who first spread the poisonous tale about him.

'I don't know, sir,' said Marmion, stoutly. 'If I ever find out, I'll box his ears then drag him along here. There's great respect for you among the men.'

That, too, was well short of the truth but it seemed to mollify Chatfield.

'Let's get back to the case in hand,' he said.

'You forgot to mention the reaction of Maureen Quinn's parents, sir.'

'I was coming to that, Inspector. Her mother, Diane, was horrified but her father – Eamonn, was it? – tried to turn you away by saying his daughter was in bed. When that lie was exposed, he insisted in sitting in on the interview and trying to browbeat Maureen. You had to shut him up to get anything substantive out of her.'

'Mr Quinn has no time for the police, sir.'

'Yes,' said Chatfield, picking up a slip of paper, 'you told me that and gave it as your opinion that he'd been in trouble with the law. You're right. I checked.'

'What did you find out, sir?'

'He's been fined twice for causing an affray.'

'Quinn is a strong man,' said Marmion. 'I wouldn't want to get too close to him when he's had too much to drink. He's the kind of person who likes to settle an argument with his fists.'

'Then there's a possible motive behind the bomb blast.'

'I'm not sure that I detect it, sir.'

'Wake up, man. Quinn probably has dozens of enemies. One of them may have wanted to get back at him by killing his daughter.'

'Then why not attack her on her own?'

'The birthday party presented an irresistible opportunity.'

'No,' said Marmion, 'I'm afraid that your theory doesn't hold water. How would this supposed enemy of Eamonn Quinn even be aware of the party? It was in Hayes and Maureen lives miles away. Someone local who nursed ill will against her father wouldn't even know where the Golden Goose was.'

'He would if he worked at the factory as well,' argued Chatfield.

'I don't think that Quinn is the key factor here, Superintendent. We have to look in more depth at the private lives of the five victims and the survivor. There has to be a connecting thread somewhere.'

'You won't find it if you alienate the parents as you did earlier today.'

'Mr Ingles was overwrought. We've seen it happen before.'

'Are you going to have another go at him tomorrow?'

'We'll talk to the neighbours first,' said Marmion, reflectively. 'Florrie was a real extrovert. They'll all have a tale to tell about her. And I don't care how lovable she was supposed to be. We *all* have enemies – even someone like you, sir.'

Chatfield's ears pricked up. 'Have you heard rumours to that effect?'

It was late when Keedy picked her up from her flat but the café at the end of the road was still open and they were able to find a table in a quiet corner. Over a light supper, Alice told him about her brother's imminent return from the front and he was thrilled at the news. She also talked about her day and basked in the pleasure of seeing him again, albeit for a short time. Keedy pounced on one remark she made.

'Inspector Gale has been hounding you again?'

'She likes to put me down, Joe.'

'Then you should learn to avoid her,' he counselled. 'When I first joined the police, I had this bully of a sergeant who liked to use me as a punch bag. So I learnt to keep out of his way and – when that wasn't possible – I always made sure that there was someone with me. The sergeant didn't hector me half as much when I had a witness. In the end, he switched his attention to another new recruit and made *his* life a misery instead.'

'Gale Force doesn't make my life a misery,' said Alice. 'She just pecks away at me and it's always about the same thing – Daddy.'

He grinned. 'Don't I get a mention?'

'Yes, you do, because she knows that you're working on the case as well.'

'Ah, I see. She thinks you're getting a whiff of a murder investigation while she's confined to more mundane matters. She envies your privileged position, Alice.'

'It's a double-barrelled privilege, that's what really upsets her. I not only have a father with an unparalleled record as a detective, I'm engaged

158

to the most handsome man at Scotland Yard.'

'Well, I can't disagree with that bit,' he said, complacently.

'Don't be so vain,' she scolded.

He laughed. 'I can't help it if I was born with such good looks.'

'No, but you can help boasting about it.'

She prodded him playfully. In fact, he was not at his best at that moment. The long hours at work were taking their toll. Keedy's eyes were red-rimmed and his frown lines were accentuated. Even the delight of seeing her hadn't enabled him to shake off his fatigue. While she knew that he'd pay no heed to the advice, she told him that he needed more sleep, then she guided him gently around to the subject of the investigation. He held up both hands.

'Stop there, Alice.'

'Why?'

'Your father says that I'm not to discuss the case with you.'

'Daddy isn't here at the moment, is he?'

'Are you asking me to disobey a senior officer?'

'I'm asking you to tell me what you've been up to, that's all. It's not a state secret, is it? Nobody else will ever know. Where's the harm in it?'

Keedy hesitated. 'I shouldn't be doing this, Alice. Your father is bad enough but the super-intendent would go berserk if he knew that I was revealing details of the case to someone who had no right to hear them. You're not qualified, Alice.'

'I'm going to be your wife – what better quali-fication is there than that? Besides,' she added, 'I'm doing you a favour by asking.'

'That's ridiculous.'

'Is it? In telling me about what happened today, you'll be going through the evidence you picked up. Daddy always says that you can't do that enough. He sifts evidence time and again.'

Keedy was persuaded. He gave her an attenuated version of events and stressed that she mustn't breathe a word of it to anyone else. Alice not only listened attentively, she asked some pertinent questions and amazed him by showing she'd forgotten nothing of what she'd been told earlier. She remembered every name and every shred of evidence. While being shocked at the antics of Alan Suggs, the promiscuous driver, she was surprised at the ease with which anyone could borrow the key to the outhouse. The landlord had to bear the blame for that. When Keedy had come to the end of his account, she singled out one name.

'Maureen Quinn went to church?'

'She was consumed with guilt, Alice.'

'Did you speak to the parish priest?'

'No – why should I?'

'Well,' said Alice, 'if she was there for hours on end, somebody would have noticed her and passed on the information. Roman Catholic priests keep a close eye on the families in their congregation.'

'But, according to Mrs Quinn, they never went to church.'

'That's all the more reason why Maureen would have been spotted and reported. One of the women I work with is a Roman Catholic. Her priest is always dropping in at the house. She calls him a spy for the Almighty.'

Keedy was thoughtful. 'You might be on to something there, Alice.'

'It's only a guess but I think it's worth looking into. The priest will know the family and be able to give you more information about them. He'll also be aware of that explosion in Hayes. It's common knowledge now. Maureen needs comfort and he'll surely want to provide it.'

Seated around the kitchen table, the four of them ate their supper in comparative silence. Diane Quinn made a few comments, Lily asked when she'd be going back to school and her father told her that he'd make the decision in due course. Maureen said nothing. Unaware of their presence, she ate her food without really tasting it. She gazed down at her empty plate and replayed in her mind the moment when she heard the explosion. It had blown her whole world apart. She didn't hear Lily being sent off to bed or see her father pouring himself a glass of beer from a flagon. Only when her mother moved Maureen's plate to the sink did she come out of her reverie. Diane sat down again and glanced across at her husband before speaking.

'There's something we need to discuss,' she ventured.

'I don't think so,' said Quinn, peremptorily. 'She doesn't go.'

'Maureen must make her own decision, Eamonn.'

'She's not strong enough to do that. I'll make it for her.'

161

'What are you talking about?' asked Maureen, looking up.

Quinn flicked a beefy hand. 'It doesn't matter.'

'Yes, it does,' argued Diane. 'It matters a lot.' She turned to her daughter. 'We're talking about the funerals, Maureen. They can't be far off. Your father doesn't want you to go to any of them.'

'I'm not having everyone staring at her,' he said.

'She can't stay away. They were her friends. What will people say?'

'Who cares?'

'I do,' said Diane, meeting his glare. 'The families of the other girls will be very hurt if Maureen can't even make the effort to go. They'll feel betrayed.'

'We have to put our daughter first, Di. She's bad enough as it is. If she has to sit through five funerals, it will be a terrible strain for her. I want to spare her that.'

Diane touched her daughter's arm. 'What do you think?'

'I don't know,' replied Maureen in a daze.

'I'll come with you.'

'Steer well clear,' said Quinn. 'That's what I'll do.'

Diane ignored him. 'I know it will be an ordeal for you, Maureen,' she said, softly, 'but I'll help you through it. Think how upset Mrs Radcliffe will be if you don't turn up. Then there's Shirley's family. She was a good friend – you played in the football team with her. And don't forget Florrie. It was her birthday party. That's where this whole thing started.'

162

Maureen looked hopelessly confused and unable to come to a decision.

'There you are,' concluded Quinn. 'She doesn't *want* to go.'

'Maureen hasn't said that.'

'It would be cruel to force her, Di.'

'Think how it will look if she *doesn't* go.'

'You can be there instead of her. Say that she's too poorly.'

Diane paused to consider. 'Perhaps we should ask Father Cleary,' she said at length. 'He'll be able to advise us.'

'Keep that nosy old so-and-so away from here.'

'He's our parish priest, Eamonn. He'll know what the decent thing to do is.'

'I'm not letting him back into my life again,' said Quinn, bitterly. 'I had enough of Father Cleary when we first moved here. He was always calling in to cadge a cup of tea and tell me how to bring up my children. He was here so often that he might as well have moved in with us.'

'Don't exaggerate.'

'He downright pestered us, Di. In the end, I was sick of the sight of him.'

'We're not talking about you,' she reminded him. 'When he came to see Maureen, he helped. That's all I care about. He soothed her. Father Cleary knows how people feel when there's been a disaster in their lives. He understands what Maureen must be going through.'

'Well, he can keep his advice to himself.'

Diane looked at her daughter again. 'Would you like to talk to Father Cleary?'

'I don't know.'

'Shall I ask him to call again?'

'I don't know, Mummy.'

'You must have been thinking about the funerals.'

'I have,' admitted Maureen. 'I've been thinking of nothing else all day. If I go to one of them, it will bring it all flooding back and I don't think I could bear that. I don't want to let anyone down, Mummy, but to be honest, I'm *terrified* of going.'

'There you are,' said Quinn, triumphantly. 'I was right.'

After his meeting with the superintendent, Marmion went to his office and sat at his desk while he reviewed the facts of the case once more. If only one victim had been targeted and killed, his job would be much more straightforward. There'd simply be one person's background to explore instead of five. When he added Maureen Quinn to the list, he realised what a mass of material they would assemble, most of it turning out to be irrelevant in the course of time. Other investigations had left him starved of information. In this case, he had far too much of it. When he opened his notebook, he was daunted by the number of names he'd already recorded in connection with the crime, and he suspected that there would be many more before the case was solved.

It was time to leave. Having dismissed his driver for the day, he travelled home by bus and walked the last few hundred yards down streets that had a reassuring familiarity. Nobody else was about. Marmion hoped that his wife would have had the sense to go to bed. He was always overcome with remorse if he kept her up late. When he saw the light through the living room curtains, he knew that Ellen was still there and reproached himself for not leaving Scotland Yard earlier. He let himself into the house and hung up his coat and hat before peeping into the living room. Ellen was sound asleep, slumped in a chair with an open book in her lap. Marmion smiled and crossed the room to plant a delicate kiss on her head. As he picked up the book, an envelope fell out of it and landed on the carpet. He retrieved it at once.

'Hello,' he said to himself, 'what do we have here?'

CHAPTER ELEVEN

Exhaustion finally got the better of June Ingles. Though she tossed and turned for hours, she finally fell into a deep sleep. She came out of it when the birds were heralding a new dawn. The first thing she noticed was that her husband was wide awake, sitting upright beside her and frowning with concentration. June made an effort to shake off her drowsiness.

'Did you get any sleep?' she asked.

'No, I didn't.'

'You need it, Brian. We both do. Let the doctor prescribe sleeping pills.'

'I don't need any pills,' he said, bitterly. 'The only thing that would make me sleep again is to have Florrie back with us, and that's not going to happen.'

'We have to get used to the fact.'

'It will take time, June.' He suppressed a yawn. 'I've spent half the night thinking about the letter I'm going to write.'

'What letter?'

'It's that headline in the newspaper,' he said. '"Five Dead Canaries" – it was tasteless, indecent and incorrect. Florrie wasn't a canary. She was a wonderful daughter with a lovely disposition. She was an individual, June, and deserves to be treated as such, not tossed into a common pot labelled "canaries". It's demeaning.'

'You shouldn't have read that paper if it was going to upset you.'

'How could I help it? Someone put it through our letter box.'

'Yes,' said June, 'but they didn't mean to offend you. They thought we might be interested in what was being said about the explosion.' She sat up and put the pillow at her back. 'What else have you been thinking about?'

'It's that idea of Mr Kennett's.'

'Oh, I'm not at all sure about that,' she said, worriedly.

'Neither was I when he rang yesterday evening but I've been mulling it over. It's very kind of the factory to make the offer. After all, Florrie's birthday party was a private matter,' he emphasised. 'It wasn't the management's responsibility. Yet Mr Kennett says that they'll bear the cost of the funerals for the victims.'

'But is it what we *want?*'

'It will relieve us of the burden of organising it.'

'Yes, but Florrie will just be one of five people lowered into a grave. There'll be nothing *personal* about her funeral. It will be shared.'

'They died together and should be buried together.'

'A moment ago,' she noted, 'you were complaining about that newspaper headline robbing our daughter of her individuality. The funeral will do the same.'

'No, it won't. It's a different matter altogether.'

'I'd still like Florrie to have a service of her own.'

He was insistent. 'Do you want us to be the odd one out, June? What if the other four families opt for a joint funeral and we refuse? We'd get a lot of criticism.'

'Who's to say that everyone else will accept Mr Kennett's offer? I'm not sure that they will. Apart from anything else,' she pointed out, 'the victims didn't all go to the same church. Jean Harte, I know for a fact, didn't go to *any* church.'

'Mr Kennett made allowances for that,' he said with a touch of impatience. 'He realised that the services themselves might take place in different churches but the burials would all take place together at the cemetery. It's only a question of timing, June. Florrie might have a separate service but a shared burial.'

'I still don't like the idea.'

'But it will simplify everything.'

'That's what I've got against it, Brian.'

'It will also save us money.'

'That's an awful thing to say,' she complained.

167

'I'm surprised at you for even mentioning it. This is Florrie we're talking about. No expense should be spared at her funeral. We can afford it and we should pay it willingly.'

'We'll foot the bill for the flowers, naturally.'

'What about after the funeral?'

'We join the others at the hotel.'

'Exactly,' she said. 'We mourn our daughter in the midst of strangers.'

'Don't get so worked up about it, June. They're not all strangers. We know Jean's father and Shirley's husband and we've bumped into Agnes Collier and her mother a few times while out shopping. We're in this together,' he reasoned. 'It's a tragedy common to all five families and we mustn't imagine we're not part of it.'

June was both wounded and puzzled. She strongly disapproved of the notion of a shared event and she couldn't understand why her husband had agreed to it. As a rule, he always put privacy first. She was surprised when he even gave Kennett's invitation serious consideration. The revelation that he viewed it as a means of saving money was a profound shock to her. His salary enabled them to live a comfortable life. Her husband was generous and June lacked for nothing. Yet he was now trying to cut back on funeral expenses. There was another shock in store for her.

'June...'

'Yes?'

'Something else has been on my mind as well.'

'What's that?'

'I'm wondering if we should sell the house and

move to somewhere smaller.'

Harvey Marmion was in a good mood when he climbed into the car beside Joe Keedy. The news about his son's forthcoming leave had given him a real fillip. Hoping to surprise his companion with the information, he was taken aback when he learnt that Keedy was already aware of it.

'You didn't tell me that you'd be seeing Alice last night,' he said.

'You didn't ask, Harv.'

'How is she?'

'As pleased as the rest of us that Paul is coming home,' said Keedy. 'He's had a hard time over there. A break was long overdue.'

'There's only one problem, Joe. It increases the pressure on us.'

'I don't follow.'

'We don't want to be bogged down in this investigation when my son comes home. We need to have the whole thing done and dusted.'

Keedy's laugh was hollow. 'You've got a hope!'

'We'll get a breakthrough soon. I can feel it coming.'

'I can't say that I share your enthusiasm. It's still early days.'

The car was driving swiftly towards Hayes and taking a route to which it was becoming accustomed. Knowing exactly how long they had before they got there, the detectives planned the day ahead.

'I'd like to learn more about Florrie Duncan,' said Marmion.

'Her father won't even let you through the front

door, Harv. The same goes for Reuben Harte, by the way. He's the one who thought you looked shifty.'

Marmion was piqued. 'Don't keep ribbing me about that.'

'I told Alice. She thought that it was funny.'

'I hope that's *all* you told her about this investigation,' said Marmion, sternly. 'I don't want you divulging information. One detective is enough in any family.'

'The subject never even came up,' said Keedy, looking through the window. 'We had other things to talk about.'

'Keep it that way. As for Florrie Duncan, I'd like to know what the neighbours thought of her. I'm not going to do any snooping myself. If her father caught sight of me in the road, he'd probably chase me away with a garden fork.'

'We can deploy some of our men there. They've finished house-to-house calls in the vicinity of the Golden Goose. That turned out to be a futile exercise.'

'It had to be done, Joe. It's unfortunate that nobody saw suspicious behaviour near the pub. Customers came and went all the time. The neighbours were so used to seeing traffic in and out of the Golden Goose that they stopped looking at it.'

'The bomber must have come at night.'

'How would he have got into the outhouse?'

'With the key, I expect.'

'That would have meant breaking into the pub after dark and that would have been dangerous. No,' decided Marmion, 'the landlord is pretty lax about security but I still bet that he'd check that

170

the outhouse key was on its hook before he went to bed. Whoever borrowed it, did so during the day and slipped off to plant his bomb when everyone else was boozing in the bar.'

'Are you going to speak to the landlord again?'

'That's my starting point, Joe.'

'What about me?'

'I'd like you to talk to Maureen Quinn again. Try to get her on her own. Her mother owes you a favour after the way you found her daughter at the church. Tell her you'd like a private word with Maureen.'

'There's something I'd rather do before that, Harv.'

'Oh – what's that?'

'Another visit to that church may pay dividends,' replied the other. 'The priest lives in the house next door to it. I reckon he'll have been made aware of the fact that Maureen spent hours in church yesterday. He may even have called on her. At all events, he'll know the Quinn family and be able to give us the sort of information we might not get from anyone else.'

Marmion was impressed. 'That's a good idea, Joe. I wish I'd thought of it.'

'So do I,' said Keedy under his breath.

Since he had no telephone, the message was delivered to Jonah Jenks by hand. When he heard the envelope drop through the letter box, he thought at first that it would be another card from one of the neighbours, expressing their sympathy at his loss. Instead, it was a letter from the munitions factory on headed paper. Bernard Kennett, the

171

works manager, offered his condolences and raised the possibility of a joint funeral for the five victims. Since they'd been employed at the factory, he'd been authorised to say that all expenses would be met from management coffers. The letter stressed that no compulsion would be involved. The families of the deceased were free to make their own decision about the funerals of their respective daughters.

Jenks was touched by the unexpected sign of compassion. He viewed the munitions factory as an enemy, a huge, relentless machine that enslaved thousands of women and sent them home with ruined complexions. It had cut short his daughter's burgeoning career as a musician, eating into her practice time and coarsening her hands so much that she could no longer conjure the same mellifluous notes out of piano and violin. Enid had denied that filling shells had had a deleterious effect on her playing but her father knew what he heard. Her talent had been compromised. After reading the letter again, he decided that the factory owed his daughter something and that the invitation should be accepted.

Putting on a coat and hat, he went off to discuss the matter.

Things had changed at the Golden Goose. Now that detectives had finished searching through the rubble for bomb fragments, the lumps of stone and charred timbers were being loaded onto the back of a lorry. The pub might be losing its outhouse but it had gained some scaffolding. It now surrounded the building, holding it in like a metal corset. Men were already on the roof, mending the chimney and replacing the dislodged slates. Houses nearby had also improved in appearance. Windows had been installed and the shards of glass on the pavement swept up. There had even been some repairs to damaged brickwork and to front doors from which large splinters of wood had been gouged out. The area was getting back to normal.

What could not be removed so easily were the ugly memories of the blast. People were still complaining angrily about it and comparing the damage it had done to their properties. There was sympathy for the victims but it was relegated to a secondary position. Leighton Hubbard could not leave his pub alone. Drawn back to the Golden Goose that morning, he stared up dolefully at it, trying to work out if it was doomed to distinction or a phoenix about to rise from the ashes. One thing was certain. He and his wife would never feel safe inside it again.

The police car drew up and Harvey Marmion stepped out. After an exchange of greetings with Hubbard, he looked at the work going on.

'The mess will soon be cleared away, sir,' he said.

'But what am I left with?' asked Hubbard. 'I'll have a pub with a jinx on it. Customers are already starting to say they won't come back. Others have deserted me for my rivals. I've been put out of business for good.'

'I doubt that, Mr Hubbard. I've talked to a lot of people around here and they speak well of you and your pub. Rely on their loyalty. They'll be back.'

'The big question is this, Inspector – will *I* be back?'

'Is there any reason why you shouldn't be?'

'Yes,' said the landlord. 'That bomb has given my missus the shakes. She won't even hear about moving back in yet. She's lost her nerve completely.'

'I'm sure it will return in time,' said Marmion, facing him. 'Did you do what I asked you to do?'

'Yes,' said Hubbard, thrusting a hand into his pocket, 'but I can't see that it will be of any use.' He handed over two crumpled pieces of paper. 'Those are all the names that I could remember. Frankly, I was amazed how many there were. Some just pop in now and then, of course, so they may not count. Regulars like Ezra Greenwell were in the Goose almost every night.'

Marmion ran his eye down the list on the first page, then studied the second one. He noticed that Royston Liddle had a mention and so did Alan Suggs. It was as well that the landlord didn't know what the two of them had got up to at the pub.

'Did you see much of Alan Suggs in here?' asked Marmion.

'He wasn't one of my regulars,' said Hubbard. 'Alan's more interested in chasing women than playing darts in my bar. When he did come in, he had that smile on his face as if he'd been having fun somewhere else. He even tried to flirt with my missus once.' His expression hardened. 'I wasn't having that and neither was she. After we'd both had a go at him, we didn't see him in here for months.'

'What are these ticks against certain names?'

'Those are men who've been coming here for years, real dependables.'

'What about the crosses? Do they indicate men employed at the munitions factory?'

'Yes – it's what you asked for, Inspector.'

'Thank you, sir,' said Marmion, pocketing the two pieces of paper. 'It could turn out to have been a profitable piece of homework. One of the patrons on your list might have been the bomber.'

Hubbard was incensed. 'I deny that,' he said, hotly. 'I know everyone who comes into the Goose. Not one of them would dare to do such a thing to me.'

'But they didn't do it to *you* – they did it to five young women.'

'It amounts to the same thing. It was on my premises.'

'Which would have been worse?' asked Marmion, looking him in the eye. 'A bomb planted in the outhouse or one hidden in your cellar?'

'One in the cellar, of course – we'd all have been killed then.'

'Please bear that in mind, sir. Instead of moaning about being a victim, you should be grateful that you're a survivor.'

But the landlord could only see the explosion in terms of what it had cost him. He drifted away to talk to one of the workmen. His place was taken by Royston Liddle, grinning and nodding simultaneously.

'Good morning, Inspector,' he said.

'Hello, Mr Liddle. Perhaps you can help me.' Marmion took out the lists given him by Leighton

175

Hubbard. 'Have a look at those, please.' The grin vanished and Liddle took a step backwards. 'Ah, I see. You can't read. In that case, I'll go through the names of people in whom I'm interested. Tell me what you know about them.'

'I can read a bit,' said Liddle, 'but I'm very slow.'

'Let's start off with Les Harker.'

'Oh, he comes in here a lot. He works at the factory.'

'All the people that I want to hear about work there.'

There were over a dozen names on the list. Marmion went through them one by one. Liddle knew them all by sight and was able to supply a lot of detail about some of them. The last name required no comment from him.

'You've already told me enough about Alan Suggs,' said Marmion.

'He said that you talked to him.'

'Oh, I did. We had a long and fruitful conversation. Mr Suggs has a very complicated private life, but I daresay you know that.'

'Alan came after me.'

'Did he threaten you in any way?'

'He did more than that, Inspector,' said Liddle, rubbing his shoulder gingerly. 'He pushed me so hard against a fence that I've got bruises. I saw them in the mirror. He chased me down the alleyway. If I hadn't run so fast, he'd have really hurt me.'

'I warned him against reprisals.'

'What are they?'

'Never mind,' said Marmion. 'I'll speak to him again.'

'Tell him that I didn't mean to get him into trouble. I'm his friend.'

'He might take some convincing on that score.' Folding the pieces of paper again, he slipped them into his pocket. 'But thank you for your help with those names. You've saved me bothering with most of them.' The praise made the other man beam. 'Keep your eyes open. If any of the people we talked about show up here at night just to gloat, let me know.'

'I've always wanted to be a policeman,' said Liddle, excitedly.

'Don't wish too hard,' cautioned Marmion. 'The hours are terrible, the work is never-ending and a lot of people think it's their mission in life to tell you dreadful lies. You're better off doing odd jobs, Mr Liddle. It's a lot safer in every way.'

When he was shown into the room, Keedy was astonished to see how barely furnished it was. Apart from the desk and the chair behind it, there were only two upright chairs and a bookcase. The floor was uncarpeted and the only wall decoration was the large crucifix above the fireplace. Father Cleary was amused by his reaction.

'What did you expect, Sergeant?' he asked.

'It's so Spartan.'

'The Catholic priesthood is not a road to luxury, you know. This study is ideal for me. It has no clutter and nothing to distract the eye. That's my idea of an ideal environment.'

'It wouldn't suit me, Father Cleary. I like a bit of comfort.'

'Then we're clearly not soul mates.'

177

Keedy had arrived to receive a cordial greeting. The priest seemed to expect him and waved him to a chair. On the desk in front of him were neat piles of paper and a Bible. There was a chill in the air.

'Once February is out, I manage without a fire,' explained Cleary.

'You're a model of self-denial, Father.'

'Oh, I don't flatter myself that I occupy that status. Models are for people to copy. You won't find any of my parishioners taking up their carpets and throwing out half the furniture.' He smiled benignly. 'You've come about Maureen Quinn, haven't you? I had a feeling you would, sooner or later.'

'To be frank,' said Keedy, 'I've come about the whole Quinn family. I was hoping that you could tell us more about them. Maureen seems very nice but her father couldn't wait to get us out of the house.'

'Eamonn was never very hospitable.'

'He stopped the children coming to church, I believe.'

'Yes, and it was a crying shame because they learnt so much while they were here, Maureen especially. Her brothers were a bit of a handful, mind you, and I don't think their father liked it when I told him about their little tricks.'

'Tricks?'

'When they came to Sunday school, each of the children was given a penny for the collection. Maureen and Lily always put theirs dutifully on the plate but the lads kept the money and tried to palm us off with blazer buttons and the odd foreign coin. I soon put a stop to that. But all credit to them,' Cleary went on, 'they might have been little devils as children but, when war broke out, Liam and Anthony were among the first to volunteer for the army.'

Hands clasped and shoulders hunched, he went on to give Keedy a brief history of the family and of its fluctuating interest in the church. Diane and her daughters had last attended a service at Christmas. It was years since Eamonn had been near the place. In Cleary's judgement, he was essentially a man's man and missed his sons badly. He'd spent most of his free time with them and taught them the rudiments of carpentry in the garden shed. Liam had gone on to be apprenticed to a cabinetmaker. Anthony had worked in a foundry. Keedy was given the image of a relatively happy and close family whose lives had been fractured by the war. Maureen had been a major casualty. In spite of a good education and other assets, she'd ended up toiling in the munitions factory to contribute to the family budget.

'What was your view of her father?' asked Cleary.

'He likes to let his family know that he's in charge,' said Keedy, 'which is a polite way of saying that he's an uncouth bully.'

'He has his better qualities.'

'We weren't allowed to see them.'

'I'm sure you know that he fell foul of the law.'

'Yes, he was fined twice for causing an affray.'

'Oh, he caused trouble more than twice,' said Cleary with a laugh. 'Eamonn is quick to anger and slow to cool down. He's been banned from a couple of pubs for threatening behaviour. Even with watered beer, he can get horribly drunk.'

'I feel sorry for his wife and children.'

'They've learnt to live with him.'

'Do they have any choice?' Keedy took out his notebook and consulted a page. 'This is my record of our interview with Maureen. She was deeply shocked, of course, as anybody would be when friends have died in such horrible circumstances. But there was something more than shock in her face.'

'It was guilt, Sergeant. They died while she lived. That fact will haunt her.'

'I'd taken account of that, Father Cleary. There was something else as well.'

'What was it?'

'That's the trouble – I don't know. And we were unable to draw it out of her because her father was sitting beside her. Inspector Marmion had the same reaction as I did. We didn't get the full truth out of Maureen, somehow.'

'You must allow for her confusion,' warned the priest. 'After a ghastly experience like that, the poor girl must be totally bewildered. Give her time.'

'We don't have unlimited time to give her,' said Keedy. 'In cases of murder, we find that the first forty-eight hours after the event are crucial. That's when memories are fresh and we're likely to get a clearer idea of what actually happened. The longer an investigation goes on, the more difficult it sometimes becomes. Witnesses are less reliable, evidence disappears and the killer is given valuable time to get far away from the scene.'

'I don't think he's far away at the moment, Sergeant. He's right here.'

'What do you mean?'

'It has to be a local man, hasn't it? You're looking for someone familiar with the Golden Goose and with the fact that a birthday party was being held there.'

Keedy blinked. 'Well done, Father. That's exactly who we're after.'

'And you think Maureen can help you find him?'

'I just feel that she may be hiding something.'

Cleary's smile was enigmatic. 'I'll be interested to hear what it is.'

CHAPTER TWELVE

Reuben Harte was reading his way carefully through a pile of cards from friends and neighbours but he drew no comfort from them. The messages were sincere and the condolences well meant but they washed over him without leaving any trace. His grief was too deep to be relieved by kind words and pretty cards. When there was a knock on the door, he sat up. Not wishing to see anyone, he was prepared to make an exception for the detectives from Scotland Yard. When he twitched the net curtain aside to peer out, however, it was not Marmion and Keedy who'd come calling. It was Jonah Jenks. Though not close friends, the men knew each other well. Harte

181

relented. The visitor deserved to be admitted. He was a fellow sufferer.

Harte opened the front door and stood aside to let him in. Jenks was subdued.

'Good morning, Reuben,' he said, shaking his hand.

Harte shut the door. 'Go into the living room.'

They traded a few pleasantries then sat down. Jenks took out an envelope.

'Have you had one of these from the factory?'

'It came first thing by courier.'

'What did you think?'

'To be honest, Jonah, I haven't given it a great deal of thought. Jean's death has blocked everything out. It's the same for my wife,' said Harte. 'She can't stop talking about it. She's had to go to her sister to be looked after.'

'So you've not discussed the letter with her?'

'I'm not sure that I will.' He appraised Jenks. 'How are you coping?'

'I try to keep busy,' replied Jenks. 'I must have cleaned every room at least twice. And I've turned the piano into a kind of shrine to Enid. I polished it until I could see my face in it and put every photo I could find of her on top of it. Oh, yes,' he continued, 'and I put the sheet music of her favourite Chopin nocturne on the stand as if she was just about to play it.' He smiled wanly. 'I was humming it on my way here. Do you like Chopin?'

'I'm not much of a one for music, Jonah, but my wife loves a good tune.'

There was a long pause. Conjoined by their grief they let it have its way for a few minutes before they attempted to shrug it off. Harte stretched an arm to take an envelope from the mantelpiece. It matched the one brought by his visitor.

'All I did was to glance at it,' he said.

'It's a good offer and I'm ready to accept.'

'All five of them are to be buried together? I have reservations about that.'

'Such as?'

'It just doesn't seem right somehow.'

'Why not?'

'Well, *we* want to make the decisions about Jean's funeral, not leave it to this Mr Kennett. I've never even met the man.'

'Enid used to speak well of him.'

'I still feel he's intruding.'

'I didn't feel that at all. It's high time the factory did something for the women they employ there. This is a first example. Enid would approve.'

'I can't say that Jean would.'

'Oh?'

'She wouldn't mind sharing her funeral with Florrie Duncan. They were good friends. There'd be some meaning in that. As for the others...'

'It will be interesting to see how their families respond.'

'That's anybody's guess, Jonah. I don't know Agnes Collier's family. They live over towards Uxbridge.'

'What about Shirley Beresford?'

'Oh, I've met her husband lots of times. Neil coaches the football team and Jean was one of the reserves. Whenever she played, I used to stand on the touchline and cheer her on. Neil Beresford must be beside himself,' said Harte. 'He's not only lost a lovely wife, he's had to see his hopes of

183

winning that cup match crumble into dust. He gave *everything* to that team.'

'Then he'll probably agree with me about this offer. From what I can gather, two of the victims played in the football team – Shirley Beresford and your daughter, Jean. It seems fitting that they should be laid to rest together.'

Harte was not convinced. He let Jenks advance his arguments in favour of a collective burial but they made no impact on him. He resisted what he saw as a breach of his daughter's private rights. The factory had controlled her life from the moment she started to work there. It felt wrong to let them dictate the terms of her funeral as well. There was another factor that influenced him.

'We're not churchgoers, Jonah,' he admitted.

'You were married in a church, weren't you?'

'Well, yes – we were.'

'Then you've nothing to worry about. Everyone in the parish is entitled to a Christian funeral. You'll be given the same consideration as any of us. We were all there every Sunday, of course,' said Jenks, 'because Enid loved going. There was even talk of letting her become the assistant organist. I'd have been so proud of her if that had happened.' He smiled at Harte. 'Where does that leave us, Reuben?'

'You want to accept the offer and I don't.'

'Make sure you think it over properly.'

'My wife won't like the idea, I can tell you that.'

'What about the others?' asked Jenks, holding up his envelope. 'Suppose – for the sake of argument – that the families of Florrie Duncan, Agnes Collier and Shirley Beresford all agree to

184

the suggestion. That would mean we outvote you four to one.'

'I won't be forced into changing my mind,' said Harte, resolutely.

'Nobody would dream of using force in a situation like this. It would be wholly out of place. What I wish to know is this,' said Jenks, slyly. 'What would it take to persuade you that the five of them should be buried at the same time?'

Harvey Marmion was not entirely sure about the motives behind the offer. Bernard Kennett told him that it was a gesture of goodwill and that the factory felt an obligation to its employees, but Marmion wondered if other reasons had prompted the management to act. If accepted, their offer would garner some good publicity for the munitions factory and it was always in dire need of that. Newspaper articles about its operations always focused on the dangers faced by the women who worked there. Serious accidents at the factory – and it had had its share of them – could not be hidden from the public and stories of that kind made recruitment more difficult. In this case, however, the explosion took place at a pub some distance away. To give it extra prominence would not reflect badly on the factory.

Talking to the works manager, Marmion also wondered if guilt had played a part in the decision. The offer to pay the funeral expenses could have been triggered by the need to atone for the rigours that the women were put through on a daily basis. The victims were not five anonymous employees. They had a real presence at the factory. Two of them were members of the football team that had brought such kudos and a third, Florrie Duncan, was the official representative of the National Federation of Women. A fourth woman, Enid Jenks, had more than once entertained diners at the canteen piano during the lunch break. Accompanied by her, Agnes Collier had sung a few popular songs with more gusto than musical talent. Because they were widely known and liked, their deaths were felt more keenly.

After chatting in Kennett's office, Marmion had asked to see the football pitch. It was on a fairly barren patch of land at the rear of the factory. They stood on the touchline and looked at the tufted grass and the undulations.

'We have a big advantage over teams who've never played here before,' said Kennett. 'Our ladies know where the bumps and dips are. They exploit them.'

'Is this where the cup final will be played?'

'No, Inspector, that's at a neutral venue in Camberwell.'

'How good is the opposition?' asked Marmion.

'The question to ask is how badly weakened is our team now that we've lost some of our best players? I was talking to my secretary about it – she watches all our games. She reckons that Shirley Beresford was the real difference between the two sides. And Maureen Quinn, the goal-keeper, will hardly be in a fit state to play after what she's been through. Jean Harte was also in the team for the cup final.'

'The biggest loss is their coach,' said Marmion. 'Neil Beresford has moulded that team together

186

and obviously knows what he's doing. But the death of his wife has rocked him. When I called at the house, he was so upset that he wasn't even able to answer a few questions. His mother had to take over instead. Mrs Beresford thinks that a supporter of the Woolwich team must have planted that bomb.'

'That suggestion is not as absurd as it may sound, Inspector.'

'Oh, I haven't ignored it.'

'Passions run deep in the world of ladies' football.'

'That's why I've sent two of my men to Woolwich to make some discreet enquiries,' said Marmion. 'But I'm still inclined to dismiss the theory because it presupposes that someone from a munitions factory several miles away was both aware of the date of Florrie Duncan's birthday and the fact that three members of your football team – I'm including Maureen Quinn – would be helping to celebrate it. Then, of course, we come to the small matter of the pub itself. How would a complete stranger know where it was and that the party would be in its outhouse?'

'Perhaps he wasn't such a stranger,' said Kennett, darkly. 'What if we have a rabid Woolwich supporter here in the factory?'

'It's possible but a trifle unlikely.'

'Why is that, Inspector?'

'Because I think he'd know that there's a much easier way of sabotaging the football team than by blowing up some of its players. His target would be Neil Beresford. He's the key to the success of your team,' said Marmion. 'Kill or

187

disable him in some way and you've more or less handed that cup to Woolwich.'

Neil Beresford looked and felt a little better but his mother was still worried about him. Reassured by the fact that he was able to get dressed and come downstairs, she was troubled by his occasional bursts of tears. Having known him as a strong, resilient person, she was surprised by his collapse in the wake of the disaster. Since her son now seemed more robust, she felt able to broach the topic of the funeral.

'Would you like to talk about that letter we received?'

'No,' he said.

'A decision will have to be taken, Neil.'

'Then let Shirley's parents make it.'

'But you're her husband,' said May. 'By rights, *you* should take charge of the funeral arrangements. It's your duty.'

'I'd rather not think about it.'

'Well, it can't be put off indefinitely. The factory will want to know.'

Beresford made no comment. He was sitting in the armchair beside the fireplace and his mind was wandering. May went off into the kitchen and made a pot of tea, putting it on a tray with two cups and saucers along with the milk jug and the sugar bowl. Bringing it into the living room, she set it down on the table. Beresford was a study in concentration. His forehead was wrinkled, his eyes gleaming and his teeth clenched. Saying nothing, his mother poured two cups of tea and added milk and sugar to both before stirring them in with a teaspoon. Her son was still wrestling with a thorny problem. All of a sudden, he announced a solution.

'I'll go back to work tomorrow.'

'But you can't,' she protested. 'You're not ready for it yet.'

'I've got to face up to it, Mum, and show some strength for a change. I can't just stay at home and brood. It's driving me mad. I need to occupy my mind. And there's another thing I've decided.'

'What's that?'

'I can't let the rest of the team down. We were due to have a practice session after work tomorrow and I want to be there to lead it.'

May was aghast. 'You can't worry about football at a time like this.'

'I have to – the cup final is less than ten days away.'

'Let someone else take over, Neil.'

'There *is* nobody else, Mum. I'm their coach. They rely on me.'

'They won't expect anything from you now,' argued May. 'You're in mourning. We all are. There's been a dreadful tragedy and you need to recover from it before you even think of going back to the factory.'

'I've always been a fighter,' he said, banging his thigh with a fist, 'and I'm ashamed of the way I behaved. We have to win that cup now. Shirley may not be able to play but she'll be our inspiration. It will give the whole team a lift.'

May picked up a cup and saucer. 'Have your tea, Neil.'

'I've been working it out,' he said, ignoring her

offer. 'Audrey Turner can take over Shirley's position as centre forward. She may not be as fast or as clever at dribbling but Audrey is nearly six feet. She'll win everything in the air. The other person I can bring into the forward line is...'

His eyes were gleaming more than ever now as they sighted a victory against the odds at the cup final. He explained in detail how he would defeat the opposing team. It was impossible to stop him. May put the tea back on the tray and reached for the other cup. Though she was pleased to see him so animated, she was alarmed by the edge of frenzy in his voice. It had ceased to become a football match to him and had turned into a mission. Beresford was driven to succeed for the sake of the factory, the players who'd worked so hard under him and, most of all, for his wife who'd been the undisputed star. Deprived of a chance to raise the trophy herself, Shirley Beresford would nevertheless lead them to a triumphant win.

May was disturbed. She didn't think her son was fit to return to work, let alone coach a football team. It was as if he was in the grip of a fever. Unable to check him, she tried to humour him, agreeing with everything he proposed and even managing a supportive smile. While she knew little about the game of football, she understood its significance in the household. Having heard her son and her daughter-in-law discuss the team at length, she knew all the names of the players and – though she didn't understand the finer points of the game when she stood on the touch-line – she had a good idea of their individual worth. When he paused for breath, she took the opportunity to step in and remind him of something.

'At least you won't have to find a new goal-keeper.'

He stared at her blankly. 'What did you say?'

'Maureen Quinn survived the blast. She can still play for you, Neil.'

'I wouldn't dream of asking her,' he said with a note of shock in her voice. 'You should know better than to suggest it. She was nearby when that bomb went off. It will have shattered her nerves.'

'Supposing that she *wants* to play?'

'There's no chance of that, Mum. All she'll want to do at the moment is to stay well away from the factory and the team. Maureen was a good goalkeeper but we'll have to do without her. It would be cruel even to approach her.'

'How do you feel now, Maureen?'

'I just feel so ... numb.'

'That's not unusual.'

'I do things without really noticing that I'm doing them. For instance, I ate breakfast this morning but can't tell you what I had.'

'What about sleep?'

'I did get some last night.'

'That's good to hear.'

After his visit to the priest, Joe Keedy had moved on to Maureen's house, making sure that he ar-rived after her father had gone off to work. Talking to her in his presence was frustrating. As it was, it took him a long time to persuade her mother to let him interview Maureen on her own. Though she had no real objection to it, Diane was afraid of what her husband would say if she allowed a detective to question Maureen alone. It would be one more thing to hide from him. They sat opposite each other in the living room. Keedy decided that the sight of his notebook might inhibit her so he relied on memory instead.

'Does your father know that you went to church yesterday?' he began.

'No – we didn't tell him.'

'Why did he stop you going there on a Sunday?'

'He said that we'd grown out of it.'

'Is that what you think, Maureen?'

She hunched her shoulders. 'I have to do what my father tells me.'

'What about your brothers?'

'They were braver than me,' she replied with a smile. 'They were very naughty sometimes. Liam was the worst.'

'But you're pretty brave yourself, aren't you?' he asked. 'If you play in goal for a football team, you have to have a lot of guts. That ball must come at you very hard and sometimes from a short distance.'

She nodded. 'I broke a finger once,' she said, 'trying to save a penalty. I didn't realise till after the game. You get carried away when you're playing. You don't always notice the pain.'

'I know. I used to be in a soccer team at one time.'

'We have a lot of injuries. Everyone takes it so seriously.'

'And so they should. The competitive urge is

very important. It's what drives us on to take chances and push ourselves to the limit.' She appeared to be listening but Keedy wasn't sure that he had her full attention. 'I'm told that Father Cleary came to see you yesterday.'

She sat up in surprise. 'Who told you that?'

'I called in to see him before I came on here. He said that you'd been a keen churchgoer at one time. You enjoyed the services.'

'It's true – I did.'

'You certainly enjoyed them more than your brothers.'

She smiled again. 'They could be wicked when they wanted to be.'

'What did they think when they heard you'd taken up football?'

'They laughed at first. They said that girls couldn't play football because they were too slow and too weak. When they came home on leave, I took Liam and Anthony to the park and we put a couple of coats down to mark the goalposts. I stood between them,' she recalled, warmed by the recollection. 'They were amazed how many goals I saved. They stopped laughing after that.'

'Tell me about the other girls at the birthday party.'

She became wary. 'I've already done that, Sergeant.'

'You told us a little about them, Maureen, but I'm sure that you left a lot out. It was too soon afterwards. You couldn't be expected to remember everything.' Her reluctance was almost tangible. 'You'll have to talk about them at the inquest.'

'The inquest?' she echoed, cowering on the settee.

'It's a legal requirement in cases like this.'

'But why do I have to go to it?'

'Your testimony is vital,' he told her. 'As the only survivor, what you say will carry a lot of weight. You'll be asked about things you saw when you first arrived in that outhouse and what the general mood was.'

Maureen was transported for a moment back to the birthday party. She heard the excited chatter, saw the presents being opened by Florrie Duncan and remembered the song they all sang with such passion. They were barbed memories now.

'Will I have to be there?' she asked.

'I'm afraid so,' replied Keedy. 'That's why the more you talk about your friends to me, the easier it will be when the coroner asks you questions. He'll want to know about the sequence of events but I want to delve a little deeper.' Maureen was watchful. 'You do want the person who planted that bomb caught, don't you?'

'Yes, of course.'

'Then we need your assistance.'

She looked hunted. 'There's nothing else I can tell you, Sergeant.'

'Oh, I think you can. You just don't realise it yet. Let's start with a comment you made when we first came here,' he suggested. 'You talked about Florrie Duncan looking out for you.'

'That's right – she was older and more experienced than the rest of us.'

'You said that she stopped men at work from

194

pestering you. Is that true?'

'Oh, they never bothered me very much.'

'What about the others?' pressed Keedy. 'We can leave out Florrie because she obviously wouldn't stand any nonsense and Shirley Beresford was married so she was protected in a sense. The same goes for Agnes Collier. She had a husband and a baby. But that still leaves Jean Harte and Enid Jenks.'

'Jean lost her fiancé at the front. She never looked at another man.'

'What about Enid?'

Maureen's head fell to her chest and her body seemed to shrink into the settee. Keedy watched her struggle with feelings of guilt and betrayal. He was sorry that he had to put her under such pressure but believed that it was necessary. The women were bonded by the job they did and the visible consequences of doing it. They were likely to confide in each other. Maureen was a quiet, sensitive young woman whom the others could trust. She'd know what was happening under the surface of the lives of her friends.

She raised her eyes. 'Will I have to say this at the inquest?'

'No, Maureen, the questions will be confined to what happened at the pub.'

'I wouldn't want her father to know about it, you see.'

'We certainly won't tell him.'

'He didn't want Enid to have a boyfriend. He was very strict about that.'

'Go on,' he whispered.

'But there was someone at the factory that Enid

liked and it was obvious that he liked her. He was always there when she arrived and when she left the factory. In the end, he asked her out. She was too afraid to go at first. But,' she recalled, 'he didn't give in. There were little presents and he was always very polite to her. So Enid took a chance. She told her father she was going out with some of her friends but she went off with this man instead.'

'What happened?'

'I don't know,' said Maureen, 'but she was very strange the next day. All she'd say was that she never wanted to see him again.'

'Was that the end of it?'

'No, Sergeant,' said Maureen. 'It was the start of something else. He didn't bother her at work because he knew that Florrie would go for him, but he followed Enid home and stood outside her house. When she went to church one Sunday, he was in the congregation even though he lived miles away from that parish.'

'Didn't she complain to her father?'

'How could she? It would have meant telling him that she went out with the man and her father would have raised the roof. Enid was being persecuted and there was nothing she could do about it.'

'Was he still stalking her at the time of that birthday party?'

'Yes,' she replied. 'To be honest, I'd forgotten all about him until you asked me about Enid. He really made her suffer. He kept sending her these little notes to say she'd never escape him. Enid showed me one. It was horrible.'

'What did it say?'

'It said that, if *he* couldn't have Enid, then nobody would.'

Keedy took out his notebook. 'I'll need the man's name.'

CHAPTER THIRTEEN

Royston Liddle was up early that morning to help the milkman on his rounds. He enjoyed the work because it gave him the opportunity to meet a large number of people in the area as he ladled milk out of the churns and into their jugs, basins or other receptacles. Liddle was also allowed to drive the horse and cart, a real treat for him. He yearned for a time when he had a milk round of his own even though he knew, in his heart, that it would never come about. He could never master the sums involved in charging the right amount of money. As an assistant, however, he did everything that was asked of him and it gave Liddle a sense of well-being. On his way back home, he passed the stricken pub once again. The landlord was standing outside, talking to Ezra Greenwell. Liddle joined them in time to hear the old man voice his uncompromising opinions.

'Good riddance to them!' snarled Greenwell.

'That's a shocking thing to say,' Hubbard rebuked him.

'But for those damned women, I'd have got

back safely to my house that night instead of being rushed to hospital with a mouth gushing with blood.'

'You got off lightly, Ezra. The five of them were killed.'

'Don't ask me to mourn them. I'd prefer to give three cheers.'

'That's very bad of you,' said Liddle, inserting himself into the discussion with his inane grin at variance with the seriousness of his argument. 'The police told me it was murder. Nobody deserves to be blown up like that, Ezra. How would you like it if your daughter had been in the outhouse at the time?'

'She'd have more sense than to take a job at the munition works,' said Greenwell. 'Martha knows that a woman's place is in the home.'

'My wife knows that,' Hubbard chimed in, 'but, in her case, staying in the home means working in the pub as well because we live above it. We used to, anyway. Those days could be over now.'

'Then you should be blaming those stupid women as well.'

'They didn't *ask* to be killed by a bomb, Ezra.'

'They brought bad luck and disaster to the Goose.'

'It's not their fault,' said Liddle.

'What do you know about it, you ignoramus?'

'Royston is entitled to his opinion,' said Hubbard.

'Not when he starts talking out of his arse.'

Liddle was offended. 'That's rude, Ezra.'

'Then bugger off. Nobody asked you to butt in.'

198

'All I did was to say I'm sorry about those poor women.'

'And so am I,' added Hubbard, casting a jaundiced eye at the pub, 'even though *I've* been left to pick up the pieces.'

'When do you want me back?' asked Liddle.

'I'm not sure that I do, Royston.'

'But you always said that I worked hard for you.'

'It's true – you did. And if we carry on at the Goose, I'll want you there as usual. Do we start all over again or sell the pub to someone else? It's not an easy decision to make, Royston.'

'If you leave,' boasted Liddle, 'I'll take over the Goose.' The others laughed scornfully. 'What's the joke?'

'You are,' said Greenwell, cackling.

'Running a pub is a complicated job,' explained Hubbard. 'I grew up in the trade because my father was a publican. It's beyond you, Royston.'

'I could *learn*.'

'You haven't even learnt your ABC properly,' sneered Greenwell.

'Yes, I have.'

'Forget it, Royston,' said the landlord with a fatherly hand on his shoulder. 'The Goose is not for you. What you can do, you do very well. Be satisfied with that.'

Liddle accepted the truth of the advice. Since he was feeling hungry, he decided to go home for a late breakfast. As he walked away, he could hear the two of them still laughing at him. It was dispiriting but he soon shrugged off his irritation. After a lifetime of being derided, he found that mockery no longer hurt him. He was about to take a short cut through an alleyway when he remembered what had happened the last time he'd been that way. Alan Suggs had ambushed him and handled him roughly. Even though he knew that Suggs was probably at work, he took no chances of a second encounter, choosing instead to make a long detour. When he eventually came into his own street, he told himself that Suggs was not a danger to him. Having made some vile threats, he hadn't carried them out. Besides, Liddle had Inspector Marmion on his side. He was protected.

Letting himself into the house, he went through to the scullery, gathered up some lettuce and let himself out into the garden. Ready as he was for breakfast, he had to feed his rabbits first. They brought him a companionship he could never get from a human being so he always treated them with the greatest care. Liddle reached the hutch and unlocked the door, only to recoil in horror.

His beloved rabbits were no longer there.

They met at the local police station which had become their unofficial headquarters during the investigation. Keedy was interested to hear about the offer to pay the funeral expenses of the five victims, especially in view of the categorical way in which the works manager had refused even to consider the idea of paying any compensation to the female munition workers for the way that they changed colour and suffered ill health. He was also intrigued to learn more about the ladies' football team and how much it had improved during its relatively short existence. Neil Beresford, he agreed, must be a truly outstanding coach. When he heard Keedy's report, Marmion was intrigued to hear the latest revelation.

'I knew that you'd winkle something out of Maureen,' he said.

'Some of the thanks must go to Father Cleary,' Keedy pointed out. 'He told me a great deal about the Quinn family and helped me to understand Maureen a little more. This news about Enid Jenks gives us another possible suspect.'

'He may be more than that, Joe. If he works at the factory, the likelihood is that he's capable of making explosives. Alan Suggs clearly wasn't. That makes this chap – Herbert Wylie, was it? – sound much more promising.' He gave a wry smile. 'So much for Jenks's claim that his daughter was never interested in boyfriends. I saw the photo of her. Enid was gorgeous. They must have come after her in swarms.'

'Wylie was only her boyfriend momentarily, Harv,' said Keedy. 'After one night out together, she never wanted to see him again. He changed from a friend into a stalker. Wylie seems to have dogged her wherever she went.'

'We need to speak to him as soon as possible.'

The room they were using was cold and cramped but it did have a telephone. Marmion snatched it up from the desk. He was soon talking to Bernard Kennett once again. When he rang off, he replaced the receiver.

'He's going to find out if Wylie clocked in this morning,' he said. 'If he did, we'll go straight over there and haul him out of the Cartridge Section.'

'It could be another false hope,' warned Keedy.

Marmion was more optimistic. 'I'm starting to feel that we may be on to something, Joe.'

'Enid Jenks obviously had a torrid time with this chap.'

'It's that threat to kill her that interests me.'

'Even the most tenacious unwanted admirer gives up after a while. Not in this case,' noted Keedy. 'It became an obsession with Wylie and we know the kind of extremes that that can drive people to. On the other hand,' he continued, 'I'm not getting too excited. He sounds like our man but, then, so did Alan Suggs.'

'He was a different kettle of fish altogether. Suggs was no unwanted admirer. According to him, he was wanted by dozens of women at the factory. They were queuing up to go out with him, apparently.'

'Well, he won't be able to entice any of them into that outhouse again.'

They chatted for a few minutes until the telephone rang. Marmion took the call and nodded away as he listened. He then wrote something down in his notebook. After thanking the works manager, he put down the receiver and turned to Keedy.

'Well, well, well,' he said.

'What did Mr Kennett say?'

'Supposing that you'd planted that bomb, Joe. When it went off, what would you do next?'

'I'd run like hell,' replied Keedy.

'It looks as if Wylie did the same. He hasn't been at work since the night of the explosion.' Marmion tapped his notebook. 'I've got his address here. Let's pay a visit and see if he's hiding under the bed.'

Diane Quinn was increasingly worried about her daughter. Maureen was somnolent, withdrawn and looking distinctly unwell. Whenever her mother suggested calling a doctor, however, she insisted that there was nothing wrong with her. She just wished to be left alone. Diane couldn't even prise out of her the details of her conversation with Joe Keedy. Once the detective had left, Maureen had effectively clammed up. Diane was preparing lunch when she heard the door knocker. Fearing that it might be some more reporters, she went to the door with trepidation. When she opened it, however, she was astonished to see that her visitor was Sadie Radcliffe. They embraced impulsively, then Diane brought her into the house and took her into the living room. They stayed in each other's arms for minutes. Sadie then broke away.

'I came to apologise,' she said.

'There's nothing to apologise for,' insisted Diane.

'Yes, there is and that's why I had to come. I was so shocked by what happened that I lashed out in all directions. I said things about Maureen that...' she paused in order to dab at moist eyes with a handkerchief '...that I regret very much. Instead of moaning because she survived when Agnes died, I should be sharing your relief. Maureen is a lovely girl. She was a good friend to my daughter.'

'She loved Agnes. They got on so well together.'

'That's what I should have remembered, Di.'

'Sit down,' invited Diane, easing her onto the

settee and sitting beside her. 'I wanted to come and see you but the truth is that ... Eamonn thought it best not to.'

'He was right. I was in a terrible mood when I first heard. I'm ashamed of what I said. And I was even ruder when you called on me, Di.'

'That's all in the past. No need even to think about it again.' Diane looked at the grief burnt into the other woman's face. 'It must be unbearable for you.'

'I'll get by. It's Terry I feel sorry for, not myself. He'll have heard by now. They sent a telegram.'

'Is there any chance that they'll let him come back for the funeral?'

'I don't think the army does things like that. But I'm glad you mentioned the funeral. It's something I wanted to discuss with you.'

She told Diane about the offer made by the factory and how it had thrown her into confusion. Annoyed at first that they should even think of trying to take over something as private as a family funeral, she'd come to see that there was some worth in the gesture. It would enable her daughter's remains to be buried alongside those of her friends. She believed that that was what Agnes would have wanted.

'What would you do, Di?' she asked. 'If it was Maureen, I mean.'

'I wouldn't make the decision – Eamonn would.'

'And what would he say?'

'I think he'd look for the advantages,' said Diane. 'If someone else was paying and taking over the arrangements, he'd think it was a load off his back.'

'But would he want to share the actual burial?'

'He might – but, then again, he might not. Eamonn is funny sometimes.'

'I've no idea what the other families think about it. I wish I did. What I really came for was to ask Maureen's opinion. She knew all the parents.'

A voice piped up behind them. 'What did you want to ask me, Mrs Radcliffe?'

They turned to see Maureen standing in the doorway. Sadie's response was to leap to her feet and wrap her arms around her with an amalgam of fondness and remorse. Maureen was perplexed. Agnes's mother had never been quite so demonstrative before. Diane explained about the offer from the factory management. All three of them sat down to talk about it.

'What do you think the other families will do, Maureen?' asked Sadie.

Maureen shook her head. 'I can't really say.'

'Put yourself in their shoes.'

'I don't know that I can, Mrs Radcliffe.'

'Just try,' urged her mother. 'How will Florrie's parents react, for instance?'

'I fancy they'd be against it,' said Maureen. 'They're nice people but Mr Ingles does give himself airs and graces sometimes. Florrie used to tease him about it. Because he earns a lot of money, he thinks that he's above most people. My guess is that he wouldn't want to share anything.'

'What about Jean's family – or Enid's – or Shirley's?'

'I really don't know,' replied her daughter in obvious discomfort. 'To be honest, it's something I'd rather not discuss.'

'I don't have that luxury,' said Sadie. 'They want an answer fairly soon.'

'Why not contact one of the other families?' suggested Diane.

'I don't really know them.'

'You're Agnes's mother. They're bound to be sympathetic.'

'I was hoping that Maureen might help out.'

Maureen tensed. 'What can I possibly do?'

'Well, you've met them all and been to their houses. I wondered if you'd be kind enough to come with me if I caught the train to Hayes. I'm sure that you'd like to express your condolences to them, in any case,' Sadie went on. 'You can introduce me and I can ask about that letter from Mr Kennett.'

'Yes,' said Diane, 'you could do that, Maureen, couldn't you?'

'No,' said her daughter, flatly.

'But it would be such a help to Mrs Radcliffe.'

'It would,' endorsed Sadie. 'I'd be ever so grateful.'

'I'm sorry,' said Maureen, jumping to her feet, 'but I just can't do it. You'll have to find someone else, Mrs Radcliffe. I simply want to be left alone.'

Without another word, she flounced out of the room and could be heard running up the stairs. Diane was crimson with embarrassment.

In telling her to avoid confrontation with a senior officer, Joe Keedy had given Alice Marmion sound advice. It was, however, easier to accept than to follow. Though she did her best to evade Inspector Gale, she couldn't disobey a summons to meet her. Before she went into the office, she made sure that she smartened her uniform. Her tap on the door was met with a curt command so she went in. Thelma Gale was studying a report. Without even looking up, she beckoned Alice towards her then kept her standing there for several minutes. It was a deliberate means of humiliating her but Alice didn't complain, even though she could see that the inspector was not actually reading the words in front of her. When she finally sat back and looked up at Alice, the other woman was disappointed not to be able to find fault with her appearance.

'I'm going to send you out on patrol,' she said, crisply. 'Your introduction to the police service has been far too cosy.'

Being rapped over the knuckles every day was not what Alice would have called 'cosy' but she didn't respond. Getting out of the building would be a boon to her. Apart from anything else, it took her well beyond the inspector's reach.

'Too many girls are being drawn into prostitution,' said Thelma, 'and they need to be warned about the risks to their health and – in some cases – to their lives. We've had some of them so badly beaten that they're disfigured for life. There have also been two murders.'

'The war is partly to blame, Inspector,' suggested Alice. 'Soldiers have had a dreadful time at the front. They've seen friends die all around them. When they come back on leave, they're desperate for some female company and – if they have no wife or girlfriend – they're more than ready to pay for it. Sometimes, they get carried away and don't realise how violent they're being.'

'You seem remarkably well informed. Have you been talking to Daddy?'

'No, Inspector – it's common knowledge.'

'And how knowledgeable are you about the services these girls provide?'

'On that score, I'd have to admit that I'm rather ignorant.'

'Then patrolling the streets will be an education for you,' said Thelma. 'It will open your eyes to the ways of the world and take your mind off this major crime that you're helping your father to solve.'

'I'm doing nothing of the kind,' retorted Alice.

'Don't take that tone with me, young lady!' snapped the other.

'I'm sorry, Inspector.'

'I'm entitled to obedience and respect, or didn't your father tell you that?'

Alice bit back a rejoinder. 'You're right,' she said at length.

'If he didn't, then Sergeant Keedy should have done so. He's been here long enough to appreciate the structure of command.' Thelma narrowed her eyelids. 'Has he been telling you how the case is proceeding?'

'We see very little of each other, Inspector.'

'What do you think he'll say to this latest assignment of yours?'

'Sergeant Keedy knows that I'll do what I'm told and that it's the essence of police work to take orders and act on them promptly.'

'Ah,' said Thelma with a cold smile. 'You *have* been listening, after all.'

'To whom do I report?'

'Don't rush off. I haven't finished talking to you yet.'

'As you wish...'

Thelma appraised her shrewdly. 'Has something happened?'

'I don't know what you mean.'

'Oh, I think you do. Ever since you came into this office, you've been trying to hide a smile. Do I look comical to you? Is that it?'

'No, it isn't, I assure you.'

'Perhaps you think that the women police are a subject for amusement.'

'Not at all,' said Alice, firmly. 'Had I done so, I'd hardly have been so eager to join. If you do detect a smile, it's because we've had some good news.'

'Are you ready to share it with me?'

'It's of no interest to you, Inspector.'

'Everything about you is of interest to me,' said Thelma, sitting forward, 'because it affects the way you do your job. What is this good news?'

'Paul – that's my brother – is coming home on leave next week.'

'When did you last see him?'

'It was ages ago,' recalled Alice. 'It's getting on for the best part of a year.'

'Where is he stationed?'

'He's in a camp near the Somme.'

'When he gets back here, he'll be very relieved.'

'We're giving him a welcome party.'

'Is he married?' asked Thelma.

'No, Inspector.'

'Does he have a sweetheart?'

'Paul is single and fancy-free.'

'Then you'll be in a position to offer him some guidance, won't you?' Alice looked confused. Thelma had a gibe ready. 'When you eventually discover what it is that ladies of the street actually do, you'll be able to tell your brother to keep away from them or he may be going back to France with a nasty itch.'

It took them a long time to find the address they'd been given. There were three streets with very similar names and they went astray. Marmion wished that he'd asked Kennett to spell the name of the street. It would have saved them a lot of trouble. In the end, the car did find the right place and it nosed its way along the gutter before pulling up outside a Victorian artisan's cottage. Herbert Wylie, they learnt from the landlady, rented a room there and was an ideal tenant. He always paid her on time and spent most evenings alone in his room. Mrs Armadale was a garrulous old woman with hair dyed an unnatural ginger colour. Having lost her husband the previous year, she'd taken in a lodger because she felt so lonely. From the way that she talked about Wylie, it was evident that he'd become a friend and did all kinds of odd jobs for her. He'd even taken over the little garden at the rear of the house.

When asked to describe him, she had nothing but praise. A picture slowly formed in the detective's mind. Wylie was short, slim and in his thirties. Whenever he went out, he always took care with his appearance. The landlady spoke with approval of the attention he lavished on his shoes, polishing them every day and making them gleam if ever he went out of an evening. She was unaware that he'd briefly had a girlfriend named Enid Jenks.

'When do you expect him back?' asked Marmion.

'I don't know, Inspector,' she replied. 'A few days or so, he said.'

'And he didn't tell you where he was going?'

'No, he didn't.'

She was very happy to answer their questions until they asked if they could see Wylie's room. Suddenly, she became defensive, wondering what had really brought them there and why they were so keen to speak to her tenant. Keedy took over and invented a plausible story concerning an accident at the factory that Wylie had witnessed and about which he'd promised to deliver a written report. The combination of Keedy's charm and Marmion's rank persuaded her that she should let them have their way. Once inside the room, they began a thorough search.

'Thanks, Joe,' said Marmion, opening a wardrobe. 'You saved us the trouble of getting a search warrant.'

Keedy sniffed. 'Would you want to live in room like this? It stinks.'

'I think that Wylie came to the same conclusion.' He indicated the empty wardrobe. 'The cupboard is bare. What's in those drawers?'

The sergeant opened them one by one. 'Nothing – he's made a run for it.'

Wylie had taken almost all of his clothing and personal items. All that he'd left behind were a few books and a grubby shirt hung on the back

211

of the door. They could find nothing that indicated where he'd gone. Marmion was disappointed that they'd found no evidence to connect Wylie to the explosion at the pub. The man had either been careful to remove all trace of it or had not been implicated in the first place. They were about to leave when Marmion caught sight of the little shed in the garden. If Wylie looked after the lawn and the flowerbeds, he'd have free access to the shed. The landlady was puzzled by their request to go into the garden but she raised no objection. Keedy led the way and lifted the hook on the door of the shed. There was barely room for the two detectives to step inside. It was filled with garden implements. Marmion managed to trip over a watering can and Keedy's shoulder dislodged a flowerpot from a shelf.

But the visit yielded a clue that made the pair of them grin broadly.

'Do you see what I see, Joe?' asked Marmion.

'I do, indeed,' replied Keedy.

CHAPTER FOURTEEN

The news that her son was at last coming home on leave had filled Ellen Marmion with a delight that never faded. As she did her housework that morning, she was almost radiant. Her only complaint was that she'd not yet had time to discuss with her husband or daughter the welcome they should prepare for their returning hero. Paul's letter had talked about his need for a long rest but there would be other members of the family eager to meet him, so there had to be a big celebration. Plans for a party began to form in her mind. Taking wartime food shortages into account, Ellen even went through the meal that would be served. It was when she got to her son's bedroom that she felt real exhilaration. Though he'd been away for a long time, she'd cleaned the room regularly and dusted all of his trophies. Paul had been a talented sportsman. He'd won cups for his prowess at athletics and tennis, but the award he valued most was the shield his football team had acquired when winning the league title in their last full season. A photograph of the eleven players stood on the mantelpiece and Ellen could see her son smiling proudly in the back row.

Her stomach lurched slightly as she glanced at some of the other young men. Heartened by the fact that they could all be in the same regiment if they joined up together, the whole team had rushed off to the recruiting office. Some of the players had already been killed and others had been sent home with missing limbs and disturbing memories. While luxuriating in her own pleasure, Ellen spared a passing thought for families less fortunate than her own. When she picked up the photo to examine it more closely, she was struck by something that Marmion had told her about the investigation. Some of the victims were members of a ladies football team. Such a thing had never existed in her youth and Ellen was not sure that it ought to exist now. While she saw the necessity for change, she was fearful of the way that the boundaries between the two sexes were being blurred and, in some cases, eradicated altogether. Women now played football, drove buses, ran canteens and refugee centres, filled shells in munition factories, joined the police service and did almost everything else that had once been the exclusive territory of their male counterparts. Some, like Ellen herself, sewed and knitted with varying degrees of skill in order to send gloves, socks and other items to soldiers at the front.

It was unsettling for a woman with the values of her generation. Particularly worrying for Ellen was the rise of the suffragettes. Having suspended their campaign at the outbreak of hostilities, they'd devoted themselves to unflagging war work as a means of attesting their patriotism and of proving that they could match what men did and should therefore be given an equal right to vote. That was going too far, in Ellen's view, and she was unnerved by the support that Alice gave to the notion of female emancipation, hoping that her daughter's marriage to Joe Keedy would return her to a more traditional role. Dusting the photo before replacing it, she wondered what her son would make of the way that Alice had changed since the outbreak of war. As children, they'd been very close but they'd slowly drifted apart. Ellen had watched with disquiet as her daughter had gone from being a teacher to wearing a police uniform. An army uniform might have wrought even more profound changes in her son. He would certainly not be the person they'd waved off after his last leave. All of a sudden, her elation began to dim slightly.

'What's the fellow's name?'

'Herbert Wylie.'

'Where did he work?'

'In the Cartridge Section at the munitions factory.'

'When did he last turn up there?'

'On the day of the explosion,' replied Marmion.

'What did you find at his digs?'

'We saw evidence of bomb-making ingredients, sir.'

'Anything else?' asked the superintendent.

'It looks as if he's flown the coop.'

After their visit to Wylie's house, the detectives had returned to the police station. In view of what he felt was a significant discovery, Marmion had rung Claude Chatfield to tell him what had been found in the garden shed. He praised Keedy for drawing the information out of Maureen Quinn that one of her friends had been stalked by a man at the factory who was frighteningly obsessive.

'What do we know about him?' enquired Chatfield.

'We know very little, I'm afraid,' said Marmion. 'Mr Kennett only knew him by sight and Wylie's landlady gave us an idealised portrait of him. She seems to treat him like the son she never had. If he can win her over so completely, he must have some redeeming features.'

'Did you tell her that he's now a suspect in a murder inquiry?'

'No, sir – it seemed too cruel to shatter her illusions. Besides, we don't know that he *was* the bomber. We've had strong evidence in the past

215

that turned out to be annoyingly misleading.'

'My instinct tells me we've picked up the scent of the man we want,' said Chatfield, emphatically. 'I'll release his name to the press and say that we're anxious to trace him. He's gone to ground somewhere and we need to flush him out.'

'I agree, Superintendent.'

'What will you and the sergeant do in the meantime?'

'Sergeant Keedy has gone back to the factory to talk to people who knew Herbert Wylie rather better than the works manager. With luck, there might even be a photograph of employees that includes the man. I know that there are group photos of female workers because I saw one on the wall in Mr Kennett's office. Hopefully, they pointed the camera at the men as well.'

'You haven't told me what *you'll* be up to, Inspector.'

'I'm going to pay a second visit to Mr Jenks.'

'I thought he denied that his daughter had any interest in boyfriends.'

'He did,' said Marmion. 'What he's going to learn about Enid will come as a severe blow. Jonah Jenks felt that he controlled his daughter's life.'

Jonah Jenks sat at the piano and played a few chords. The sound was still echoing when the door knocker introduced a note of disharmony. He answered the door and, moments later, brought Neil Beresford into the living room. Though they'd never met before, their mutual sorrow gave them an immediate rapport. After declining the offer of a cup of tea, Beresford explained why he'd called.

'By rights,' he said, 'I should be at work but I overslept this morning. I'd set the alarm when I went to bed but my mother removed the clock while I was asleep and I woke up far too late.'

'Your mother probably did you a favour, Mr Beresford.'

'I've told her I'll go back tomorrow but she thinks it would be too soon.'

'I'm inclined to agree with her. I've taken leave from work for the foreseeable future.'

Beresford looked as if he needed as much rest as he could get. Fatigue had painted his features a deep grey and hollowed his cheeks. Yet there was an intensity and animation about him that contradicted his appearance.

'I really came to ask you about the letter from Mr Kennett. Have you reached a decision yet?'

'Yes,' said Jenks. 'I've come round to the view that the offer should be accepted. I'd like Enid to be laid to rest with her friends.'

'Mr Ingles wants his daughter to be part of a joint burial,' Beresford told him. 'He called round to see me early on and persuaded me that it's the right thing to do. That makes three of us who are of the same mind. I can't speak for the others.'

'Reuben Harte is against the idea.'

'How do you know?'

'I tackled him about it earlier but he wouldn't commit himself to the notion. He prefers a quiet funeral involving only the immediate family.'

'What about Agnes Collier?'

'I don't know her family at all, Mr Beresford. Agnes lived near Uxbridge close to Maureen

217

Quinn. We'll have to wait and see how they react to the offer. My hope is that – seeing three of us in favour of it – they'll decide to join us. If it's a case of four to one,' Jenks continued, 'then the pressure will tell on Reuben Harte. His resistance might well crumble. What do you think?'

Beresford was distracted and the question had to be repeated for him.

'I'm sorry,' he said with a disarming smile, 'I was admiring that photo of your daughter. She was a beautiful young lady.'

'One newspaper described her as a canary – along with your wife, I may say. It's a dreadful name. I hate it. But you know Reuben Harte, don't you?' Jenks went on. 'Whenever his daughter played in the football team, he came along to support her.'

'Yes, he was always there on the touchline. A lot of parents were.'

'What will happen to the team now?'

'We'll fight on,' said Beresford with conviction. 'We owe it to the players we've lost to play and win that cup final. Woolwich may think it's theirs for the taking and that will make them complacent. We'll take them by surprise.'

'I wish you good luck.'

They sat down and discussed the apparent lack of progress in the police investigation. Neither of them could offer any clue as to the identity of the person who'd planted the bomb or what his motives could possibly be.

'My mother feels that it could be a Woolwich supporter,' said Beresford, 'but even a fanatic would have more respect for human life than to kill five innocent women. I'm wondering if it was a tragic accident.'

'It was certainly tragic,' said Jenks, sadly.

'Why would anyone deliberately want to cause such pain and suffering?'

'The German army is doing just that as we speak, Mr Beresford.'

'You expect horrors in a war,' said Beresford, 'but not on your doorstep.'

'When did you first hear?'

'I knew that something had gone wrong when...' he paused to grapple with his emotions '...when Shirley didn't come home after the party. The Golden Goose is less than twenty minutes' walk away. I was about to go there when a police car pulled up outside the house. Hearing the news was like being hit by a thunderbolt.'

'I felt the same. Enid was my sunshine. I couldn't believe she'd died.'

'My wife used to say what a fine musician she was.'

'We'll never know just how good she could have become,' said Jenks, flicking his eyes to the photograph on the piano. 'The war robbed her of a chance to develop her talents and the explosion robbed her of her life. It's so unjust.' He took a deep breath before conjuring up a smile. 'Have you had any reporters hounding you?'

'Quite a few have come to the house but my mother sent them away.'

'They're like vampires, feeding off the dead.'

Beresford was philosophical. 'I suppose they'd say that they were only serving the public interest. It's a big story that must have got national

coverage. Every newspaper wants inside information.'

'Well, they won't get it from me.' He looked up
as he heard the door knocker. 'If that's another of
them, he's going to go away empty-handed.' He
got up from his seat. 'Excuse me.'

Jenks went out of the room and opened the door.
The caller was Harvey Marmion. After apologising for disturbing him, the inspector asked if
they might speak in private. Jenks brought him
into the living room. Marmion was surprised to
see Beresford there but pleased to have caught the
two of them together. It enabled him to ask about
the funeral arrangements. Both men confirmed
that they would accept the offer and that Brian
Ingles planned to do so as well. Jenks hoped that
Marmion had brought some good news about the
investigation.

'Do you have something to tell us, Inspector?'
he asked.

'It's really for your ears only,' said Marmion.

'You may speak freely in front of Mr Beresford.
After all, he's rather more than an interested
party.'

'That's true,' said Beresford. 'I'd like to hear
what you've found out.'

Marmion looked from one to the other before
putting a question to them.

'Does the name Herbert Wylie mean anything
to either of you?'

'No,' replied Jenks. 'I've never heard about him.'

'What about you, Mr Beresford?'

'There's a chap at work called "Herbert" but
I've no idea what his other name is. He puts

220

detonators into shells.'

'That sounds like our man. Could you describe him, please?'

After explaining that he didn't really know the man, Beresford gave enough details about his appearance to convince Marmion that it was indeed Wylie. The description tallied with that given by his landlady.

'Why are you so interested in this fellow?' asked Jenks.

'What I'm looking into is Wylie's interest in your daughter,' said Marmion, gently. 'I suspect that you didn't realise that Enid once went out with him.'

'That's nonsense!'

'We have it on good authority, Mr Jenks.'

'Enid would have told me. She wasn't deceitful in any way.'

'This occasion was the exception to the rule, sir. Wylie did take her out and your daughter chose not to mention it to you because the evening ended unhappily. Enid told him that she never wanted to see him again.'

'Wait a moment,' said Beresford, snapping his fingers. 'My wife used to work beside Enid at the factory. I vaguely remember her saying that someone was pestering Enid. I didn't realise that it was Herbert.'

Jenks was puce with anger. 'I still refuse to believe that my daughter went out with any man,' he asserted. 'Her whole life was here with me and her music. What else did she need?'

'Whatever it was,' said Marmion, she obviously didn't find it in Wylie. For his part, he was livid

221

at being rejected and determined to win her over. It seems that he pursued her with single-minded dedication. He even turned up in the church congregation at one point, simply to be close to her.'

'You're making this up,' said Jenks.

'I'm only reporting what I was told, sir.'

'And I can support it,' said Beresford. 'Now I recall it, Enid always lurked at the factory gate so that she could go in with Shirley. I thought she was just being friendly but it's more likely that she needed a bodyguard.'

Jenks was furious. 'If Enid was being harassed, she'd have told me.'

'It's precisely *because* you're her father,' argued Marmion, 'that she couldn't turn to you. It would have meant owning up that she'd once encouraged this man's interest in her.'

'Where did you get this monstrous tale?'

'If only it were monstrous, sir.'

'Who is your informant?' demanded Jenks.

'It was Maureen Quinn. Your daughter confided in her and Maureen would hardly have invented a story like that. She struck me as a truthful young woman.' Marmion looked at Beresford. 'You know her well, Mr Beresford, because she is in your football team. Would you say that Maureen was honest by nature?'

'Yes,' said Beresford, 'I would. She's very honest.'

Marmion turned back to Jenks. 'Facts are facts, sir, however distasteful they may be. You'll simply have to accept the truth.'

Jenks was dazed. The daughter whom he'd loved and trusted was changing before his eyes and it was a distressing transformation. He was so shocked that he dropped down into an arm-chair with his head in his hands. All that Marmion and Beresford could do was to wait until he began to rally. Sitting up straight, Jenks looked at Marmion with apprehension.

'What other revelations do you have about my daughter?' he asked.

'I know of nothing to her discredit,' said Marmion. 'The fault, it seems, lies entirely with Wylie. When you read a newspaper tomorrow morning, you'll see that he's been identified as a chief suspect.'

'Then why, in God's name, haven't you arrested him?'

'He's disappeared and we don't know where he is.'

'Have you been to his house?'

'Sergeant Keedy and I called there earlier. What you need to know, Mr Jenks, is that Wylie kept sending notes to your daughter. One of them is of special interest to us because,' said Marmion, solemnly, 'it contained a threat that, if *he* could not possess Enid, then nobody could.'

'It was Herbert!' cried Beresford. 'I bet he planted that bomb.'

'We're working on that supposition, sir. The search has begun.'

Jenks was horrified. 'Are you saying that Enid *caused* this disaster?'

'Not at all,' stressed Marmion. 'She was an inno-cent victim and so were the other four people at that birthday party.'

'If she'd told me, I could have tackled this devil

and sent him packing.'

'Perhaps she found it difficult to confide such things in you, sir.'

'I still can't accept that she lied to me, Inspector.'

Beresford stood up. 'How sure are you that Herbert was behind the crime?'

'The evidence speaks for itself, sir.'

'Well, he'd certainly know how to make a bomb. It was his job.'

'We found items at his address that proved he had the means to construct an explosive device. And when someone suddenly vanishes from the scene, it's often because he wants to escape justice.'

'I'd like to tear him apart,' growled Jenks, rising to his feet.

'So would I,' affirmed Beresford.

'He must have put my daughter through hell. If he turned up at church, Enid must have realised that there was nowhere to hide. The poor girl must have been at her wits' end.' He wrung his hands. 'Why ever didn't she turn to me?'

'That's a question only you can answer, sir,' said Marmion, quietly.

Everyone to whom Keedy talked said the same thing about Herbert Wylie. He was a quiet, industrious, rather lonely man who did his job but who made few friends at the factory. Those who realised that a detective would only take an interest in their colleague if he was suspected of something expressed their surprise. Alf Rutter, the foreman under whom Wylie worked, refused

224

to countenance the notion that the man was capable of committing a crime. Rutter was a bull-necked man with a bald head and a toothbrush moustache that wiggled as he talked. He was also very fond of gesticulating as a means of under-lining any points he was trying to make. Keedy felt that it was like talking to a human windmill.

'Herb Wylie?' said Rutter. 'He wouldn't say boo to a goose.'

'What about a Golden Goose?' asked Keedy.

'You've got the wrong man, Sergeant.'

'Did he have a girlfriend?'

'No, he was far too shy. A barmaid only had to smile at him and Herb would blush bright red. Now, in my case,' boasted Rutter, hands whirring away, 'it was different. I was in the merchant navy. I saw a bit of the world, if you take my meaning.'

'What about hobbies?'

'There's no time for hobbies in this place. You work till you drop then stagger home to bed. The only thing that any of us have any time for is a reviving pint and a natter with the missus.'

'But Wylie wasn't married.'

'He had this landlady who doted on him. She couldn't do enough for Herb. That was his idea of a girlfriend – someone old, kind and wanting to look after him.'

'What about his family?'

'I don't think he had anything to do with them, Sergeant. He left home years ago. He was from Sheffield originally and came south to look for work. God knows how he ended up in Hayes but he did. As for his work,' said Rutter, arms still flailing away, 'I got no complaints. Herb was slow but he kept at it. He was ... what's the word?'

'Tenacious?' suggested Keedy.

'That would sum him up perfect. He was tenacious.'

'You mean that once he got his teeth into something, he'd never let go.'

Rutter grinned. 'I couldn't have put it better myself, Sergeant.'

It was an aspect of Wylie's character that indicated he could well be the person described by Maureen Quinn. When he went through what he knew of the victims, Keedy could see why the reportedly shy Wylie had settled on Enid Jenks. Florrie Duncan would have been too daunting a challenge for him while Jean Harte was still mourning the death of her fiancé and repelled all male interest. Shirley Beresford and Agnes Collier were both married, the former having a husband on the premises. When he added Maureen Quinn's name to the list, Keedy decided that she'd be more able to stand up for herself, especially with Florrie at her back. Of the six women who went to the birthday party, Enid Jenks was the most likely recipient of Wylie's unsought addresses. She was, by all accounts, a quiet, gentle soul with few interests outside her music. Because of her father's vigilance, she had no opportunity to find a boyfriend or to enjoy some experience of real adult life. As a target, she would have been docile and unable to strike back. Wylie had watched her for a long time before moving in.

'Where would he go if he wanted to hide?' asked Keedy.

Rutter was combative. 'Who says he's in hiding? I reckon he's just gone off for a few days' holiday. To tell the truth, he looked a bit odd last time he was here, like he was ill or something.'

'Was he jumpy?'

'No, he just did his job then rushed out.'

'Thank you, Mr Rutter. You've been very helpful.'

'I've saved you a lot of wasted time, Sergeant. There's no need to go after Herb. He wouldn't have the courage to look at them girls, let alone blow them up.'

He semaphored with both arms then turned on his heel and strode off. Keedy was glad to have spoken to the foreman. Unwittingly, the man had told him something about the suspect that confirmed his potential as a suspect. When he returned to Kennett's office, a bonus awaited him. The works manager had dug out an old photograph of some employees about to depart on an outing. A dozen or more men were standing on a platform at the railway station and grinning happily. Wylie was lurking on the edge of the group as if he was not really part of it. Head bent forward and eyes screwed up in concentration, he stared defiantly at the camera.

'Can we borrow this, Mr Kennett?' asked Keedy.

'Yes, of course,' replied the other.

'I'd like the inspector to see it and it will enable us to give the press a more detailed description of the wanted man.'

'It will be a stigma on us if he does turn out to be guilty.'

'Why is that, sir?'

'It will look bad, Sergeant – very bad. Personally,

I feel very uneasy at the thought that we may be harbouring a killer in this factory.'

'Then there's something you haven't noticed,' said Keedy, unable to resist the comment. 'Everyone who works here is engaged in the production of dangerous weapons. It looks to me as if you're harbouring several thousand killers.'

CHAPTER FIFTEEN

Eamonn Quinn was less than pleased with what his wife told him.

'Sadie Radcliffe came *here?*'

'Yes.'

'Then why the hell did you let her in?'

'She came to apologise, Eamonn.'

'I'd have sent her on her way,' he said, vengefully.

'She's Agnes's mother,' Diane reminded him, 'and you should have some sympathy for her. Because our daughter left that party early, we were very lucky. Sadie wasn't. I admire her. With all that she has to cope with, she nevertheless felt that she wanted to say sorry for things she said about Maureen.'

'I'll never forgive her for that.'

'We'd have done the same in her position. If our daughter had died and Agnes had survived, we'd have been bitter and said things we didn't really mean.'

Quinn was adamant. 'I always mean exactly

228

what I say.'

After washing his hands in the sink, he dried them and took his seat at the table. Diane prodded the potatoes and decided that they needed a few more minutes in the saucepan on the stove. She told her husband how her visitor had asked for advice with regard to the offer made by the factory. Her husband's reaction was instant.

'Stupid woman!' he exclaimed. 'She should snatch their hands off.'

'Sadie was undecided.'

'Think of the money she'd save.'

'She has to put Agnes first. Money doesn't really come into this.'

'Yes, it does,' he insisted. 'The factory owes those girls something. They work their fingers to the bone and come home looking like refugees from Peking. The least they deserve is to have their funeral expenses covered.'

'It's the idea of a burial all together that worries me,' said Diane, 'and I think it would worry Father Cleary as well.'

'Why?'

'We're Roman Catholics and the other families are not. Father Cleary would want us to keep apart from them.'

'I'd do what I wanted and not listen to him.' He sat back as she put four plates on the table. 'What did Sadie decide in the end?'

'She really wanted to know what the other families thought. Since they're all strangers to her, she asked if Maureen would go with her because she knew where the parents of the other victims lived.'

'Then she's got a damn cheek, if you ask me!'

'It was a simple enough favour to ask, Eamonn,' said his wife. 'Agnes would have done the same for me if she'd been the one to survive. As it was, Maureen refused. It really upset her to be asked. She just ran off upstairs.'

'Maureen did the right thing.'

Diane went to the door and called to her daughters. Maureen and Lily came into the kitchen and took their places at the table. Their mother put out the cutlery before draining the potatoes. She then served them directly onto the plates. Thin slices of mutton followed with some peas. Bread and thinly-spread butter were already on the table. Quinn began to eat the moment that food was put in front of him. His daughters waited for their mother to slip off her pinafore and join them at the table. After giving Maureen a warning glance, Diane braced herself.

'We had another visit from Sergeant Keedy,' she said.

Quinn glared. 'Why is he still bothering us?'

'He wanted to talk to Maureen alone.'

'Well, I hope you told him that he couldn't. I don't care who he is, Di. He can't come barging in here and bombarding Maureen with questions. She's still recovering from what happened.' He pointed his knife at Diane. 'You should have refused outright. Did you?'

'No – but they were only alone together for a short while.'

'Two minutes would have been too long!' he protested.

'He felt that Maureen could help the investigation.'

'I didn't mind,' said Maureen, coming to her mother's aid. 'Sergeant Keedy was very nice. He didn't make me feel uncomfy or anything. He just wanted to know a little more about the others.'

'The best way to do that,' said Quinn, 'is to talk to their families.'

'No, it isn't,' said Diane. 'They're still struggling with the shock of what happened at that pub. Besides, they could only say what their daughters were like at home. Maureen knew them at work where they behaved differently.'

His gaze shifted to Maureen and there was menace in his tone. 'Don't you dare tell me that you talked to him about our family. I warned you against that.'

'Sergeant Keedy didn't ask about us,' said Maureen.

'So what *did* you tell him?'

'I just told him the truth. I liked them all. They were friends. I miss them. The person that the sergeant was really interested in was Enid.'

'Enid Jenks – she the one who plays the violin?'

'Yes, she played the piano as well.'

'And what did you say about her?'

Maureen hesitated, looking at her sister to indicate that Lily was perhaps too young to hear the information. Quinn became restive. He spoke through a mouthful of half-chewed potato.

'Well – what did you say, girl?'

'I told him that Enid was having trouble with a man at work.'

'What sort of trouble?'

231

'He wouldn't leave her alone.'

Meals of any kind always posed a problem during an investigation. Marmion and Keedy had to eat on the hoof, grabbing whatever they could at whatever unlikely time it might be. It was mid-afternoon before they finally managed to have some lunch. Back at the police station, they munched sandwiches and sipped lukewarm tea. Keedy's visit to the factory had given them a much more rounded picture of their chief suspect and the photograph was an added bonus. As he reached for another sandwich, Marmion studied the face of Herbert Wylie.

'What do you see when you look at him, Joe?' he asked.

'I see an ugly little bugger in a decent suit.'

'You'd never think he was off on a works outing, would you?'

'Maybe he didn't want to spend a day with a load of other men,' said Keedy. 'His idea of fun is to be alone with Enid Jenks.'

'Alan Suggs was no oil painting but, compared to this sour-faced chap, he was dazzlingly handsome. If he wanted to impress women, why didn't Wylie learn to smile properly?'

'Who knows?' He looked over Marmion's shoulder at the photograph. 'There's a mean glint in his eye. You can imagine him stalking his prey.'

'That's only because you know what he did to Enid Jenks,' said Marmion. 'If you didn't, you'd probably have said that he needed spectacles. I mean, look at this character over here,' he went on, pointing to a plump individual in the middle of the group. 'He's got the face of a merciless killer, if ever I saw one, yet he's probably a devoted husband and father who's led a spotless existence. The camera *does* lie sometimes.'

'That's a fair point,' conceded the other. 'I daresay that anyone looking at a photo of me would think I was a homicidal maniac. And remember how Harte reacted when he first set eyes on you? You're a highly respected detective inspector yet he thought you looked shifty.'

'There's no need to bring that up,' complained Marmion.

'It shows you that you should never judge a sausage by its skin.' Keedy glanced at the telephone. 'Are you going to ring Chat for a chat?'

'He'll be too busy claiming credit for unmasking our new suspect.'

'We do the digging and he gets the pat on the back.'

'It was ever thus in the police force.'

'You could have been superintendent, if you'd really wanted the job.'

'I like it the way it is, Joe.'

'Really?'

'Yes, I'm serious.'

'But it would have meant more money, more power and regular meals.'

'It would also have kept me caged up in Scotland Yard, missing the dubious pleasure of your company. I'm good at what I do and I'll settle for that.'

Keedy drank some tea. 'How did you get on with Enid Jenks's father?'

'It was much as I expected.'

'Did he refuse to believe that his daughter had deceived him?'

'Yes, he did – and I had some sympathy with him there. It rattled him,' said Marmion, pressing on quickly before Keedy could respond to the veiled reference to Alice. 'He thought that Enid did everything that he told her and that she'd never developed a mind of her own. He knows differently now.'

'Didn't he have the faintest inkling that she was being hounded?'

'No, Joe, he's not the most observant of men. In retrospect, of course, it was another story. When I told him that Wylie had turned up at their church on one occasion, he said that he knew when that must have been because his daughter began to behave strangely one Sunday. She not only dragged him away as soon as the service was over, she held his arm all the way home and she hadn't done that for years. When he asked if something was wrong, Enid said she felt unwell.'

'It must have been a torment for her, suffering in silence like that.'

'She just didn't feel able to confide in him. By chance,' continued Marmion, 'Neil Beresford was there when I called. He's made an amazing recovery. Last time I saw him, he was almost at death's door. He'd come to see Jenks to discuss the letter they'd both received from Mr Kennett.'

'What was their verdict?'

'They're both going to accept the offer.'

'That's very sensible of them.'

'So is Mr Ingles, apparently.'

'I remember him,' said Keedy. 'He threw us out

234

of the house.'

'We touched a sensitive spot, Joe.'

'My memory of Mr Ingles is that he was a compound of sensitive spots. You had to be careful what you said. Talking to him was like walking barefoot over broken glass. Next time you go there, Harv, you go alone. There was one thing in his favour, mind you,' he went on, unable to hide a smirk. 'At least he didn't think you were shifty.'

Sadie Radcliffe was in the middle of putting wet dungarees through the mangle when the visitors called. Drying her hands, she went to the door and opened it to a smartly dressed couple whom she'd never seen before. Brian Ingles introduced himself and his wife and asked if they might speak to her. Since the living room was full of baby things, Sadie was embarrassed to take them into it but she had no alternative. After waving them to the settee, she perched on a stool beside the fireplace. She noticed the quality of June's coat and the pearl necklace at her throat. Ingles took control. Accustomed to giving orders at work, his question sounded more like a demand.

'Have you come to a decision concerning that letter, Mrs Radcliffe?'

'Yes,' replied Sadie. 'I have more or less.'

'Then I trust that you had the sense to accept. That's what my wife and I have done and I can speak for Neil Beresford, Shirley's husband, as well. I talked to him earlier. I also know that Jonah Jenks is sympathetic to the idea because Reuben Harte told me when I went to see him today.'

'Mr Harte is against it,' said June.

235

'I'll persuade him,' said her husband, testily. 'I rarely fail to win people over to my viewpoint.' He smiled condescendingly at Sadie. 'May I take it that you'll follow where we lead?'

'Yes, Mr Ingles.'

'It will simplify everything,' said June.

'It will also make it possible to set a date for the funeral,' added her husband. 'All I have to do is to get Reuben Harte on our side and the job is complete. The five victims can be interred together, as is only right and proper.'

There was an awkward pause. Sadie wondered if she ought to offer them some refreshment but held back because she felt that their tea service would be markedly superior to hers. When she did speak, she blurted her question out.

'You're the ones with the big house in Hayes, aren't you?'

'Yes,' said June, smugly.

'Agnes told me that you have a garden at the front and the back.'

'It's everything we ever wanted, Mrs Radcliffe.'

'Though, actually,' said Ingles, 'were about to put it on the market.'

'We can't do that, Brian,' urged June. 'I love that house.'

'So do I, my dear, but it's far too large for our needs.'

'I'd rather have too much room than too little,' said Sadie.

'That's my feeling exactly,' said June. 'Besides, the house holds so many fond memories for us. I'd like to stay there indefinitely. My husband thinks that the place feels empty now that Florrie

236

has died but she hasn't lived there since she got married.' She looked at her husband. 'You never worried about it being too big when Florrie was alive. What's changed?'

'Need we discuss this here?' he said, irritably.

'I'd just like to know.'

'Very well – I'll tell you. What changed are the associations with the house. As you said earlier, it holds fond memories but they've been over-shadowed by Florrie's death. As long as we stay there, we'll be reminded of it. I'm sorry, June,' he went on, 'I know it's difficult for you to grasp but we have to get well away from there and make a fresh start. We have to build our lives anew.'

'I wish I could do that,' moaned Sadie. 'I'd love to be able to sell up and move far away but there's no chance of that happening. We're stuck here for ever.'

'I want to get far away from that confounded factory,' declared Ingles. 'And I want a smaller house that's easier to manage.'

'It can't be *much* smaller, Brian. That would be intolerable.'

'Leave this to me.' He stood up. 'Thank you, Mrs Radcliffe. I'm glad that the journey here has paid dividends. I can go back to Reuben Harte and tell him that he's the fly in the ointment. He must accept the majority decision.'

'I agree,' said June, now on her feet.

'God willing, I should be able to phone Mr Kennett later this afternoon to tell him what we've all decided. The funeral will be a harrowing experience for us all. If the five of them are buried at the same time, however, we can each draw support from others in the same unfortunate position.'

Sadie led the way. 'I'll show you out.'

She was relieved to get rid of them. June had been looking around the living room with polite disdain and Ingles had annoyed her by the way in which he'd taken the arrangements for the burial into his hands. Sadie felt that she hadn't been given free rein to express her opinions. As she watched them going off down the street, she could still hear them arguing about whether or not to sell their house.

'Who cares about your bloody house?' she said to herself. 'In case you forgot, Florrie died in that explosion with Agnes. How can you think about anything else but your daughter?'

Harvey Marmion felt that Leighton Hubbard deserved to know about the emergence of a suspect before he read it in the newspapers the next day. As a courtesy to the landlord, therefore, he and Joe Keedy drove to the pub in search of him. Repairs were still under way and the landlord was watching like a hawk. When the car drew up beside the pavement, he ambled across to it. The detectives got out and surveyed the scene of the bomb blast.

'It looks very different now, Mr Hubbard,' said Keedy.

'They tell me that it will have to look worse before it looks better,' said the landlord. 'The scaffolding is there to hold the Goose up. They discovered cracks in the brickwork almost everywhere. The work will cost a fortune.'

238

'I take it that you're insured,' said Keedy.

'Yes, Sergeant – the bills will be paid in full. What you can't insure against is all the heartache we suffered and all the customers we must have lost. It's been such a trial that there've been times when I wished *I'd* been blown up with those women.'

'You can't really mean that, sir.'

'Everything we loved about this place has been destroyed.'

'Then perhaps you'd like some news to raise your spirits,' said Marmion.

Hubbard's eye kindled. 'You've made an arrest?'

'We hope to do so before very long.'

'Who's the villain? Is it one of my rivals?'

'He's not a publican, sir. He works at the munitions factory. Thanks to that list you gave me, I was able to see that he was a patron of yours.'

'What's his name?'

'Herbert Wylie.'

'Do you recall him?' asked Keedy.

Hubbard nodded grimly. 'Yes, I do. He's not one of my regulars.'

'We've seen a photograph of him and I talked to his foreman. It seems that Wylie was not really a sociable type.'

'He wasn't, Sergeant. He'd only come into the Goose now and then and never had more than a pint. I could never work out if he was mean with his money or just not thirsty. Anyway, he didn't mix with the other customers. He liked to sit in a corner and stare into his beer. You get people like that.'

'What else can you tell us about him?' asked Marmion.

'That's it – excepting that he didn't stay long. He always slunk off early.'

'He's slunk off again. It may only be a coincidence but he hasn't been seen at work since the explosion. We went to his address but he'd taken most of his things and gone off somewhere.'

'Wylie is on the run,' decided Hubbard, scowling. 'Tell me where he is, Inspector, and I'll go after him, however far away he might be.'

'Leave him to us, sir.'

'Yes,' said Keedy. 'His name and description will be in every newspaper tomorrow. Everyone will know that we're hunting for Herbert Wylie in connection with what happened here. He'll find it almost impossible to avoid being seen.'

'Are you certain that it was him?' asked the landlord.

'You can never be completely certain in this game.'

'But we're confident enough to release his name to the press,' said Marmion. 'We've linked him closely to one of the women at that birthday party. We know that he's an expert bomb-maker. We found evidence that he'd been constructing one at the house where he lived. And you confirmed that he drank at your pub and was therefore aware of the fact that the key to the outhouse could easily be borrowed from its hook.'

Keedy spread his arms. 'What more evidence do we need?'

'Herbert Wylie,' said Hubbard, grinding his teeth. 'I didn't realise he was such a scheming

240

little runt.'

'We're assuming that he acted alone.'

'In his mind,' said Marmion, 'he probably saw it as a crime of passion.'

'That's not how I see it, Inspector. It was premeditated murder. Either way,' said Keedy, 'he'll face an appointment with the public executioner.'

'Let's not prejudge him. He has to be considered innocent until proven guilty.'

'What was this about him knowing one of those women?' asked Hubbard.

'He was rebuffed by the young lady. That may have given him a motive.'

'Oh, I see. That's all it takes, is it? Because some girl won't let him put a hand up her jumper, he thinks it's all right for him to kill her and her friends then destroy part of my pub into the bargain.'

The sight of the detectives brought neighbours out of their houses in search of information about the latest developments in the case. Marmion and Keedy didn't even get the chance to repeat the news because Hubbard did it for them. Accepting Wylie's guilt as proven fact, the landlord launched into a long denunciation of him and wished that he'd had the forethought to poison the man's beer. The knot of people grew into a small crowd. Seeing no reason to linger, the detectives moved to the car. The landlord hurried after them.

'Hang on a moment,' he said. 'I have to pass on a message.'

'Who gave it to you?' asked Marmion.

'Royston Liddle.'

'What's his problem?'

'He's been the victim of a terrible crime, Inspector.'

'Oh?'

'Someone's stolen his rabbits.'

'With respect to Mr Liddle, we can't marshal the full force of Scotland Yard in a search for missing rabbits. I think you'll agree that the murder of five innocent young women must take priority.'

'Don't forget the damage to my property.'

'I don't think you'll ever *let* us forget it, sir,' said Keedy, 'and you're right to do so. As for the rabbits, whoever stole them has probably had them in a stew by now. You can't charge someone with a crime when the evidence has been eaten.'

The sense of injustice festered inside Royston Liddle. He had a number of chores to complete throughout the day and he did them in a daze. All that he could think about was the atrocity in the rabbit hutch. The culprit was obviously Alan Suggs. He'd not only sworn to get back at Liddle, he knew just how much the rabbits meant to him. Stealing them would cause lasting pain to their owner. Suggs had been a friend once and Liddle had got both amusement and excitement out of watching him with a naked woman in the outhouse. It was Liddle who'd made that tryst possible and this was his reward. He tried to think of an appropriate act of revenge but he knew that he was too law-abiding to inflict it on Suggs. The crime had to be solved by the police.

As he trudged home after a day's work in

various places, he was bereft. The rabbits were far more than pets. They were part of the family. Instead of letting himself into the house by the front door, he went to the back entrance. As he came into the garden, he had a strange feeling that his rabbits had come back. Suggs had either relented or been overcome with guilt. Liddle was thrilled. Rushing to the hutch, he pulled the door open and looked inside. The rabbits were indeed there but not in their entirety. All that remained of them were their heads.

CHAPTER SIXTEEN

Because he'd never even made it past the front door on his previous visit, Marmion paid a second call on Reuben Harte. He was hoping to find the man in a slightly more hospitable frame of mind. Fortune favoured the detective. As he approached the house, Marmion was spotted through the window by Brian Ingles. Identified by him, he was allowed in by Harte and ushered into the living room. Sensing that the visitor might have brought news about the investigation, both men were markedly more welcoming than they had previously been towards him. With an apologetic smile, Ingles was quick to explain away his behaviour at the earlier meeting with Marmion.

'You caught me at a difficult time, Inspector,' he said.

'I appreciate that, sir.'

'Only someone whose child has been murdered could understand the pulverising effect that the news can have. It leaves you utterly bewildered.'

'Brian is right,' said Harte. 'I felt exactly the same. Losing a loved one knocks you for six. I'm still stunned.'

'And so was I,' said Marmion, seizing the opportunity to show them that he'd been through a similar experience. 'It shook me to the core. My father was killed while on duty as a policeman, you see. It took me days to accept the awful truth. When I did that, other feelings took over. I had this overpowering urge to go after the man who'd committed the murder. That led in time to my joining the police force.'

The information had a different effect on the two men. While Ingles had more respect for Marmion after the revelation that he'd been through the same horror, Harte was both annoyed and hurt, as if the inspector had somehow reduced his status as a father mourning a murder victim. Ingles was more open but Harte came close to sulking.

'I'm glad to find the both of you together,' Marmion began.

'I was just on the point of winning an argument,' explained Ingles. 'I daresay that you can guess what it was about.'

'Was it the offer made by Mr Kennett?'

'Indeed, it was.'

'I've agreed to nothing,' said Harte, stonily.

'But you were at least listening to sense at last,' said Ingles. 'And now that four of us are in agreement, you're feeling uneasy at being isolated.'

'You don't know *how* I feel, Brian.'

Ingles was tactful. 'Then I'll not press you on the matter. In any case,' he went on, 'I'm sure that the inspector didn't come here to join in the discussion.'

'That's true,' said Marmion.

'What news do you have for us?'

'We've identified a suspect.'

Harte perked up immediately. 'Who is he?'

'It's a man by the name of Herbert Wylie.'

'I've never heard of him.'

'No more have I,' said Ingles.

'He worked at the munitions factory,' Marmion told them. 'At least, he did until the day of the explosion. After that, he seems to have packed his bags and vanished. We've released his name to the press and there'll be a nationwide search for Wylie. We're very anxious to speak to him.'

'When police use that phrase, it usually means that they think a particular person is almost certainly guilty. Am I right, Inspector?'

'You can deduce what you wish, sir. We need to find this individual as a matter of urgency but there's no absolute guarantee that he's our man.'

'What can you tell us about him?'

'Simply that he was in the right place at the right time,' said Marmion. 'He knew the pub in question and seems to have had a thwarted passion for one of the young women attending that party. Neither of your daughters, I hasten to say,' he added, 'was the person in question. They had the misfortune to be there when this man – as the evidence suggests – took his revenge.'

'How did you find all this out?' asked Ingles.

'We are fortunate enough to have a survivor of the blast.'

'Ah, of course – Maureen Quinn.'

'She supplied the name that led to a series of productive enquiries.'

Ingles was overcome with relief. 'Thank heaven!' he exclaimed.

'Why didn't she tell you about this man earlier?' asked Harte.

'For the same reason that you wouldn't let me into your house on my first visit, sir,' said Marmion with a half-smile. 'She was stunned by what happened and couldn't begin to think straight. Her instinct was to withdraw into herself. It's exactly what I did when my father was murdered. I just brooded for hours on end.'

'I can understand that only too well, Inspector.'

'Anyway, I wanted you both to know about Wylie in advance so that it won't come as a complete shock when you read the newspapers tomorrow. But I must emphasise that the case is very far from being closed,' said Marmion. 'We still have some way to go so don't make any assumptions.'

'Thank you so much for your consideration,' said Ingles, beaming. 'I can't speak for Reuben but this news has really lifted my spirits. I can't tell you how pleased I am.'

'Yes,' conceded Harte. 'It is a consolation.'

'If this fellow was not pursuing either Florrie or Jean, who was he after?'

Harte turned to Marmion. 'Was it Maureen Quinn, by any chance?'

The pastoral care of his flock weighed heavily

with Father Cleary and every day apart from the Sabbath consisted of a series of visits to people in distress or requiring comfort. In the course of an exceptionally busy afternoon, he made time to call on Maureen Quinn. Over a cup of tea, he chatted with Diane and her elder daughter. Pleased to see that Maureen looked and sounded better than at their previous meeting, Cleary was alarmed to hear of the offer made to the grieving families of the victims.

'They're advocating a *collective* burial?' he said, gaping.

'That's what we've been told,' replied Diane.

'I find the very notion of it abhorrent – and I hope that you do.'

'To be honest, Father Cleary, it worried me a little but my husband thought it was a good idea. Eamonn said that, if Maureen had died in that blast, then he'd have accepted the offer.'

'Goodness gracious.'

'It would have saved us a lot of money we don't have.'

'That's a secondary consideration, Mrs Quinn,' said the priest, sharply. 'Besides, we're always prepared to help out financially in cases of genuine need. We have a fund set aside for that purpose. It's other aspects of the situation that are paramount.'

'What do you mean, Father?' asked Maureen.

'A funeral is, by its very nature, a very private event.'

'Yet they have mass funerals in France and Belgium,' said Diane. 'As you know, Liam and Anthony are both serving at the front. They've attended funerals where dozens of men have been buried at the same time.'

'That's a regrettable consequence of war, Mrs Quinn. Where large numbers are involved, they have to resort to such exigencies. There are only five victims here and they deserve a burial service that preserves their individuality. Had Maureen been in that situation,' he continued, 'I'd have done everything in my power to persuade you and your husband that, from start to finish, the funeral service should follow the established practice of the Roman Catholic Church. I'd hate to think that it would be diluted in any way.'

'Sadie Radcliffe's daughter was one of the victims. She came to ask my advice on the subject.'

'What did you tell her?'

'That I was glad I wasn't put in the same position.'

'I hope you pointed out that you wouldn't have made any decision without consulting me.'

'I'd have had to talk it over with my husband first,' said Diane.

'It was your duty to refer the matter to your parish priest.'

'Luckily, the situation never arose.'

'I sometimes wish that it had,' said Maureen under her breath.

'In none of the five cases,' resumed Cleary, 'is it a normal funeral. Most of the services at which I officiate relate to old people who've withdrawn gently from life and whose demise was inevitable. Here we have an instance of the most violent and heinous crime. Young women with whole lives before them have been summarily killed. In each case, the funeral needs to be handled with extreme sensitivity.'

'I can see that, Father Cleary.'

Diane could also see that he'd really come to talk with her daughter alone. Withdrawing to the kitchen on the pretext of making another pot of tea, she left the pair of them together. Cleary's smile was filled with kindness and concern.

'How are you, Maureen?'

'I'm bearing up, Father Cleary.'

'Have you been saying your prayers?'

'I say them night and day.'

'At a stroke,' he said, 'you lost five good friends. It's a heavy cross to bear. As the survivor, you have responsibilities to the other families. Have you been in touch with any of them?'

'Agnes's mother – that's Mrs Radcliffe – called here but I don't feel that it's right for me to visit any of the other parents. They might not wish to see me.'

'I can't see why you should think that. You could offer solace.' She looked doubtful. 'You could, Maureen. For one thing, you could give them precious details of what happened at the party. It might give them a modicum of cheer to know that their daughters died while they were happy. There might even be last words you can remember some of them saying. It would be something for parents to hold on to.'

Maureen shuddered inwardly. She was dreading a meeting with the families of the victims. Even the conversation with Sadie Radcliffe had been a trial for her. Others might not be in as forgiving a mood as Agnes Collier's mother. Yet

249

she had to face them all sooner or later. The inquest was imminent and so were the funerals. If they did indeed all take place on the same day, she'd be spared the agony of having to attend all five separately and of being under intense scrutiny at successive events. From purely selfish motives, she hoped that the collective burial would take place at the cemetery. Her ordeal would be over in one fell swoop and the fact that so many people would attend meant that she'd be largely hidden in such a massive crowd.

Father Cleary leant forward to take her hands and look into her eyes.

'What's troubling you, my child?' he asked, softly.

'Everything.'

'I fancy that there's something in particular.'

'No,' she replied. 'I just have this feeling all the time.'

'What sort of feeling?'

'It's difficult to explain, Father. I keep thinking how ... unworthy I am.'

'You must never think that, Maureen.'

'I can't help it. As soon as I wake up, it's still there.'

'And is there no special reason for this sense of guilt?' She lowered her head. 'I asked you a question, Maureen.'

She met his gaze. 'There's *no* special reason, Father Cleary.'

But there was a distinct tremble in her voice.

It fell to Joe Keedy to apprise Sadie Radcliffe of the latest development in the case. Marmion had already told Jonah Jenks and Neil Beresford about their new suspect, and he'd planned to go on to the homes of Reuben Harte and Brian Ingles. That left only Agnes Collier's mother unaccounted for so Keedy paid her a visit. Having just put the baby down for a sleep, she spoke in a whisper as she hustled him into the house. Only when she'd closed the living room door behind them did she talk in her normal voice. Unsurprisingly, she looked harried and careworn.

Keedy told her about the identification of Herbert Wylie as a suspect.

'I've heard that name before,' she recalled.

'Do you remember what was said about him, Mrs Radcliffe?'

'No, not really – it was one time when Maureen had called on Agnes. They were talking about the men they worked with and that name cropped up. It was something to do with the football team. Yes, that's it,' she decided. 'Neither of them liked him. He used to turn up when Maureen and the others played in a match. He didn't really have any interest in watching the game.'

'A lot of men are like that, I'm afraid,' said Keedy. 'The opportunity of watching attractive young women running around in shorts is too good to miss for some of them.'

'The person that Wylie was watching was Enid Jenks.'

'I didn't know that she was part of the team.'

'She wasn't, Sergeant, but she liked to support them now and again. That all stopped when this strange man kept turning up to stare at her.'

'Did you overhear your daughter saying anything else about him?'

'Only that she felt sorry for Enid,' said Sadie, 'because she didn't really know what to do. Agnes was married so the men steered clear of her. And the few that didn't got the cold shoulder. Agnes was very friendly with the men at the factory but that was as far as it went. Enid – at least, this is what I gathered – had no idea how to handle them. That's why she was frightened of this man you mentioned.'

'His name will be in the national newspapers tomorrow.'

'Are you going to say *why* you want him caught?'

'No,' replied Keedy. 'It's just a general request for the public to keep their eyes peeled. What you've told me about Wylie ties in with what we already know. He persecuted Enid Jenks but her name will be kept out of the newspapers. We don't want to cause her father any undue embarrassment.'

'Does he know that you're on this man's tail?'

'Oh, yes – Inspector Marmion went to tell him in person.'

'In a way, it's his fault – Mr Jenks, I mean.'

'I'm not sure that I follow you.'

'Well, I'm only going on what Agnes told me, of course,' said Sadie, 'but it seems that Enid wasn't allowed to have a boyfriend. Her father made her spend all her time and energy on her music. He cut her off from the world. That's unhealthy.'

'I agree, Mrs Radcliffe.'

'Enid just didn't know how to cope with men.'

As she expanded on her theme, Keedy could see that she'd taken a close interest in her daughter's

252

friends. Of the other four victims, she knew them all by name and character traits. Sadie had anecdotes about each one of them. But she'd clearly done more than catch the odd reference to Enid Jenks. She talked so knowledgeably about her that Keedy suspected she'd eavesdropped on conversations between Agnes and Maureen Quinn. When she was describing Florrie Duncan's pre-eminence in the group, she remembered something.

'Her parents called to see me,' she said.

'I'm surprised they were ready to venture out of their home,' said Keedy. 'When we visited them, Mr Ingles wasn't really prepared to talk to us.'

'I couldn't stop him talking.'

'And you say that his wife was with him?'

'Yes, I don't know how they found out my address but they did somehow. They came to discuss this offer we've had from the factory. To be more exact,' she said, 'they were here to push me into accepting it.'

'How did you react?'

'In fact, I'd more or less decided that I'd go along with the idea so there was no real argument. But I was upset, Sergeant. I can make up my own mind without having them telling me what to do. Agnes used to say how bossy Mr Ingles could be.' Her eyes flashed. 'And there was something else as well.'

'Oh?'

'It was as if they were doing me a favour by coming here,' she said, resentfully. 'The pair of them talked down to me.'

'They had no call to do that, Mrs Radcliffe.'

She adopted a combative stance. 'I won't stand for it. I don't care how big their house is, they've got no right to treat people like that. Next time that Brian Ingles comes anywhere near me, I'll shut the front door in his face. As for the daughter they're so proud of,' she went on, harshly, 'I could tell them a few things about Florrie that would wipe the smiles off their faces.'

'Really?' said Keedy. 'What sort of things, Mrs Radcliffe?'

The longer he stayed, the more Harvey Marmion was learning about the five victims of the explosion. Brian Ingles and Reuben Harte had reached the stage of open competition, each one boasting about the achievements of their respective daughters and talking about the unfulfilled dreams of the women. It was not only Florrie Duncan and Jean Harte who were revealed in greater detail, the three women who'd died with them also came into sharper focus. Maureen Quinn was not omitted. Both men described her as being on the fringe of the group, popular by dint of her skill as a goalkeeper but never a leading figure. Ingles called her immature while Harte considered her to be rather sly without actually being able to justify his claim. What both men did agree was that the six of them were natural allies and that their mutual friendship gave them a sense of belonging to an elite group.

'Florrie always set the tone,' said Ingles.

'Jean wasn't slow to assert herself,' Harte reminded him.

'My daughter liked to be in charge.'

'Mine didn't suffer from that defect, Brian.'

'It's not a defect,' retorted Ingles. 'It's a fact of nature. Some of us are born to lead and the majority are born to follow. You're a perfect instance of that, Reuben. Had you possessed a leader's instinct, you'd now be a bank manager instead of a humble clerk who toils in the shadow of superiors.'

Harte was stung. 'My job carries many responsibilities.'

'You'd have even more if you'd had an ambitious streak.'

'I'm not sure that this debate is at all useful,' said Marmion, intervening before the acrimony developed. 'Our thoughts should be with the victims and not with a petty squabble about who does what job.'

'Thank you, Inspector,' said Harte. 'You're right to chide us. I'm afraid that no conversation with Brian is complete without him reminding you that he has a very important position.'

'There's no point in hiding my light under a bushel,' said Ingles.

'You're incapable of doing so.'

'That's an unnecessarily spiteful remark, Reuben.'

'Then stop provoking me.'

'With respect,' said Marmion with a reproachful glance at each in turn, 'each of you is as bad as the other. Common grief should unite you, not set you at each other's throats. From everything I've heard about your daughters, my sense is that they were both exceptional young women in their own way. Maureen Quinn talked about them with great

255

fondness. Florrie was very kind to her and Jean was involved in the football team with Maureen. Sport is one of the best ways for people to bond.'

'We're justly rebuked again,' said Harte, ashamedly.

'I apologise, Inspector,' said Ingles. 'We're bickering like children.'

'Nerves are bound to be frayed at a time like this, sir,' said Marmion, glad that they'd both calmed down. 'I suggest that we forget the whole thing.' The other men exchanged a nod. 'You've both been informed of the date of the inquest, I take it?'

'Yes, we have. I'll be interested to hear what Maureen will have to say.'

'So will I,' said Harte.

'We're still puzzled as to why she left the party early.'

'Apparently,' explained Marmion, 'she was not feeling well.'

'What a stroke of luck!'

'Maureen doesn't *feel* lucky, Mr Ingles – far from it. She's very confused, of course, but she's also contrite. She feels guilty that she survived when her friends didn't. Like anyone in that situation, she wonders why she was spared.'

'So do I,' murmured Harte.

'Well,' said Ingles, consulting the watch he'd taken from his waistcoat pocket, 'I must be off. I have an appointment with an estate agent.'

'Are you thinking of selling your house?' asked Marmion.

'It's ... a possibility, Inspector. It never does any harm to keep abreast of current property values.

I anticipate that our house will be worth a decent sum.'

'Then why do you wish to leave?'

'I like to keep my options open,' said Ingles, evasively. He turned to his host. 'Goodbye, Reuben. Bear in mind that you have to reach a decision by the end of the afternoon. It's disrespectful to Mr Kennett to keep him waiting and we need to set arrangements in train. Weigh my arguments in the balance,' he continued, 'and you'll accept that you simply must fall into line with the rest of us.'

'We shall see,' grunted Harte.

After trading farewells with Marmion, Ingles was shown out of the house by Harte. When the latter came back into the living room, he was obviously pleased that the other man had finally gone.

'I've had quite an invasion today,' he said.

Marmion prepared to leave. 'Well, I won't bother you any more, sir.'

'That wasn't a hint to you, Inspector. Given the news that you brought, you're very welcome. It's Brian Ingles's visit I could have done without. He's an invasion all by himself.'

'Yes, he does like to take control, doesn't he?'

'I won't be browbeaten by the likes of him. He was almost manic before you arrived to rescue me. He only calmed down when you told us about Wylie.'

'I'm glad I was able to pour oil on troubled waters,' said Marmion. 'I must say that I find it odd that Mr Ingles is talking about selling his house at a time like this. I would have thought he had more pressing matters on his mind.'

'It's not the only thing that was odd,' observed Harte. 'My suggestion really upset him for some reason.'

'What suggestion was that, sir?'

'I just wondered if we might club together to commission some sort of memorial for the five victims. It needn't be anything too elaborate but it would preserve their memory. If all five of us put in an equal amount,' said Harte, 'then the cost wouldn't be prohibitive.'

'Why was Mr Ingles upset by the idea?'

'I can't really say but it was decidedly odd. I mean, he has more money than the rest of us put together. I should know, Inspector – he's a client of my bank.'

CHAPTER SEVENTEEN

Having started work early that morning, Alice Marmion came off her shift in the middle of the afternoon. Instead of returning to her flat, she decided to call on her mother. Knowing that Ellen would not be at home, she went to the centre where a group of women were contributing to the war effort by knitting and sewing. They were absorbed in their work when Alice entered in police uniform. Her sudden appearance led to a flurry of concern. It was soon stilled. Delighted to see her daughter, Ellen was glad to be rescued from the tedium of her voluntary work. Over a snack in a nearby café, they were able to chat at leisure.

'Thank you for coming to my aid,' said Ellen.

'I thought that you liked your Sewing Circle.'

'Actually, we do more knitting than sewing and, yes, I do enjoy it as a rule. I've made some good friends there. Some of them are in the same boat as me with sons at the front. Mrs Fletcher, who runs the group, has all three of hers in France.'

'She must be worried to death,' said Alice.

'She manages to hide her anxiety. What she can't hide,' confided Ellen, 'is that she's hopeless with a pair of knitting needles in her hands. You should see the socks that she produces. The wool is too coarse and the feet are always too small. But she's a good-hearted woman so we daren't criticise her.'

'You won't need to send any socks to Paul. You can give them to him.'

'I know, Alice. I can't wait for him to come home.'

'Neither can I,' said her daughter. 'I just wish that I knew how he felt about me and Joe. I wanted him to be happy for us.'

'And I'm sure that he is. All he can think about at the moment, however, is surviving the war. Casualties are mounting every day. That's why I want him safe and sound at home.'

'It's only a short leave, Mummy,' Alice reminded her.

'Then we'll have to make the most of it.'

They drank their tea and nibbled at their cakes. Ellen chuckled.

'When you came through that door, I didn't

recognise you at first. I thought I was about to be arrested for knitting gloves that don't fit.' She squeezed Alice's hand affectionately. 'What have you been up to?'

'You wouldn't believe me if I told you.'

'Why?'

'I've been consorting with prostitutes.'

When she was told about the new assignment, Ellen was nonplussed.

'I thought they were called "ladies of the night". Are you telling me that they come out in the day-time as well?'

'Don't look so shocked,' said Alice, laughing. 'Apparently, it's a twenty-four-hour profession. There's a demand throughout the day.'

'I'm sorry that you have to deal with such people.'

'They're not the sort of women you imagine, Mummy. Very few of them do it by choice. They're driven into it by poverty or by some cruel person who has a hold over them. Some are still only girls, really,' Alice went on. 'One of them told us that she turned to prostitution when her husband was killed at the front. It was the only way she could support herself and the baby. We tried to point out the dangers to her.'

Ellen pursed her lips. 'It's such an unsavoury side of life.'

'That's why the inspector gave me the job. She wanted to open my eyes.'

'It sounds as if she wanted to punish you, Alice.'

'Gale Force does that in various ways every day.'

'You don't have to put up with it, you know.'

'If I'm not in the building,' said Alice, cheerfully, 'then I'm out of her range. Also, I'm getting an education, of sorts.'

'Your father had that kind of education when he was on the night shift. He was a bobby on the beat in those days, of course. To spare my blushes, he didn't tell me about some of the encounters he must have had. But if you really want to know about prostitutes,' said Ellen, 'you should talk to your Uncle Raymond.'

Alice laughed. 'Why? I didn't think he'd have any dealings with them.'

'He doesn't, in the sense that you mean. But work in the Salvation Army makes him look in the darkest corners of London. He offers help to anyone in need, regardless of how they earn a living.'

'I'd forgotten that. Maybe I *will* have a chat with Uncle Raymond.'

'I know that he shielded a prostitute on one occasion,' said Ellen. 'She was terrified of being beaten up by the man who tricked her into selling her body. Your uncle let her stay there for the best part of a week.'

It was a sobering reminder of the routine work that the Salvation Army did in the capital. Raymond Marmion was a tireless man with a huge fund of compassion. He gave advice, sympathy and practical assistance to a wide circle of people. A talk with him might well prepare Alice for some of the sights she was bound to come across in the course of her patrol.

'When are you going to see Joe again?' asked Ellen.

'I wish I knew, Mummy.'

'It doesn't get any better with the passage of time.'

'Are you trying to warn me off marrying a policeman?'

'I'd never do that, Alice. You've made the right choice. Stick by it.'

Alice was sad. 'If only I could hear Daddy say that!'

'You will one day,' said Ellen. 'He's already starting to mellow.'

'Well, why didn't you say so, you fool?' yelled Marmion, angrily. 'The car must be available at all times. It's your job to make sure that it is.'

'I'm sorry, Inspector.'

'If you knew there was a problem, you should have reported it.'

'Yes, sir,' said the driver, cowering under the onslaught.

'That's why we have mechanics. They keep our vehicles on the road.'

'I didn't think that the problem was serious.'

'Get it fixed.'

'I don't have any tools.'

'Then find someone who has,' said Marmion, pointing a finger down the road. 'We passed a garage on our way here. When you heard that noise in the engine, why didn't you stop and ask for help?'

He made an effort to rein in his temper. Ordinarily, the driver was extremely dependable, working at all hours without complaint. But he had slipped up on this occasion. As a result, the car had broken down and both of them were now standing on the pavement beside it. To get to the police station would only take Marmion a ten-minute walk but that wasn't the point. Reliability of transport was vital. Had they been speeding to an emergency, the breakdown could have had critical results. The driver clearly didn't need to be told that. He was writhing with embarrassment.

'It's never happened before, sir,' he argued in his defence.

'I know,' said Marmion, anger subsiding, 'and it's my fault as much as yours. I heard that strange noise when you did. I should have insisted you pulled into that garage. Sorry I lost my temper.'

'I deserved it, Inspector.'

'I'll go on foot now. Bring the car when it's been repaired. And if it turns out to be beyond repair,' he added, 'we'll have to borrow one from the police station. We can't solve a murder case by riding around on bicycles.'

The driver's laugh was more out of relief than amusement. He was grateful that his reprimand was over. Marmion rarely lost his temper but, when he did, he could be very scathing. The driver was still feeling the force of the blast.

Marmion set off with long strides. His brisk walk got him to the police station where he found Joe Keedy awaiting him. He got no sympathy from the sergeant.

'Now you know how I have to manage,' said Keedy. 'While you've had a chauffeur, I've had to walk everywhere or use public transport.'

'We can't all have a car at our disposal, Joe.'

'Neither of us does at the moment.'

Marmion sat opposite him and heard about the visit to Sadie Radcliffe. He was intrigued to learn new intelligence about Florrie Duncan. It transpired that she was not the dutiful daughter that her parents had spoken about. According to Sadie – working on information supplied by Agnes Collier – there'd been a serious rift in the family before Florrie's marriage. Because of her parents' strong objections to her choice of husband, Florrie had moved out of her home and into a flat. Neither her mother's pleas nor her father's hectoring had been able to bring her back. In the wake of their son-in-law's death, the parents had expected their daughter to turn to them for comfort but Florrie made a point of avoiding them.

'I talked to the men who've been knocking on doors in the area,' said Keedy, 'and they told a similar story. It's not a happy family and Mr Ingles is disliked by his neighbours.'

'That's because he's so objectionable,' said Marmion. 'But you haven't told me what it was that was likely to wipe the smile off his face and that of his wife.'

'I'm not sure if this is true or just idle tittle-tattle.'

'What did Mrs Radcliffe tell you?'

'Her daughter had the feeling that Florrie was pregnant.'

'That could be good news if it was her husband's child.'

'It can't possibly be, Harv. The dates don't fit.'

'Well,' said Marmion, sitting back to absorb the news, 'that could mean that there were six victims

264

of that explosion. From her parents' point of view, it might be just as well that the post-mortem didn't reveal signs of pregnancy. How certain was Mrs Radcliffe that her daughter was telling the truth?'

'Agnes Collier had a child of her own. She knew the signals.'

'Did she have any idea who the father was?'

'No, Harv, but it does show Florrie in a different light. She was obviously a young woman who enjoyed life,' said Keedy. 'We'll never know if the baby was an accident or a deliberate means of scandalising her parents.'

'I'd go for the first explanation, Joe. Florrie may have fallen out with them but she'd know the terrible stigma that a child born outside wedlock would bear. It would make life very uncomfortable for mother and child. No woman would want that.'

'I wonder if the father *knew* about what had happened. They could always have got married, I suppose.'

'Not if he was already married,' Marmion pointed out. 'Or he could have been some careless chap who simply wanted a bit of fun and wasn't prepared to face the consequences. Either way, he'd have left Florrie to cope on her own.'

'Unless…'

They were both thinking the same thing. Someone who was confronted with the information that he'd fathered a child might have taken extreme measures to get rid of it. If he and Florrie had been close, he'd know the date of her birthday and be aware that the party was taking place in the

265

outhouse at the pub. Again, the likelihood was that the man worked at the factory and therefore had access to materials that could be used to fashion a bomb. Marmion slipped a hand into an inside pocket and took out the lists that Leighton Hubbard had drawn up for him. One of the names could well belong to Florrie Duncan's lover. They might have a second suspect. Herbert Wylie had apparently acted because he'd been rejected by a woman. It was the opposite case here. A man's advances had been welcomed and he'd taken his pleasure with Florrie. What could have moved him to contemplate murder was the pressing need to remove her and her child from his life.

'What will Chat make of it all?' asked Keedy.

'The superintendent has a mind that none can fathom, Joe.'

'Are you going to tell him?'

'I'll wait until he rings me.'

'I still think that Wylie might be our man.'

'We can't dismiss this new suspect,' said Marmion, 'whoever he might be. Thank goodness you called on Mrs Radcliffe. What sounded like idle tittle-tattle may turn out to be the solution to the crime.'

'What about you, Harv?'

'Oh, I uncovered no interesting new evidence. I did have some luck, though. When I got to Mr Harte's house, he not only let me in, he had Brian Ingles there. It saved me a second visit.'

'What did they have to say for themselves?'

Marmion gave him an abbreviated account of his time at Reuben Harte's house. In view of what he now knew about Florrie Duncan, he could see that most of her father's grandiose claims about her had been so much hot air. Ingles was blissfully unaware that his daughter had a new man in her life and that he'd impregnated Florrie. It would have been shattering news to her parents. Keedy was so enthralled by what he heard that he forgot to mention that Harte had earlier thought that Marmion looked shifty.

'Ingles has a lovely house,' he said, enviously. 'Why sell it?'

'That's what I wondered.'

'He surely can't want anything bigger.'

'Not when there are only the two of them there, Joe. I can tell you this, though. When my father was killed, the last thing my mother was thinking about was selling the house. It's such a peculiar thing to do.'

'Perhaps it's his way of taking his mind off the funeral.'

'We may never know,' said Marmion. He looked at the telephone. 'I suppose that I ought to contact Chat. No,' he decided. 'I'm not ready for him yet. He can wait. Let him stew in his own juice for a while.'

Claude Chatfield had learnt very early in his police career that overwhelming evidence could be deceptive and might dissolve under close examination. When he heard about Herbert Wylie's abrupt disappearance, he was quite certain that they'd found the man who'd planted the bomb. When releasing the name to the press, however, he was careful to describe Wylie as a person of interest to the police rather than as a definite culprit.

And while he nursed the hope that they were in pursuit of the right man, he was experienced enough to brace himself for disappointment. A request from Marmion had helped him to unearth the fact that Eamonn Quinn had had convictions in the past and that drove Chatfield on to make further enquiries about him. Because the detective assigned to do the research had not come back to him, the superintendent assumed that he'd found nothing worth reporting.

He was wrong. When he returned to his office after a long session with the commissioner, Chatfield found a file on his desk. Flipping it open, he read the information with gathering concern. As soon as he'd finished, he moved across to the bookshelf and reached for a map of the British Isles.

Maureen Quinn was still totally confused. Conflicting emotions filled her mind and reduced her to a state of near paralysis. Father Cleary's visit had been simultaneously reassuring and disturbing. While he made her feel that he cared for her plight, he unwittingly deepened it. After he left, she was more guilty, isolated and depressed than ever. When there was a tap on the door of her bedroom, Maureen felt as if someone was knocking on the top of her skull. She leapt up.

'Is that you, Lily?' she asked.

'No,' replied her mother, 'it's me. Can I come in?'

'Yes – if you want to.'

Diane opened the door and entered. Seeing the distraught look on her daughter's face, she reached out to embrace her. Maureen stifled her tears and took strength from her mother's love. At last, Diane pulled back.

'I have to go out.'

'What about Lily?'

'I'm taking her with me. She's been cooped up in here too long.'

'Will I be left on my own?' asked Maureen, worriedly.

'It will only be for a short time.'

'Where are you going?'

'There's shopping to do. I'd ask you to come with us but I don't suppose you'd want to do that.' Maureen shook her head vigorously. 'No, I thought not. It's best if you stay here. Is that all right?'

'Don't be long, Mummy.'

'We won't be, I promise. Is there anything you want?'

'No.'

'I could go to the library for you.'

'Please don't bother. I just want to stay in here on my own.'

'Then we'll get out of your way. Your father will be home before too long. He said that he'd try to finish early today.' She hugged Maureen again. 'You get some rest. We'll be off now.'

Diane went out and closed the door behind her. Maureen could hear her descending the stairs and calling for Lily to join her. When the two of them left the house, Maureen went to the window in the front bedroom to watch them walk off down the street. She was in a quandary. Needing to be alone, she nevertheless wanted someone else in the house with her. She felt that she'd been cast adrift now and it was alarming. Her first impulse was to leave and find sanctuary once more in church but that would be unfair on her mother and sister. Returning to find her absent, they'd be very hurt even if she left a note for them. In any case, Maureen was not ready for another conversation with Father Cleary. His instinct was too sharp and his questions too probing. All that Maureen could do was to remain in her bedroom and go through the tragic events yet again, mourning each of the victims in turn.

As she sat on the bed and stared ahead of her, a loud noise broke into her reverie. It was the sound of the letter box opening and shutting. Since it was far too late for the postman to call, she wondered what had been delivered. Opening the door, she crept downstairs with tentative steps. On the mat was a white envelope. When she picked it up, her heart constricted as she saw her name written on it. At first, she was quite unable to open it and stood rooted to the spot. Then she rushed into the living room, tore open the envelope and read the letter. Her face and body burned with embarrassment. After reading the words again, she took instant action. Scrunching up the letter and the envelope, she tossed them into the empty fireplace. Maureen then grabbed the box of matches from the mantelpiece and set the paper alight. Down on her knees in front of the little blaze, she didn't move a muscle until the letter had been burnt out of existence.

Harvey Marmion was on the point of making

contact with Scotland Yard when the telephone rang. He pulled his hand back as if the receiver were red hot. Joe Keedy laughed. After shooting him a look of reproof, Marmion picked up the telephone.

'Inspector Marmion here,' he said.

'Why haven't you been in touch?' demanded Chatfield.

'I was just about to do so, sir.'

'Don't lie to me. I expected a call an hour ago.'

'Sergeant Keedy and I have been very busy.'

'I haven't exactly been twiddling my thumbs here, Inspector. What have you discovered?'

'We learnt a number of things.'

'Well, come on then – spit them out!'

Marmion told him about the visit to Reuben Harte and how surprised he'd been at Brian Ingles's decision to sell his house. It led on to the information that Keedy had gleaned from Sadie Radcliffe. Normally, every time he rang the superintendent, Marmion's sentences would be routinely interrupted by Chatfield as he sought greater clarification. Chatfield remained unusually silent now, listening intently. Marmion could hear his heavy breathing down the line. When he came to the end of his report, Marmion added a rider.

'We must remember that all this is pure specu-lation, sir,' he said. 'We have unsubstantiated evi-dence of a pregnancy but no concrete proof. On the other hand, I think you'll agree, a significant new factor may have entered the investigation.' The silence continued at the other end of the line and he could no longer hear the sound of heavy breathing. 'Are you still there, Superintendent?'

271

'Where, in God's name, do you *think* I am!' said Chatfield's rasping voice.

'I'd value your opinion.'

'My opinion is that you should have rung me the moment this information came into your possession. Is Sergeant Keedy with you?'

'He's sitting beside me,' replied Marmion.

'Then you can let him take a share of the blame. The sergeant should have insisted that you communicated with me at the earliest possible juncture. Pass that message on to him.'

The order was unnecessary because Keedy could hear his voice clearly.

'He deserves something other than your strictures, Superintendent. It was during his visit to Mrs Radcliffe that this new evidence was collected. I would have thought it merited praise rather than condemnation.'

'You'll get all the praise you want when the killer is caught and convicted.'

'Who will it be?' mused Marmion. 'Is it Herbert Wylie or the nameless father of Florrie Duncan's child?'

'It may be neither,' said Chatfield.

He spoke rapidly to impart some news and Keedy was unable to catch what he was saying, but he judged from the expression on Marmion's face that something of importance was being divulged. Making notes as he listened, Marmion nodded away and was only allowed to speak when he bade the superintendent farewell. As he put down the receiver, his expression was one of sheer wonderment.

'What a day!' he said. 'This case is moving too

fast for me, Joe. There's only one thing worse than uncovering a completely new suspect to muddy the waters of an investigation. Do you know what it is?'

'Tell me.'

'It seems that we now have *two* new suspects. The superintendent has been burrowing into the Quinn family's history and he's turned up a fascinating coincidence – if that's what it really is. Do you recall a man by the name of Niall Quinn?' Keedy looked mystified. 'Think hard, Joe. His picture was on the front pages of the papers a year ago.'

Keedy smacked the table. 'He was that Irish lad caught planting a bomb.'

'And where was he arrested?'

'Remind me.'

'It was somewhere perilously close to where we're now sitting.'

'Is that why Chat is getting so excited?'

'He discovered an interesting fact,' said Marmion. 'It seems that the Irish nationalist has a definite connection with this area. He's Eamonn Quinn's nephew.'

'So what? He was arrested and sent to prison. Niall Quinn is behind bars.'

'Not any more, I'm afraid. He escaped last week. Chat has been putting two and two together. A known bomber is at liberty and Maureen Quinn, a relation of his, is the only person to escape from an explosion that he might, or might not, have engineered. Was it chance or design?'

'I haven't a clue. What are we supposed to do?'

'We have to look into it immediately so just

pray that the car's been repaired.'

'Where are we going, Harv?'

Marmion grinned. 'We're off to a whisky distillery in Wales.'

CHAPTER EIGHTEEN

The pain would not go away. It had subsided to a dull ache but it was always there. The only way that Neil Beresford could cope with it was to throw himself wholeheartedly into frenetic activity. His mother was amazed when he started to clean the house and do a range of odd jobs that he'd hitherto postponed. For the first time she could remember, he even worked in the garden with enthusiasm. His bursts of energy provided a distraction without actually curing the underlying condition. Anguish pulsed away inside his brain, giving him a permanent headache. While the death of his wife might have weakened the football team he'd so lovingly created and coached, he was determined that it wouldn't falter completely. Thanks largely to the brilliance of Shirley Beresford, they'd reached the cup final. It fell to the remaining members of the team to end the season on a note of triumph.

Beset as he was with worries about the inquest and the funeral, Beresford never lost sight of the importance of the cup final. When he ran out of things to do at home, therefore, he walked to the factory with a football under his arm. Recognised at the gate, he was allowed in and given some words of commiseration. He strolled out to the pitch on which so many training sessions and games had been played. His overriding memory was of the goals that his wife had scored there. Dropping the ball to the ground, he dribbled it the length of the pitch then smashed it past an invisible goalkeeper. Beresford reclaimed the ball from the net and set it on the penalty spot. He did exactly what his wife had been taught to do and aimed for the top right-hand corner of the goal. It left the invisible goalkeeper hopelessly stranded. He was taking his third penalty when, out of the corner of his eye, he saw someone coming towards him. Beresford broke off and turned to face the newcomer.

He was slightly alarmed when he saw Bernard Kennett, assuming that the works manager had come to scold him on the grounds that, if he was able to play football, he was fit enough to return to his job. In fact, Kennett gave him a welcoming smile tinged with sadness.

'I saw you walk past my window,' he said, 'and guessed that you might be coming here. You have my deepest sympathies, Neil. I was shocked to learn of the death of your wife. Football meant so much to the pair of you.'

'Yes, sir,' said Beresford. 'Shirley was a wonderful all-round athlete but this was the sport at which she excelled.'

'Between you and your wife, you put Hayes Ladies' Team on the map.'

'It wasn't only down to us, Mr Kennett. There were ten other players ready to give blood for the team. Shirley couldn't have scored goals if she hadn't been given a steady supply of the ball.'

'There's a rumour that we may yet take part in the cup final.'

'We'll do more than take part, sir – we'll win the game!'

Beresford's conviction was absolute. His single-mindedness was inspiring. With huge numbers working in the Cartridge Section, Kennett could only know the bulk of them by sight. Neil Beresford was an exception. Because of what he'd done for the reputation of the factory, he was a familiar figure there. Kennett had often spoken to him and they were on friendly terms.

'I had a phone call from Inspector Marmion,' said the works manager. 'He told me that they've identified a prime suspect.'

'I know,' said Beresford. 'I was at Mr Jenks's house when the inspector arrived. It was good of him to show us such consideration.'

'It was reassuring to hear that a culprit had been tracked down but, I must admit, that I'd rather he didn't work here. If this Herbert Wylie really *is* guilty, it will leave a nasty stain on the factory,'

'The police have to catch him first.'

'Inspector Marmion and Sergeant Keedy are both very able.'

'Yes, sir,' said Beresford, 'but Wylie would have had a head start on them. Arranging that explosion would have taken a lot of forethought so he's obviously a calculating man. That means he'd have planned his escape well in advance.'

'There's nowhere for him to hide. Police forces

all over the country will have been put on the alert. There's a full-scale manhunt for Wylie.'

'I still think he'll prove elusive.'

'They'll catch him somehow.'

'What if he's gone abroad?'

'Then they'll go after him,' said Kennett. 'Nothing daunts them. According to Sergeant Keedy, they had two suspects last year who went off to France with their regiment. They were pursued, arrested and brought back to face justice. I have faith in Inspector Marmion and the sergeant. They'll travel *anywhere* to get their man.'

The driver insisted on going. Even though he'd be committing himself to several hours behind the wheel, he wanted to atone for what he felt was his incompetence. Knowing that there was a mechanical fault with the car, he should have reported it and taken an alternative vehicle from Scotland Yard. Fortunately, the car he'd been driving was easily repaired and he was able to pull up outside the police station just before Marmion and Keedy emerged. Startled by the news that they were going to North Wales, he adjusted quickly and volunteered his services. It meant that the detectives could sit together in the rear of the car and discuss the case.

The journey was long, cold and uncomfortable. It was late March and the wind still had considerable bite. Since there was no source of heating in the car, its three occupants were soon shivering when evening plucked all vestiges of light from the sky. With headlamps giving them only restricted vision of the road ahead, they were reduced to a moderate speed. Keedy had the uneasy feeling that they'd never reach their destination.

'This is madness!' he complained. 'We're going to the back-of-beyond in a car that could easily run out of petrol.'

'Orders are orders,' said Marmion. 'Every time we find a petrol station, we'll fill the tank.'

'Why couldn't we go tomorrow in broad daylight?'

'The superintendent can't wait until tomorrow.'

'Then it's Chat who should be freezing his balls off in here and not us. If he wants answers today, let him come and get them. Better still,' he went on, 'why not simply ring this place for the relevant details?'

'He tried that, Joe. What we're after is classified material. It won't be given over a telephone with no safeguards in place. If we want it, we go and get it.'

'What's the place called?'

'Frongoch – it's a former distillery used as a prisoner-of-war camp.'

'Why does it have to be so remote?' said Keedy.

'To make it more difficult for prisoners to escape,' replied Marmion. 'If they do get out, they find themselves in the Merionethshire wilderness.'

'I feel as if *we're* the ones in the wilderness, Harv. If we do have to go there, why didn't Chat send us by train? Surely, it would have been quicker.'

'You're maligning our superintendent unfairly. The first thing he did was to check the timetables and where we'd need to change trains. London to

Frongoch usually takes six hours but it would have taken half as long again this evening. Believe it or not,' said Marmion, 'this is probably the fastest way.'

Keedy grimaced. 'Walking would be faster!'

'Try to be philosophical about it, Joe. There was a time when you liked the adventure of going to strange places and there's nowhere stranger than Frongoch.'

Marmion passed on the information given him by Claude Chatfield. Over twenty-five years earlier, a whisky distillery had been built beside a clear stream near Bala but it had been unable to compete with its Scottish rivals and went out of business. It was taken over at the start of the war and converted into an internment camp for German prisoners. Its isolation and strict regime also recommended it for use as a prison for Irish republicans who'd launched terrorist attacks in mainland Britain.

'So Niall Quinn is being held as a *political* prisoner,' said Keedy.

'That's right.'

'Then it's out of our jurisdiction. This is a case for Special Branch.'

'The superintendent feels that we have an interest as well and he's managed to secure permission for us to speak to the governor. They want Niall Quinn caught by whoever tracks him down first.'

'Supposing that he's hopped on a boat back to Ireland?'

'Why do you keep inventing obstacles for us?'

'Because I think we're on a wild goose chase.'

279

Marmion smiled. 'I'm very partial to the taste of wild goose.'

'I'm serious, Harv. Okay, maybe this Irish hothead likes to set off bombs but there's nothing to connect him with the crime that we're investigating. I know that Sinn Fein are taking advantage of the fact that our police force has been depleted by the war,' said Keedy, 'but why on earth should one of its members take an interest in an obscure pub in Hayes, Middlesex?'

'There's something you ought to know, Joe.'

'What is it?'

'Niall Quinn came over from Ireland with the express purpose of blowing up a stretch of railway line near Uxbridge station. Moreover,' Marmion went on, 'he was arrested at his uncle's house with bomb-making equipment in his possession.' He raised a quizzical eyebrow. 'Now why didn't Eamonn Quinn mention that to us?'

When the meal was over, he sent the children upstairs so that he could talk to his wife in private. Maureen and Lily were glad to run off. Their father was in a surly mood and that never boded well. Left alone with her husband, Diane Quinn had a piece of news to pass on.

'Who told you that?' he asked.

'I met Sadie Radcliffe when I was out shopping.'

'That woman is a witch.'

'Eamonn!' she exclaimed.

'She said some nasty things about Maureen and I'll always remember that. How did she hear about this Herbert Wylie?'

280

'Sergeant Keedy went to see her.'

'Do the police think that he put that bomb in the outhouse?'

'They seem to have good reason to name him as a suspect,' she said, 'and all because Maureen told them about the man. It's a feather in her cap.'

'I'm not happy at the way they keep on at her.'

'They've only been here a few times, Eamonn.'

'They're badgering our daughter,' he argued, 'and she's not in a fit state to be questioned time and again. What if she blurts out something she shouldn't?'

'Maureen wouldn't do that. She has more sense.'

'I'll give her another warning.'

'No, don't do that,' advised Diane. 'She's not feeling well.'

'What's wrong with her?'

'I'm not sure. All I know is that she's been behaving in an odd way since I got back from the shops. Maureen was fine when I left. Well,' she corrected herself, 'as fine as she could be, that is. Later on, she was shaking all over. I thought she'd caught a chill or something and wondered if I should take her to the doctor.'

'No,' he decreed. 'Doctors cost money.'

'We can't let her carry on like that, Eamonn.'

'I didn't see anything wrong with her.'

'Well, I did and it worries me. It's something to do with her mind.'

'That's why I want to keep those detectives at arm's length,' he said, jabbing a finger at her. 'They always ask too many questions. If they

281

keep on and on at her, she might forget what I told her.'

'She won't mention Niall, I promise you.'

'It could be awkward for me, if she did.'

'I don't see why.'

'Use your head, Di,' he chided. 'Niall spent the night here. If the police had found that out, I'd have been in the dock beside him. It was only because I talked my way out of the situation that I didn't get arrested.'

'It might have been safer if you'd turned Niall away.'

'He's family. I got loyalties.'

'He frightened me,' she admitted. 'He's full of such anger at the government. Why does he have to get involved in politics at all? He's Maureen's age. He should be thinking about settling down.'

'Niall has a mission.'

'I know – and it involves killing people.'

'All he was trying to do was to cause a disruption on the railway. He was going to take great care that nobody was hurt. Niall is not a killer, Di. He's a brave lad who sticks by his principles.'

'Yes,' she said, 'but what terrible principles they are. He'll stop at nothing to get what he wants. Why can't he live a normal life like the rest of us?'

Quinn was peremptory. 'There's nothing wrong with what he believes in,' he said, tapping his chest. 'I share his convictions. Ireland has been ground down by the British for far too long. We need people like Niall. More power to his elbow!'

Diane was quietly horrified. She'd never heard him speak like that before.

The installation of the telephone at the Marmion house brought many benefits. It meant, for a start, that he could no longer be hauled out of bed in the small hours by a messenger rapping on the front door. A summons from Scotland Yard could be made by telephone. It also enabled Marmion to contact his colleagues directly from home and to arrange for a driver to pick him up. Yet it remained a novelty to Ellen and she still viewed it with mixed feelings. Its loud ring always unsettled her even when she was expecting a call. The sound caught her off guard that evening and she almost dropped the cake tin she was about to slip into the oven. Putting it on the stove, she wiped her hands on her apron and went into the hall. The ring seemed to have an accusatory note. She lifted the receiver cautiously.

'Yes?'

'It's me, Ellen,' said Marmion.

She relaxed at once. 'Where are you?'

'We're on the other side of the Welsh border. I'm ringing from a police station in a town whose name I wouldn't even try to pronounce. It has no vowels in it.'

'Whatever are you doing in Wales?'

'Joe is cursing the superintendent for sending us here and I'm hoping that it's not a wasted effort. I can't go into details, love. I just wanted to warn you that I'll be back very, very late tonight. Don't wait up for me.'

'I can't sleep properly when you're not here.'

'Try a bit harder. There's a possibility that we may have to spend the night at the camp. In that case, you won't see me until tomorrow.'

'What camp are you talking about?'

'I'll tell you when I see you.'

'Have you got a suspect?'

'We have two at the moment, love, and a third on the horizon.'

'This case is getting more and more complicated.'

'That's its attraction,' he said, breezily. 'It would be far more convenient if we were operating entirely within London but we have to go where the evidence takes us. Is there any news at your end?'

'I knitted another pair of socks today.'

'Well done!'

'Oh – and Alice called in to see me at the centre. That inspector of hers has sent her out on patrol, looking for prostitutes.'

He chortled. 'She'll find plenty of those roaming the streets.'

'It's nothing to laugh at, Harvey.'

'I'm glad, for her sake. Alice will be out in the fresh air and she'll get some experience of the seamy side of life. It will toughen her up.'

'I don't want her toughened up. I want her to stay as she is.'

'We all have to grow and develop, Ellen. Anyway,' he said, 'I must be on my way. Joe sends his love and has made a decision about where he and Alice will spend their honeymoon.'

'Oh, that's good. Where will they go?'

'Anywhere but Wales – that's official.'

He rung off and the line went dead.

Royston Liddle had never felt his weakness so

284

keenly. Convinced that Alan Suggs was responsible for the outrage, Liddle wanted to avenge the deaths of his rabbits but he had neither the strength nor the cunning to do so. All that he could do was to follow the killer whenever he could and watch his every move from the shadows. That way, he could at least direct his hatred at Suggs. The explosion at the pub had been a major event and Liddle had been unable to take in the enormity of it all. The murder of his pets was another matter. It was more personal and direct. In his limited codex, five dead canaries couldn't compete against two dead rabbits.

Having waited for Suggs to return home from work, he hid nearby and kept the house under surveillance. When a light came on in the bedroom, he decided that his quarry had gone upstairs to change out of his working clothes. There was another wait in a doorway while – as he assumed – the driver made himself a meal. Liddle was patient. The longer he stayed out of sight, the darker it was getting. When he finally came out, Suggs was wearing a suit and had changed his flat cap for a trilby. Walking with a swagger, he made his way to the nearest pub and went in for a drink. Liddle could see him through the window, quaffing a pint and chatting to some of the other patrons. At one point, Suggs came over to the window and Liddle had to duck sharply to avoid being seen. It was a false alarm. In fact, Suggs hadn't spotted that he was under scrutiny. Having removed his hat, he used the window as a mirror in which to check his appearance.

Half an hour later, he came out of the pub and

looked in both directions to make sure that he was not observed. He then moved off furtively down a side street until he reached the house on the corner. After a second check that nobody else was about, he knocked on the front door. It was opened almost immediately and he was whisked inside. Royston Liddle gave a silent cackle. Perhaps there was a way to get his revenge, after all.

Silhouetted against the night sky, Frongoch camp looked all the more forbidding. Its high perimeter fence was topped with barbed wire. Guard dogs could be heard barking. The building that had once housed the whisky distillery was now largely given over to staff accommodation. Internees and other prisoners were locked away in crude huts fitted with wooden bunks. It was late when the detectives arrived and they had to show their credentials to the armed guards at the gates before they were let in. The interminable drive along winding roads had been an ordeal for the chauffeur. Left alone in the car, he fell instantly asleep.

Once inside the fence, Keedy's curiosity got the better of his discontent. He looked around with interest, noting the number of armed guards on patrol. Marmion was grateful to be liberated from the car. It had explored every pothole on its way there and he was aching all over. When the visitors were conducted to the governor's office, they rallied at the sight of the bottle of whisky on his desk.

Major Hugh Gostelow was a genial host. He beamed at his guests.

'Welcome to Frongoch, gentlemen,' he said,

cheerily. 'May I offer you something to keep out the cold?'

'Yes, please,' replied Marmion.

Keedy was more wary. 'It isn't *Welsh* whisky, is it?'

'No,' said Gostelow. 'It's the best Scotch – single malt, of course.'

He poured the drinks and handed them to the newcomers, reserving a generous portion for his own glass. After introductions had been made, they all sat down. Tall, angular and still in his forties, the governor had an air of gentlemanly authority. His uniform was impeccable and he was noticeably well groomed.

'What's this all about, Inspector?' he began. 'When I spoke to your superintendent, he only told me what he felt was necessary to get my cooperation.'

Marmion gave him a fuller version of the investigation. When he heard details of the explosion, Gostelow winced. He asked some pertinent questions and thanked the inspector for being so articulate and concise. Then he reached for a folder on his desk and handed it to Marmion.

'That's your man,' he said as the detectives read the file together. 'As you can see, Quinn has packed rather a lot into the twenty years he's been on this planet. The police want him for a string of offences in Dublin and he's suspected of being involved in many Republican activities on this side of the Irish Sea. Pity, isn't it?' he added. 'He's a good-looking young fellow.'

Marmion and Keedy looked at the photograph of Niall Quinn. He had close-cropped dark hair and a faint resemblance to his cousin, Maureen. The scowl on his face couldn't hide the fact that he was arrestingly handsome. He looked older than twenty and his gaze was challenging.

'How did he escape?' asked Keedy.

'It was during the night,' said Gostelow. 'He'd bribed one of the Germans to take his place at roll-call so that we thought he was still with us. It was hours before we found the tunnel. Quinn was a human mole. He'd been working on that tunnel for months, by the look of it.'

'Did nobody else go with him, Major?'

'No it was a solo run.'

'Was a search mounted?'

'Of course it was, Sergeant. We scoured the whole county for him but there are lots of places to hide in Merionethshire. My feeling is that he went to ground somewhere. We know he'd been hoarding food so he wasn't short of rations.' He gave a short laugh. 'The rogue even helped himself to a bottle of my Scotch.'

'He sounds like an enterprising chap,' said Marmion.

'He was, Inspector. When he put his mind to it, he could be quite engaging. It was only a means of camouflage, however. He tried to convince us that he wasn't really so eager to plant bombs in the name of Sinn Fein but we weren't fooled.'

'Do you have many Irish prisoners here?'

'They've increased in number recently and I fancy that we'll have many more. I don't know how conversant you are with events across the water,' said Gostelow, 'but Sinn Fein and the so-called Irish Citizens Army have both stepped up

288

their activities. It's only a matter of time before something really serious happens. My fear is that it will spill over into this country.'

'Do you have room for more prisoners?' asked Keedy.

'Not if they come in substantial numbers. If that's the case, our German guests will have to be moved to Knockaloe Camp on the Isle of Man. That's a shame because most of them are perfectly harmless individuals with the misfortune to have German parentage. The Irish are different. They hate us simply because we're British. If they had the chance to blow Frongoch up, they'd take it.'

Having perused the documents, Marmion handed them back to the governor.

'Thank you,' he said. 'I notice that Niall Quinn was arrested under Defence Regulations.'

'It's a vital tool in a wartime situation,' said Gostelow before taking another sip of his whisky. 'It saves us the time and trouble of going through the courts. DORA has been a boon to us. I know that it produced howls of protest from people who thought their freedom was being taken away, but the Defence of the Realm Act was one of the best pieces of legislation passed by the government.'

'How well did you get to know Quinn while he was here?'

'Oh, it was very well – he made sure of that. Prisoners tend to keep their heads down and keep clear of me but Quinn had the cheek of the devil. He spoke up whenever he had the chance and he was always causing trouble. I had him in here on many occasions to answer charges of various kinds.' Gostelow smiled at the memory. 'He's the only prisoner I've ever met who could be both obsequious and taunting at the same time. He made two failed attempts to escape before he actually did get away. In one sense, I'm glad to be rid of the little so-and-so.'

'What do you think he'll do with his freedom?' asked Keedy.

'Oh, there's a short answer to that, Sergeant,' replied Gostelow. 'He'll go straight back to what he was sent to this country to do – planting bombs.'

'Will they be designed simply to damage property or are they likely to kill people as well?'

'Quinn has no concern for human life. One of the guards overheard him boasting to his friends that he was ready to blow up British men, women and children to achieve his ends – particularly young women.'

'Why is that?'

'They bear children. Murder them and you stop British babies being born.'

Keedy exchanged an uncomfortable glance with Marmion. Both were thinking of Florrie Duncan. They let Gostelow ramble on. Everything they heard about Niall Quinn marked him out as a ruthless and dedicated young man.

'In his file,' said Marmion, 'I saw that he had a few regular visitors.'

'Yes,' said the governor. 'They were Irish Members of Parliament. As soon as we lock up anyone from the Emerald Isle, they're here to protest about poor food, dreadful accommodation, punitive discipline and so on. It's all nonsense, of course, but they feel they have to speak up for their fellow countrymen. What really upsets them, however, is that we limit visits to a mere fifteen minutes.'

'That would upset me as well,' volunteered Keedy. 'It's a hell of a long way to come for a quarter of an hour of conversation.'

'At least, they get to speak to someone, Sergeant. As Members of Parliament, they have that right. People who just roll up at the gates are usually turned away. That's what happened to the first visitor who tried to see Niall Quinn,' explained Gostelow. 'When I knew that you were coming, I looked up his name out of interest.'

'Who was it?' asked Marmion.

'It was his uncle – a Mr Eamonn Quinn.'

CHAPTER NINETEEN

June Ingles was puzzled. At a time when all she could think about was the gruesome murder of their daughter, her husband was talking about selling the house. It disturbed her at a deep level. It not only intruded upon her grief, it suggested that Brian Ingles was not as preoccupied with mourning Florrie's death as he should be. She'd accepted that he was at times arrogant and high-handed but he'd never been so determined to ignore her wishes before. A decision such as moving house was something that ought to be discussed with her in full and at a more appropriate moment. The sense of being disregarded gnawed away at her. The moment that June woke up that morning and saw that her husband was sitting up in bed, she returned to the subject.

'I still don't understand why you went to that estate agent yesterday.'

'I wanted a rough valuation,' he replied.

'Why? We don't need to sell it, Brian, and I certainly don't want to.'

'No more do I.'

'Then what's all the fuss about?'

'It's just a precaution, that's all,' he told her. 'What happened to Florrie has made me think. All the plans we ever had for her disappeared in a flash. And it could happen to either of us, June.' He flicked a hand. 'I don't mean that we're likely to be blown up as she was but there are other reasons for sudden death. We could be killed in a car accident or die from some terrible disease.'

'Don't be so morbid.'

'I'm just being practical. If I were to have a fatal heart attack tomorrow, you'd be in the most awful position. You'd be stuck in this big house with no idea of any outstanding financial commitments. It would be a nightmare. Moving to a smaller property would mean that everything was simplified for you.'

'I'm not a child,' she protested, 'so you can stop patronising me.'

'There'd be money in the bank. You'd have a safety net.'

'But I already have that, Brian. This house is my safety net in every way.'

He got up and drew the curtains on the bay

292

window, peering out to see a fine drizzle falling. A neighbour opposite was setting off to work with an umbrella. The milkman was working his way along the road. A stray dog was prowling.

'Come back to bed,' said June.

'I'm up now.'

'We need to settle this once and for all.'

'No, June,' he snapped. 'It's already settled. There's nothing else to be said.' By way of appeasement, he put a hand on her shoulder. 'I'm sorry to be so short with you but the fact is that I'm the breadwinner here and therefore entitled to make the major decisions about our future.'

'Not without consulting me.'

'You *have* been consulted.'

'No, I haven't,' she said. 'This idea came completely out of the blue. You'd made up your mind before you even spoke to me.'

'Yes – and I've just explained why.'

'This is ridiculous. You're not going to have a heart attack, Brian. At your last check-up, the doctor said that you were as fit as a fiddle. And the chances of either of us being knocked down by a car are very remote.' She hauled herself up and rested against the headboard. 'Something's going on, isn't it? And you're not telling me what it is.'

'I'm just asking you to trust me.'

'Why can't I know the full truth?'

'You already know it, June,' he said. 'Now why don't we stop fighting over this issue and have a cup of tea instead? I'll go and make one.'

'You're doing it again,' she complained. 'As soon as I ask you a question, you either cut me off or find a reason to change the subject. What's going on, Brian?'

'I'm making sensible plans for our future.'

'There's more to it than that.'

'Florrie's death has made me face reality.'

'But you've always done that. What you've never done before is to threaten to sell this lovely house.'

'It's not a threat, June.'

'It sounds very much like it to me.'

He inhaled deeply. 'It's just one option I'm considering,' he said, irritably. 'It may not be necessary. I hope that it isn't. But I wanted to take stock of our situation. Now will you please stop nagging me?'

June brightened. 'So we may be able to stay here, after all?'

'It's ... a strong possibility.' He took his dressing gown off its hook. 'Can I go and get that cup of tea now?'

'Yes, please. You've cheered me up. Thank you, Brian.'

Putting on his dressing gown, he gave her an ambiguous smile and left.

None of them had ever spent a night behind bars before but that's what happened at Frongoch Camp. All three of them had locked up prisoners in the past but it was their turn to be ushered into cells. It was the only accommodation available for Marmion, Keedy and their driver. Each of them was given one of the cells in the segregation unit. Reserved for prisoners who needed to be kept in solitary confinement, they were small, bare and featureless, containing little beyond a bunk, a table bolted to the floor and a chair. Blank walls pressed in upon them, though closer inspection showed that they were not entirely plain. Earlier occupants had scratched their names or their artwork into the rough plaster. There was a plethora of obscenities and, in Harvey Marmion's cell, the name of Niall Quinn was proudly recorded. The Irishman had left his mark on the camp in a number of ways.

The visitors were grateful that they didn't have to face another long drive through the night. Marmion had already warned Ellen that he might not be home until the morrow, Keedy had nobody waiting up for him and their chauffeur, although married, had schooled his wife to accept that he'd be forced to work uncertain hours. All three of them enjoyed a hearty breakfast before being given a quick tour of the camp by Major Gostelow. Security was tight. The dogs were trained to attack. In order to escape, Niall Quinn had shown both courage and ingenuity.

Having entered Wales at night and having endured endless bumps and bends in the road, Joe Keedy had had an unfavourable impression of the country. Daylight helped him to revise his opinion. Early morning mist had been burnt off by the sun and they drove through areas of breathtaking natural beauty. A car was a rare sight in some of the tiny hillside villages so they always got attention and friendly waves. Now that the driver was able to see exactly where he was going, he could avoid the worst hazards along the way.

Marmion remembered the name scratched into

the wall of his cell.

'Niall Quinn is dangerous,' he said.

'We knew that before we set out,' Keedy reminded him. 'I'm not persuaded that we needed to come to Frongoch at all.'

'When did you last drink such an excellent whisky?'

Keedy grinned. 'Yes, I have to confess that it was rather special.'

'So was the experience of being locked up in solitary confinement.'

'My door was left open.'

'I was speaking metaphorically, Joe,' said Marmion. 'As for our visit, I'd say that it might have provided us with another suspect. We learnt that Niall Quinn would have no compunction about blowing up young women.'

'But why would he want to?' asked Keedy. 'And how would he know that the birthday party was taking place in that pub?'

'There's an easy answer to that – his cousin told him.'

'Are you saying that Maureen Quinn *wanted* her friends killed?'

'I'm reminding you that she wasn't there when the bomb went off.'

'Yes, Harv, and we know why. She was unwell.'

'Was she?' Marmion ran a ruminative hand across his chin. 'If she'd been that poorly, she wouldn't have gone to the party in the first place. And she didn't look unwell when we saw her. She was jangled, yes, but who wouldn't be? What I didn't see were any signs of illness.'

'Are you suggesting that she lied to us?'

All I'm saying is that I knew when either of my children was unwell. You only had to look at their faces – Alice, especially. They were either flushed or pale. If they had a temperature, you could spot it straight away.'

'I still can't see Maureen Quinn as part of a conspiracy.'

'Neither can I,' admitted Marmion, 'but she could unwittingly have helped her cousin. She might have mentioned the party and he saw his opportunity.'

'But why blow up five innocent young women?'

'It was to get attention, Joe. Publicity is what Sinn Fein is after and they got plenty of that. Yes,' he went on, anticipating Keedy's rejoinder, 'I know that they didn't claim responsibility. That means nothing. They're out to cause maximum disruption and spread fear. And consider a crucial fact. Someone like Quinn wouldn't see the victims as innocent young women. In his eyes, they're munition workers. Because they make weapons, they symbolise the hold that we have over Ireland.'

'Only some brainless fanatic would think that.'

'Quinn *is* a fanatic.'

'No,' said Keedy, thinking it over, 'I'm not convinced. If an escaped prisoner turned up on Maureen's doorstep, she's more likely to have reported it to the police.'

'What about her father?'

'He's different. He wouldn't lift a finger to help us.'

'Then don't rule his nephew out.'

Keedy was adamant. 'My feeling is that Herbert Wylie is still our best bet.'

'What about the anonymous father of Florrie Duncan's baby?'

'We can't even be certain that there *was* a baby, Harv. At best, it was only guesswork. No,' he continued, *'you* can add Quinn and Florrie's secret lover to your list. It was Maureen who gave us our breakthrough. The culprit is Wylie.'

To burn off some of the energy that was coursing through him, Neil Beresford went for a run that morning, padding around the streets in shorts and singlet. The drizzle had stopped now and a wind had sprung up. He tried hard to still the ugly memories that clouded his mind. He'd got used to the idea that Shirley was a permanent fixture in his life. They'd known each other since school and a long courtship had followed. Married for almost four years, they were looked upon as the ideal couple. Since they worked at the same factory and were key figures in the football team, they were invariably seen together. A vast hole had suddenly opened in Beresford's life and nothing could ever fill it. Though he pushed himself hard, he couldn't outrun the agonising truth that he'd never see his wife again.

The physical effort finally began to sap his energy and make him puff hard. Slowing down as he approached a run of shops, he came to a halt and needed a couple of minutes to get his breath back. Beresford then went into the newsagent and bought a copy of the morning paper. As he stepped back onto the pavement, a car drew up at the kerb and came to a halt. When the engine was switched off, Brian Ingles got out of the vehicle and looked him up and down.

'Good morning!' he hailed.

'Oh, hello,' said Beresford, almost defensively.

'You've been running, I see.'

'I had to get out of the house, somehow. I felt trapped in there.'

'Yes, the associations are powerful, aren't they? Wherever you look, you must be reminded of your wife. It's different with us because Florrie didn't live at home.'

'She told Shirley that she liked her independence.'

'We still saw a lot of her,' said Ingles, airily, 'because she wasn't far away. We've always been a close-knit family.'

It wasn't what Beresford had been told by his wife. He was well aware of the fact that Florrie had been almost estranged from her parents but he didn't dispute Ingles's version. All that he wanted to do was to get away from the other man because he hated people who had a need to dominate a conversation.

'It looks as if the collective burial will go ahead,' said Ingles.

'Does it?' muttered Beresford. 'I'm glad.'

'I think that I was responsible for that. I not only persuaded Agnes Collier's mother, I finally battered down the walls of Reuben Harte's opposition. He's fallen into line with the rest of us.'

'Good.'

'What does it say in the paper?'

'I haven't really looked,' said Beresford, lifting it up so that he could see the front page. 'It's the

299

main story – POLICE NAME PRIME SUS-
PECT.'

'My God!' exclaimed Ingles. 'He did it, I'm
sure. Wylie did it and he'll hang for the crime.
Excuse me,' he went on, moving away. 'I want to
get my own copy and read the details.'

He went into the shop and left Beresford
wondering why the man was in such a buoyant
mood. His daughter had been killed in an explosion yet Brian Ingles was grinning happily as
if she were still alive. Beresford had plenty to
think about on the jog back to his house.

It was a flying visit but Ellen was delighted to see
him. Marmion had returned to the house to
apologise for his absence in the night and to
change his clothing. He gave her very few details
and she didn't press for any. Having him back
under the roof was enough for her. All she wanted
to talk about was their son's return and he found
it easier to agree with everything that she suggested.

'How was Alice when you met her yesterday?'
he asked.

'She's fine in herself, Harvey. Only one thing
worries her.'

'Is it that inspector who's taken a dislike to
her?'

'I think that she can cope with that.'

'So what is it that's troubling her?'

'It's Paul,' she replied. 'He's been told about
Alice and Joe but he's made no comment about it.
That really hurt her. Joe is going to be his brother-
in-law yet Paul couldn't even be bothered to

acknowledge the fact.'

He shrugged. 'Perhaps he didn't even get her letter. Mail does go astray.'

'Alice wouldn't believe that. She thinks that Paul definitely knows.'

'He forgot to mention it, that's all, love. It may be at the forefront of Alice's mind but our son is more interested in fighting the enemy. Family matters don't strike you as so important when you're in that situation.'

'I'd say that they were even more important,' she contended. 'Look how thrilled he was to be given leave. Paul couldn't wait to get back to us. All of his previous letters were about the things he missed here.'

He patted her back. 'It was your cooking that he really missed, Ellen. And he did send his love to Alice in his last letter. Isn't that enough for her?'

'No, Harvey. She thinks that he may support *you*.'

'I'm not taking sides,' he claimed, hands held aloft.

'Yes you are so don't try to pretend otherwise. You still can't accept that Joe Keedy and our daughter are going to be married.'

'It's an established fact – I have to accept it.'

'Then do so graciously.'

'I must be off,' he said, moving away.

She grabbed his arm. 'It would make such a difference to Alice.'

'Our daughter has made her choice, Ellen. I can't change that.'

'Then why can't you make an effort to get used to the idea? Joe Keedy is a good man – nobody

301

knows that better than you. He'll make a fine husband. More to the point, he'll make Alice very happy. Why do you have to cast such a shadow over her happiness?'

Marmion was about to reply when a car horn sounded outside the house.

'My driver has arrived,' he said, kissing her on the cheek. 'Goodbye...'

After the long journey back, Joe Keedy had also wanted to change. He was far more aware of his appearance than Marmion. When he got to his flat, he stripped off, put on fresh underwear and a clean shirt then hung up his crumpled suit and reached for the other one. After straightening his tie in the mirror, he was ready to leave. The car was waiting outside to take him back to Hayes. On their way there, Marmion gave him his orders. When he was dropped off, the first place that Keedy called at was the Quinn house. Answering the door, Diane was not overjoyed to see him.

'Maureen is very tired,' she said. 'She hasn't been getting much sleep.'

'I see.'

'Could you come back another time, Sergeant?'

'I don't need to speak to your daughter, Mrs Quinn,' he told her. 'I only came to have a word with you.'

She was taken aback. 'Oh – why is that?'

'If you let me in, I'll be able to tell you.'

Reluctant to do so, she nevertheless allowed Keedy into the living room. It would mean some harsh words from her husband when he found out but that was unavoidable. They sat down. Hat in his hand, Keedy tried to calm her with a smile.

'Something has come to our attention,' he said, quietly. 'It appears that your husband has a nephew by the name of Niall Quinn.'

Diane started. 'How ever did you find that out?'

'It doesn't matter. It's true, isn't it?'

'Well, yes, but we never see anything of Niall. He lives in Ireland.'

'I think you know that that's not the case, Mrs Quinn. He was arrested a year ago for activities relating to a campaign run by Sinn Fein. He's been imprisoned in a camp in Wales.'

'I did hear some vague rumour about that,' she admitted.

'Your memory is letting you down, I'm afraid. He was caught in this very house with incriminating material in his possession.' Biting her lip, she lowered her head. 'There's no point in denying it, Mrs Quinn.'

'I didn't want him here, Sergeant. He's no relation of mine.'

'How long was he in the house?'

'He just popped in to see us for that one afternoon.'

'So he didn't stay here at all?'

'No,' she said, raising her head.

'I'm sure you know the penalty for harbouring a fugitive.'

Diane was roused. 'We did nothing wrong. When a member of the family knocks on your door, you don't turn him away. Besides, we'd no idea that Niall was involved in ... the things that got him sent to prison. It's unfair of you to make me feel guilty. Anyway,' she added, 'it was a long

303

time ago. I've tried to forget it.'

'Did you know that Niall escaped recently?'

'No, I didn't.'

'He hasn't been in touch, then?'

'I swear that he hasn't,' she said, vehemently. 'If you've come to accuse us of helping him to escape, you might as well leave now. Neither I nor Eamonn had the slightest idea that he'd got out of prison.'

'It's an internment camp called Frongoch. I think you knew that.'

'No, I didn't.'

'But your husband paid a visit there.'

She was bemused. 'When?'

'It was not long after his nephew had been moved there.'

'He never mentioned it to me.'

'Are you sure?'

'I don't even believe that it's true.'

'Oh, there's no question about that, Mrs Quinn,' said Keedy. 'Inspector Marmion and I drove all the way to the camp last night to interview the governor.' She recoiled from the information. 'He told us about your husband's visit. We also discovered what a very nasty young man Niall Quinn was.' Diane was confused and hurt. He could see her flitting between bafflement and discomfort. 'Why didn't your husband tell you that he was going to Wales?'

'I don't know,' she confessed.

'Is he in the habit of keeping things from you?'

'No,' she said, resenting the implication. 'Most of the time I know where Eamonn is. But he does go off with friends from time to time. They have

304

outings. I don't mind that. My husband has a tiring job. He deserves a treat.'

Keedy wanted to ask her why she wasn't allowed an occasional treat herself but he felt that it would be too cruel. Diane clearly knew little about Niall Quinn's movements and had been embarrassed to have him in her house. Evidently, she had no idea why her visitor was even asking about him.

'Is your husband interested in politics?' he asked.

'He never discusses anything like that with me, Sergeant.'

'That wasn't what I asked. Does he go to meetings of any kind?'

'He likes a drink at the pub, that's all.'

'Would that be an exclusively Irish pub, by any chance?'

She hunched defensively. 'What are you getting at?'

'I'm wondering if your husband supports the aims of Sinn Fein.'

'I told you. He never talks about things like that to me.'

'Yet you must have known that Niall was involved in their activities. Did your husband approve of what he was doing or condemn it?'

About to fling back a retort, Diane was checked by the painful memory of her husband's declaration in favour of Irish nationalism. It had been under the surface all the time but it had never burst out like that before. Keedy watched her closely and wondered if he should apply more pressure. He was prevented from doing so by the

305

arrival of Maureen Quinn. Having been listening to them outside the door, she wanted to protect her mother from further questioning.

'What's going on?' she asked. 'Did I hear Niall's name being mentioned?'

It was mid-afternoon when Marmion got to the police station in Hayes. He'd already rung Claude Chatfield from his home to report on their visit to Frongoch and hoped that he wouldn't have to speak to the superintendent again until the end of the day. Yet, as soon as he went into the room he was using as his office, he saw the note left on the table for him. It asked him to contact Scotland Yard immediately. He rang the number and heard the telephone being snatched up at the other end.

'Is that you, Marmion?' asked Chatfield.

'Yes, sir.'

'I expected you to ring earlier than this.'

'I've only just arrived here,' said Marmion. 'The traffic was heavy on the drive here and I had to drop Sergeant Keedy at Maureen Quinn's house.'

'Have you seen this morning's paper?'

'I caught a glimpse, sir.'

'It's done the trick,' said Chatfield, excitedly. 'We've had a response. In fact, we've had several but most of them could be easily discounted as hoax calls. One of them, however, has the ring of truth about it.'

Marmion was alert. 'That's very gratifying, Superintendent,' he said. 'Have you received a tip-off about Herbert Wylie?'

'The tip-off came from the best possible source.'

'Oh – what's that?'

'It was from the man himself, of course. Having seen his name in the paper, he walked into the nearest police station and gave himself up.'

'Are they *sure* it's Wylie?'

'They are,' said Chatfield, 'and so am I. As he was being described to me, I was looking at that photograph you obtained from the works manager. In every detail, the description fitted him.'

'What about his voice?' asked Marmion. 'If he came from Sheffield, he'd have had a Yorkshire accent.'

'He's got one.'

'Where is he being held?'

'He's at Rochester police station. I think that congratulations are in order,' the superintendent continued. 'It was down to you and Sergeant Keedy that this man was identified. That was good detective work.'

'Thank you, sir,' said Marmion, savouring a rare compliment.

'Well, off you go, then. Drive straight to Rochester and take this man into custody. When his confession has been verified and he's been formally charged, I can release the information to the press.' He gave a ripe chuckle. 'Herbert Wylie is waiting for you. Go and get him.'

CHAPTER TWENTY

Staring at the notepad on the kitchen table, Neil Beresford was so engrossed in what he was doing that he didn't hear the knock on the front door. It was only when there was a much louder knock that he sat upright. His mother had a key so it couldn't be her and he wasn't expecting any visitors. After the initial burst of sympathy from his immediate neighbours, he'd been left completely alone and he valued the freedom. His first thought was that it must be the detectives calling on him. When he opened the door, however, it was the anxious face of Jonah Jenks that confronted him.

'Hello, Mr Beresford,' said the visitor. 'I wonder if I might have a word.'

'Yes, yes, of course you can. Come on in, Mr Jenks.'

Jenks followed him into the kitchen and they sat on either side of the table. Since he'd only met the man once before, Beresford wondered why he'd called. Arrangements for the funerals had been finalised so there was no need for further discussion. Jenks seemed unwilling to explain the reason for his visit. Looking down at the notepad, he saw the list of names in a triangular pattern on the page.

'I've obviously come at an inconvenient time,' he said.

'Not at all,' said Beresford. 'I was just working out the team for the cup final.'

Jenks was startled. 'It's still going ahead?'

'My mind is set on it.'

'But in the circumstances...'

'If we pull out now, we hand the cup to Wool-wich and I'm damned if we're going to do that. They're going to have to fight for it. Mind you,' he went on, 'I really ought to give them an apology. When that bomb went off, I was too quick to think that they had something to do with it and it was wrong of me. According to Inspector Marmion, they had no connection with it at all. He sent some of his men to Woolwich to investigate and that was their conclusion.'

Jenks indicated the notepad. 'Why are the names separated like that?'

'I can see that you're not a football fan, Mr Jenks.'

'To be honest, I know very little about sport of any kind.'

'This is the formation,' explained Beresford, pointing to the names in turn. 'We have the goal-keeper here at the back. Then we have two full-backs with three halfbacks in front of them. These five players here are the forwards. As a result of what happened, I've been forced to make some changes.'

'But you've still got one player left from that bomb blast,' Jenks reminded him. 'Maureen Quinn survived the explosion. I remember Enid telling me that she was a very good goalkeeper. At least, you have her in your team.'

'No, I don't. It would be too much to ask of her.'

'But she might *want* to play.'

'She won't have the chance,' said Beresford. 'For her own sake, I'm not selecting Maureen. The pressure on her would be immense. Now, then,' he went on, 'what did you come to see me about?'

Jenks cleared his throat. 'It was that visit from the inspector.'

'I thought he gave us good news. They have a suspect.'

'Yes, but only because of his link with my daughter. Can you imagine how dreadful that makes me feel? I had no idea, Mr Beresford – none at all. What kind of father does that make me?'

'Don't be too hard on yourself,' said Beresford, moved by his obvious distress. 'It was something that Enid didn't feel able to confide in you, that's all.'

'But why – what's wrong with me?'

'The fault may have been with her, Mr Jenks.'

'She deceived me,' said the other, solemnly. 'That's what I can't accept. Enid was the soul of honesty yet she told me a lie to hide the fact that she was going out with this man.'

'Perhaps she felt that you'd object.'

'I most certainly would have done so.'

'Then she was forced to deceive you.'

'And look what her deception has led to!' wailed Jenks. 'If she'd felt able to approach me in the first place, she'd still be alive and so would your wife.'

Beresford reacted as if from a pinprick. 'There's no way of knowing that,' he said. 'This man, Wylie, pursued her because she rebuffed him. Telling you

310

about him wouldn't have stopped him doing that.'

'Yes, it would. I'd have warned him off.'

'He doesn't sound like a man who'd pay attention to warnings. From what the inspector told us, Wylie was in the grip of an obsession. You couldn't have frightened him off with a few stern words.'

As he battled with unpleasant memories, Jenks looked even more anguished.

'Do you have any children?' he asked.

'No, Mr Jenks.'

'Then you can't really understand what it feels like.'

'That's probably true,' said Beresford with irritation. 'But, if that's all you came to tell me, I'm afraid that I have work to get on with.'

'Don't send me off,' pleaded Jenks. 'What I really came for was information. I know it will be very painful but I'd like to hear it all the same. You told me that Enid confided in your wife that this man was hounding her at work and elsewhere. I know that my daughter was friendly with Shirley. What exactly did your wife tell you?'

Marmion took pity on his chauffeur. Having subjected the man to two marathon drives, he elected to go to Rochester by train instead. In the event, it was a quicker mode of travel. Having returned to London, he and Keedy changed trains and headed down into Kent. The sergeant was optimistic. Since he'd decided that Herbert Wylie was the man who'd caused the explosion, he was delighted that they were finally about to meet him. Marmion, as always, was more cautious.

'It sounds too good to be true, Joe,' he said.

'The only thing that sounds too good to be true is hearing Chat giving us three cheers for our excellent work,' said Keedy. 'Getting praise out of him is like getting blood out of a stone.'

'It's the confession that worries me.'

'Criminals are not all hard-hearted monsters. Some have a conscience.'

'Then why didn't it prompt Wylie to hand himself in earlier? If he was sorry for what he'd done, he could have come straight to Scotland Yard.'

'You've got to remember the state he must have been in,' argued Keedy. 'He planted that bomb in order to kill Enid Jenks. Once the explosion was over, he'd done what he set out to do and fled the scene. That makes sense, doesn't it?'

'Yes – up to a point.'

'It was only when he'd had time to reflect on it that he realised there'd been other victims. Beforehand, that wouldn't have troubled him. They were simply incidental casualties. Afterwards, however,' said Keedy, 'he came to see them as real human beings whose lives he'd ended needlessly.'

'You could be right,' conceded Marmion, 'but I reserve my judgement.'

'Can't you enjoy a bit of luck when you see it, Harv?'

'All that I see is a possibility – and it's no more than that – of an arrest. Even if it is Wylie, there's no guarantee that he was actually the bomber.'

'Why else should he confess to the crime?'

'We'll soon find out, Joe.'

Having been to Rochester before, Marmion

made sure that they sat on the right-hand side of the compartment so that they had a good view of the River Medway as it curved in a graceful arc towards the town. On the other side of the river were the ruins of the Norman castle with its tower soaring up into the sky. Beyond it was the cathedral, a structure notable for its solidity rather than for any architectural majesty. Rochester was a quaint little town with a number of half-timbered old houses and with close associations with Charles Dickens. It was Keedy's first visit but he saw none of its abundant attractions. As soon as they left the train, they went straight to the police station and introduced themselves.

The detectives were shown the signed statement made by the man claiming to be Wylie. It was short and explicit, naming all five of the victims. Marmion and Keedy were conducted along a passageway to an interview room. The door was unlocked for them and they were left alone with the prisoner. He was sitting with his arms resting on the table in front of him and barely lifted his eyes to them. He looked slightly broader than he had been in the photograph of him but there was a definite resemblance to the man on the works outing. There was the same grim expression and the same strange intensity about him.

They sat in the two vacant chairs and appraised him. He remained motionless. Marmion performed the introductions and warned him that everything he said would be taken down. Keedy produced a notebook and pencil. The interrogation began on a relatively calm note.

'What's your name?' asked Marmion.

313

'Herbert Wylie,' replied the man.

'Can you prove it?'

'Why should I lie to you?'

'Do you have any form of identification on you?'

'No, I don't.'

'Why is that?'

'I threw everything away when I left Hayes,' said the other. 'I wanted to start a new life with a different name. That's why I came here.'

His northern accent was faint but unmistakable, his voice heavy with remorse.

'Did you plant a bomb in the outhouse of the Golden Goose?'

'Yes, I did, Inspector.'

'Why did you do it?'

'I wanted to kill someone.'

'The bomb killed five young women. Was that your intention?'

'I can't remember. It's all scrambled in my mind now. When I placed that bomb there, I knew what I wanted. Afterwards, it was different.'

'Where were you born?'

'Sheffield.'

'Where did you work?'

'At the Hayes munition factory – I was in the Cartridge Section.'

'How long had you been there?'

'I got a job there soon after it opened.'

'Where did you live?'

'I rented a room from an old lady.'

'What was her name?'

'It was Mrs Armadale.'

'Right,' said Marmion, raising his voice. 'Almost everything you've told me so far could have been found in the newspapers. Let's see how well informed you are about people and events that have *not* been in the public domain.'

'I'm Herbert Wylie,' insisted the other. 'What more do you need to know?'

'Did your landlady wear spectacles?'

'Yes, she did.'

'How did you get into that outhouse?'

'That would be telling.'

'What's the name of the works manager?'

'The only thing that matters is *my* name, isn't it? I'm Herbert Wylie, the man who planted a bomb. Arrest me for the crime. Put my picture in the papers. Tell everyone what I did.'

'What you did,' said Marmion with utter disgust, 'is to waste our time and distract us from the search for the real killer. You're not Wylie,' he added, rising to his feet. 'You're just a pathetic little creature who wants the perverse thrill of being regarded as a mass murderer.'

'It's not true!' exclaimed the man, thumping the table. 'I'm Herbert Wylie.'

'Then you should know that Mrs Armadale doesn't wear spectacles. She told us how particular her lodger was about cleaning his shoes.' He glanced down at the man's dirty boots. 'Oh, you'll be arrested and charged, I promise you, but not as the killer you're pretending to be.'

It was too much for the man. Pulsing with fury, he jumped up and swung a fist at Marmion. It was easily parried. Before he could throw a second punch, he was overpowered by Keedy who leapt up and grappled with him before slamming him against a wall. It took all resistance out of the man. The commotion brought two uniformed constables into the room.

'Lock him up,' said Keedy, handing him over. 'And find out his real name.'

The man was still yelling at the top of his voice as they dragged him out.

'I had a horrible feeling that we'd find someone who simply craved attention,' said Marmion with a resigned smile. 'His statement gave him away.'

'How?'

'He was so eager to convince us that he set off that bomb that he listed all five victims. The real Herbert Wylie wouldn't have done that. He probably didn't even know all the names. The one person he was interested in was Enid Jenks. The others didn't matter.'

'I should have realised that,' admitted Keedy.

'Yes, Joe, you should have. As a penance, you can be the one to ring the superintendent to break the bad news to him.' Marmion gave him a friendly pat. 'Don't forget to wear ear plugs. He can be vindictive.'

At the end of a taxing day, Alan Suggs clocked off at the factory and walked home. Having driven his lorry considerable distances at work, he was glad to be back on his feet again. As he was going through the factory gates, another shift was streaming towards him. He spotted a pretty young woman with dimpled cheeks and a full figure. When she saw him grinning at her, she turned away and quickened her step. Their friendship had been brief and, on her side, demeaning. Suggs, however, had stirring memories of their time together and he celebrated them with a guffaw. It was a long walk back to his house but he moved along with alacrity. Behind him was the world of work; ahead of him was a night of pleasure.

His route took him past the Golden Goose and he saw Royston Liddle lurking nearby. He couldn't resist the opportunity to taunt him.

'Shouldn't you be at home feeding your rabbits?' he asked with a smirk.

'I can't,' said Liddle, 'and you know why.'

'I haven't a clue what you're talking about, Royston.'

'You killed them.'

Suggs feigned righteous indignation. 'That's a downright lie!'

'I can't prove it but I know it.'

'You'd better be careful what you're saying.'

'It's the truth.'

'Come out with nonsense like that and everyone will know that you've lost what little sense you have. That means only one thing,' he said, menacingly. 'They'll lock you up in the lunatic asylum. Best place for you, if you ask me.'

Liddle was wounded. 'I don't belong in an asylum.'

'Then stop making stupid accusations.'

'Everybody talks to me proper, Alan. Why can't you?'

'Because I think you're a streak of shit with as much use as a dead rabbit.'

'That's cruel!' whined Liddle, backing away.

'Keep out of my way.'

Pushing him roughly aside, Suggs strode on, his

derisive laughter echoing along the street. In the gathering gloom, he didn't realise that Liddle waited for a while then followed him at a distance. The driver went through his usual routine. He let himself into his house, washed in the kitchen sink then went upstairs to get changed. When he came back down, he cooked himself a frugal meal then spent minutes in front of the mirror with a comb, slicking his hair down and admiring himself. Slipping on his coat and hat, he left the house and went straight to the pub. Over a pint of beer, he was soon trading coarse jokes with some of the other patrons.

Offered a fresh drink by a friend, he glanced at the clock on the wall and declined the offer. Suggs drained his glass in one last gulp and left. As before, he checked to see that nobody else was about. His walk became more furtive now and he kept glancing over his shoulder. When he reached his destination, he had one last look up and down. Satisfied that he was unobserved, he was about to knock on the door when he saw that it was slightly ajar. The invitation could not be more obvious. Responding to the show of readiness, he let himself in and shut the door behind him before bolting it. He walked down the passageway and went into the room at the rear of the house. Back turned to him, she was waiting. Suggs was disappointed. She was fully dressed. He clicked his tongue.

'Somebody forgot her promise, didn't she?' he said, warningly. 'You'll be sorry for that. You know I love to look before I touch.'

As he walked towards her, she turned slowly around to face him. The sight of her face stopped him in his tracks. Both eyes were blackened and there were dark bruises on her temples. A trickle of blood from her nose had dried in place.

Hearing a noise behind him, he tried to turn round but he was too slow even to see his attacker. The first blow sent him reeling and the second battered him to the ground. He was kicked, stamped on and belaboured with a pick handle. Long before the assault had ended, he lost consciousness. When it was all over, he was dragged along the passageway. The front door was opened and Suggs was thrown out bodily onto the hard pavement, collecting fresh wounds on impact. He lay there in a pool of blood that slowly increased in size. It was the last tryst at that particular address.

There was quiet laughter in the darkness.

After their futile visit to Rochester, they returned by train to London, then were driven out to Hayes again. Herbert Wylie remained their chief suspect but Marmion wasn't ready to discount the other two people who came into the reckoning. Niall Quinn still interested him and there was the putative father of Florrie Duncan's child. Since the pregnancy was not confirmed, the detectives decided to call on a person who might be able to help them. Reuben Harte gave them an ungracious welcome but he did at least let them into the house. However, he took care not to invite them to sit down. The conversation took place in the middle of the living room with the three of them standing in a triangle.

'What do you wish to know, Inspector?' he asked.

'How close was your daughter to Florrie Duncan?'

'They were very close. I told you that.'

'Did Jean often talk about her?'

'Naturally,' said Harte. 'They worked side by side and spent a lot of their spare time together. Jean talked about her all the time. Florrie was always up to something, not least trying to organise the women into a union.'

'Was there much opposition to that at the factory?' asked Marmion.

'A great deal of opposition, Sergeant. No boss likes to be told that he's not paying his workers enough or that their working conditions are appalling. It would be bad enough coming from a male employee. Coming from a woman, it would have been even harder to take.'

'Mr Kennett implied that,' recalled Keedy. 'He and Florrie had a couple of brushes, apparently. While he liked her as a woman, he probably detested her as the spokesperson for the other women – even though he'd be too polite to show it.'

'I'm more interested in what Florrie did away from the factory,' said Marmion. 'If the photos of her are anything to go by, she was a striking young woman. Is that correct, Mr Harte?'

'Oh, yes – no camera could catch her vitality, Inspector.'

'That must have made her a target for the men at the factory.'

'She was always getting approaches from them but Jean said that she just shrugged them off with a laugh.'

'Did that go for *all* of them, sir?'

'What do you mean?'

'Well, her husband died some time ago,' said Marmion, 'and she'd got used to the idea of being a widow. Florrie must have reached the point where she started to look at other men with interest again. She couldn't stay in mourning for ever.'

'She didn't,' said Harte. 'Her natural ebullience wouldn't allow it.'

'There's a social club attached to the factory, isn't there?' noted Keedy.

'That's right, Sergeant.'

'Did Florrie and your daughter ever go there?'

'Yes, they enjoyed an evening there on occasion.'

'So they would have met plenty of men.'

'If you're insinuating that my daughter was looking for someone to replace her fiancé,' said Harte, bristling, 'then you're quite wrong. Jean will only ever love one man and that was Maurice.'

'What about Florrie Duncan?'

Harte was about to terminate the conversation and send them on their way when he was reminded of something. It took him a moment to gather his thoughts. They could hear the pain in his voice as he talked about the fatal birthday party.

'There might have been somebody,' he said, thoughtfully, 'but if there was, then I don't think it came to anything. At least, that's the conclusion I'd draw. Jean passed on a remark that Florrie had made to her. It meant nothing to me at the time but – in view of what you're asking – I fancy it may be relevant.'

321

'What was the remark she made to your daughter?' asked Marmion.

Harte winced. 'I feel embarrassed to be talking about such things, Inspector.'

'I can understand that, sir.'

'Do you have children?'

'Yes, I have two – a son and a daughter.'

'Then I daresay that you'd feel awkward, discussing what goes on in your daughter's private life.'

Marmion said nothing. Standing next to Keedy, he felt more than awkward. During a critical period, he'd been excluded from Alice's private life and it rankled. He upbraided himself for his lapse into self-pity. Harte had lost a beloved daughter in the most horrific way. All that Marmion had done was to experience the humiliation of being deceived by Alice and Keedy. A sense of proportion was needed. Beside their host's plight, Marmion's was negligible. Reuben Harte was a father with a wound that would never heal.

'I'm sorry to put you in this position,' said Marmion, 'but any information you have about Florrie Duncan is of interest to us. What was the remark that she made to your daughter?'

'She said that she was going to drink herself into oblivion at the party.'

'Isn't that what we all do on our birthdays?' asked Keedy with a grin.

'Not in Florrie's case – she was quite abstemious, actually.'

'Everyone lets themselves go at a party.'

'I don't, Sergeant, and neither did my daughter.'

322

'How do you interpret the remark?' wondered Marmion.

'I can only hazard a guess at what she meant, Inspector.'

'So?'

'It could have meant that she was planning to drink heavily in order to forget something. Alcohol can be a good sedative if you're mourning a loss. I've found that out.'

'If there *had* been a man in Florrie's life,' suggested Keedy, 'then she'd have celebrated her birthday party with him, wouldn't she?'

'Good point,' said Marmion.

'Or the remark could simply have meant that it was the last time all six of them would be together,' said Harte. 'That's why Florrie was going to overindulge. It was because there'd never be an occasion like that again.'

'Why not, sir?'

'She was going to leave the factory soon.'

'Nobody told us about that.'

'Jean was the only person she confided in and it rocked my daughter. She hated the thought of losing her. I can't think why Florrie would even consider leaving. She was part and parcel of the factory.'

'I wonder if her parents knew about her plans,' said Marmion.

'It's unlikely. They weren't on the best of terms with Florrie.'

'So we gather.'

'She went out of her way to shock them sometimes.'

Marmion smiled. 'I can imagine that they'd be

easily shocked.'

'I don't flatter myself that I've been a good father,' said Harte, soulfully, 'but I've made a far better fist of it than Brian Ingles. Although we had differences, Jean and I were always able to talk, whereas he more or less drove his daughter away from that big house of theirs. Ingles is not so high and mighty as he appears,' he said with a sly grin. 'I learnt something about him today that I didn't know.'

'What was that, sir?'

'A colleague of mine from the bank called to offer his condolences and see how I was.' He lowered his voice. 'I'm telling you this in strictest confidence, mark you.'

'Yes, of course,' said Marmion.

'We won't breathe a word,' added Keedy.

'It will show Ingles in a very different light,' said Harte. 'In spite of the lordly way he behaves, he's in no better position than we ordinary mortals. He loves to give the impression of being well off but, according to my colleague, he took out a huge loan at the bank and is having trouble paying it back.'

Maureen Quinn found herself alone that evening. Her father had gone out to the pub and her mother had taken Lily to visit the children's aged grandmother. Not wishing to leave the house, Maureen remained in her room, reflecting on what Father Cleary had said to her and reading passages from the Bible that he'd recommended. Though the exercise gave her a measure of solace, it could not assuage the feeling of guilt. The in-

324

quest and the funerals would be separate ordeals but there was also her return to the factory to contemplate. Maureen would be stared at as a freak, the sole survivor of a grisly event that would lodge in the collective mind. In the wake of the explosion, she'd had a weird urge to go back to work but she wondered now if she'd ever do so. It would never be the same again. Every time she went through the factory gates, she'd think of her five missing friends. No amount of prayer could obliterate frightening memories.

A banging noise from the garden caught her attention. She looked through the window but could see nothing in the dark. Going downstairs, she picked up the little torch in the kitchen then inched the back door open. She scanned the tiny garden but the beam was too weak to be of any real use. Yet she was sure that someone or some animal was there. When she heard a second noise, she realised that it came from the ramshackle shed. Moving the beam of the torch onto it, she saw that the door had swung partly open. The last time that the latch had slipped, a cat had climbed over the fence and got into the shed, knocking over some flowerpots. Assuming that the same thing had happened again, she went out and opened the shed door wide.

'Shoo!' she cried out.

It was the only sound she was allowed to make because a figure was instantly conjured out of the darkness. Before she knew what was happening, Maureen was grabbed firmly and a hand was clapped over her mouth.

CHAPTER TWENTY-ONE

Back at the police station in Hayes once more, Marmion and Keedy reviewed the situation. It was mid-evening but they were loath to call it a day and return home. New developments had set their minds working and given them fresh energy. While both of them were annoyed about the impostor who'd lured them on a pointless journey to Rochester, the incident had proved one thing. The plea for information about the whereabouts of Herbert Wylie had been widely circulated and prompted a response. The impostor was only one of a number of people who'd contacted the police. According to Claude Chatfield, more people had come forward throughout the day to claim sightings of the missing man. When he'd rung the superintendent to tell him about their setback in Rochester, Keedy had heard about information that had come in from places as far apart as Torquay, Bradford and Perth. The claims were being investigated by local police. Only when the evidence was compelling would the detectives be dispatched again from their base in Middlesex. With the whole nation on the alert, their suspect could not elude them for ever.

Herbert Wylie was at the top of their list. Marmion had put Niall Quinn in second place but had now dropped him down to third position. After their visit to Reuben Harte, both he and

Keedy felt sure that Florrie Duncan had been involved in a romance at one point and that the man concerned was almost certainly employed at the munitions factory. She would not have been the first single woman there who'd become pregnant. Hasty wartime marriages would have been arranged in some cases but that was not an option available to Florrie – or so it appeared. The man in question might well have wished to get rid of the unwanted problem completely.

'Why did she decide to leave the factory?' asked Marmion.

'The answer is that she had to go before the baby became too obvious,' said Keedy. 'Although they were very close, she didn't confide that in Jean Harte. It was Agnes Collier who noticed the signs. She was the only mother in the group.'

'There is another explanation, Joe.'

'I don't see it.'

'Well, if the man worked at the factory, Florrie might have been embarrassed to go on seeing him every day. A blighted romance can leave you feeling sensitive.'

Keedy chuckled. 'Do you speak from experience, Harv?'

'No,' said the other, pointedly, 'I don't. As men, we tend to have it easy. We not only have a monopoly on making the first move, we usually set the pace. If things don't happen the way certain men want, they back away. Look at Alan Suggs, for instance. He picks women up and casts them aside all the time.'

'I don't think Florrie Duncan would fall for someone like that.'

'Maybe not, but the factory could still hold unpleasant memories for her. She'd want to leave in order to put them behind her.'

Keedy was sceptical. 'That doesn't ring true, Harv,' he said. 'Remember what everyone told us about Florrie. She was a fighter. If it was only a case of a blighted romance, then she'd be more likely to drive the man concerned out of the factory than quit her own job. Then, of course, there was that remark about drinking herself into oblivion.'

'Yes, that could be significant.'

'It reminded me of a woman I arrested when I was on the beat. She was roaring drunk and swearing at passers-by. I had to manhandle her to get her back to the station,' recalled Keedy. 'She was barely seventeen, far too young for strong drink. I had to feel sorry for her. When she'd recovered, she told me her story.'

'Was she pregnant, by any chance?'

'It was worse than that, Harv. She'd got hold of the idea that if she drank enough, she could actually get rid of the baby. Instead of that, she ended up with a terrible headache and a charge of being drunk and disorderly.'

'And she was still carrying the child.'

'Yes.'

'That can't have been the reason that Florrie Duncan reached for the bottle,' said Marmion. 'She was a married woman. She'd know that you can't secure an abortion that way.'

'As a married woman,' said Keedy, 'you'd expect her to know something about contraception as well.'

The comment brought the exchange to a stop. Marmion was keenly aware of the situation in their private life. As a healthy and passionate man in his thirties, Keedy was more or less bound to have had sexual experience in his earlier relationships. It raised the question of whether or not he and Alice had been to bed together. Though he did his best not to think about it, the question kept popping up at random to jab away at Marmion. He forced himself to resume the conversation.

'The person we really need is Agnes Collier,' he said.

'Why is that?'

'She could have told us exactly why she thought Florrie was pregnant.'

'It was just a feeling she had – that's what she told her mother, anyway.'

'Who else did she tell?'

'What do you mean?'

'I'm wondering if Agnes spoke to anybody else about it.'

'There's one obvious candidate,' said Keedy, 'and it's Maureen Quinn.'

'They saw a lot of each other and travelled to work together every day. Also, they were the only two members of the group who didn't live in Hayes.' He got up from his seat. 'I can well imagine Agnes saying something to her friend.'

'Where are you going?'

'I'm going to call on Maureen,' said Marmion, 'and you're coming with me.'

'The Quinn family won't be pleased to see us.'

'This is a murder investigation, Joe. I don't care

329

if they barricade themselves in and pour boiling oil down on us. Whatever it takes, I mean to speak to Maureen.'

Before he could move, however, the telephone rang.

When she'd been grabbed in the dark, Maureen Quinn had been seized with a feeling of shock and pain. There was worse to come. She was hustled into the house and warned not to scream because her attacker meant no harm. In fact, he apologised for frightening her. It was her cousin, Niall Quinn. She didn't recognise him at first. He had thick stubble on his face and his hair was much longer than she remembered. In the year they'd been apart, he'd changed a lot. What had remained, however, was the beguiling lilt in his voice and the sense of purpose that he radiated. Niall was a very determined young man.

'I didn't mean to scare you, Maureen,' he said.

'What are you *doing* here?' she demanded. 'I know that you escaped because the police told us you had. It's dangerous for you to come here, Niall.'

'I wasn't intending to stay.'

'You were somewhere in Wales, weren't you?'

'That's right. It was a nasty place called Frongoch. I was honest with them. The moment they locked me up, I warned them that they wouldn't be able to hold me.' He smiled at her. 'Aren't you glad that I got free?'

'I'm not sure,' she confessed.

'I'm your cousin, Maureen. Blood is thicker than water.'

'It terrifies me, having you here like this.'

'I was only intending to come and go without disturbing any of you. If you hadn't come out to the shed, you'd never have known I was even there.'

She was nonplussed. 'I don't understand.'

'I came back for something,' he told her. 'I hid it in the shed when I was here last time. The police carried out a search when they arrested me but they never found the hiding place.'

'What did you put in there, Niall?'

He produced a gun from inside his jacket. 'It was this.'

When he held it up, Maureen almost fainted. Seeing her distress, he thrust the weapon out of sight again. It was too much for her. Maureen wished that she hadn't reacted to the noise she heard from the garden. The news that a gun had been hidden in the garden shed all this time unnerved her. She knew that Niall had been arrested for trying to plant a bomb and she'd believed his claim that nobody would have been harmed by the explosion. The possession of a gun couldn't be so easily explained away. It turned her cousin into a potential killer because she sensed that he'd be ready to use the weapon. Maureen had immediate proof of the fact. The sound of the front door key being inserted into the lock made her jump but it had a more dramatic effect on Niall. Fearing discovery, he drew the weapon once again.

'It's only us!' called Diane as she entered the house.

Realising there was no danger, Niall put the gun

quickly inside his jacket again. A moment later, Diane came into the kitchen with her younger daughter. She froze when she saw the stranger there.

'It's Niall,' said Maureen.

'Dear God!' exclaimed Diane.

'I thought you were in prison,' said Lily, goggling at him.

'Go upstairs.'

'But I want to talk to Niall.'

'Go upstairs to your room now!' ordered Diane, easing the girl through the door. 'This doesn't concern you.'

Lily went off reluctantly, leaving her mother to assess the situation.

'Your uncle will have to be told,' she decided.

'I wasn't meaning to stay,' said Niall.

'You can't stay. Maureen will explain while I go and fetch Eamonn. He'll know what to do.' She looked him up and down. 'I know you're family, Niall, but you've come at a very bad time.' She moved away. 'I won't be long.'

Niall turned to his cousin and gave her a winning smile.

'What is it you need to explain to me, Maureen?'

Before they left the police station in Hayes, they were delayed by a long telephone call from Scotland Yard. The superintendent wanted to defend his position. While exonerating himself from the charge of having sent them to Rochester on a fool's errand, he reserved the right to criticise them for their naivety in believing that they were

332

off to arrest their prime suspect. When Marmion told him they were seeking confirmation that Florrie Duncan might have been pregnant, he took care not to mention contraception. The subject was anathema to a strict Roman Catholic like the superintendent. While he didn't put it into words, he was very unsympathetic towards Florrie's predicament, clearly blaming it on the sin of having sexual intercourse outside marriage. When the call finally ended, Marmion rubbed his ear.

'I've just listened to a sermon,' he complained. 'I'm surprised that Chat doesn't have a pulpit erected in his office.'

'You should have known better than to let him get on to religion.'

'I couldn't stop him, Joe.'

'He roasted me earlier on,' said Keedy. 'Now it was your turn.'

'Let's be off before he rings again,' said Marmion, reaching for his hat. 'We need to get to Maureen's house before she goes to bed.'

They went out to their car and the driver set off. For most of the journey they travelled in silence, each wrapped up in his own thoughts. The purpose of their visit was to establish that Florrie Duncan was pregnant but it was something else altogether that made Keedy eventually speak.

'What Mr Harte told us was very interesting,' he said.

'Yes,' agreed Marmion. 'We learnt a little more about Florrie Duncan.'

'It was the bit about her father that surprised me. Brian Ingles goes out of his way to impress

people. You'd think he was rolling in money.'
Keedy turned to him. 'Why should he need a
large loan from the bank?'

Eamonn Quinn was very unhappy about being
dragged out of the pub and having to leave an
unfinished pint of beer on the table. The sight of
his wife urging him to leave drew sniggers from
the other men. Once outside, Diane told him
why she was there and his ire subsided at once.
They hurried back to the house to find Niall and
Maureen in the living room. Quinn shook his
nephew's hand.

'It's always good to see you, Niall,' he said, 'but,
as Maureen will have told you, this is not the
ideal moment to call on us.'

'Say the word, Uncle Eamonn, and I'll be off.'

'You can stay the night, if you need to.'

'That's asking for trouble!' cried Diane.

'Keep out of this, woman.'

'Remember what happened last time.'

'I told you to keep out of it, Di,' he snarled.

'It's better for everyone if I just go,' said Niall.

'Yes, it is,' added Maureen.

'I don't want to cause any problems for you all.
I'm on the run. If I'm caught on your property,
you could face a spell in prison yourself.'

Quinn was perplexed. Common sense told him
to let his nephew go but family loyalty had a
bigger pull. He was ready to take the risk of keeping Niall there.

'It's why you came to us, isn't it?' he asked,
clapping his nephew on the shoulder. 'You knew
that you could rely on us.'

'Niall only came to get something,' said Maureen. 'He hid a gun here.'

Diane gasped. 'A gun!'

'They're after me,' said Niall. 'I need to defend myself It was hidden under the floor in the garden shed. I nailed the wood back down again.'

'This changes everything, Eamonn,' said his wife. 'He can't stay here with a gun. Think of the consequences.'

'Calm down,' ordered Quinn. 'Flying into a panic will get us nowhere.'

'Get him out of here, that's all I ask.'

'P'raps it would be all for the best,' said Niall.

He stiffened as he heard a car draw to a halt outside the house. His hand went instinctively to the gun. Maureen drew back the curtain to peep out.

'It's Inspector Marmion and the sergeant,' she said.

Quinn took charge. 'Right,' he said. 'Get upstairs, Niall. You can go into Maureen's room. The detectives are not here about you. They're only interested in the explosion in that pub.' Niall scampered off upstairs. Quinn turned to his wife and daughter. 'You stay in here. I'll get rid of them.'

Shutting them into the living room, he went to the front door. As soon as he heard a knock, he flung it open and blocked the doorway with arms folded.

'Can't you give us a moment of peace?' he demanded.

'We'd like to speak to Maureen, please,' said Marmion. 'And before you tell me that she's gone

335

to bed, I should warn you that we saw her clearly when she pulled back the curtain just now.'

'You can't talk to her.'

'You can't stop us, Mr Quinn.'

'What are you going to do?' challenged the Irishman.

'Well, if you continue to refuse us entry, I'll ask Sergeant Keedy to arrest you on a charge of obstructing police officers in the execution of their duty. That will mean a night in custody for you and an appearance in court.' Marmion gave him a meaningful stare. 'Do you really want that to happen?'

Quinn took a full minute to size up the situation. He then gave in.

'You can talk to her for five minutes but one of us must be present.'

'I won't have a time limit set on it,' said Marmion, 'but I'm happy for a parent to be present. Given the subject, I suggest that it's Mrs Quinn.'

After further protest, Quinn moved away to let them into the house. The detectives went into the living room and exchanged greetings with Maureen and Diane. Both of them looked distinctly uncomfortable. Quinn lurked outside the closed door to eavesdrop on what was being said. When the four of them had sat down, Marmion explained that they'd come to ask questions on a delicate subject that might have a bearing on the case. Maureen seemed to relax when told that she'd be asked about Florrie Duncan. Her mother, however, glanced uneasily towards the door.

'You travelled to and from work with Agnes Collier,' began Marmion.

'That's right, Inspector.'

'Did she talk a lot?'

'Agnes never stopped talking.'

'Did she ever say anything about Florrie Duncan?'

'Of course,' replied Maureen. 'She was our friend.'

'I'm wondering if she mentioned her suspicion to you,' said Marmion. 'You see, the sergeant had a conversation with Mrs Radcliffe.'

'I did,' said Keedy, taking his cue, 'and she told me what her daughter had told her. Agnes had the feeling that Florrie might be pregnant.'

'Never!' protested Diane, horrified at the idea.

'Did Agnes say anything about it to you, Maureen?'

'It can't be true. Florrie was such a sensible woman.'

'Let your daughter answer, Mrs Quinn.'

All three of them turned their gaze on Maureen. She wilted slightly.

'It's not a difficult question,' said Keedy.

'If she'd told her mother,' reasoned Marmion, 'we felt certain that Agnes would have told you as well. Did she?'

'Yes,' admitted Maureen, shyly.

'What did she say?'

'Agnes saw her being sick one morning and ... there were other things.'

'This is quite unseemly, Inspector,' said Diane, hotly. 'My daughter shouldn't have to talk about it.'

'There are only two things we wished to know, Mrs Quinn. Maureen has already told us the first of them. The second follows from the first.' He looked back at Maureen. 'Did Agnes know the name of the man involved?'

'No, she didn't,' said Maureen.

'Did he work at the factory?'

'I can't say. Agnes only saw them together once.'

'How did she describe him?'

Before Maureen could answer, her sister interrupted her. Running to the top of the stairs, Lily yelled out to her father.

'Come quickly, Daddy. Niall is climbing out of the window!'

Niall Quinn was tired of waiting. As long as detectives were in the house, he was in danger. Moreover, he was putting his relations in a difficult situation and it was unfair on them. His paramount concern was to get away and he'd hoped to do that as quietly as possible. All that he'd come back for was the gun. It was a vital asset to someone being hunted. As well as giving him reassurance and a means of defending himself, it enabled him to get the money he needed. Theft was a much easier crime when you could poke a gun at somebody. They handed over their cash instantly. That's why he made the effort to come all the way back to Middlesex. The gun was his passport out of the country and back to Ireland.

He barely heard Lily's shout inside the house. He was too busy dropping from the window ledge. Landing awkwardly, he twisted his ankle and had to rub it before hobbling off towards the fence at the bottom of the garden.

338

Marmion and Keedy had reacted like lightning. Flinging open the door, they'd pushed Quinn aside and hared up the stairs. They went into the back room and saw the window wide open and the curtains flapping. Though they only caught a fleeting glimpse of the fugitive, they learnt an important fact. He was limping. That would slow him down. Keedy didn't stand on ceremony. Climbing through the window, he clung onto the ledge then dropped down. He then followed the same route as Niall Quinn, hauling himself over the wooden fence and finding himself in a narrow lane. Unsure which way to run, he turned to the right and sprinted off.

The inspector, meanwhile, descended the stairs to face Eamonn Quinn.

'You've got a lot to answer for, sir,' he warned.

'He wasn't here to stay,' insisted Quinn.

'You obviously didn't learn your lesson.'

'We didn't ask him to come back, Inspector. I swear it.'

'But you went to visit him in Frongoch.'

'That was my sister's idea. She wrote from Dublin and begged me to see how he was getting on. Niall has always been a bit wild.'

Diane and Maureen joined the two men from the living room. Conscious that she may have done the wrong thing, Lily threw herself into her mother's arms.

'My husband is telling the truth,' said Diane. 'Eamonn didn't even know that he was here until I went to the pub to tell him. Niall turned up out of nowhere. It was Maureen who saw him first.'

'I heard a noise in the garden,' explained Maureen. 'When I went to see what had caused it, Niall jumped out on me. He said that he hadn't meant us to know that he'd come and gone. He was only here to collect something.'

'What was it?' asked Marmion.

'He hid it in the shed the last time he was here.'

'Was it more equipment to make bombs?'

'No, Inspector,' she said with a glance at her father, 'it was a gun.'

'Why did you have to tell him that?' snarled Quinn.

'It's the truth, Daddy.'

'But it makes everything worse, you stupid girl.'

'No, it doesn't,' said Marmion. 'It's a vital piece of information and we're very grateful to have it. Forewarned is forearmed. What Maureen's just told us could save lives.'

After a dash of almost thirty yards, Keedy came to the conclusion that he'd either gone in the wrong direction or that his quarry had concealed himself somewhere along the way. He'd now reached the end of the lane and decided to walk around the corner and approach the house from the front. His exertions had made him pant but his frustration far outweighed his lack of breath. In pursuit of a man with a limp, he should easily have caught him. When he came back into the street, he trotted towards the car. Marmion was standing beside it.

'He got away, Harv,' he apologised as he reached the house.

'Be grateful that he did.'

'Why?'

'He's got a gun, apparently.'

'Blimey!'

'He's determined not to be caught.'

'Well, he can't get far with a limp like that.'

'Agreed,' said Marmion. 'That's why I fancy he'll try to catch a bus or a train. Get in the car,' he went on, opening the door. 'We'll drop you off at the railway station, then round up some reinforcements from the local nick.' He climbed in after Keedy. 'I'll then use the car to trawl around the streets.'

'Let's go,' said Keedy.

The car shot away with a squeal from its tyres.

Having shaken off the initial pursuit, Niall Quinn skulked in a doorway and puffed hard. His ankle was hurting and he was unable to run at any speed. There had to be a better way to travel. He soon found it. An old man rode up slowly on a bicycle and dismounted nearby. Niall was on him at once, pushing him violently away so that he could have the machine. He pedalled away from the outraged cries of the old man. His ankle still made him wince as he pressed down on it, but he was able to move much faster. As he gathered pace and came to a downward gradient, he was even able to freewheel. There was another thing in his favour. The detectives were looking for a pedestrian with a limp and not a cyclist. He'd found a useful disguise.

When he reached the railway station, he abandoned the bicycle. His first thought was to buy a ticket for the next available train but that would only give him away. The clerk would surely remember a dishevelled young man with an Irish accent. He had to sneak unnoticed onto the train. Creeping along the railings, he came to a place where he was able to climb over without too much difficulty. The problem came when he landed. His injured ankle was jarred and the pain increased. Retiring to the shadows, he sat down to rest.

Having dropped Joe Keedy off at the railway station, Marmion was taken by car to the police station where he asked for assistance. Only a couple of constables were available and neither of them looked happy when informed that they were after a desperate man with a gun. Before they could leave the station, they saw an old man stagger in to report the assault on him and the theft of his bicycle. When he heard the rough description of the attacker, Marmion knew that it must have been Niall Quinn.

'Which way did he go?' he asked.

The old man blinked. 'He rode off towards the railway station.'

He was there. Keedy couldn't see him and no-body on duty reported noticing the Irish fugitive but the sergeant nevertheless sensed that he was there. He began to work his way systematically around the place, going up and down each plat-form and looking into every room. There was no sign of Niall Quinn but that only meant that he was hiding somewhere. Keedy was about to widen his search by jumping down on the track when he saw Marmion trotting towards him with two uniformed constables.

'He's here somewhere, Joe,' said Marmion.

'I know that.'

'He stole a bicycle and headed this way.'

'If we spread out,' said Keedy, 'we can comb the whole area.'

The constables didn't take kindly to the notion of getting down onto the track, especially as they could hear a train approaching. It came out of the gloom at a moderate pace and they could see that it was a goods train. Wagon after wagon clanked past in what seemed like an endless procession. Marmion watched them but Keedy's eye was on the bridge between the platforms. A figure had suddenly appeared above them.

'There he is!' he yelled, pointing a finger.

They looked up in time to see Niall Quinn, clambering over the side of the bridge before dropping into a passing wagon. Keedy was furious.

'We've lost the bastard!'

CHAPTER TWENTY-TWO

As a rule, June Ingles didn't get to see a morning newspaper. Her husband always bought one on his way to work, read it during his lunch break then discarded it before coming home. There'd been a radical change that day. Brian Ingles had not only bought three different newspapers, he kept reading their front pages at intervals as if he'd forgotten what news was being featured. When she caught him glancing at the headlines of one paper yet again, she was curious.

'You must know that article off by heart now,' she observed. 'Why do you keep picking it up?'

'I find it reassuring, June.'

'Well, I don't. I hate seeing Florrie's name mentioned in print like that. It brings back that awful moment when we were first told what happened.'

'But the police *know* who did it,' he said, tapping the newspaper.

'They only think they know, Brian.'

'Inspector Marmion wouldn't have released this name if he wasn't pretty sure. People all over the country will know that this Herbert Wylie was responsible for the explosion. Someone is bound to spot him.'

'What good is that to us?'

'He'll be caught, convicted and hanged.'

'That won't bring Florrie back, will it?'

'No,' he conceded, 'but it will give us the satisfaction of knowing that the person who murdered her will get his just desserts.' He put the paper aside. 'I intend to be in court to see it happen.'

They were in the living room. The only bonus of their daughter's death was that June had been able to enjoy her husband's company for successive evenings. After work, he often dined at his club or went to a meeting of one of the societies of which he was an active member. It was only at weekends that they spent any time together. Though irritated by his regular recourse to one of the newspapers, she was pleased to see that his spirits had lifted. Immediately after the news of the explosion, Ingles had been close to despair. Instead of consoling his wife, he'd been in need of consolation himself. It was June who'd had to find the strength to carry the two of them through the initial horror. That had changed now. Ingles had recovered his habitual self-confidence and shrugged off his earlier torpor. What pleased his wife was that he was no longer talking about selling the house. She could now think of ways of improving their existing home.

'We need new curtains in here,' she said.

'No, we don't.'

'Take a proper look at them, Brian. They've faded badly.'

'There's nothing wrong with them.'

'But you promised me that I could choose some new ones.'

'Did I?' he said in surprise. 'When was that?'

'Months ago – don't you remember?'

'There are more important things to spend our money on, June, so you can forget about the curtains.'

'But you said that we'd go to London one day to look at fabrics.'

'That will have to wait,' he said, brusquely.

'I've been waiting for ages already.'

'For heaven's sake, June, stop blathering on about curtains!'

His harsh tone alarmed her. 'I'm sorry.'

There was a hurt silence. He tried to make amends for his momentary outburst by offering her a conciliatory smile and a pat on the knee. After another glance at the headline in the newspaper on his lap, he changed the subject.

'Did I tell you that I saw Neil Beresford this morning?'

'No,' she replied, 'you didn't.'

'He'd just been to the newsagent's. It was quite cold but he was wearing a singlet and a pair of shorts. Apparently, he'd been out running.'

'Why?'

'You'll have to ask him. It seems a strange thing to do at a time like this.'

'I envy him,' she admitted. 'Neil Beresford lost his wife but he's young enough to find another one. We can never replace Florrie.'

'Don't go on about it, June.'

'But it's true.'

'I know,' he said, squeezing her hand, 'but we mustn't let it cloud our thoughts indefinitely. We have to build our lives anew – and so will the families of the other victims.'

Seeing the deep sorrow in her eyes and the sag in her shoulders, he tried to cheer her up. He put his newspaper aside and crossed to examine the curtains.

'I can't see them properly in this light,' he said, holding the fabric, 'but they do look as if they've faded a bit.'

'We've had them for five years, Brian. We need a change.'

'Perhaps we do. Let me think about it.'

'Thank you.'

The telephone rang in the hall. Ingles was on the move at once.

'That might be the inspector,' he said, hopefully. 'I asked him to ring the moment he had any

346

positive news.'

He left the room and lifted the receiver with a smile on his face. But it was not Marmion at the other end of the line. It was a voice that chilled him to the bone.

'Hello,' said a man. 'Do you remember me?'

The stationmaster was a mine of information. He knew the times of departure of every passenger train that came there during the day and he also knew when the regular goods trains were due. The detectives had not lost Niall Quinn, after all. They knew where he was going. According to the stationmaster, the goods train on which the Irishman had contrived a free ride was heading for a marshalling yard some fifteen miles or so away. Since it would maintain a reasonable speed all the way, it would give Quinn little opportunity to get off in transit. If they could get to the destination before the train, they stood a chance of catching the fugitive. It meant a mad dash in the car and considerable discomfort for the two passengers as they were thrown about in the rear seats but Marmion and Keedy raised no protest. They were willing to endure anything in order to overtake Niall Quinn.

'We'll just have to hope that the train doesn't slow down at any point,' said Marmion, 'or he may be able to jump off.'

'I don't think he'll be jumping anywhere, Harv. Didn't you see the way he hung from that bridge so that he didn't have so far to fall? That limp tells us that he's hurt one of his legs,' argued Keedy. 'Otherwise, he'd have leapt off that bridge like the daredevil that Major Gostelow described. In any case, didn't the stationmaster say that the goods train wouldn't stop until it reached the marshalling yard?'

'There could always be an emergency stop.'

'Niall Quinn will want to go as far as the train will take him.'

'You're probably right,' said Marmion, 'and we do have one thing in our favour – he thinks he's shaken us off. He doesn't realise we're after him.'

'The surprise element is always useful, especially when someone is armed.'

'We must take no chances, Joe.'

'I'd feel a lot happier if we had guns as well.'

'You're not trained to use a firearm.'

'I ought to be and so should you.'

'Take it up with the commissioner,' said Marmion, 'though you'd be spitting in the wind. It's a matter of pride to him that, in the main, we're not armed. I know that constables on night patrol in certain areas do carry weapons but they're the exception and their pistols are not always reliable. Don't forget what happened at the Siege of Sidney Street.'

'How could I?' said Keedy, bitterly. 'It was a disgrace. Our guns were useless and our so-called marksmen couldn't shoot straight.'

It was only five years since the siege and it remained fresh in the memory. Three policemen had been shot dead while trying to arrest a gang of Latvian burglars. Just over a fortnight later, the police received information that two of the gang were hiding in a flat in Sidney Street. A gun battle developed. While the police used bulldog revolvers, shotguns and firearms more suitable for a rifle range, they were up against men with Mauser pistols capable of rapid and accurate fire. Eventually, the police had to ask for volunteer marksmen from the Scots Guards.

'It really showed us up,' complained Keedy. 'When they saw how inadequate our guns were, they withdrew them from service, then reissued them as soon as the war broke out. Do we never learn?'

'It's a question of budgets, Joe. It always is.'

'It's a question of common sense.'

They swung hard to the left as the car turned a corner at a speed that took two of its wheels briefly off the ground. As it straightened, it was racing down a road that was parallel with the railway line. A passenger train thundered past in the opposite direction, half-hidden in billowing smoke. Buildings and trees obscured the line for a few moments but it soon came back into view. Seeing something ahead, their driver increased speed until he drew level with a goods train.

'Do you think that's the one Niall Quinn is on?' asked Keedy.

'I'm sure it is, Joe.'

'How can you be certain?'

Marmion chuckled. 'Didn't you see him wave to us?'

Convinced that he was safe, Niall Quinn lay back and rested. Some of the wagons had been carrying coal but he chose one with a tarpaulin over, it in the hope of a softer landing. He was in luck. Beneath the tarpaulin were large cardboard boxes.

349

While he had no knowledge of what they contained, he was grateful for the way they'd softened his fall from the bridge. His first task had been to inspect the swollen ankle. Nothing was broken but it really hurt. Accustomed to improvising, he tore a long section off the bottom of his shirt to use as a bandage and give his ankle support. Feeling marginally better, he was able to relax and consider how best he could get to Anglesey and thence to Ireland. He was sorry to complicate the lives of the Quinn family by turning up unexpectedly and he was especially sad to have terrified his cousin, Maureen. Under other circumstances, he'd have liked the chance to get to know her better. But his commitment to the ideals of Sinn Fein came first.

Remaining in England was too dangerous. As long as he was there, he'd be hunted and he'd vowed never to be incarcerated in Frongoch again. Once he'd got back to the safety of Dublin, he decided, he might send a cheery postcard to Major Gostelow. The governor had a sense of humour. He'd appreciate it.

Their car had long since lost sight of the goods train and they had no idea if they were still ahead of it or indeed if it was the right one. They were in open countryside now with trees looming out of the dark.

'I take it that Niall Quinn is no longer on your list,' said Keedy. 'If he only came back to the area today, he couldn't possibly have set off that bomb at the pub.'

'I accept that, Joe. He's not the man we're after.'

'Then why are we chasing him?'

'Would you rather let him go?' asked Marmion.

'Oh, no – he's a danger to the public while he's on the loose. When we've got a chance of nabbing him, we've got to take it. I'm not quite sure what Chat will make of it all, though.'

'I think I do. If we arrest Quinn, he'll rap us over the knuckles for straying away from our investigation, then he'll enjoy bragging rights over Special Branch because we did their job for them. Chat always wants it both ways.'

'What about the Quinn family?'

'Technically, they were harbouring an escaped prisoner.'

'They were doing it reluctantly,' said Keedy. 'I believe Maureen. Her cousin popped up like a jack-in-the-box and there was nothing she could do about it. If he hadn't needed to reclaim his gun, Niall Quinn wouldn't have gone anywhere near the house. We should remember that.'

'We will, Joe. In fairness to Niall, he didn't mean to get them into trouble. We happened to arrive on their doorstep at the wrong time.'

'I'd have thought it was the right time.'

'It is, in one sense,' said Marmion. 'When we found Niall there, we struck gold. He's the one to blame, not the family.'

'Maureen told us the truth,' said Keedy, 'I'm certain of it. I'm less certain that she told us the full truth about the night of the explosion.'

'What makes you think that?'

'There's always this sense that she's holding something back.'

'Most of the time, it will just be tears.'

351

'Perhaps I'm not the best person to question her.'

'I'd say that you did very well, Joe. After all, you were the one who got the name of Herbert Wylie out of her. That marked a huge advance for us.'

'There's more to come, if only I knew how to draw it out.'

'We'll both have a go at her next time.'

'I'm not sure that that's the answer, Harv. We're men and she's a young woman in a tragic situation. With the best will in the world, we can't ever win her over completely.'

'Why not?'

'It's a job for a woman,' suggested Keedy. 'Maureen needs someone who can console her and gain her trust. That's where the feminine touch has the advantage.'

'We don't have female detectives,' said Marmion.

'We have policewomen. In fact, you've got one in the family.'

'Let's not drag Alice into this.'

'But she'd be the ideal person to talk to Maureen,' said Keedy. 'She's patient, softly spoken and full of sympathy for anyone in distress. Also, she's fairly close in age to Maureen. I think that Alice would know instinctively what to say to her. She'd win Maureen's confidence in a way that we could never achieve.'

Alice Marmion got off the bus and walked in the direction of her flat. Though she was not directly involved in the case, she knew enough about it to make deductions of her own. It was a more pleasurable exercise than tramping the streets as she'd done when on duty that day. She envied her father and Joe Keedy. They were at the heart of a multifaceted investigation that kept throwing up new lines of enquiry. She longed to face such challenges. When she got to the house, she let herself in and instantly forgot all about the case. Waiting for her on the table was a letter sent from someone whose handwriting she'd recognise anywhere. Seizing the envelope, she tore it open and read the letter from her brother.

It was full of loving apologies for forgetting to say anything about her engagement to Keedy in his earlier letter. He admitted the mistake and gave her his warmest congratulations. Paul was less enthusiastic about her decision to join the police service but he admired her courage in doing so. Alice was ecstatic. Her anxiety had been unfounded. Her brother was ready to welcome Keedy into the family. She would count the days until she saw Paul again.

When he felt the train gradually slowing down, Niall Quinn craned his neck over the side of the wagon and saw lights ahead. They were coming into a marshalling yard. Even with the bandage on, his ankle would barely take his weight. It led him to wonder if he should stay where he was for the night. It was unlikely that the wagons would be unloaded until the next day. Even if someone came to check the cargo, he could evade prying eyes by crawling under the tarpaulin. On the other hand, he warned himself, escaping in daylight meant taking obvious risks. Anyone seeing him would take note of his limp and he couldn't hope to outrun any pursuit. On balance, it was better to withstand the discomfort of travelling on foot and make his exit under the cover of darkness. As the train got ever slower, therefore, he braced himself to take a chance.

At least they knew that it was the right train. Having got to the yard five minutes ahead of it, the detectives had established that it had to be the one on which Niall Quinn had obtained a lift. There was no guarantee that he was still on it, however, but they remained optimistic. They watched the locomotive haul its load into a siding and come to a halt, hissing steam into the air. Marmion and Keedy set off. Keeping either side of the train, they walked towards the rear and checked every wagon. The fugitive had boarded the train somewhere about halfway down but it was not impossible that he'd made his way forward during the journey. Someone who could escape the high security of Frongoch had to be extremely resourceful. They made allowances for the fact, moving stealthily and careful not to show their hand too soon.

It was Marmion who saw him first. As he made his way along the wagons, he saw a head appear some twenty yards or so in front of him. Kneeling down in the shadows, he waited until a leg came into view. It was followed by the body of Niall Quinn, lowering himself gingerly to the ground. Since his back was turned to him, Marmion risked an attack. He stood up and ran towards the Irishman, hoping to catch him unawares. In seconds, he was staring down the barrel of a gun. Roused by the noise of footsteps, Quinn had swung round to face Marmion. Still yards away from him, the inspector came to a dead halt. He was able to take a good look at him and identify the man whose photograph he'd seen at the prison camp. It was definitely Niall Quinn. Knowing that Keedy was nearby on the other side of the wagons, he raised his voice and sought to distract the Irishman.

'Don't be stupid,' he said. 'If you go back to Frongoch, all you'll have to face is a longer sentence. Use that gun and you'll be signing your death warrant.'

Niall was puzzled. 'Who the devil are you?'

'I'm Inspector Marmion of Scotland Yard and I've followed you from the home of your uncle, Eamonn Quinn. The game is up, lad. Why don't you hand that weapon over?'

Extending a hand, Marmion took a few paces towards him.

'Stay back!' warned Niall. 'I'll shoot if I have to.'

'That will rouse the whole place. Dozens of people will come running. You can't kill the whole lot of us, Niall. There's no escape.'

'Yes, there is.'

'I'm only trying to make it easy for you.'

'How did you get here?'

'We followed you in the car.'

Niall was wary. 'Who are "we"?' he demanded.

'Me and my driver,' replied Marmion, careful not to mention Keedy.

'Where's the driver now?'

'He's still in the car.'

'Then I can borrow him for a while,' said Niall, limping towards him. 'I've got a hostage, you see. You're my way out of here, Inspector.'

'What if I refuse to go with you?'

'Then I'll shoot you dead where you stand.'

It was no idle threat. When the gun was levelled at him, Marmion knew that his life was in danger. But help was very near. Having worked his way along the wagons, Keedy had ducked under the buffers and come out on the other side. He was well behind Niall and creeping towards him. Marmion played for time.

'Take the car,' he said. 'You don't need us.'

'I can't drive with my ankle like this.'

'Then accept that you've got no hope of getting away.'

'There's always hope.'

'What happens when we take you where you want to go?'

'That depends on how cooperative you are.' He motioned with the gun. 'Lead the way to the car and keep your back to me.'

'As you wish, Niall,' said Marmion, humouring him.

The two of them set off. It was the moment for Keedy to strike. Coming up behind Niall, he tried to dive on his back but the Irishman had a sixth sense. He spun round and lashed out with the gun, catching the sergeant hard on the side of the head and knocking his hat off. Keedy slumped to the ground. Before Marmion could move to his aid, the gun was pointed at him again.

'How many more of you are there?' asked Niall.

'There's only the driver – I swear it.'

'Then keep moving.'

'Let me see to the sergeant first.'

Niall put the barrel of the gun against Marmion's forehead. It left its imprint on the inspector and persuaded him to do as he was told. With Keedy still motionless on the ground, the two of them walked along the track, Quinn at the rear, until they came to an exit that led to the place where the car was parked. Marmion was less worried about his own dilemma than about the injury suffered by Keedy. The gun had hit him with vicious force. He didn't relish the thought of describing to his daughter what had happened. There was still some way to go and Marmion didn't hurry. With his ankle causing him searing pain, Niall was content with the slow pace.

Keedy was still groggy as he hauled himself to his feet. It had been a glancing blow and his hat had taken some of the sting out of it but it had been enough to stun him and to draw blood. After rubbing his head gently, he made sure that he'd regained his balance before setting off. Dim figures were moving ahead in the middle distance. He could see that Marmion was taking an unnecessarily long route to the car. It gave him his opportunity. Keedy lurched after them, then struck off to the right, taking a short cut that would save him minutes. His head was pounding and his vision was blurred but he forced himself on. Marmion was at the mercy of a desperate man with no compunction about killing a police officer. He had to be rescued.

Niall Quinn stayed close behind his captive. When they reached the shade of a warehouse, he ordered Marmion to halt and put his arms out wide.

'I don't have a weapon,' said Marmion.

'I know that or you'd have drawn it on me when you had the chance. I'm not looking for a gun,' said Niall, reaching inside the other's coat. 'I'm after this.'

With a deft flick of the wrist, he extracted Marmion's wallet and slipped it into his own pocket. Then he nudged his prisoner forward with the point of his gun.

'That's very kind of you, Inspector. You not only lend me your car, you give me some money as well.'

'You're welcome to the money, Niall, but I would like the photographs inside it, please. They're very important to me.'

'You're in no position to ask favours, Inspector, and I won't grant you any.'

'The photos are no use to you.'

'Yes, they are – I'll have fun burning them.'

Marmion struggled to prevent himself from turning round to confront him. Niall was heartless. Provoking him in any way could be a fatal mistake. As they reached the back of the warehouse, the car came into view. There was enough light for Niall to see that the only person in it was the man behind the driving wheel.

'Thank you for your help, Inspector. This is where we part company.'

Before he could reply, Marmion felt the gun crash down on the back of his head. It sent him into oblivion. Stepping over him, Niall went towards the car.

Keedy, however, had got there before him and was bent down on the other side of it. Having warned the driver what to expect, he'd armed himself with the starting handle. Niall limped across to the car and pointed the gun at the driver, jamming it against the glass. It was as far as he got. Keedy suddenly came round the car and flung his weapon at the hand holding the gun. It was knocked from Niall's grasp and fell to the ground. The driver then swung his door open, hitting the Irishman with enough force to make him fall backwards. Keedy rushed forward to kick the gun out of reach then dropped onto Niall, punching away at face and body. Flailing away with both fists, Niall fought back with a real ferocity, spitting into his attacker's face and trying to bite him. But he was no match for two trained police officers. When the driver came to Keedy's assistance, they soon overpowered the Irishman, turning him over and snapping handcuffs onto his wrists. He writhed madly on the ground and turned the air blue with expletives.

'Save it for the trial,' said Keedy, lifting him by the scruff of the neck and pushing him against the car. 'You can swear all you like then.'

Picking up the gun, he thrust it under his belt then hurried across to Marmion, who was starting to move slightly. He brought an unsteady hand to his head.

'What happened?' he asked.

'We caught him,' said Keedy, gasping for breath.

Though they both needed hospital treatment, the detectives insisted on driving back to Scotland Yard first to hand over the prisoner. Claude Chatfield was still there. Unsure whether to praise them for their success or upbraid them for straying away from the murder investigation, he took pity on them and said that a full report could wait until the next day. The priority was to have their wounds examined. Knowing that she'd still be up worrying about him, Marmion rang his wife to assure her that he wasn't seriously injured but that a driver was on his way to pick her up. In the event, Ellen got to the hospital before they did. When her husband appeared, she rushed over to him and saw the gash on his head.

'Are you sure you're all right?' she asked.

'I'm fine, love,' he replied, hugging her. 'You can order a coffin for Joe but I'll be back on my feet tomorrow.'

Realising that she'd ignored Keedy, she turned to embrace him as well. His head wound would also require stitches. Marmion sent him off to be seen to first, then sat down with Ellen.

'I'm so glad that Alice didn't see Joe like that,' she said, anxiously. 'It would really have upset her.'

'She's a policewoman. Alice knows that we have a spot of bother from time to time.'

'It's more than a spot of bother, Harvey. That man could have beaten your brains out.'

'I've got a thick skull and so has Joe. Besides, we both had hats on.'

'They didn't stop you from being knocked out.'

'Don't remind me,' he said, one hand to his head. 'The pain only eases when I can forget about it. Just be thankful I'm safe and sound. It's all over now.'

Ellen was distraught. 'He had a gun – you could have been killed.'

'But I wasn't, love. What does that tell you?'

'It tells me that you take too many chances.'

'We couldn't let him get away.'

'Has the superintendent given you time off to recover?'

Marmion laughed. 'Claude Chatfield wouldn't give us time off if we'd been run over by a train. He'll expect us back to work tomorrow on the dot.'

'That's cruel.'

'It's the way the Metropolitan Police works, Ellen, and you know it.' He kissed her on the cheek. 'Isn't there something you've forgotten?'

'I don't think so.'

'A word of congratulation wouldn't go amiss.'

'I just feel terribly sorry for the pair of you.'

'We've caught a dangerous criminal,' he told her. 'He was sent to this country to cause havoc by setting off bombs. Joe and I will get a big round of applause in the press for this – and there'll be cheering in Frongoch as well.'

'Is that the place you went to in Wales?'

'Yes, love. The governor is going to be very pleased with us.'

'Then I should congratulate you as well,' she said. 'Well done, Harvey.'

'The real hero is Joe. He actually arrested Niall Quinn.' Marmion winked at her. 'Would you like

361

to know why?'

'Yes, I would.'

'When he held a gun on me, Quinn took my wallet. Joe saw him do it. I bet that's what incensed him. Joe must have known there was a lovely photo of Alice inside it,' said Marmion. 'Nobody was going to get away with that.'

CHAPTER TWENTY-THREE

Unconfirmed reports of sightings of Herbert Wylie had come in regularly. Claude Chatfield had collated them and dismissed those that were clearly of no use to him. Some were deliberately misleading, sent in by people who patently derived a thrill from causing mischief. He was still sifting through the latest batch when Harvey Marmion appeared in the open doorway. Chatfield glanced at him. For a man sometimes on the verge of looking scruffy, the inspector was noticeably smart for once. He saw the question in the superintendent's eyes.

'It's my best suit, sir,' he explained. 'The one I had on yesterday got rather dirty. My wife refused to let me go out in it.'

'That's very commendable of her,' said Chatfield, 'but I wasn't expecting you for another hour.'

Marmion held up some sheets of paper. 'I had a report to write. You'll want to know all the details of yesterday's adventures.' He handed the pages over. 'It's not fully accurate. I missed the actual arrest. Sergeant Keedy will tell you about that.'

'How are you now.'

'I'm feeling much better, sir.'

'No permanent damage, I hope?'

'When the stitches are taken out, I'll be as right as rain.'

'The commissioner is going to be singing your praises.'

'I'm always glad to get plaudits from Sir Edward.'

'Well, don't rest on your laurels,' said Chatfield, becoming businesslike. 'There's still a murder investigation to be resolved. Don't expect an ovation from me until it's all over and done with.'

'Is there any more news about Wylie?'

'There's far too much. The British public seems to have invented a new game. The object is to befuddle us by making false claims.'

'That's an indictable offence,' said Marmion, 'as our friend in Rochester found out. Did you ever discover his real name?'

'Forget him. The real Herbert Wylie is still at large. If I hear anything reliable, I'll phone the information through to you. Make sure that you check your calls at regular intervals.'

'I will, sir.'

'Where will you begin today?'

'At the place where we left off yesterday,' said Marmion, 'and that's the Quinn house. They'll want to know what happened to Niall and whether or not they'll be prosecuted. You'll see from my report that I recommend leniency. They didn't invite him there and he had no intention of going into the house when he returned there. All he was after was the gun he'd hidden.'

'Nevertheless, he was on the premises when you called there.'

'That was a coincidence.'

'They gave sanctuary to a man on the run.'

'That's not quite what happened, Superintendent.'

Chatfield sniffed. 'I'll make my own judgement about that when I've read your report.'

'Fair enough,' said Marmion. 'You'll notice that I've given our chauffeur a special mention. While I was still seeing stars, he was assisting in the arrest of an armed man. He and the sergeant should be singled out for their bravery.'

'And so should you,' said the other, grudgingly. 'Has the sergeant arrived yet?'

'Yes, sir, he was here before me. Sergeant Keedy is very resilient.'

'That's something we must all strive to be. Is he waiting in your office?'

'No,' replied Marmion, 'I believe he had someone to see.'

Alice Marmion was shocked to learn of the injuries to her father and to Joe Keedy. When the sergeant met her outside Scotland Yard, he explained how the bruising on his face had got there and how he and the inspector had finished up in hospital. She scolded him for not sending for her but he told her that he didn't want to disturb her at that time of night and that her mother had been able to supply enough succour for both of them. Alice insisted on seeing the head wound and there was a sharp intake of breath when she saw the stitches.

'They won't stay in for long,' said Keedy, re-placing his hat.

'You shouldn't have tackled an armed man, Joe.'

'What were we supposed to do – buy him a train ticket and wave him off?'

'I'm serious. You might have got hurt.'

He indicated his head. 'I *was* hurt, Alice. But my pride would have suffered far more if we'd let him escape. I've been cursing Chat for sending us all the way to Merionethshire but it seems worthwhile now. We caught the man who escaped from there even though it wasn't really our job.'

'How's my father?'

'You can ask him yourself. He'll be out in a moment.'

'Over the years, he's had so many injuries on duty.'

'They haven't deterred him, Alice – or me, for that matter.'

She hugged him impulsively and he pulled her close. They were still entwined when Inspector Gale marched up. She cleared her throat to indi-cate displeasure and the two of them stood apart.

'I warned you when you first joined,' she said, oozing disapproval. 'I don't allow fraternisation with male officers. It's unprofessional behaviour.'

'Sergeant Keedy and I are engaged,' Alice re-minded her.

'Not when you're on duty. Domestic matters are irrelevant then.'

'That's a matter of opinion, Inspector.'

365

Gale's eyes blazed. 'Do you dare to criticise me?'

'Of course not,' said Keedy, acting as a conciliator. 'Alice understands that the job takes precedence. It's a lesson she's learnt from her father.'

'Well, she still has several other lessons to learn,' said the older woman, tartly, 'when she can spare the time to learn them, that is.'

On that sarcastic note, Thelma Gale headed for the door and went into the building. Alice tried to suppress her irritation. Keedy stepped in to lift her chin up with a finger so that he could kiss her on the lips.

'If that's unprofessional behaviour,' he said with a wicked grin, 'then I have to say that I'm all in favour of it.'

The events of the previous evening had left the Quinn family in disarray. Diane feared that they'd all be arrested, Maureen blamed herself for letting her cousin into the house and Lily was chastised by her father for raising the alarm and alerting the detectives. Eamonn Quinn himself swung between bravado and apprehension, boasting that he'd defy any attempts by the police to arrest him, then sharing in the general unease. When he went off to work, he warned them once again to say as little as possible to Marmion and Keedy.

Left alone together, the female members of the household began to speculate.

'What do you think happened to Niall?' asked Lily.

'I'm sure they'll tell us,' said her mother.

'Well, I hope that he got away.'

'I don't,' said Maureen.

'He's our cousin. You don't want him caught, do you?'

'I don't like the idea of him being on the loose with that gun, Lily. Somebody could easily get killed. Besides,' Maureen went on, 'if they did arrest him, it could help us. Niall could tell them that we weren't really hiding him at all.'

'Daddy would have let him stay here all night, if need be.'

'There's no point in going on about it until we know what's happened,' said Diane. 'Inspector Marmion and Sergeant Keedy have got to know us quite well by now. They'll realise that we wouldn't willingly break the law.'

'Daddy did,' Lily piped up.

'That's different.'

'He got himself banned from that pub.'

'Be quiet, Lily. You don't know anything about it.'

'Yes, I do. The girls at school told me about him being arrested.'

'That's all in the past,' said Diane with a gesture to indicate that the discussion was over. 'What are you going to do today, Maureen?'

'I thought I might go to church,' she replied.

'Do you want to see Father Cleary again?'

'In time, perhaps – I just want to be somewhere where I can sit and think.'

'Lily and I might come with you.'

'But Daddy doesn't like us going to church,' said Lily.

'He doesn't have to know, does he?' asked Diane, giving each of them a stern look. 'Since

Maureen survived that explosion, we have a lot to be thankful for. It's high time we got down on our knees to pray.'

June Ingles had spent so many years letting her husband pay all the bills and make all the decisions that she never dared to challenge his authority. It suited her to accept his domination because she was also cosseted most of the time. She was permitted an occasional whinge but it rarely went beyond that. As she watched him that morning, however, she saw that he was a changed man and decided that it was perhaps the moment that she underwent a transformation herself. Lost in thought, Ingles was walking up and down the living room. She planted herself in front of him.

'This has gone far enough, Brian,' she said, firmly.

'What are you talking about?'

'I'm talking about the state you're in, of course.'

'There's nothing wrong with me.'

'Yes, there is. Ever since you took that phone call yesterday, you've been in the most peculiar mood. You wouldn't even tell me who rang you.'

'It's none of your business, that's why,' he snapped.

'Was it the police? Was it someone at work?' When he turned away from her, she walked around to face him once more. 'We never used to have secrets. Why start now?' He avoided her gaze. 'We're in the middle of a crisis, Brian. We've simply got to stick together.'

'I know,' he mumbled.

'So who was it on the phone?'

368

'It was ... a friend of mine.'

'Is it someone I know?'

'No, June,' he said, evasively. 'He's more of an acquaintance than a friend. He just gave me some useful information, that's all.'

'What about?'

'It doesn't matter.'

'Will you please stop lying to me,' she begged. 'I've lived with you long enough to know when something's getting you down. You look hunted and in pain. What on earth did this acquaintance of yours tell you?'

'I'd rather not go into it.'

'Is it something to do with your job?'

'Yes,' he replied, 'yes, it is. I don't want to bother you with the details, June. It's all rather petty, to be honest.' He dredged up an unconvincing smile. 'As for being hunted, nothing could be further from the truth.'

'It's all part of a pattern,' said his wife, trying to work it out in her head, 'and it started before Florrie was killed. You were more tetchy than usual and you stayed out later. Also, you began to drink more. I assumed that you'd had a bad time at work. Then came the news about Florrie and I thought you were going to have a heart attack. The next minute, you were talking about selling our home.'

'That may still be on the agenda.'

'But you said that we could stay here,' she protested.

'I said that it was a possibility.'

'You were even ready to talk about new curtains.'

'Well, you might as well forget about those,' he said with controlled fury. 'because we're not going to buy them. I have things to sort out, June. Is it too much to ask that I can be left alone without having you breathing down my neck all the time? Stop being such a confounded nuisance, woman.'

June was aghast. They'd had their disagreements before and warm words had been exchanged but she'd never been put down with such venom and it was humiliating. All she could do was to stand there and stare at him open-mouthed. Overcome with guilt at his outburst, he hung his head. The telephone rang and he stiffened visibly.

'Do you want me to answer that?' she asked.

'No,' he grunted. 'Stay here.'

Going out of the room, he closed the door firmly behind him.

Before they could leave for church, they saw the car pull up outside. When they let the detectives into the house, they demanded to know what had happened to Niall. Tense and frightened, all three talked excitedly at once. After calming them down, Marmion told them that he'd been caught and arrested. No decision had yet been made on whether or not they'd be prosecuted but he had recommended sympathy for their predicament. Lily was sent up to her room so that the visitors could talk alone with Maureen and her mother. Both of them gasped when Keedy removed his hat to reveal the stitches in his head wound. Marmion's wound was also clearly visible but he forbore to tell them how the injuries had been acquired. He wanted to concentrate on the investigation into the explosion. Diane was ready with a question.

'Why were you asking about Florrie's private life?' she said. 'I don't see that it has anything to do with the case.'

'We have to explore every avenue, Mrs Quinn,' he told her, 'and this is a valid one. If Florrie really *was* pregnant, the man involved may have been very upset by the news.'

'He could equally well have been pleased, Inspector.'

'I don't think so. We have evidence to suggest that she'd been let down by whoever it was. Why did she hold that party in the first place? If she was in love with a man, he was the obvious person with whom she'd have celebrated the birthday.'

Keedy looked at Maureen. 'You told us that she was very happy when you got to that outhouse,' he recalled, 'but that she began to drink as soon as you arrived. Was she maudlin in any way?'

'Well...' said Maureen, uncertainly.

'Was she tearful, sentimental or full of remorse about something?'

'I didn't really stay long enough to find out.'

'Wait a moment,' said Diane in disbelief. 'Are you saying that this man might have planted the bomb? I thought you already knew who did that.'

'We believe we know,' said Marmion, 'but this other man is of interest to us as well. That's why we need Maureen's help. Yesterday,' he went on, 'we were interrupted at a crucial point. I asked you if Agnes Collier had ever described this friend of Florrie's to you.'

Maureen nodded. 'She told me a little bit about

him, Inspector.'

'And?'

'Well, she only saw them together that once. It was an evening when I'd stayed behind for a meeting of the football team. Agnes wasn't in that, so she went home on her own for once. I remember her telling me that she was making her way to the railway station when this car pulled up at a junction.' Maureen shrugged. 'She saw Florrie in the front seat beside the driver. He was an older man.'

'It could have been her father,' said Diane.

'It couldn't have been Mr Ingles because Agnes had met him. Anyway, this man wasn't as old as that. She said he might be in his late thirties.'

'Go on,' encouraged Marmion.

'Agnes only saw him for a few seconds but she did say he was handsome and had a dark moustache. Also,' she said, slowly, 'it was a new car.'

'Didn't she ask about it the next day?'

'Of course – but Florrie said it was just an old friend who'd given her a lift. Agnes didn't believe her because she was all dressed up. She didn't dare to have a row about it with Florrie. You didn't argue with her, Inspector.'

'How long was this before the birthday party?'

'Oh, it was two or three weeks at least.'

'And she was never seen with the same man again?'

'Does that satisfy you?' asked Diane, worried at the pressure that her daughter was clearly feeling. 'There's nothing else Maureen can tell you.'

'Yes, there is,' said Keedy. 'Let's go back to the party.'

Maureen gulped. 'I'd rather not.'

'You left early because you were feeling unwell.'

'That's right.'

'Did you feel ill when you were at work?'

'No, I didn't.'

'What exactly was wrong with you?'

'I don't see what this has got to do with the case,' complained Diane.

'Answer my question, please.'

'I had an upset tummy,' said Maureen, feeling her stomach.

'It must have been bad if you were forced to leave a celebration like that.'

'It was, Sergeant.'

'Were you sick when you got back here?'

Maureen moistened her lips. She looked from Keedy to Marmion and back again. Both were gazing at her intently. She felt as if a great weight was pressing down on her. It seemed to get heavier and heavier. Her heart began to race and her cheeks were burning. The pain was steadily increasing. When she could no longer bear it, she burst into tears and buried her head in her hands.

Diane put an arm around her and glared at the detectives.

'Do you see what you've done to her now?' she said, angrily.

Neil Beresford was still trying to distract himself from his grief with frantic activity. Dressed in shorts and singlet once again, he was pushing himself harder than ever. On the last leg of his run, he sprinted the length of the street, then paused at the corner to recover, using the lamp to support himself.

'Someone is feeling energetic this morning,' said a voice.

Beresford looked up. 'Oh, it's you, Mr Jenks.'

'You won't find me doing anything like that.'

'I like to keep myself fit.'

'That's what Enid told me,' said Jonah Jenks, who'd just come round the corner. 'The first time she came to watch a football match, she saw you jogging around it before the match with the whole team.'

'It was a good way to warm them up and it paid off. Most of the teams we beat just couldn't match us for fitness. We wore them down in the last fifteen minutes.'

'Are you still planning to contest the cup final?'

'Oh, yes,' said Beresford, 'I've written to everybody who'll be in the team. My wife and Jean Harte are no longer here, of course, and I've had to leave out Maureen Quinn. It would be an imposition to include her.'

'She may want to come and watch the match.'

'That's highly unlikely, I'm afraid.'

'Well,' said Jenks. 'You know her best. She'll be at the inquest, no doubt. I was hoping they'd have made an arrest before that takes place. I'm still shocked that my daughter was indirectly involved. This whole business started when Herbert Wylie took an unhealthy interest in Enid.'

'That's no reflection on her.'

'Why haven't they caught that monster yet?'

'Have patience,' advised Beresford. 'The search is nationwide. It's only a question of time before

374

they find Herbert Wylie.'

With his collar turned up and his hat pulled down over his forehead, the man let himself into the church and closed the heavy door behind him. The only other person there was the cleaner, using a dustpan and brush in the side chapel. He hurried across to the bell tower and went in, climbing the first of many stone steps on the circular staircase. He was slow but methodical, going ever higher as he brushed his shoulder against the ancient wall. When he reached the bells, he didn't even pause to look at the dangling ropes. He simply opened the little door that led to a second flight of steps. They seemed to curve up to infinity and his legs began to tire. By the time he finally reached the top, he was panting for breath and aching all over. Unlocking the last door, he went out onto the balcony and stared over the parapet. People moving below resembled a colony of giant ants, darting in all directions.

It took a supreme effort to haul himself up onto the parapet. After a prayer for forgiveness, he fell forward and hurtled through the air towards destruction.

Over a cup of tea at the police station, Marmion and Keedy wondered why Maureen Quinn had reacted so dramatically to their questioning. Keedy had felt all along that he'd never got the full details from her of the events on the day of the birthday party. He was more convinced than ever now that she was hiding something but it was difficult to prise it from her when her mother was there to protect her. One way or another, the Quinn family was causing them a lot of problems.

'Oh,' said Keedy, 'I forgot to mention something that Alice told me.'

'What was that?'

'She'd had a letter of her own from Paul. He wanted to make it clear that he was very happy with the fact that she and I had got engaged.'

'I see.'

'It meant so much to Alice – and to me, of course.'

'Could we keep our minds on the case, please?' asked Marmion with undue sharpness. 'We're not here to discuss family matters.'

'I thought you might be interested, that's all.'

'And I might be at a different time.'

'You can't keep shying away from it for ever, Harv,' said Keedy, reasonably. 'I'm going to marry the woman I love and that just happens to be your daughter.'

'I hear the message loud and clear.'

'I just don't want it to come between us.'

'Then stop going on about it every minute of the bloody day!'

Marmion immediately regretted his momentary loss of control and he gestured an apology. The telephone rang several times before he picked it up. Claude Chatfield was on the line and he gave Marmion scant opportunity to say anything. For the most part, the inspector was confined to nods of agreement and expressions of surprise. When he put the receiver down, he slumped into his chair.

'Bad news?' asked Keedy.

'Yes – they've found Herbert Wylie.'

'That's good news, surely. Where was he?'

'Splattered all over the ground,' said Marmion. 'He chose a church with one of the tallest spires in London and committed suicide by jumping from it.'

'It will save the cost of a trial, anyway.'

'There would've been no trial, Joe. He didn't plant that bomb. Wylie left a long suicide note, explaining why he was innocent of the crime. He fled because he couldn't bear the thought of staying at the factory where he'd met Enid Jenks. After some sleepless nights in a cheap hotel,' said Marmion, 'he decided that he couldn't live without her. You know the rest.'

Keedy needed a few moments to assimilate the information. Having been so certain that Wylie was the bomber, he was flabbergasted to hear of the man's innocence and death. It emphasised the full intensity of his unrequited love for Enid Jenks. While condemning the man for stalking her, he also felt very sorry for Wylie. A sad life had been ended in a grotesque way.

'We've got a problem, Harv,' he admitted. 'We're running out of suspects. We lost Niall Quinn and we can now cross Herbert Wylie off the list. That only leaves the supposed lover of Florrie Duncan. At least the other two suspects did actually exist. Our third man could turn out to be a figment of our imagination.'

'He *was* real,' Marmion argued. 'Agnes Collier saw him.'

'What she saw was Florrie being given a lift by a nameless man. He could have been a friend, a relative or someone with whom she did business.

There's nothing that identifies him as her lover,' said Keedy, 'still less as the father of a baby who may turn out to be another false assumption.'

'Don't lose faith, Joe. We need to trace this man.'

'I know. He's all we've got.'

Maureen Quinn went to church with her mother and her sister and they all prayed together. When it was time for the others to leave, she insisted on staying there alone. Diane withdrew with Lily, telling her elder daughter that she mustn't wallow in guilt because no blame was attached to her for the tragedy. Maureen watched them go and stayed near the confessional box until she saw Father Cleary coming towards it. As soon as he disappeared behind the curtain, she entered the box on the other side.

'Forgive me, Father,' she said, 'for I have sinned.'

The Golden Goose looked forlorn. Still covered in scaffolding, it gazed down on the detritus of the building site. Almost every vestige of the outhouse had been taken away, leaving a gaping hole. Leighton Hubbard was arguing with one of the workmen and didn't hear the police car draw up. It was only when the detectives hailed him that he became aware of their presence. The landlord came quickly over to them.

'Have you caught him?' he demanded. 'Have you arrested the blighter who ruined my pub?'

'I'm afraid that we haven't, sir,' said Marmion.

'Why ever not?'

'He's rather elusive, Mr Hubbard, and we don't have unlimited resources.'

'But you've got his name and photograph. What more do you need?'

'Herbert Wylie didn't blow up your outhouse, sir. That line of enquiry has been abandoned because he is no longer a suspect. Sadly, Mr Wylie committed suicide in London today.'

When he recovered from his shock, the landlord berated them for their incompetence and Marmion had to assert his authority, warning him that they deserved respect for their efforts. He explained why they'd returned to the pub.

'We missed something,' he said. 'When we first interviewed you, we were dealing with a man who was in a state of despair.'

'Do you blame me? I lost everything.'

'That's not true,' said Keedy, indicating the pub. 'You still have the main premises and you'll be back in business.'

'When you gave your account of what had happened,' resumed Marmion, 'it was rather garbled. We're not blaming you for that. You told us about events immediately before the birthday party. We should have gone back a bit further.'

Keedy referred to his notebook. 'What the inspector means,' he said, 'is that we didn't ask about how Florrie Duncan came to book the outhouse in the first place.'

Hubbard hunched his shoulders. 'I thought I told you that.'

'Remind us when the booking was made.'

'It was two or three weeks beforehand.'

'Did she come here on her own?'

'Yes,' replied the landlord, 'though she was anxious to be on her way. I showed her the outhouse and gave her a price. We shook on the deal and off she went. That's all I can tell you.'

'She wasn't alone,' said a voice.

Royston Liddle had crept up so that he could overhear the conversation. When the three of them turned to him, he giggled readily, pleased at the attention.

'I was here,' he continued. 'I was on duty that evening.'

'What happened?' asked Marmion.

'Don't trust him,' sneered Hubbard. 'He's got a memory like a sieve.'

'What happened?' Keedy repeated.

'She came in a car,' said Liddle. 'I remember her getting out of it and going into the bar. He stayed out here.'

'Who did?'

'The driver, of course – he was reading a paper. I know I forget most things,' he went on, 'but I remember that because it was such a nice car. I haven't seen many like that around here.'

'Can you describe the man?' asked Marmion.

Liddle pointed at Keedy. 'He was about *his* age – maybe older – only he was better looking. And he had this little moustache.' He grinned inanely. 'I've always wanted to have a moustache but I can't seem to grow one.'

'Let's go over this again,' said Marmion, curbing his impatience. 'This man brought Florrie Duncan–'

He broke off when he saw a uniformed constable cycling towards him. The man was semaphoring with one arm. When he reached them, he put the message into words.

'There's someone to see you, Inspector,' he said, adjusting his helmet. 'I'm sorry to interrupt but you're to come back to the station urgently.'

When she finally emerged from church, Maureen Quinn was both chastened and relieved. The terrible burden of guilt she bore could never be wholly removed but it already felt lighter. It had been a continuous ordeal in the confessional box. The effort it had taken to get her there had been immense and it had told on her. Maureen was now sagging with fatigue. All she wanted to do was to go back to her bedroom so that she could collapse on the bed. But somebody was now standing in the way.

'Hello, Maureen.'

She backed away. 'What do you want?'

'I saw you go into church with your mother and sister. You were in there for ages. I thought you were never coming out again.'

She raised a palm. 'I don't want to talk.'

'Did you read my letter?'

'I burnt it.'

'But I meant what I said, Maureen.'

Neil Beresford had kept her house under observation until he saw her come out with Diane and Lily. After trailing them to the church, he'd waited in a lane on the opposite side of the road. When he saw her mother and sister leave, he knew that he'd have the opportunity to accost Maureen alone. Beresford gave a nervous smile.

'It's so good to see you again,' he said.

'Leave me alone, Neil.'

'I've thought so much about you.'

'I want to go home.'

'And you've thought about me as well – admit it.'

'Yes,' she said, anger rising, 'I did think about you and I felt ashamed. What we did was terrible, Neil. It was sinful.'

'But we didn't actually do anything,' he complained. 'You were on your way to my house when that bomb went off. Shirley would have stayed at that party for hours. We'd have been alone at last.'

'It was a punishment for us. The bomb was our punishment.'

'That's what I thought at first and I felt as guilty as you did. But there was another way of looking at it. Instead of being a punishment, it was a blessed release. Shirley was only a wife in name,' he told her. 'She had such a horror of childbirth that she slept alone most of the time. I wasn't allowed to touch her. That's not a real marriage. We can be together now,' he went on, taking her by the shoulders. 'I don't mean right away. There'd have to be a decent interval first. But later on – when it's proper – we can have what we've both wanted.'

'No,' she said, stepping back out of his hold. 'Everything has changed, Neil. I don't want anything to do with you ever again. It was wrong of us and it was cruel to Shirley. She was your wife. You shouldn't have come after me.'

'I don't remember you complaining,' he said with rancour. 'You were as willing as I was.' Beresford's tone became more conciliatory. 'Look, I'm

382

sorry. I don't mean that the way it sounds. Give it time, Maureen. Wait until all this goes away. If you read my letter, you know how I feel about you. We were meant to be together,' he insisted. 'Don't worry about what happened in the past. Nobody will ever know about that.'

Maureen glanced at the church. 'Someone already does.'

It took a cup of tea and several minutes before they could calm June Ingles down enough to get articulate information out of her. She seemed ready to lapse into hysteria at any moment. Marmion and Keedy were alone with her at the police station. With a combination of patience and understanding, they drew the story out of her.

'What makes you think your husband is in trouble?' asked Marmion, gently.

'I listened,' she replied. 'Brian had two phone calls and started to behave wildly. He refused to tell me what was going on. So I listened, Inspector. When he made a phone call himself, I opened the door of the kitchen and eavesdropped.' Tears welled up in her eyes again. 'He was telling the estate agent to come to the house as soon as he could to give him a valuation. Why?' she cried. 'We love the house. It's ideal for us. The other day, Brian said we wouldn't have to move. All of a sudden, he's putting the house on the market.'

'Did you challenge him about it, Mrs Ingles?' asked Keedy.

'Yes, I did. It made me livid.'

'What did your husband say?'

'I've never seen him so angry,' she replied. 'When he realised that I'd been listening, he used the most disgusting language. And then he...'

The memory was too fresh in her mind to bear repetition. June needed a few more minutes before she could go on. Marmion assured her that there was no hurry. Taking down her statement, Keedy was equally considerate. Both of them recognised the significance of what she was telling them. When she was ready to continue, she made a pathetic effort to put on a brave face.

'What did your husband do, Mrs Ingles?' prompted Marmion.

'I still can't believe it.'

'Why?'

'We've always been so ... contented together. Brian's been a good husband,' she declared, anxious to say something in his defence. 'Some people might say that he spoilt me. And it meant so much to me, you see.'

'What did?'

'My jewellery – he demanded that I sold it at once.'

They'd heard more than enough to be convinced that Ingles had been plunged into some sort of financial crisis. Petrified at the death of his daughter, he'd rallied soon after and regained something of his former swagger, but phone calls to the house had given him an edge of desperation. He was even about to sell off the jewellery he'd bought his wife throughout their marriage. The urgency of it all was frightening.

'What did you say, Mrs Ingles?' asked Keedy.

'I refused,' she replied. 'I put my foot down and

refused to hand over my jewellery. It was very precious to me – and I don't mean in terms of its value.'

'How did your husband react?'

There was another strained silence as she fought to compose herself.

'He hit me,' she said, lower lip trembling. 'Brian went berserk and slapped me across the face. He's never done anything like that before. He wouldn't have dared. Then, instead of apologising and trying to comfort me, he went charging off upstairs to grab my jewellery box. My husband's lost control,' she wailed, 'and it's all to do with those phone calls he took.'

'Where is he now?' asked Marmion.

'He's at home. Brian said that I had to leave for a couple of hours because he had an important business meeting. Just think of that,' she said, eyes widening in despair. 'We've been married for thirty years and I get thrown out of my own house. You've got to help me, Inspector. Since that bomb went off, I've been living with a madman.'

Brian Ingles sat white-faced on the edge of an armchair in his living room. The man who stood over him was tall, lean, well featured and almost twenty years younger. Wearing an expensive suit, he fingered his moustache as he looked down at Ingles, relishing the power he had over him. He listened to a long list of promises from the other man.

'It's not enough,' he said, coldly, 'and it's not soon enough.'

'You have to give me more time,' pleaded Ingles.

385

'You've already had far too much time. Debts must be paid.'

'And I'll pay them in full if only you'll bear with me for a while. It's the worst possible moment. We're in mourning for our daughter, for God's sake! Doesn't that mean anything to you?'

'It means a great deal.'

'Then show some compassion.'

'You exhausted my supply of that a long time ago.' He took some sheets of paper from his inside pocket and held them up. 'We have a contract. I expect it to be honoured.'

'I did honour it,' asserted Ingles. 'I paid you thousands.'

'All you were doing was to pay off some of the interest. You're nowhere near settling the whole debt. The longer you delay, the higher the interest becomes,' he went on with a taunting smirk. 'You borrowed so much that the bank won't give you any more credit. Find the money elsewhere. It will take more than this house and a jewellery box to get me off your back.'

'You're bleeding me dry, you bastard!'

'I didn't ask you to catch the gambling bug. When you risk your future on the turn of a card, you have to be ready to pay a high price. You're a loser, Brian, a born loser. You've had such success at everything else in the past that you thought you couldn't fail. But you did,' said the man with grinning satisfaction. He stuffed the contract back into his pocket. 'You failed and failed again. Failure costs money.' His face hardened. 'I warned you that I wasn't a man to be trifled with. You pushed me to the limit.'

386

'I thought it was someone else,' said Ingles, head in his hands. 'When I heard that they had a suspect, I really believed that the police knew who'd done it. It was such a relief. You hadn't carried out your threat, after all.'

'Yes, I had – I don't make idle threats, Brian.'

'I never thought you'd stoop to murder.'

'Oh, I stooped much lower than that,' said the other, exultantly. 'When I was in the army, I learnt three vital lessons, you see. I learnt how to make an explosive device that went off when I wanted it to. I learnt how to play cards and win because there's a lot of spare time when you're a soldier. And – most important of all – I learnt that, when you've got hold of an enemy, you *never* let him go.'

'I should have gone to the police at the very start.'

'You signed a legal document. It's binding.'

Ingles tried to get up. 'I'll ring them now and tell them the truth.'

'Sit down,' ordered the man, pushing him back down. 'You're not stupid enough to get the coppers involved. It's the one thing in your favour. You know what I'd do, Brian. Cross me and you won't have a house left to sell.' He looked around the room. 'It will burn very nicely.'

'You'll never let us off the hook, will you?'

'It's where you deserve to be.'

Ingles was horrified at his impotence in the face of his visitor. After luring him into a token friendship, the man had slowly stripped him of almost everything that he held dear and the worst of it was that Ingles could do nothing about it. Naked fear paralysed him. Even though the man had been responsible for the death of his daughter, Ingles felt powerless against him. It was almost as if he were hypnotised. 'What did you mean?' he asked, quietly. 'When you said that you'd stooped lower, what did you mean? Wasn't cold-blooded murder enough for you?'

'I hate waste,' said the man, airily. 'Florrie was an attractive woman and she was feeling lonely. So I got to know her a little. We became friends. When I heard it was her birthday, I even drove her to the pub to make the arrangements. Florrie was going to tell them, you see. When we had the party, I was going to be unveiled as the best birthday present she'd ever had. But I disappointed her,' he went on with a callous laugh. 'I dropped her like a stone and let her go off with the rest of those doomed canaries.'

Ingles sat forward. 'You *knew* Florrie? You spent time with her?'

'We did more than spend time, Brian. I'll let you into a secret.' The man leant forward to whisper. 'You and June were about to become grandparents.'

The horror of it all was too much to endure. When he realised what his tormentor had actually done, Ingles lost his fear and his inertia. The man had not only seduced Florrie then killed her in an explosion, he was glorying in villainy. Ingles's rage surged and he leapt up to grapple with the visitor. The brawl was quickly over. The man was younger, stronger and far more accustomed to fighting. After subduing him with some heavy punches, he got a hand to his throat and held

Ingles at arm's length. He was about to administer further punishment when he heard a loud knock at the front door. Swinging round, he saw a face peering at him through the window.

The evidence given them by June Ingles had sent the detectives to her house. For her own safety, they'd left her at the police station. While Keedy knocked on the door, Marmion moved to the front window and looked in. One glance was enough to tell him that Ingles was in difficulties.

There was a lengthy delay, then the door was opened by a stranger.

'Can I help you?' he asked, politely.

'We've come to see Mr Ingles,' said Marmion.

'He's not available at the moment, I'm afraid. We're in the middle of a business discussion.'

'And do your business discussions always involve physical assault?'

'I really don't know what you mean.'

Marmion looked him in the eye. 'I saw you with your hand around Mr Ingles's throat.'

The man laughed. 'Oh, that was all in fun.'

'I'd like to hear Mr Ingles confirm that, sir.'

'Who are you?'

'I'm Inspector Marmion from Scotland Yard and this is Sergeant Keedy.' He indicated his companion. 'We're investigating a murder that occurred at a public house in Hayes. Mr Ingles's daughter was one of the victims.'

'Yes,' said the man with apparent sympathy. 'I was sorry to hear about that. In fact, I was just offering my condolences to him. I came here to discuss the sale of his house. He and his wife have decided to move.'

'That's not what Mrs Ingles told us,' said Keedy, looking him up and down. 'Her husband is planning to sell the house against her will.'

'Might we have your name, sir?' asked Marmion.

'Yes, of course,' replied the other, reaching inside his coat. 'I'll give you my business card.' But what he pulled out was a gun that he pointed menacingly at them. 'Out of my way,' he ordered. 'Don't give me an excuse to kill you because I'd be happy to take it.'

They backed away so that he could hurry past them to his car. He got in, gave them a wave then drove off. They were after him at once. Running to their own vehicle, they leapt in and slammed the door behind them. The driver needed no instruction. He set off at once.

As they picked up speed, Marmion and Keedy realised that their quarry answered the description they'd been given of Florrie Duncan's alleged admirer. He was dark, handsome, wearing a moustache and approximately the right age. Also, the car they were following was the latest Daimler. While the police vehicle was older and less flashy, it had an expert driver at the wheel. Even though the Daimler turned corners without warning, it could not shake off the pursuit. Every move was matched by the police car, dodging oncoming vehicles, braking wildly and even mounting the pavement on occasion. After a hectic chase through Hayes itself, they accelerated past the munitions factory and on into open country. The Daimler was fast but the police car nevertheless slowly began to overhaul it.

'What do you want me to do, sir?' asked the driver.

'Stop him,' said Marmion.

'It could cause a lot of damage, sir.'

'I don't care two hoots.'

'Superintendent Chatfield will care a lot and I'll be answerable to him.'

'You can leave Chat to me,' said Marmion, determinedly. 'That man is a suspect. Whatever you have to do, just do it.'

Relieved of responsibility for any damage to the vehicle, the driver took it up to its full speed. Ordinarily, the Daimler would have been too swift to catch but there was extra power under the bonnet of the police car. It surged forward and was about to draw level when a lorry came round the bend directly ahead and sounded its horn angrily. The police car had to drop back to avoid a collision. As he shot past, the driver of the lorry waved a fist. Marmion was more interested in the man behind the wheel of the Daimler. If he had a gun, they needed to neutralise its danger somehow. There was no point in stopping his car when he had a weapon to hand.

'Force him off the road,' he urged.

'Yes, Inspector.'

'Make him crash the car.'

The driver accelerated once again, caught up with the Daimler, waited for the right moment, then moved alongside it and slowly edged in front of it. Waving the gun with one hand, the man couldn't fire accurately because he needed to keep his eyes on the road ahead. When he did pull the trigger, the bullet went harmlessly past the other car. A second shot was equally wide of the mark. As they approached another bend at top speed, the man needed both hands to keep his vehicle on the road. The police car suddenly cut across the Daimler at an angle, forcing it to veer sharply to the left to avoid a collision. Both cars were going far too fast to negotiate the bend safely. The police car went into a skid, turning round and round in circles on screeching tyres until it landed up on a grass verge, facing the wrong way. The Daimler had fared far worse, leaving the road and bouncing off a tree before careering uncontrollably along the verge, then plunging into a ditch.

Keedy was out of the police car before it actually came to a halt. Running across to the Daimler, he saw that the driver had been thrown forward at the moment of impact and had smashed through the windscreen. Rivulets of blood ran down his face and he was clearly dazed. Before the man could even think of using his gun, Keedy yanked open the door, pulled him out, then seized the weapon from his hand. He tossed it to Marmion who'd now come to help him. Danger was past. The man revived enough to offer some token resistance but Keedy quickly overpowered him and snapped handcuffs onto his wrists. Stuck at an acute angle in the ditch, the Daimler was badly damaged. One of its wheels had come off and there was a huge dent in its bodywork. The windscreen had been shattered.

The man was absolutely horrified at the state of his vehicle.

'Look what you made me do!' he howled. 'My car is ruined.'

'Don't worry, sir,' said Marmion, pulling out a handkerchief to stem the blood on the other's face. 'You won't need a car where you're going.'

Ellen Marmion could not have been happier. They were all together for once. Her daughter helped to prepare the meal and set out the cutlery beforehand. Harvey Marmion was home early and he brought Joe Keedy with him. Since Paul Marmion would soon be joining them on leave, they had a cause for celebration. While Ellen was simply glad that the investigation was finally over, Alice hunted for details.

'What was his name?'

'Eddie Gregg,' said her father. 'And I was right about him being a local man. Gregg was born and bred here. In younger days, he'd drunk at the Golden Goose. He was as ruthless as he was cunning. When he came out of the army, he worked at a gambling club and gradually took it over.'

'He had a nose for people's weaknesses,' explained Keedy. 'Once he'd identified a target, he simply reeled them in. Brian Ingles is a case in point. He was given blandishments at first – free drinks, discounts on meals – and, of course, he was allowed to win small amounts until he was addicted to the card table. Gregg could then begin fleecing him.'

'What a horrible man!' exclaimed Ellen.

'You don't know half of it.'

'I'm not sure that I *want* to know.'

'The full story will be in the papers, love,' said

Marmion, taking a long sip of his beer. 'Gregg had two strings to his bow. He was a crooked club owner who made sure that he always won in the end and, when his customers ran out of money, he loaned them more so that they could go on playing in the vain hope that they could recoup their losses. They'd usually had a fair bit to drink before they signed a contract for the loan and didn't realise that they'd be charged exorbitant rates of interest.'

'He was a shark,' said Keedy. 'He ate his victims alive.'

'When that bomb went off, Ingles thought Gregg had planted it because he'd threatened to kill Florrie if Ingles didn't pay off his debt. But then,' Marmion went on, 'we named Herbert Wylie as our main suspect. Ingles must have danced with joy at that point because he thought it proved that Gregg was not the bomber, after all. He knows better now.'

'The person I'm sorry for is Mrs Ingles,' said Ellen. 'Imagine how she'll feel when she learns about the terrible mess her husband landed them in. Indirectly, he was responsible for the murder of their daughter.'

'It will haunt him for the rest of his life,' said Marmion.

'Underneath her self-confidence,' suggested Keedy, 'Florrie Duncan must have been a vulnerable woman. She was lonely, widowed and she scared off most men. Then someone rolls up to pay court, tell her she's wonderful and spend lots of money on her. Gregg was obviously a charmer when he wanted to be and he was wealthy. His car was expensive and the suit he was wearing made me green with envy.'

'Murder and intimidation,' said Alice. 'Those were his weapons. I get plenty of intimidation from Gale Force,' she added with a laugh, 'but, to give her credit, she's unlikely to start detonating bombs. When I hear what Mr Ingles had to endure, I think that I get off lightly at work.'

'You could always go back to teaching,' Ellen reminded her.

'It's too late,' said Keedy. 'She's one of us now.'

'And that's the way it will stay,' decided Alice. 'Police work can be gruelling but there are wonderful rewards.'

'Yes,' said Marmion, chuckling, 'we had two of them earlier on. When we got back to Scotland Yard, the superintendent promised to recommend us for a King's Police Medal for tackling two armed men – Niall Quinn and Eddie Gregg.'

'That's marvellous, Daddy!' cried Alice, clapping her hands.

'It doesn't mean that we'll get it,' said Keedy.

'It's the thought that counts,' said Marmion, ironically. 'Our other reward is more tangible. Major Gostelow was so delighted that we shipped an escaped prisoner back to Frongoch that he's sending us a bottle of his excellent whisky.'

'I'll enjoy helping you to drink it, Harv.'

'I thought we'd save it until Paul gets back.'

'Oh, yes,' said Ellen, 'he'd appreciate that.'

'We'll just have to hope that nobody gets murdered before he comes, love,' said Marmion. 'We pulled out all the stops to solve this case and be free to welcome Paul home. I'm going to be on that platform when his train pulls in,' he vowed. 'It will be wonderful to see him. We'll be a complete family once again.' He smiled at Keedy. 'That includes you, Joe.'

This Large Print Book for the partially sighted, who cannot read normal print, is published under the auspices of

THE ULVERSCROFT FOUNDATION